P9-ELD-523

TALKER 25

JOSHUA McCUNE

GREENWILLOW BOOKS
An Imprint of HarperCollins Publishers

Talker 25

Copyright © 2014 by Joshua McCune

www.epicreads.com

The text of this book is set in 12-point Fournier MT

Book design by Paul Zakris

Library of Congress Cataloging-in-Publication Data

McCune, Joshua.

Talker 25 / Joshua McCune.

pages cm

"Greenwillow Books."

Summary: The fifteen-year-long war between man and dragons seems nearly over until Melissa becomes an unwilling pawn of the government after she—and those driving the beasts to extinction—discover that she can communicate with dragons.

ISBN 978-0-06-212191-2 (hardback)

[1. Dragons—Fiction. 2. Human-animal communication—Fiction. 3. Telepathy—Fiction. 4. Adventure and adventurers—Fiction. 5. War—Fiction. 6. Science fiction.]

I. Title. II. Title: Talker twenty-five.

PZ7.M4784157Tal 2014

[Fic]—dc23   2013046186

14 15 16 17 18 LP/RRDH 10 9 8 7 6 5 4 3 2 1

First Edition

 GREENWILLOW BOOKS

To Mom, for being my first editor, even when it was all crap;
to Dad, for being my first believer, even when belief was hard;
and to Christina, for putting your sleeping bag next to mine
all those years ago

PART I
KISSING DRAGONS

1

When Trish called and begged me to go dragon hunting, I should have trusted my instincts. Now I'm stuck in a car with her and a pair of wannabe farmboys whose idea of Friday night fun is sneaking onto the rez to get their pictures taken next to Old Man Blue.

While she's riding shotgun, laughing at Konrad Kline's lame jokes about tonguing lizards, I'm crammed in the back with Preston Williams, a self-proclaimed dragonologer with greasy black hair, clumps of facial fuzz on his cheeks, and beady brown eyes that too often find their way to my neckline.

Konrad steers his BMW to the side of the road and parks next to the cornfield that adjoins the rez. He and Trish walk a few yards ahead of us, their flashlights making zigzags in the darkness, the soft crunch of trampled corn mingling with their whispers. Preston chirps in my ear about his favorite band—Loki's Grunts—or maybe it's a band he's forming. I stop listening, but nod and smile as my gaze drifts skyward.

A glittering blanket of stars covers us. I won't miss much about Kansas when I leave for college, but I'll miss this. The nights are planetarium black here, and when I'm by myself, deathly peaceful.

As always, staring into that vastness of space makes me think of Mom. Not burned and screaming, like in those last minutes before she slipped into a coma, but in a transcendent way, like maybe she's watching over me. What does she think of me? She'd want me to be nicer to the farmboys, I bet. She'd want me to forgive the dragons—

"Watch out." Preston grabs my wrist and jerks me back. My focus snaps from the stars to the forearm-thick barbed wire a foot in front of me.

"Better pay attention, Callahan, we're entering enemy territory." He sets his hand at his waist and grins. "Piles of crap this high. Doesn't smell much, but man, it will stain your clothes something fierce."

After crossing over, we follow Trish and Konrad across flattened pasture toward Dragon Hill. The massive mound of rock and dirt is nothing but a shadow across the horizon, the blue light atop it another star in the heavens.

Except for Old Man Blue, the dragons are out of sight. But I can still feel their eyes on me. Neither hostile nor friendly. Neither angry nor afraid. Just there, watching. Like I'm the one who is trapped and under examination.

I've felt this before, the few times I've been in the car when Dad's needed to stop by the rez to check on a patient—his term, not mine. I know these Blues aren't dangerous. Not usually anyway.

Konrad calls us together near Dragon Hole. "Rule one of the hunt: never wake a sleeping dragon. Luckily, that's not something we'll have to worry about." He points his flashlight at the blue glow atop the adjoining hill. "Brightest one in the bunch, but nobody's ever seen the old man awake. Each day the other Blues dig their hole. It gets deeper and Dragon Hill gets taller. The old man's got to get up and climb to his new position at the top, right?"

Trish nods, eyes wide.

"My father figured the same thing," Konrad says, "so he posted men to monitor the old man at night. Each morning the guards were asleep and the old man had moved up the hill."

Preston wiggles his fingers at us. "Dragon magic."

Trish rolls her eyes but leans in closer to Konrad. "What about the rest?"

"Eager for some lizard action, huh?" He takes her hand, leads her to the edge of the hole.

"Wow," she says. "How many are there?"

"Two hundred or so."

Every one of them watching me.

Konrad clasps Trish around the waist and spins her toward Dragon Hill. "You like those, wait until you see one up close."

Preston waves me over. "You gotta check this out, Callahan. It's Jedi badass."

I hesitate, then think of Mom. She believed every decision boils down to two choices, whether it be as simple as yes or no, or as complex as right or wrong. I can stay here in the darkness, afraid of the dragons and everything they represent, or . . .

I glance skyward and offer a silent prayer before shuffling forward.

The closest dragons nestle in caves a dozen yards from the top, their blue bodies sparkling like giant sapphires. A ramp spirals down, caves and dragons on either side. Farther down, blackness swallows the ramp, but the twinkling blue lights continue into the infinity.

Staring into the abyss reminds me how little we know about these creatures. They exploded into our world fifteen years ago, full grown and lethal. Everybody's got theories, most of them stupid, but nobody knows how they got here. Just like nobody knows why they're digging this giant pit in the middle-of-nowhere, Kansas. When Army inspectors attempted to investigate, a few months into the excavation, the dragons nearly destroyed the rez and half of Mason-Kline with their thunderous stomping.

But at rest, they're not scary at all. They're beautiful.

The dragon luminosity mesmerizes me, and the sensation that they're watching me dissolves, along with my apprehension. A peacefulness I haven't felt since Mom's death creeps over me.

Preston's nasal laugh ruins it. "Kon thinks they're searching for treasure," he says. "Me, I'd put my money on dwarves. Let's see if the old man will give us his opinion."

When I look away from the hole, I expect my unease to return, but it doesn't. Maybe the dragons have seen me and are satisfied now.

Or maybe I'm just crazy.

It's a hundred feet to the top of Dragon Hill. Made of huge clumps of torn earth, the mound more resembles an irregular landfill than a hill. The ten-minute climb leaves me sweating and out of breath.

Even lying down, Old Man Blue's taller than a double-decker bus. If his neck were longer, he'd resemble an iridescent blue brontosaurus. It's the most stunning thing I've ever seen, marred only by the silver fire restrictor cinched about his neck.

"Time for a smooch," Preston says. For a horrible moment, I think he's talking to me.

"How we want to do this?" Konrad asks.

"We'll make this an easy one for our novices," Preston says as he pulls out his phone. "Kon, you ride the old man, and we'll have the ladies kiss him on the cheeks."

"No."

"Don't be scared, Callahan," Preston says. "The old man's harmless."

"Yeah, if earthquakes and gunfire can't wake him, a little peck on the scales ain't gonna do it," Konrad says.

"I'm not scared. How would you like someone to come into your bedroom, jump on your neck, and kiss you while you're sleeping?"

"Depends on who's doing the kissing." Konrad winks at me. "Come on, Melissa, lighten up. Look, Trish is doing it."

Ah, farmboy logic. Beats real logic every time in Mason-Kline.

Trish appears as if she'd rather be tiptoeing through a field of scorpions as she edges toward the enormous Blue. Konrad laughs and swings himself onto the dragon's snout.

"Did you see that?" I ask Preston.

"See what?"

"He brightened when Konrad jumped on."

"Hey, Kon, the old man's got his light saber up for you,"

Preston says. He removes a pair of sunglasses from his jacket. "Put these on if it's too bright for you, Callahan. We don't want you squinting like you're blocked up or something."

I ignore him and march into place.

"Okay, ladies, we want this to be good. Wanna spark some fires," Konrad says, and gives us his all-American smile. "How 'bout you lose the shirts?"

Trish shrugs at me, then wriggles out of her sweater. Guess she's not worried about the dragon anymore.

"Very, very nice, Patricia Potter," Konrad says.

She grins. "Your turn, dragon hunter."

Konrad complies with farmboy enthusiasm. He flexes his biceps in various poses; Trish whistles her approval.

"Sometime this century, Callahan," Preston says.

"You're wearing a bra, aren't you?" Trish whispers over the dragon's snout, but from Konrad's smirk, it's obvious he heard.

"That's not the point," I hiss. "I don't want Dad seeing this. Why don't you ride the dragon? Konrad and Preston can kiss it, and I'll take the picture."

"I'm not getting on that thing."

"Your dad won't care," Konrad says. "He knows what happens on these hunts."

"She won't change her mind," Trish says. "She's got that stubborn look."

Stubborn look? At least I don't have the whore look.

"Actually, Callahan's idea ain't bad," Preston says. "We'll mean mug it, Jedi style. She already looks pissed anyway." He holds up his sunglasses. "But you'll have to wear these."

"You mean Trish, right?" I say.

"If you won't take off your shirt," Trish says, "I won't ride the dragon."

Touché.

A minute later, Preston and Konrad have stripped to their boxers and I'm straddling Old Man Blue's head. The dragon's skin is harder than rock and smells of iron, and there's a faint warmth to it, like I'm sitting on a stovetop with the oven turned on.

Trish directs her phone's camera at us. "Two sexy studs and a sultry dragon rider," she says, then snaps the picture. Good thing Preston's sunglasses hide me rolling my eyes, otherwise I might ruin their work of art.

"So much sarcasm for one so young."

I remove the sunglasses and glare at Trish. "What did you say?"

"Two sexy studs and—"

"No, not that. After that. You said 'so much sarcasm for one so young.'"

Konrad shakes his head. "No she didn't. You okay, Melissa?"

"We're not here to hurt you." It's the same voice as before. Sounds like Trish, but a bit deeper.

I slide off Old Man Blue and scan the hilltop. Nothing but darkness and shadows. Plenty of places for somebody to hide.

"Mel, what's wrong?" Trish says.

"Stop it, guys. This isn't cool."

Preston's smartass smile makes me think they're up to something, but Konrad's approaching me as if I were a feral dog. "Come on, Melissa, let's get out of here."

I don't know what's happening, but I allow them to herd me away from Old Man Blue. I look over my shoulder several times, but there's nobody there. Except for a few brief exchanges between Trish and Konrad, everything's quiet.

I've convinced myself I'm losing my mind when something tells me to check one last time. Squatting, I pretend to tie my shoes until Trish and Konrad pass. Preston stops beside me, but his attention is focused on the sparkling blue bodies winking back at us from Dragon Hole.

When I turn around, I expect someone to be standing next to Old Man Blue, but there isn't. I smile uneasily, glad to have come, but much happier to be going. "Bye, old man."

The dragon opens its eyes—giant brown orbs that bore into me. "Good-bye, Melissa."

"Preston," I say in a voice softer than a mouse squeak. "Preston!"

But he must not hear me. He's crouched a few feet away, staring into the sky. Two quick steps and I'm at his side, shaking his shoulder.

He grins at me. "What's wrong, Callahan? Still hearing voices?"

"Old Man Blue's awake."

Preston's grin fades as he glances over his shoulder, but returns a second later. "Almost had me there."

My breath catches. The dragon's eyes are closed. "He was awake. He looked right at me." Preston regards me with a mixture of incredulity and concern. "I'm not crazy, Preston. I know what I saw."

But what about what I heard? Did Old Man Blue actually speak to me?

"It's probably a trick of the light," he says.

"I'm not crazy," I murmur.

"Maybe just a bit scared." Preston grabs my elbow and leads me down Dragon Hill. "It's okay, Melissa, these dragons aren't going to hurt you."

2

Trish and the farmboys drop me off at home around midnight. I tiptoe to my bedroom. Dad's light is on, but he's snoring. Good. I just want to go to sleep and forget about my trip to Dragon Hill.

But sleep won't come. I can't stop thinking about Old Man Blue and his (her?) band of dragons. Was it all in my head, or can they really talk? If so, why did the old man talk to me and nobody else?

Those and a dozen more questions plague my thoughts. I'd text Trish, but she and the others already think I'm on the train to Crazyville. At some point I even consider waking Dad, but he'd schedule an appointment with my shrink the second after I finished a sentence with the words "dragon" and "telepathy" in it.

2:14.

3:06.

3:51.

4:34.

I look from the clock to the moonlit picture of Mom on my bedside dresser. Her arm's wrapped around my shoulder. She's smiling, flashing a peace sign. Two months before she died, happy and oblivious. It's been more than three years, but it feels like I was sitting next to her only a minute ago, holding her heavy, limp hand as her coma went eternal.

All because of the dragons she loved, dragons she believed intended us no harm.

And then it's eight o'clock and my alarm's going off. No way I'm going to soccer practice today. Unfortunately, there's also no way I'm going back to sleep.

I dress in my Saturday outfit of choice—sweatshirt and sweatpants—and throw my hair into a ponytail before trudging to the kitchen. I grab breakfast and sit at the table beside the window that overlooks the cornfield behind our house.

I'm wondering if Dorothy would trade me her twister for my dragons when Sam says, "What's floggin' your noggin, Mel?"

I glance up from my bowl of uneaten Cheerios to find my brother examining me, a hand stroking his chin and a spoon balanced on his nose. As far as younger brothers go, Sam ranks pretty high on the nuisance list, but he's always good for a cheap laugh.

"'Floggin' your noggin'? What's that even mean?"

He taps his head. "The hamsters are busy."

I snatch the spoon from his nose. "Keep talking like that and wearing silverware and you're never going to find a girlfriend."

He grins. "Speaking of which, how'd your date go?"

"It wasn't a date."

"Touchy, touchy. You look like ass this morning, you know?"

I throw a Cheerio at him. "Don't you have somewhere to be?" He's dressed in an MK cross-country sweatshirt a size too big and shorts that show too much of his skinny white thighs. "Run along, little man."

"Sam, stop teasing your sister," Dad says as he enters the kitchen, a cup of coffee in one hand, a computer tablet in the other.

"Why am I getting in trouble? She threw food at me."

Dad smiles at Sam. "I'm sure you deserved it. You ready to go?"

"You're driving him?" I say. "Don't be lame, Sam. Run there."

"It's on my way," Dad says. "Want a ride?"

I'm about to say no, but reconsider when I notice the foot-long dragon Taser tucked into his utility belt. "You're going to the rez?"

He waves the tablet at me. "It seems another group of miscreants broke into the sanctuary last night. Can't possibly imagine who that was. Did you get pictures?"

"Unfortunately."

"You didn't do anything stupid, did you, Melissa?"

I shake my head. "I don't want to talk about it, Dad." Sam makes exaggerated kissing faces behind Dad's back. I throw another Cheerio at him.

"See, completely unprovoked."

"Sam, that's enough." Dad checks his watch. "If you want a ride, Mel, you've got two minutes to get your gear."

I return a minute later with my tennis shoes.

"What happened to your cleats?" Dad asks.

"I'm not going to soccer today."

After unloading Sam at the school, Dad steers the Prius onto the thoroughfare that connects Mason-Kline to the rez. Reservation Road, wide as a runway and unmarked by signposts or mile markers, is empty except for us. I keep my gaze fixed on the spears of golden corn blurring by the window.

"What's going on, Mel? Why did you want to come to the sanctuary?"

I shrug.

"Something to do with your date last night?"

"It wasn't a date. I don't want to talk about it, okay?"

"Hopefully not all bad?"

"No." I know he won't drop it. Maybe I can divert his attention by asking one of the questions bothering me—a question that won't get me in trouble. "Dad, how do you tell the difference between male and female dragons?"

"Once we're back home, I'll forward you some public literature."

"There's classified stuff on this?" Dumb question. If the army researched the mating habits of sheep, it would deem half the material top secret. "I'm sure it's thoroughly boring. Could you just highlight it for me?"

"Since we've never seen them mate or reproduce, we have to dissect them."

"Can't you . . . um . . . just look at their business?"

He laughs. "They have no external business."

"Aren't there easier ways? X-rays or something?"

"Nothing like that works. We don't know half as much as we think we do about them. What's going on, Mel?"

"Nothing." I glance at the blinking red light on the haft of his Taser. "You need to charge your Taser. You promised."

"You know these Blues aren't dangerous."

"How do you know that? You can't even tell the difference between boys and girls until you do an autopsy."

"I just know."

"Kind of like how Mom knew?"

"That's enough. You know that's different."

"It's not any different. Mom trusted dragons and they killed her."

"It wasn't their fault," he says softly.

"No, Dad, it's never their fault. They're just animals that got out of control, right? It's Mom's fault she's dead, isn't it?"

Dad grabs my thigh and squeezes hard before letting go. "That's enough, Melissa."

"You're angrier at me than you ever were at them." I blink back tears and swallow a bitter laugh.

Five minutes later, Dad parks in the small lot adjacent to the rez's guard post. He doesn't say anything until he's halfway out of the car. "You coming?"

I don't answer.

He mutters something and slams the door shut.

Only after the crunch of boots on gravel fades to nothing do I open my eyes. Dad's at the guardhouse, talking with a soldier wielding a machine gun. Moments later, the tank-wide gate swings open. Dad glances my way, shakes his head, and strides into the rez.

The lot's a quarter mile from the entrance to Dragon Hill; Old Man Blue is little more than a glowing sapphire at this distance. A couple of dragons have lumbered from their hole for a midday snack, which consists of wild grass and charred cow. One of them stands near the fence, lazily chomping a rib bone.

I watch the Blues graze for several minutes. Not once do they look at me. Not once does a strange voice pop into my head.

After sufficient flirting, the guard opens the gate. The Blues pay me no heed as I pass, their attention drawn to the column of smoke rising from the nearby fire pit. The cows on the opposite side of the pit, separated from the rest of the rez by a twenty-foot-high electric fence, take turns mooing as one of their brothers is roasted whole in a giant hearth.

A man stripped to the waist and covered in soot takes a break from working the spit to wave. I wave back, blanch against the stench of burning flesh, and quicken my pace.

I'm almost to Dragon Hill when I see Dad. He notices me, goes from angry to all-out pissed. He thrusts his fist in the air and stomps over.

"What were you thinking?"

Before I can answer, he opens his fist and drops a decapitated toy soldier to the ground. He grabs my arm and drags me away from the hill.

"Dad, let go. You're hurting me."

"I can't believe you did this."

I shake free. "I didn't do anything."

"Really? This came into our system a few minutes ago. I expected more from you, Melissa Anne," he says through clenched teeth, a dark hue spreading up his neck into his cheeks. He thrusts his tablet at my face.

Two dozen headless action figures—some standing wedged into the ground with arms akimbo, the rest kneeling with hands in prayer—are arranged in a semicircle facing Old Man Blue. Toy dragons of various colors loom behind each miniature soldier. I've seen some sold at Walmart, but except for the Green with its neck arched in attack mode, I don't remember any coming with crimson driblets painted around their mouths.

To make matters worse, I'm on top of Old Man Blue. Arms crossed, sunglasses on, lips pursed, I appear quite menacing, like a judge who found the soldiers guilty and ordered their decapitation via dragon. My two farmboy sidekicks have been removed.

Konrad can be a jerk sometimes, but I can't see him doing something like this. That leaves Preston, a recent transfer to MK High who I'd never really hung out with until last night. He must have gone back to the rez to play some stupid joke on me. Set up some toys, take a picture, blend it with the earlier one, put the doctored version on the net. Now the military's found it, and I look like some hardcore sympathizer or even an insurgent.

No wonder Dad's pissed.

"Preston must have set me up, Dad. Honestly, I didn't know."

"You need to find new friends, Melissa." He shakes his head. "You know what? You're going to clean it up. Wait here while I get a trash bag."

"Whatever. I didn't do anything wrong." I start toward the hill, but he grabs me before I've gone two feet.

"Where do you think you're going, missy? You don't go near the old man without me."

"You wanna put me on a leash?"

The redness reaches his temples. He's beginning to resemble a beret-wearing lollipop. "Don't push it," he says in that deathly quiet voice he normally reserves for Sam. "Wait here."

When he's past the fire pit, I give him the finger, turn around, and march right up Dragon Hill.

The scene at the summit is identical to the one on Dad's tablet, minus me and one headless toy soldier. Old Man Blue appears to be asleep.

"Hello," I whisper. No response. I step around the decapitated soldiers. "Old Man?"

The Blue remains silent. I try a few more times. Nothing. Maybe it was just another prank. Preston had one of his buddies hiding behind a boulder or something, eager to mess with the girl afraid of dragons. How come Trish and Konrad didn't hear anything then? How did they open its eyes?

How did they read my mind?

I'm kicking the toys into a pile when a shift in the shadows alerts me I'm no longer alone.

Not Dad. I cover my eyes against the sun but still can't make out more than an outline of the figure beside Old Man Blue. The trench coat makes me think it's Preston or one of his farmboy friends.

"You're one of them, aren't you?" I say.

"One of them?" There's amusement in the question. The voice is unfamiliar.

"Better scat before Colonel Callahan comes back and rips you a new one."

"Will he now, Melissa?"

I squint at him. "Do I know you?"

"No, Melissa."

"You know my name. Good for you. And you are?" I look over my shoulder. Dad's at the edge of the fire pit. A minute ago I never wanted to see him again. Now he can't get here soon enough.

"James." The voice pulls my attention back to the farmboy.

He emerges from the shadows. The farmboy in front of me looks like no farmboy I've ever seen.

Bronzed skin. Sweeping black hair. A slightly crooked nose, probably broken a couple of times. A strong jawline. And to top it all off, blue eyes that burn with intensity.

If I weren't so out of sorts, I might laugh at the rest of him. Beneath his black trench coat he's wearing a white T-shirt, blue jeans, a studded black belt, and black combat boots.

I hear my brother's voice ringing like death bells in my head—"You look like ass this morning"—and my mind reconstructs a horrid mental picture of the monster I must resemble. I'm dressed in sweats, I haven't showered since last night, I'm not wearing any makeup, I haven't brushed my teeth since yesterday morning. And my hair's in a freaking ponytail!

Glowering at him, I nod at the pile of toys. "That was a real jerk move, setting me up like that."

"Wasn't me. I wouldn't do that to you." He takes a step toward me. He smells of iron and pine trees. Strange. Another step and we're so close I can feel his cool breath against my hair.

I purse my lips and force myself to stare through him. There's a soul-searing intensity to his gaze that has likely caused many a farmgirl to swoon. Not me. No, not Melissa Callahan.

"Melissa," he says. A shiver of anticipation runs through me. God help me, I am a farmgirl. "There's another war coming, and you must decide on which side of the fence you'll stand."

The spell vanishes. "You're a real dip—"

"Melissa Anne Callahan!"

I turn around and spot Dad's lollipop head emerging over the ridge below.

"You better get out of here, James," I say, but when I glance over my shoulder, he's already gone. Typical. As Dad crests the hill, head ready to explode, I promise myself the next time I see that farmboy, I won't be played for a fool again. No matter how cute he is.

3

When we get home, a black Escalade occupies our driveway. Inscribed on its passenger door are the words BUREAU OF DRAGON AFFAIRS. As Dad parks the car along the curb, a pair of men in black suits approach. BoDA agents, aka D-men. Neither looks to have smiled in years.

"Stay here," Dad says, getting out. He meets the D-men at the front of the Prius. I crack my door a hair so I can hear. "Can I help you, gentlemen?"

The senior agent flashes identification. "Colonel Callahan, we have reason to believe your daughter is involved in the insurgency."

The younger agent looks at me and shifts sideways a step. A subtle maneuver, but one clearly designed to give him a heads-up should I decide to make a run for it. I try not to think about the fact that he's also reached inside his jacket.

Dad scowls. "What reason would that be?"

Senior shows Dad a picture.

"Those are toys."

"It's propaganda typical of the Diocletians," Senior says.

Dad glances my way, then pulls the agent out of earshot to continue the conversation.

Diocletians? Must be a new insurgency group. Most have funny names and short life spans. They rant against the continued slaughter of Reds and Greens "struggling to live a peaceful existence" in the evacuated territories and condemn the imprisonment of Blues in "research zoos."

Nobody really pays them any attention unless they turn violent or do something crazy, like attempt to fly a dragon out of the evac territories. Nobody except the Bureau of Dragon Affairs, which Mom always likened to the Spanish Inquisition. "So much as smile at a dragon, Mel, and they'll call you a heretic."

Dad's shouting. "I'll make it simple for you then. You get out of here and hope you never see me again. If you come back to Mason-Kline—"

"We'll be back, Colonel. Just hope we don't get you for obstruction." The agent gestures to his buddy, and they get in the Escalade. Dad waits until they've driven away before returning to the Prius.

I choke out a laugh. "Killing toys is pretty serious stuff these days, huh?" I say.

Dad stares off into space. After a moment of silence, he says, "They want to arrest you, but they'll have to wait until Monday for a judge. They might try to get you at school. If they do, call me right away. Under no circumstances are you to let them take you. Not unless I'm with you. You understand?"

"You're scaring me, Dad."

He looks at me. "Do you understand, Melissa?"

"Yes, sir. Who—"

"Get in the house. You're grounded until I decide otherwise."

Once I'm in my room, I Google Diocletians. The first entry talks about the Roman emperor who killed his enemies via decapitation, including Saint George, the famed dragon slayer. The second entry links to a video called "Retribution 01," uploaded a month ago.

I click on it. The screen stays black as a man begins to speak.

"Hello, world." Behind him, I hear the deep-throated growls of dragons and muffled whimpers. "Imagine this. Imagine that you wake up one day in a strange place. Imagine that you see a house in the distance, and you go there to ask where you are. Imagine that the person who opens the door greets you with a shotgun in his hands. Then, a second later, without provocation, you've got a hole in your chest. What would you do?

"If you flee, they hunt you down. They put you on TV shows and execute you for entertainment. If you fight, they call you a monster. Better to be a monster than to be dead, isn't it?"

I roll my eyes. Standard insurgent propaganda. Dragons are the victims. Just happened to kill more than eighty million people worldwide in their struggle to survive. Never mind everything else they destroyed along the way.

"You end your shows, world, and we'll end ours," the man says in conclusion.

The screen fills with light. For a moment, I'm blinded. I recover, and a part of me wishes I hadn't.

Six Greens encircle six soldiers, each tethered to a pole and gagged. The dragons stomp back and forth, impatient. The soldiers struggle futilely against their bindings. A black man in a white cloak steps into the middle of the group, somehow unafraid. A wicked scar traces his jawline. Without preamble, he lifts an arm, then brings it down, as if starting a race.

I shut off the video before the dragons commence their meal. I've seen a dozen or so insurgency videos in my life, but never anything like this. Not with execution, and most certainly not with Greens.

Six!

Reds and Blues are pack creatures, but Greens are solitary assassins—the T. rex in the dragon hierarchy. Bigger, scarier, angrier, they will kill anything on their radar, including each other.

But this guy, this Diocletian, seems to have figured out a way to make Greens get along, to control them.

I was hoping Dad was overreacting about all this, but there's no doubt those BoDA agents will be back for me. Probably first thing Monday morning.

4

Monday arrives with a loud rumble. Today's not garbage day, and it's too early for one of Mr. Henley's drunken tractor drives down Main Street. Stomping Blues? My bed's quivering, not jumping from side to side. Plaster's not falling, windows aren't cracking. No, the dragons aren't on the rampage.

I stumble out of bed and shuffle to the window. Drawing back the curtain, I'm greeted by the sharp glare of sunrise reflecting off a bumper-to-bumper convoy of black Humvees and tanks. It's the All-Blacks, the army's dragon forces unit, not the Bureau of Dragon Affairs, but I half expect them to stop at our house to arrest me anyway.

Thankfully, they roll right on by. It's ten minutes before

the last one passes, and it's another five before the vehicular earthquake subsides to a dull thrum.

"What's going down?" Sam says from behind me.

"No clue. Dad mention anything to you about Dragon Hill?" He'd spent the remainder of the weekend on the phone or at the rez. Besides reinterrogating me a couple of times about what happened Friday night, he's given me the silent treatment.

Sam taps his lip several times before flashing me his impish smile. "He said something about his stupid daughter doing stupid things with stupid people." I kick a soccer ball at him, but it hits the doorframe.

"You should have stuck to tae kwon do." He flips me off and flees down the hallway.

After changing into jeans and a thin sweater, I tiptoe to Dad's bedroom, where I find Sam with his ear pressed to the door.

I shove him aside. Dad's voice is muffled, and I can only make out snippets of his conversation.

". . . thirty APCs. Why . . ."

"What's an APC, Sam?"

"Armored Personnel Carrier."

"Huh?"

He sighs dramatically. "Looks like a tank, except without a giant gun."

". . . haven't registered any dermal signatures. Why wasn't . . ."

I glance at Sam. "A dermal signature?" Head shake.

". . . you can't come rolling into town without warning like this, Colonel."

"He's talking to a colonel. You think it's Konrad's father?"

"Maybe. It could be Colonel Sparks, the base commander at Fort Riley."

"Does he have a son?"

"A son?" His eyes widen. "Oh, that mystery guy you met on Dragon Hill."

I frown. "Answer the question."

"Beats me. Google him if you're so hot for him."

"I'm not hot for him. He might be the guy who set me up."

Sam shrugs. "Heard from your date yet?"

"He's avoiding us," I say. Dad talked to Trish and Konrad about Friday night's events, but Preston and his parents have been AWOL.

"You must have really pissed him off or—"

I wave my hand at him, barely hear Dad say, "That can't be possible." His tone has changed from angered to stunned. "You're sure about this? None of my research . . ."

When I lean harder against the door, it creaks. Sam and I share a wince.

"I'll call you back, Colonel," Dad says.

Sam darts into the hallway bathroom, leaving me stranded as the door opens. Dad's wearing his dragon camos and a dragon-sized scowl. "Were you listening to my conversation?"

I stare at the carpet. Eavesdropping may be bad, but lying's on the short list of Dad's cardinal sins. I'm about to cop to the charge when the toilet flushes.

Sam steps from the bathroom with the fakest yawn. He hooks a thumb over his shoulder. "It's all yours, sis. Word to the wise, it's gonna be toxic."

I quickstep past him, whisper a "Thanks," and close the door behind me.

I emerge from the bathroom, hair done and makeup applied, and head into the kitchen. Dad's at the table. He gives me his don't-dare-lie-to-me look. "How much did you hear, Melissa?"

"Something about a dermal signature and research, but nothing that made sense. Why are the All-Blacks here, Dad?"

"It's nothing for you to worry about."

"Does it have something to do with the Diocletians?"

"It's nothing for you to worry about, Melissa."

"How can you say that? First the D-men show and now the All-Blacks—"

He slams his fist on the table. "Dammit, Melissa!" Sam hesitates in the doorway, starts to turn around. Dad snaps his fingers at him. "Don't you two have somewhere to be?"

Sam trudges into the kitchen, head bowed. "Sorry about listening in. We're just worried."

"You let me worry. You could learn a lesson from your brother, Melissa. If you apologized—"

"Bullshit. You—"

"Watch your language, missy."

"Bullshit, bullshit, bull—"

Dad bolts from the chair. "I don't know what's gotten into you, Melissa Anne Callahan, but you'd better get your act together real fast." He takes a deep breath. "Your mother would be so disappointed in you."

"Well, she's not here anymore, as you so like to remind us," I say, blinking back wet anger.

"Get out of here!"

"Sir, yes sir!"

I'm halfway to the sidewalk when the front door opens. I spin around, expecting to deflect Dad's next volley, but it's Sam. "Wait up."

"Can't you walk yourself today?" It's been three weeks since school started, but Dad still insists I take him with me because "He's your brother."

He falls into stride beside me. "I thought you might want some company."

"Nope."

"That was really cool. You almost gave Dad an aneurysm."

"Sam, shut up," I say, scanning the area for D-men. I come up empty, but my unease remains, and not just because I expect an Escalade to appear at any moment.

Though it's an hour before school, kids stream from Mason-Kline's identical manufactured homes—one story, black siding, black roofs, small windows. Fathers or mothers stand in every doorway, most talking on cell phones or examining tablets, all in uniform.

The entire scene reminds me of a horror movie. Mason-Kline's very own *Children of the Corn*. The moment right before everyone becomes zombies.

Ten houses down, I see Trish waving at me. She's the last person I want to deal with right now. Part of me knows the past few days aren't her fault, but if she hadn't begged me to be her wing girl for her date with Konrad to Dragon Hill, I wouldn't have thought Old Man Blue talked to me, I wouldn't have gotten in those fights with Dad, and I wouldn't be on the Bureau's insurgency watch list.

Sam waves back.

"Stop that," I say.

"Just being polite. Man, does she ever not look hot?"

"Sam, if you want to live to see your next birthday, you better stop annoying me."

"I didn't see you at the play," Trish says when we reach her house. "I tried calling. You get my messages?"

I nod. A dozen to my phone, a dozen to my internet accounts. "I've been busy."

"You totally rocked Lady Macbeth," Sam says.

Trish ignores him. "Your father called yesterday to ask about our trip to the Hill. He was acting all secretive and pleasant. Everything okay?"

"Fine."

"Other than a brief little run-in with a couple of D-men in our driveway," Sam says, like he's proud of me. I want to strangle him.

Trish's eyebrows shoot up. "The Bureau came to your house? Why didn't you tell me?"

"It's no big deal."

Sam grins. "They think she's a Diocletian. They're these wicked-ass insurgents who—"

Trish shoos him. "Sometimes you're a real idiot, Sam. Scurry along and let the grown-ups talk."

Sam reddens before falling in step behind us. Normally, I wouldn't give a second thought to his sullen embarrassment, but today it's the cherry on top of the anxiety, frustration, and anger that's consumed me since my trip to Dragon Hill.

I wheel on him. "Stop acting like a baby, Sam. Trish doesn't like you. She's never going to like you. You can't even walk yourself to school like a normal person. Why don't you grow up and get a life!"

Sam looks like he wants to say something, but instead he takes a shaky step back and stumbles off the curb. When he regains his balance, he turns and flees.

The everyday sounds of Mason-Kline—the muted conversations of kids walking to school, the intermittent hum of far-off tractors, the rustle of cornstalks—fade as Sam's feet drum asphalt. His backpack thumps this way and that, zippers and mini carabiners rattling.

Startled neighbors gape and point, and he runs faster. Soon the shoulder strap breaks loose. His backpack lands with a thud in the middle of the street. Sam keeps sprinting. My heart jumps into my throat. I try to call out, but by the time I find my voice, he's disappeared around the corner.

The tears come without warning.

Trish wraps her arms around me. "It's going to be okay, Mel."

"Is it?" Between sniffles, I tell her about the doctored picture. "They think I'm an insurgent. Why would Preston do that to me?"

She frowns. "You think Preston did it?"

"Him or this other guy. He looked like one of Preston's friends. I don't know, Trish. We took the original with Preston's phone. He's a—"

"No, we took the picture with my phone," Trish interrupts. She tugs at her ear. "Shit, Mel. It could be my fault. I uploaded it to Facebook. I just wanted the world to see how damn sexy you looked."

"They took it down faster than normal," I mumble. "I checked your account Saturday afternoon." Along with Preston's and Konrad's. There were no pictures, no mentions of our trip to Dragon Hill.

The government's got a strict policy against "false representation." A pic might last a few days before administrators remove it. In the interim, anybody can grab it, alter it, then repost it.

I chew at my lip. "Whoever set me up had knowledge of these Diocletians. Didn't Preston say he was a dragonologer? Probably has a closet full of dragon toys at his beck and call."

Trish shrugs. "Sorry I got you into this, Mel."

"No, I'm sorry for being such a bitch about everything."

"Next time, pick up the phone, okay? I always got your back. Hugs?"

We embrace, and my gaze falls on Sam's backpack, torn

and abandoned in the middle of the street. "I can't believe I did that to him."

"It's for the best," Trish says. "Don't worry, he'll find someone else to fawn over."

Probably, but I humiliated him in front of the entire town today. I'll apologize when I see him at school. I don't expect he'll forgive me, but hopefully he won't hate me.

5

Trish takes me back to her house so I can clean myself up. Her mother greets us at the door. Most days, Major Potter works from home in her civvies, but today she's in her dragon camos.

"Hi, Melissa," she says with a tight smile. "Is everything okay, dear? Have you been crying?"

"It's nothing, Mom," Trish says. "Just boy trouble."

"Oh," Ms. Potter says, the worry ebbing from her voice. I start to step inside, but she doesn't move, and I have to edge by her to enter the house.

"What's up with your mom?" I ask Trish.

"Rough night with the colonel, maybe," she says, like it's not at all weird that Ms. Potter and Colonel Kline are hooking up. In a town with so many widows and widowers,

I guess it's not that surprising, but if it were me, I'd be a bit creeped out that my mother was dating my boyfriend's father.

"Don't be long now," Ms. Potter calls after us. "I don't want you being late to school."

I look at my watch. "I could take a nap and we still wouldn't be late for homeroom. It's not Colonel Kline that's eating her, Trish. Something's wrong. You saw those All-Blacks this morning?"

"You go take care of your face, and I'll get the scoop."

When I emerge from the bathroom, makeup reapplied, Ms. Potter herds me and Trish to the door. "Have a good day, you two. I love you both."

"What's going on?" I ask once out of earshot.

"It's a drill or something. They just want us at school early," Trish says. "Stop worrying, Mel."

When we arrive at MK High, a once-abandoned grist-mill now teeming with students, Trish and I head for Sam's locker, but he's not there. We check his homeroom. He's not there. She searches the small groups of underclassmen scattered throughout the hallways while I check with his friends, but nobody's seen him.

I text him an apology. His backpack rings a second later. I dig out his phone, stare at it blankly.

"He'll show up, Mel," Trish says. She grabs my hand and gets me moving again.

In the central corridor, we run into Konrad and a few of his farmboy friends. Preston's not with them.

"You seen Mel's brother?" Trish asks Konrad.

"No. You check the frosh wing?"

Trish nods.

"What the hell's going on?" I ask him.

"Standard training exercise. The A-Bs wanna have some fun with the Blues."

I snort. "Bullshit. I've got to find Sam."

"Give him some time," Trish says. "You're the last person he wants to see right now."

"He could be in danger. No way the A-Bs stormed into Mason-Kline at butt ugly in the morning to play war games with the Blues."

Konrad gives me a half smirk. "It's just a training exercise, Callahan."

"At dawn? The army does some stupid things, but they wouldn't scramble the All-Blacks for the fun of it. Something bad's happening. Something with the dragons."

"Why wouldn't they have kept us home?" Trish asks.

I think about all those parents at their doorsteps, sending their kids to school early. I speak the words as the thought forms in my head. "Because the schools have better dragon shelters than any of our homes."

"You worry too much, Mel. If there—"

The bell for first period rings.

"You coming?" Trish asks.

I shake my head. "I've got to find Sam."

I give her a quick hug, then dart into the girls' bathroom. I wait a few minutes before peeking out. The halls are empty except for Keith. Our principal usually resembles a scowling bulldog, but today he's more a bloodhound. Out sniffing for students.

Despite his intimidating appearance, magnified by the miniature swords tattooed in a spiral pattern around his neck, Keith's practically family. For almost a decade, he and Mom flew into combat zones to salvage downed dragons for the army.

On any other day, I wouldn't give a second thought to stepping into the hallway. Keith might give me a halfhearted lecture about truancy, but he'd spend the next thirty minutes reliving one of his missions with Mom.

But today I know if he sees me he'll order me to class. After he disappears around the corner, I make a beeline for the front door.

Locked.

Training run, my ass.

The fingerprint scanner above the handle glows a soft green. I press my palm to the hand outlined on the display. The scanner delivers a small electrical shock that sets my teeth on edge. The display reads *Report to class, Ms. Callahan* before returning to the outline of a hand.

It'll be a matter of moments before Keith gets notified of my truancy. If this were a conventional school, there might be a window I could escape through, but when the army converted the mill, they filled every hole they could find with cement.

Two choices. I can go to homeroom and hope Trish is right. Or . . .

I slam my heel into the crossbar. The latch gives, the door swings open.

I'm two steps outside when thunderous bursts of sound explode from the siren atop the school. For a stalled heart-beat, I think it's because of me. But I've heard this sound before. Once a month, we run drills to its sonic beat.

In the distance, the elementary and middle school sirens blare to life.

I hear a different noise coming from the horizon. It takes me a couple of seconds to spot the black jets. They rocket over Mason-Kline, the booming roar of their engines fol-lowing close behind.

When I turn to track them, I see Keith sprinting toward me. I think he's calling my name, but I can't hear above the sirens and engines.

I use Sam's phone to text Dad: *I can't find Sam.*

Keith grabs me. "We need to get inside!"

"Sam's not here."

The jets fan out, spin around, and bank up into the clouds.

"When did you last see him?"

He says something else, but my focus is consumed by the fireflylike trail of orange pulses igniting behind the gray blanket of sky. I press myself into Keith and brace for what I know comes next.

The rattling percussion of gunfire erupts louder than fireworks, and the shrieking whistles of multiple missiles scream over Mason-Kline.

"Melissa, where is Sam?" Keith shouts in my ear.

"We got in a fight."

He leans in. "What?"

"We got in a fight." My voice breaks. "He was—"

The explosion rips the sky apart. Keith and I stagger sideways as a dark shape plummets beneath the cloud line.

It's far too large to be a jet.

Even from a distance I see the gaping wound in the drag-on's flank. The monster smashes into the ground, sending up a cloud of dust and cornstalks. It's more than a thousand feet away, but the tremor knocks me off my feet.

As I push myself up, a fiendish roar—something that belongs in a myth and not Mason-Kline—booms from the heavens. Five more dragons plunge through the clouds, wings tight to their glowing bodies. I barely notice the four Reds, because at the front of the pack, the brightest by far, is a Silver.

I've never seen a silver dragon, never heard of one. Reds, Greens, Blues—that's all. Until now.

The jets race after them. Tracers and missiles paint a patchwork of fiery dots across the sky. The Silver settles in the cornfield next to its fallen comrade. The Reds encircle them, spreading their wings to form a protective perimeter.

With tremendous roars, they unleash the geysers of hell. Arcs of fire sweep the sky like spotlights. Searching, searching, searching. But they never find their targets.

Dragons can't see black. According to Dad, it's kind of like infrared to them. There, but invisible. They rely on noise to hone in on their targets, but there's too much of it now.

Missile explosions, bullet purrs, engine screams blare from every direction. The jets zip in and out, patient and methodical. The Reds bob their heads in quick circles, confused and angry, always just a second too slow.

One Red starts flickering. The fire it manages to spit out comes in sputters that don't reach more than twenty feet into the air. With one last burst, it launches itself into the maelstrom, giving its compatriots a few seconds of reprieve as the dragon jets concentrate their arsenal on it. Moments later, it crashes into the cornfield, and the DJs resume their onslaught.

The three remaining Reds adjust position to best maintain their perimeter. One screams at the Silver, then looks skyward. The others chime in, but the Silver doesn't seem to hear. It doesn't seem aware of the battle at all, its attention consumed by the dead dragon. It sniffs and prods the body, tugs at a limp wing. In the briefest moments, when the cacophony is at its quietest, I hear it mewling.

A carpet of explosions kills two more Reds. The last one flees, firing over its shoulder, clearly trying to draw the jets away. Three chase after it. The rest focus on the Silver.

The Red arcs back around to reengage, catches a missile in the chest. When the explosion clears, the dragon's glow is gone. It somersaults in a lifeless parabola toward the ground.

I look back to the main battle. The Silver's no longer huddled around the dead dragon. It's on its haunches, in attack position. Like a circus performer snatching knives in midair, it grabs the missiles from the sky and throws them aside.

I gasp. Those missiles are black. It looks like it's tracking the jets, too. It opens its mouth wide. The DJs don't change course. Sam once told me they wear armor that can withstand temperatures up to 10,000 degrees F, but it seems like suicide to dive at an angry dragon that can clearly see you.

Silver liquid erupts from the dragon's mouth. It expands out and up into a shimmering funnel that speeds toward the clouds.

The nearest plane banks too hard and spins out of control. The pilot ejects, twirling like a wobbly boomerang. The parachute attached to his seat opens but gets tangled, and he plummets into the corn.

Two more jets roar into the funnel. When they emerge from the other side, what looks like ice encases everything. They fall from the sky and shatter on impact.

A louder explosion thunders in my ears, pulling my attention to the column of smoke forming at the center of Mason-Kline.

One of the planes smashed into the middle of the housing district. The dragon shelters might provide protection for anybody who made it underground in time, but what about Sam? What if Dad got my text and was out looking for him?

I force my gaze back to the battle. The dragon continues to toss aside every missile that comes its way.

But it can't catch the bullets.

Rather than fleeing, the Silver puffs its chest, widens its stance, and seems to welcome them. Each volley knocks it a little lower, staggers it a little more, but it refuses to move from its fallen companion's side.

As the remaining jets regroup, the Silver's ice cuts out,

and it dims to a dull gray. It unfurls its tattered wings to their full extent, roars once at the heavens, then slumps to the ground beside the dead dragon.

Maybe they're brother and sister.

Keith touches my shoulder. "Inside, Melissa. You don't want to see this."

He guides me into the school. The siren is no longer blaring, and when he closes the door, the sounds of jets and gunfire fade to the background. If not for Sam's phone clutched in my hand, I might be able to convince myself I'm standing in the lobby of a movie theater, not in the middle of a war zone.

6

"Dad's not answering his phone," I say as Keith pushes me down the hallway. Outside, there's another muted explosion. The walls rattle.

"He probably took shelter."

We reach the stairwell that leads thirty feet underground, into a large metal box with enough supplies to keep two hundred students alive for a week. My phone won't get reception down there. The school shelter's got a landline, but it's a secure army channel, for priority use only. Who knows how long it will be before they let us out? It could be hours. Stuck with nothing to do but remember how the last time you were safe in a shelter, your mother wasn't.

Now Sam and Dad are both MIA.

"Can we wait up here?" I ask.

"It's not safe, Mel."

"But the dragon's almost dead, right?"

Keith grabs his mini tablet, enters a couple of passwords, and navigates to the video section of the army database. He loads a live feed that shows the Silver from afar. A soldier in body armor kneels behind a row of corn and lifts a rocket launcher onto his shoulder. Another All-Black loads the tube with a spike-tipped missile.

With this explosion, the dragon crumbles to its knees.

"It's flickering. It won't be long," I say, ear pressed to my phone. Voice mail again. I don't bother leaving a message this time. I look to Keith. "Please."

He taps a flashing icon at the bottom of the screen. Another clip pops up, this one transmitted from the cockpit of a dragon jet. The time stamp's five minutes old.

Six dragons glide through the stratosphere, wing to wing. Four Reds flank two Silvers that are identical in every way save for their brilliant luminosity.

In the next instant, bullet tracers crisscross the sky. The Reds split away. Several jets chase them off screen, but the one with the video feed stays on the Silvers.

Two missiles race into view. The brighter Silver somersaults around and opens its mouth, but nothing happens.

A blur of red sweeps up from the corner of the screen and throws itself in front of the inbound missiles. When fire and smoke clear, a dragon hovers in the air, its glow gone. It spreads its jaws, releases a tiny puff of fire, and falls head over tail into the clouds.

The other Silver dives after the dead Red, but the brighter one has vanished.

Keith shuts off the tablet.

I swallow. "Where did it go?"

"I don't know, but it could return." Keith grabs my arm. "Let's go."

We're almost to the blast door when my phone vibrates.

"Dad?" I backstep quickly before the signal dies.

"Melissa? Why aren't you in the shelter?"

"I'm with Keith. Sam and I got in a fight. He . . . he ran away. I don't know where. It's all my fault, Dad."

"It's not your fault. We'll go look for him together. Let me talk to Keith."

I hand the phone over. A few seconds into the conversation, Keith steers me up the stairs and out the front door. APCs surround the scorched field where the Silver made its last stand, All-Blacks pick over shards of ice in the MK High parking lot, and army helicopters create an airspace perimeter against the half-dozen news choppers.

"You and the young lady need to get back inside, Major," an All-Black says.

"Colonel Callahan's coming to pick up his daughter,"

Keith says as I spot Dad's Prius at the edge of the parking lot. The loud whir of helicopter blades silences his approach.

The A-B lifts a visor adorned with a patchwork of red dragon scales to reveal a face weathered by age on one side and burned by fire on the other. "This isn't open for discussion. You don't have authority here. Why don't you go back inside and teach your kids to stay in their shelters better?"

"Watch it, Sergeant," Keith says. "Let's go, Melissa."

"No, I'm waiting here," I say. The All-Black smirks at me. "Smile all you want, you don't have any authority to tell me what to do."

He runs his tongue along his upper teeth. "Feisty ragger, aren't you? Stay out of our way, girl, and if something happens I hope Daddy's here to help you, because we won't bail your pretty ass out."

I return his smug smile. With his back to the road, he didn't see Dad drive up. Busy ogling me, he must not have heard him get out of the car either.

"Daddy is here, Sergeant." My father stands beside the Prius, arms folded, jaw stiff. He opens the passenger door. "Get in the car, Melissa."

I press my middle finger to my lips and kiss it at the burned soldier as I get in.

"You ever talk to my daughter like that again—" Dad

shuts the door, cutting his sentence short, but I happily construct my own dialogue.

After Dad sends the A-B on his way and talks to Keith, he returns to the car, his features on the volcanic side of angry. I reach over and hug him. The tension in his chest softens, and he's hugging me back. "I'm sorry, Dad. I'm sorry about everything."

He releases me, then starts the car. "I don't know what I'd do if you or Sam got hurt. You have to protect him. And yourself, Melissa. Keith told me what you did." He pulls out of the parking lot wearing a sad smile. "You're too much like your mother sometimes."

Two Humvees block the road into town. Columns of smoke billow into the air from the center of the housing district. A-Bs patrol the parking lots of the adjacent Walmart and Kroger's, ordering curious shoppers back inside.

We stop at the roadblock. Dad lowers his window as an All-Black approaches. Unlike the other soldiers, he's not wearing a helmet decorated with dragon scales. He'd look young except for his eyes. He salutes.

"Any news, Captain?" Dad asks.

"Your son is at the bivouac receiving treatment for smoke inhalation." He glances at me, then leans in and says something I can't hear.

Smoke inhalation. We learn about it every year in our

Dragon Ed classes. When I was younger, they had a cartoon. I first saw it in second grade. It showed a sharp-toothed Green breathing fire on houses. Most of us laughed. The teacher shushed us as a cyclone of smoke with red eyes and a wicked grin emerged from the destruction and swept across the streets, swallowing uneducated boys and girls in its giant mouth.

Though they stopped using the video after elementary school, the message shown on the screen at the end still looms on placards in many classrooms. "Half the time it's not the fire that gets you," I whisper. It was always a joke before.

Dad frowns at me. "Thank you, Captain. I'll be back to collect samples after I check on my son."

The All-Black circles his finger in the air. The Humvees clear a lane for us.

"Is Sam okay?" I blurt the instant Dad shuts his window.

"He suffered a mild case of smoke inhalation. He'll be fine," he says in his doctor voice, the one he used when Mom was in the hospital.

"What do you mean, 'fine'?"

"He's asleep right now."

"You mean in a coma," I say. "That's what you mean, isn't it? Don't lie to me, Dad. Please don't."

"He's in an induced sleep, Mel. Not a coma."

"Then what was all that stuff the A-B was telling you?"

"It's something to do with the dragons." He steers the car around a pile of charred timbers. "Something that doesn't concern you."

"Stop treating me like I'm still your little girl. Tell me what's going on."

After a heavy silence he says, "The dragons have started to breed."

"I thought they were sterile," I whisper. In the early days of the dragon war, when terror dominated, it was this belief that gave people hope. For whatever reason, the dragons couldn't reproduce in our world. That's what the government said, that's what scientists said, that's what parents said. Their numbers were limited. One day they would be gone. But now . . . "How?"

"Cross-pollination," Dad says.

"Like lion plus tiger equals liger, except with dragons?" I say. "Red plus Green makes Silver?"

"Red plus Blue, we think. We even checked that a few years back," he says. "Just not under the right thermal conditions."

I give a bitter laugh. "It's Dragon Hole, isn't it? That's where the Silvers came from. That's why the All-Blacks came this morning."

He gives the slightest nod, stares into the smoke. "They

plan on destroying it." He sounds upset. I'm not sure why until he says, "I know it's the right thing to do, but it seems wrong to kill children."

My breath sticks in my throat as I stare out the window. That Silver was larger than Old Man Blue. Almost the size of the Green that killed Mom. "That's a child? Why's it so big, Dad? Why's it breathe ice? And it can see black, right?"

"I don't know, Melissa," he says, squeezing my hand. "We'll find out. It'll be okay."

Dad weaves the car around shattered glass, holes in the street, chunks of jet. The wreckage worsens as we near the crash site. The homes here resemble split-open doll-houses—roofs, walls, entire sections no longer exist. Street-embedded sprinklers shoot water into their charred guts, ruining whatever the fire didn't.

A slogan from a local bank back in Virginia pops into my head. "Dragon shelters save lives, not memories." I don't remember the rest—something about storing your precious keepsakes in vaults before it's too late.

There's Ellen McCormack's house. What's left of it. In the city, she would have kept her archaeologist grand-mother's artifacts in the dragon shelter. Or in that bank. But not in Mason-Kline, a military outpost in cornfield, Kansas.

What about my pictures of Mom?

"Dad, what happened to our house?"

He shakes his head. "The wind caught the fire. The sprinklers couldn't keep up. I got the cat and your brother's turtles into the shelter."

"My pictures?"

He squeezes my shoulder. "I'm sorry, Mel. We've got everything on digital. We'll get them printed once things are straightened out."

I nod and blink hard. It's not the same. She'd signed and dated them all. Most had messages, little things—*See you soon, Mel Mel*. Sometimes notes about the dragons she'd salvaged or people she'd befriended. My favorite picture had her out of uniform and on the other side of a picket line, holding a sign protesting the government's policy to relocate the Blues to dragon "sanctuaries" for observation and research. On the back it said *Don't tell your father,* followed by a smiley face and a heart. Dated five years ago, a month after the government declared victory over the dragons.

Pieces of a life more important to me than anything. Gone because I needed to have her by my bedside, to look at whenever I wanted. Gone because of the dragons.

We drive alongside the crash site, moving no faster than a walk because of the All-Blacks and mounds of debris. A layer of ash covers everything. APCs surround a crater to our right, their mechanical arms digging out remnants of charred jet. The nearby houses will need to be replaced, but anybody who was in a shelter during the battle should be safe.

I say a silent prayer of thanks. Sam will be okay, and things could have been far worse. It's amazing the jet didn't take out any—

"Oh God." I cover my mouth. On a clear day, free of smoke and A-Bs, I would have recognized where we were a long time ago.

The jet didn't miss a house. It obliterated it.

It takes me two tries to get my phone out of my pocket. Shaking, I press the speed dial. *Calling Trish Potter* appears on the screen. I'm raising the phone to my ear when Dad grabs my hand and touches the off button.

"She won't get the message for a while, and you shouldn't worry her unnecessarily." He wipes the tears from my cheeks. "Once they clear the wreckage, they'll be able to access the shelter. They're designed for high-stress impact, Melissa. There's a good chance Major Potter survived."

It's his doctor tone again, and this time I know he's lying.

7

Black. The color of America.

After the government instituted its blackout policy a decade ago, cars, houses, and cities went dark in under four months. Psychologists spoke out against what they called "the prevalence of grim," pointing to the nationwide crime increase and skyrocketing suicide rates. But there were fewer dragon attacks, and the so-called "bright psychs" lost favor with the media.

The dark world never bothered me much, except in junior high when it became trendy to dress like an A-B. I was one of the few who didn't dye my hair or wear Smoke® makeup. It was all quite ridiculous.

Mom hated it. After she died, she was buried in a white coffin in a white dress. Everybody wore pastel colors, like we were at an Easter wedding in a time before the dragons. And there were white lilies everywhere. That was ridiculous, too, but in a wonderful way.

But today there is only black.

And it squeezes me from every direction. Black smoke around the car, a constant reminder of Sam. Black soot over Ms. Potter's dragon shelter, maybe a grave now with scorched jet debris for a tombstone. All-Black soldiers everywhere, modern-day grim reapers.

Trish and I used to joke how the world would look if dragons couldn't see pink. Mom would have loved that, if for nothing else than seeing soldiers strut around in fuchsia. I'd settle for pink today, too.

Anything but black.

We drive toward the medical bivouac, an eerie carnival tent in the center of a macabre circus. I'm out of the car and sprinting before Dad finishes parking. The All-Black at the entrance lowers his gun after I find my breath and explain why I'm here.

"Red-haired kid?" he says. "Was hacking up a lung when he came in. Said something about 'meeting Smokey the Cyclone,' and laughed." I grin back tears. The soldier shakes his head. "Guess it's something with you kids."

He pulls up the entrance flap and waves me in.

Curtained sections run the length of the tent on either

side. Coughs and moans echo all around. Medical personnel move between units, practiced and proficient. I ask a nurse about Sam. He leads me to a room at the back.

I'm ready for the hospital gown, heart monitor, and IV, but the clear plastic mask covering half my brother's face makes me gasp.

"He's under sedation right now," the nurse says. "Don't try to wake him."

He closes the curtain and silence engulfs me, broken only by the wispy exhale of Sam's ventilator and the faint sound of someone crying nearby.

I slump into the chair beside my brother's bed. Even asleep, Sam looks as if he's up to no good. His lips are turned up at the corners beneath the mask, and fiery hair splays from his head like weeds.

I often asked him how we could be related—him looking like a sunburned child of mischief, complete with nose freckles and red cheeks; me having Mom's darker features, never wanting a strand out of place, a color uncoordinated. Him always acting the fool; me thinking humor inappropriate in a world with dragons.

I run my fingertip along the freckles up to his forehead. Something Mom used to do. When we were younger and afraid—me of the dragons, Sam of things that didn't exist— we'd crawl into our parents' bed. She'd go to Sam first and trace a slow line from his chin, telling him how closet goblins only came after boys who didn't eat their vegetables. Then Dad would tickle him into forgetfulness as Mom turned to comfort me.

Her soft voice would send me into a dreamy fog where I didn't have to worry about dragon shelter drills, visiting friends at the hospital, our house burning down. She somehow made the world seem safe, like we weren't in the middle of some never-ending nightmare.

Then I turned thirteen, decided I was no longer Mel Mel, and stopped running to their bedroom. Acted like dragons didn't scare me anymore, like Mom's salvage missions and Dad's research were nothing out of the ordinary. Anyway, the war was over. And even if a few dragons roamed free, Arlington was protected, never victimized by dragons because of its exemplary defense system.

Until she became another black cross in Arlington National Cemetery, Sam never stopped seeking her comfort. Must have known something I didn't. Still does. I thought Mom's death would hit him harder than me, but after we put her in the ground, he moved forward with life, figured out how to be happy in a world with dragons, in a world without Mom.

As I watch Sam sleep, a different sort of jealousy surfaces, and unexpected relief washes over me. I hurt my brother today, could have killed him, but he's stronger than I am and will survive my weakness, will probably brag about it the first chance he gets. I smile, press my hand to his cheek, feeling his warmth, his vitality.

"He needs a haircut, doesn't he?" Dad says from behind me.

"Mom wouldn't like it, but it suits him." I reach up and squeeze my father's hand.

I'm holding on to my father, looking at my brother, trying my best not to think about anything else, when Trish calls.

"Do you want me to talk to her?" Dad asks.

I shake my head and step from the room. "Hello?"

"Mel, thank God. Where are you?"

"At the medical tent."

"Sam?"

"He's okay. Smoke inhalation, but they say he'll be fine."

"You want me to come give him a kiss?"

I grin. "That would probably wake him up fast, but they want him to sleep a little longer. Where are you?"

"They let us out of the shelter, but they're not letting us out of school. A-Bs are walking the halls, making sure we're good little brats. They shut down the vid windows and cut off net access. They wanted to kill our phones, too, but Keith convinced them not to. I can't reach my mom, Mel."

"I'm sure she's fine." I try to adopt Dad's neutral tone, but I'm no good at it.

"What is it, Mel? Remember what we promised each other."

"It's nothing, Trish. I don't—"

"Shit, there's someone coming."

The line goes dead.

I'm about to pull back Sam's curtain, but a nearby voice stays my hand.

"Don't you touch her."

The voice is familiar, but I can't place it. I lean over, peep through the slit between curtain and pole.

"Son, this will go a whole lot better for you if you cooperate. It's no use struggling," says the A-B who let me in. He and a black-suited man flank a pale woman laid out on a gurney. Aside from the sheet covering her torso and thighs, she appears naked. Her silver-and-black hair falls in waves to her hips. She looks strangely beautiful.

"Please don't take her." I shut one eye, cock my head, trying to get a better view, but all I see is a tanned leg, the beginnings of a hospital gown, and an arm cuffed to a chair.

"Tell me where the rest of your group is and I'll make sure she gets a funeral," Blacksuit says. He motions to the soldier, who rolls the gurney toward the curtain.

"Hey, Trish, hold up," I say into the silent phone, then wave to the soldier as he emerges from the room. "She going to be okay?"

He shakes his head. "How's your brother?"

"Good." I study the woman's face. "What happened to her?"

"Found her"—he nods toward the curtain—"and her son at Dragon Hole. A strange lot."

"What do you mean?"

"She was dressed like Amelia Earhart and her kid was wearing this Euro punk rocker getup." He grimaces. "I'll never understand dragon riders."

My breath catches. The voice, the overdramatic farmboy words, the beauty of the dead mother . . .

"He's an insurgent?"

"So says the D-man." The A-B hooks a thumb at the curtain. "Ask me, he's a few acorns short of a tree. It's too bad you kids had to grow up in this world." He draws the sheet over the woman's face. "Glad your brother's okay."

I peek in on my way back to Sam. The D-man is on the phone, but not saying anything. I nudge back the curtain an inch. The clink of rings sliding on rod echoes loud in my ears, but he doesn't notice.

James does. Those blue eyes watch me from a face blackened by smoke and haunted with grief. I swore if I ever saw him again, he would regret it. But now I can only think of the terrible bond we share.

The curtain rattles.

Protect the children. The words come from my head. Sounds like Trish, but a bit deeper. Just like the last time atop Dragon Hill. Am I completely batshit—

The ground rumbles. The D-man pockets his phone. The rumbling intensifies into an all-out earthquake. I stumble into the curtain. The agent whirls around, his eyes widening when they find me.

"You're that—"

A sharp tremor sends him sideways. He clutches at a trembling tent pole.

"You need to get out . . . ," James says, but the rest of his words are swallowed by an explosion of dragon sirens.

The Blues are on the rampage.

8

Fissures rush through the tent, vicious subterranean claws that shred anything in their path. They come fast and straight, and when the tendrils of cracking earth reach me, they shift course and accelerate toward the D-man.

A section of asphalt shoots up through the canvas beneath his feet. He surfs the undulating chunk until a secondary tremor tips it over. He slams to the ground, and the pole he clung to moments before crashes onto his head.

"Get out of here, Melissa," James shouts above the blaring sirens. "It's the Blues. They can't control it much longer—"

"Then you'd better shut up, farmboy, and tell me where the keys are."

He nods at the BoDA agent. "Left pants pocket."

I drop and crawl over. The agent groans when I roll

him onto his side. His eyes are closed; blood pours from his scalp; a splinter of bone protrudes through his left pant leg. Biting my lip to keep from gagging, I fish through his pocket until I find the keys.

I'm lurching toward James when I hear Dad shouting my name. He sounds miles away, but when I pull back the curtain, he's on the other side of the corridor, no more than ten feet from me. Sam's slung over his shoulder. My brother's eyes blink open. He gives me a dopey smile and a gleeful wave.

I steady myself against the worsening tremors and struggle to my feet. "In here, Dad."

He spins around. "Come on!"

A nurse flashes past him, pistol in hand, and I'm suddenly aware of the patter of gunfire. Sounds like heavy rain, and it's coming closer, along with the thunder of the dragon stampede.

"Go, Dad. Get Sam out of here. I'm coming!" I yell.

He looks at the agent, at the keys clutched in my hand. "What are you doing?"

Poles clatter to the ground. Sections of tent collapse. Dad stumbles sideways and collides with a gurney, nearly dropping Sam.

"Get out of here, Melissa!" James urges.

"Sam needs you, Dad. Go!" He doesn't move. "Mom

was right about the dragons. They're not here to hurt us. And they're not going to hurt me."

Dad glances toward the exit. "You know where to meet us?"

When we're not running dragon shelter drills, we're learning evac routes. "At Henley's farm. Bet I'll beat you there."

"You better, Melissa Anne. Love you." Then he and Sam are gone.

With the earth pitching me around, it takes a couple of tries to insert the key into the cuffs securing James's hand. The latch clicks, the world shifts, I'm thrown sideways onto his lap.

He sets me on my feet, wraps an arm around my waist. Leaning on each other, we crouch-walk forward, the ground shaking every which way. We're almost to the curtain when I hear the groan behind me.

I hesitate.

Another groan. I glance back. The D-man's sprawled on a slab of asphalt that's going crimson with blood. Even with our help, there's no guarantee he'll survive. But without it, he doesn't have a chance.

"Help me get him."

James tenses. "No."

"He'll die if we don't help him."

"Good."

A tremor erupts beneath us, knocking over chairs, a cot, and the EKG machine. I stagger.

James offers me his hand. "Come on, Melissa, before it's too late."

"I'm not leaving him." I maneuver my way around fallen medical equipment, a couple of poles rolling to the earthquake's chant, and chunks of street poking through the tent floor.

The man's eyes open when I grab his jacket collar. Panic, confusion, anger cross his face. He reaches for his gun. His eyes dart from me to James, and the panic and confusion disappear.

He pulls his gun in one quick motion.

I kick at his hand, but the earth gives beneath me and I lose my balance.

I collide with something, or maybe it collides with me. I laugh but can't be sure because I can't hear, and this makes me laugh more. It suddenly seems quite funny, quite ridiculous, all of this. Terrible, but hilarious how bad things have gone, like one of Sam's twisted dreams.

Yes, it must be, because this can't be real. Why would my vision be narrowing on that hot farmboy in the hospital gown? Why would the numbness spreading through my shoulder feel so wonderful? I glance down. Red everywhere.

My favorite shirt ruined by blood. Mine? Must be a dream because I think I'd remember being shot.

Now I'm falling and spinning, a drunk ballerina on a shifting tectonic stage. The dream boy catches me in his arms, scoops me up. I blink, and we're in the remnants of the corridor. Medical equipment everywhere. A couple bodies, too. Everything vibrating to the earth's rumble.

The tent's disintegrating, the ground's splitting into a chasm. Dream boy jumps out of the way as a gurney goes tumbling by. He leaps from perch to precarious perch, somehow dodging the arsenal of growing debris.

And then we're out in the open, where All-Blacks are retreating toward us, hiding behind broken homes and abandoned vehicles to fire their weapons at the spectacular blue wall emerging from Mason-Kline's smoky center. The dragons move like a tornado, blind and wild and full of destruction. At the front is Old Man Blue.

"What's he doing?"

"She's protecting the children," James says. His voice sounds a mile away.

I look up at him and see a red dragon swooping toward us. At least a dozen more Reds plunge in and out of the clouds. Jets follow close behind. Explosions and geysers of flame illuminate the heavens.

A-Bs turn their weapons on the diving dragon. It roasts

them. As the Red comes closer, I spot the rider atop it. He aims his rocket launcher at a unit of A-Bs and fires.

The dragon hovers a few feet overhead, its airplane wide wings flapping a slow beat. A rope ladder unrolls down its side and comes to a stop a few inches from our heads. James tightens his hold on me and loops his other arm around the ladder's bottom rung. He yanks once. We spin about, and then we're gliding from the fiery devastation that's overtaken Mason-Kline.

I lift my head, close my eyes, and let the rushing wind carry me from this nightmare. It cascades over me, its soft touch tickling my skin. I unwrap my arms from the farmboy's neck and arch back. I am a bird skimming across a lake. My wing tips skip along the water's surface.

But the ride ends too soon, and when I open my eyes, the lake has become a cornfield, and I am nothing but a wingless girl in a bloody blue shirt. The Red lies a dozen yards away, munching on cornstalks.

The rider shimmies down the ladder, hurries over. Wearing a black trench coat, a fitted black cap with a chin strap, massive goggles, thick leather gloves, and a red bandana over an oxygen mask, he resembles a cross between a mad scientist and a stagecoach bandit.

He looks familiar—a sudden dizziness takes me, and a burst of agony ignites in my shoulder. My legs give out.

I start to fall, but James catches me. A black halo forms around his head, and soon there's nothing but him and me. He says something. I try to tell him I can't hear, but words won't come. He presses a finger to my lips.

Then another set of arms is beneath me, and a new face hovers in my closing tunnel of sight. The goggles are on his cap now, greasy tufts of hair protruding everywhere. Beady eyes gaze into mine.

"This day's been totally Jedi, huh, Callahan?" Preston Williams says, and then everything goes dark.

9

I awaken to groans, growls, and the dull buzz of a generator. I'm on a cot in some sort of large crate. A low-power light hangs in the corner, a red glow seeps through the gaps between slats. I lurch up. Pain burns through my shoulder, and I scream.

I'm in a hospital gown; my gunshot wound's bandaged. An IV in my hand connects to a bag of clear liquid. Maybe Preston dropped me off at the clinic, which must have lost power in the attack, hence the generator. Maybe I'm in a crate because there wasn't enough room in the building. Maybe that red glow and those growls belong to downed dragons awaiting transport to the Fort Riley dragattoir.

I hold on to those maybes as long as I can, but any hope

that I'm somewhere normal disintegrates when the wall in front of me swings back on a hinge. I'm in a stadium of a cave filled with Reds and their riders.

A middle-aged woman steps inside, introduces herself as Gretchen. She takes my pulse, unwinds the bandage around my shoulder. I barely notice, my attention fixed on the surreal world beyond the crate.

Most of the dragons lie slumped on the right side of the cave. Several leak blood through gauze-wrapped injuries; a few nurse bullet-riddled wings; one licks the stump of a lost tail. Rows of cots occupied by bruised and bloodied humans form a square on the opposite side of the cave. One of the men checking on the wounded comes our way.

Keith.

I blink several times, sure that I'm mistaken.

"You're an insurgent," I mumble as he enters the crate.

He shuts the wall behind him. "How are you feeling?"

Confused. Betrayed.

"No signs of infection," Gretchen says. I look at her as she redresses my wound. Wrinkles and scars adorn an already weathered face. A livid gash, recently stitched, runs the length of her forehead.

I chew at my lip. "Dad . . . Sam. Are they okay?"

"Your brother's fine," Keith says. "He's with your aunt and uncle in Michigan."

His words take a while to register. "Why isn't he with Dad?"

"Your father was injured pretty badly." Keith lays a hand on my good shoulder. I shrink away. "He broke his neck, Melissa. He went into surgery before I left."

"I need to see him," I say, reaching for the IV in my hand.

Gretchen intervenes. "You need to rest."

I glare at him. "Don't suppose I can call?"

Keith shakes his head. "We're in the evac territories. Even if we got a signal, it'd be too dangerous."

Too dangerous? I almost laugh. "When can I leave?"

"You're hurt," he says. "And you're flagged in the government system."

"It was just a prank—" I can't believe this. "Preston set me up. And you did, too. Why?"

"That wasn't us."

"I thought you were my friend."

"I am your friend. I—"

A thunderous rumble interrupts him. The crate trembles; the glow through the slats intensifies. Mostly red, but some silver, too. More dragons. I can feel them milling about, hear their deep-throated groans and higher-pitched mewls.

The rumble subsides, enough for me to hear someone shouting for a stretcher. Keith glances at me.

"Go, I'm fine." I'm not sure that's true. I'm not sure I'll ever be fine again.

Keith nods, opens the crate.

James is striding toward us, cast in the brilliant light of the silver dragon that prances after him. I cringe. The thing glows twice as bright as any other dragon in the cave.

A dozen more Reds crowd the floor. Most are dim. Several are bleeding. One flickers like a faulty lightbulb.

Their riders aren't in much better shape. Several stagger down their ladders; a few lie hunched over, too injured to dismount. The insurgents offer aid with the calm proficiency of people well practiced in the art of war. Or at least its aftermath.

A pair of men rush by, Preston laid out on the stretcher they carry. Blood streaks his face, some of it fresh. His eyes are closed, but I see him give a weak thumbs-up to somebody before he disappears from view.

Keith hugs James. "How'd it go?"

"We got the kids at Rez Three into the evac tunnels, but the army met us at Four," James says. He hooks a thumb at the Silver. "We were able to recover her. The others returned to Cave Eight to resupply. . . ."

Keith shuts the crate. Their voices fade.

Gretchen says she's going to get me dinner. I tell her I'll live, that she should help her friends, which it's obvious she's eager to do. She thanks me, presses a bottle of painkillers into my palm, indicates the location of the urinal pan. She's at the wall door when she hesitates, glances back with a smile.

"You look a lot like her, you know?"

I almost choke on the pills. She meant it as a compliment, but it feels more like a knife to the heart. She must have thought I'd already figured it out. Maybe I avoided the truth because today's already been hard enough, but I can't avoid it any longer.

My mother was an insurgent, too.

10

The distance between sympathizer and insurgent isn't that far, I guess, but I never fathomed that Mom could be anything but Mom, doing her army work, protesting cruelty against dragons behind Dad's back. But Mom never did anything halfway.

"You don't have any more secrets up your sleeve, do you?" I ask Keith when he returns to check on me. Things have calmed down somewhat in the cave—I guess everybody's asleep or licking their wounds—but I'm at full boil. "Dad's not an insurgent, too, is he? Were you and Mom—"

"No, Melissa. I know this is a lot to deal with, but—"

"A lot to deal with? I'm God knows where, surrounded by dragons, lying in a"—I throw my arms up to indicate the crate/hospital room, and pain explodes in my shoulder—"whatever the hell this thing is. I've been shot. The government thinks I'm a traitor. Runs in the family, evidently. And Dad . . ."

I lose it completely, dissolving into heaves and sobs. Keith holds me, rocks me, whispers words of comfort that don't make a damn bit of difference. At some point, the crate door opens. Somebody enters, but I can't make out anything more than a fuzzy silhouette.

When I'm too tired to cry anymore, Keith lets me go with a kiss to the forehead. Over his shoulder, I see James in the corner of the crate, looking anywhere but at me. He's carrying a glass of water and an MRE packet. I can think of only one reason why he brought me dinner.

I wipe my eyes and glare at Keith. "You're leaving?"

"I need to head back to Fort Riley for a debrief," Keith says. "James—"

"Take me with you," I say. "I have to see Dad. Please."

"It's too dangerous. You need to lay low until things settle down. I'll let you know how he's doing when I come back tomorrow night. It's the best I can do. *Baekjul boolgool*, right?"

"Right," I mumble.

He says something to James I can't hear, then he's gone.

"What's that mean? *Baekjul boolgool?*" James asks.

"Indomitable spirit. Some crap I learned in tae kwon do."

"You do martial arts?"

"Not anymore." Not since Mom died.

"Well, I've got something that'll make you as right as rain," he says with sarcastic cheer. He sits and waves the MRE packet at me. "Beef ravioli. Yum."

MREs (Meal, Ready-to-Eat), stocked in dragon shelters and army depots across the world, come in multiple varieties. The best ones taste like cardboard, the worst like wet cardboard. The beef ravioli's on the soggy end of the spectrum, but I am hungry.

"How's Preston?" I ask between bites.

"He cracked his head pretty good when Syren made a sharp about-face to avoid a missile." He smiles. "He's already embellishing. Listen to him tell it, and Syren was doing loop-de-loops."

"Syren's his dragon?"

"Or Preston's her human," James says with a little laugh. "They're not horses, Melissa."

"No, they're definitely not."

"They're not monsters either."

"That's what my mother thought. Look how that turned out." I take a couple of deep breaths. "Maybe they're not the evil monsters the media makes them out to be, but they are dangerous."

James regards my wounded shoulder with an exaggerated eyebrow raise. "They're not the only ones. If you talk to them, you'll understand."

"Can all of you talk to dragons?"

He looks down. "I'm one of the few left in our group anymore."

He's thinking of his mother, I suppose.

"My mom?" I ask, hoping I'm wrong.

"Yeah . . . she taught me a lot."

I look over James's shoulder, toward the mouth of the cave. The scarlet glow obscures most of the stars, but the brightest shine through. I blink a few times to clear my eyes and find Sirius.

Mom taught me the constellations early on. That way, whenever she called home during her numerous deployments, I could go outside, name one, and we could gaze at it together. Without fail, she would tell me the neighboring constellations and their major stars.

"Look at Sirius in the big dog tonight, Mel. So bright and beautiful. I wanted to name you Siri, you know, but your father wouldn't let me."

It was ridiculous because a lot of the time she was in a place where the sun hadn't set yet or the stars were different, but I didn't know that when I was young. And when I got older, we pretended anyway and laughed about it, and the world was safe for those few minutes.

But that world was a lie.

Why didn't she tell me the truth? Sam was the one who

wanted to exterminate the dragons, not me. I never hated them until they killed her. I would have understood.

Maybe she knew I wouldn't. Not really. When she sent me her first protest picture—from a march around the Pentagon to protest the government's research methods—it brightened my week. I was sharing a secret with her. But later, when I understood more, I begged her to stop. I was worried about her job, but I was more worried about myself. What would everyone at school think if it got out that my mom was a sign-carrying, dragon-loving nutjob?

She made her choice; now I have to make mine. I can hide away, build up thicker walls, pretend that everything's going to be okay, or . . .

"I want to learn," I tell James.

"Keith doesn't want you involved in this. Anyway, you're injured. You need to rest."

"If I rest, I'm gonna go crazy," I say. He starts to argue. "Please. It's the least you could do after kidnapping me."

He smiles at that, eventually nods. "Tomorrow morning, if you're better." On his way out, he pauses. "Hope you're not afraid of heights."

"Why?" I say, sure I won't like the answer.

"Before you can really talk to a dragon, you've got to fly one."

11

An icy Pegasus flaps through my dreams, the cold cutting into me with insistent sharpness until I wake. When I open my eyes, there's a silver dragon at the foot of my cot, its head crammed halfway into the crate. Crystalline blue eyes regard me with eagerness. Ice drips from the thing's snout onto the blanket.

Squinting against its brightness, shivering against its chill, and praying it doesn't think I'm breakfast, I scramble to the rear wall of the crate. I shoo it verbally and mentally, but either it doesn't understand or doesn't care. It just sniffs the air, perhaps trying to decide whether I'm edible.

"She wanted to see you," James says. With the quickest glance, I see that he's crouched in the crate corner.

"Call it off," I plead.

"You can't be scared of them, Melissa."

Perhaps emboldened by his words, the Silver stretches its neck forward until it's but a foot from me. Frost collects on my arms.

"Get away!"

The Silver retreats with a tremendous lurch, bursting through the crate. Fragments of wood fountain everywhere. I cover my head. James throws himself over me. As I grimace against the pain in my shoulder, I hear him give a couple of muffled grunts. I think he's hurt, maybe stabbed by a big splinter, but then I realize the lunatic's laughing.

I shove him away. Half of the crate's obliterated. The Silver, looking quite proud of itself, has withdrawn to a spot between two slumbering Reds on the other side of the cave. People hurry toward us, concern shifting to amusement when they see we're all right. They disperse, several of them clapping; somebody requests an encore.

James flourishes a bow I might find endearing if my shoulder weren't throbbing—never mind the fact that I'm sprinkled in glitter made of sawdust and ice. He turns to me with a sheepish smile. "That didn't go as expected. You okay?"

Breathing warmth into my fingers, I stare at him like he's a few neurons short. "What exactly did you expect? Who the hell wakes somebody up with a dragon?"

"She really wanted to see you." He surveys the destruction with pursed lips and gives a mock sigh of disappointment. "Children."

"The thing needs to be on a leash."

"You'll hurt her feelings," James says.

"Good. Maybe she'll learn boundaries."

"She doesn't understand stuff like that yet. You should be thrilled, Melissa. She likes you."

"You and I have far different definitions for thrilled. I'm thrilled she didn't eat me, if that counts for anything."

"You've got to stop looking at them like that," James says. "They're as foreign as foreign can be, and at first glance, terrifying. I understand."

"If you understand, maybe you should have eased me into it."

"I believe in the deep-end approach."

"Throw me in, see if I can swim? Seriously?"

He waves a hand at what used to be the crate wall. "Think about it. After this, flying one won't seem so bad."

I can't help but laugh. "Asshole."

"On my good days." He gives me a once-over that reminds me I'm in a flimsy hospital gown. "As much as I like the ensemble, I think we might want to get you into something a little warmer for your first flight."

"My shoulder's too stiff," I say as he clears debris from a

footlocker bolted to the floor.

"Good thing we're flying tandem then." He props open the lid to reveal a miniature thrift store of worn clothes, musty books, and random baubles. He retrieves a pair of jeans and tosses them to me.

"I still don't see how this is necessary," I say. "What's flying have to do with talking to them?"

"Nothing and everything." He chucks a basketball toward the other end of the cave. The Silver bounds after it. The floor trembles. I'm monitoring the stalactites overhead when James says, "Cartha told me that you think I'm cute."

Heat flushes my cheeks. I fold my arms over my chest and glare at him. "Who the heck is Cartha?"

"The dragon you called Old Man Blue." He holds up a hand. "I'm not trying to make you uncomfortable. Strike that, I am, but not because I care whether you think that. Not that I don't care."

Frowning, he returns his attention to the footlocker. "We're kind of like antennae, you and I. If the dragons know our frequency, they can talk to us. That's baseline. But if we're in a state of upheaval—scared, angry, that sort of thing—the signal's amplified and your thoughts become visible. Dragons become a lot more interested in you."

I think of Dragon Hill. "The watching sensation."

He nods. "Ghost eyes."

"So you give me a dragon wake-up call and want me to go fly around the block a few times to get over my fear?"

"The thing is, most dragons won't violate your thoughts if they respect you." He digs out a sweatshirt, a jacket, and a pair of thick-rimmed goggles. "Show them you can handle yourself in the sky, it gives you some street cred. Or cloud cred, I guess."

I change in another crate, which belongs to Gretchen and a dark-haired woman sedated on a cot. Hooked up to machines, she's recovering from her own gunshot wound. While I slip into my new clothes, Gretchen offers advice. Hold on tight, recognize storm clouds, stay within the perimeter, listen to James, don't disrespect your dragon, hold on tight (I get this one—quite unnecessarily—at least three more times) . . .

Dressed, I meet James outside the crate. The Silver's with him, frozen basketball between her lips. She drops it at my feet, looks at me expectantly.

I squat down slowly, my gaze never leaving the Silver. She tracks me with growing impatience. I grab the ball and hurl it. Off she goes. Wings pulled tight to her body, she barrels around insurgents and dragons with no concern in the world but retrieving that ball. On the list of things I thought I'd never do, playing fetch with a dragon ranks right near the top.

"It's really a child, isn't it?" I say.

"A baby, a beautiful baby," James says as the Silver returns with the ball.

"What about the others?"

"We saved some of them, but she's the only one big enough to fly yet."

He steers me toward a group of insurgents eating breakfast around a fire. As we walk, James plays tour guide. The crates that line the back of the cave are for the medics, those with serious injuries, and guests. He points out one in the middle. "That's mine."

"You're a medic?"

"No. I'm kind of grounded. Keith has gotten particularly paternal with me."

Over there, supply crates—food, water, drugs. We take a detour past a clothesline, a washbasin, and a couple of bathtubs to an alcove ringed with portable toilets. We pass dragon-riding equipment and a couple medics tending the Reds' injuries.

I chew at my lip. "Can I ask you a question?"

"Anything."

It takes me a couple of seconds to work up my courage.

"Why exactly do you help them?"

James regards me with a fierce expression. "Everyone thinks they're giant cockroaches who need to be exterminated." He taps his temple. "But they hurt and suffer as much as we do."

"They're the ones that showed up out of nowhere and attacked us," I remind him.

"You condemn an entire species for the actions of a few."

"A few?"

He waves his hands at the Reds. "Once the war started, were they supposed to just sit back and hope the military knew who the good ones were?"

"I don't know, James." I gesture toward a nearby pallet of weapons laden with machine guns, rocket launchers, and several objects I don't recognize. "I'm just tired of all this."

"It's not war for them. It's survival."

"Protect the children," I whisper. Old Man Blue and her army were trying to stop the military from murdering the children. But how many people did they kill in the process? I shake my head. "You can't do it this way, James."

"We have no choice."

I bite my lip before I say something I'll regret, which happened all too often in my arguments with Mom. She believed there were no bad guys, only victims. I believed she was crazy, told her so more than once. Then she died, and I didn't care about being right anymore.

We finally reach the campfire. After a whirlwind of introductions, James grabs MREs from a storage container and we sit on folding chairs beside a heavy guy with a friendly face who's busy examining a long, narrow bullet. I think his name's Howard.

"Tracker?" James asks.

"New model." He points at a microscopic hole in the casing. "They put the tracer in there. Pulled it out of Myra. We found two dozen more in the others."

"Deactivated?" James asks.

"For sure," Howard says. He grins. "We sent some out with the morning crew."

"We run sentry shifts to secure our perimeter," James says to me.

"Except this time they're going to go a bit farther," Howard says. "Activate these suckers and drop some false trails. Enough shop talk. We have more important matters to discuss."

"No, Howard. We talked about this," James says.

"You talked. I did not listen." Howard raises his voice. "Grunts, may I please have your attention." Everybody quiets. "As you know, we have a newbie in our ranks. And all newb Grunts must play our game."

"Loki run! Loki run!" the crowd chants.

"She's a guest, not a recruit," James says.

Ignoring him, Howard holds up three fingers. "It's simple, Melissa. You must tell us three things about yourself.

Two must be the truth, and the third must be a lie." He waves
an arm at the others gathered about the fire. "If we choose
correctly, you make a lap around the cave in your skivvies."

"She's not doing this," James says. "She's injured."

Jeers answer him. Three quarters of the people around
the fire are wounded. Across the way, a guy with a prosthetic left leg hobbles to his feet, strips off his shirt, and
makes a loop around the fire. He plops back onto his rock to
vivacious applause.

Everyone turns to me. Take away the dragons, the crazy
outfits, the slings and bandages, and we could be off at summer camp somewhere. Or at one of Trish's parties.

It's normal wrapped in ridiculous, or maybe ridiculous
wrapped in normal. Maybe that's the way of it, the way to
stay sane in this insane world. Or maybe it's just a way to get
a girl to take off her clothes.

"You don't have to do this," James says as the silence
intensifies.

I look around the cave, at the unfamiliar faces of these
riders—many of them my age—at the dozen Reds who sure
as hell seem like monsters, and at the Silver hunkered behind
us, who seems nothing like a monster at all.

Whether I like it or not, this could be home for a while.

"What do I get if I win?" I ask. The crowd cheers.

"You get to make one of us do a Loki run," Howard says.

"I don't think so. If I win, everybody has to."

After a discussion, they grudgingly agree.

Before I give my answers, Howard has me write them down on a piece of paper, indicating which is the lie. He tucks it in his pocket and opens the floor to me.

"Truth number one: when I was ten, I won the Northern Virginia tae kwon do championship for my age division." I stand and snap out a solid side kick.

"Sign her up!" somebody says.

"That's a big region. She'd have to be cream of the cream to win. Lie!" someone else calls.

I grin. "Number two: I have a tattoo of Canis Major on my left hip." I point at my gunshot wound. "Only thing that hurt worse was this."

"Let's have a look-see."

"She doesn't look like that kind of girl."

"Truth number three: my father was the lead scientist on the research team that discovered dragons can't see black."

"Truth!" I hear from the other end of the fire. "It was all over the news."

"Yes," I say. ARMY OFFICIALS DISCOVER DRAGONS' ACHILLES' HEEL. "But are you sure he was the lead?"

"She's got you there," James says.

Unfortunately, an older guy remembers Dad's interview on *60 Minutes*.

They debate, but end up split on the other two. Six think I'm not good enough to win the NoVa tae kwon do tournament. Six think I look too wholesome for a tattoo.

"Everett, you've got to break the tie," Howard says to James, who has stayed silent during the discussion.

"No clue," he says. "I abstain."

"Come on, man," says one of the tae kwon do disbelievers. "You must know whether she's tatted up. Don't make us go wake Preston."

"What's he talking about?" I whisper.

"You were bleeding pretty badly back in Mason-Kline. We had to get your shirt off to apply a compress," he whispers back. As I feign indifference, hoping the shadows obscure my embarrassment, he speaks up. "I didn't get a good look. She did mention that she used to do tae kwon do."

Howard switches his vote, then retrieves the paper from his pocket and unfolds it. He scowls at James. "Lying bastard."

"Perhaps he's not. Perhaps she's lying," somebody says. Calls for proof ring out.

I lift my jacket and shirt. Sirius, the top star in the constellation, and a couple of connecting lines peek out over my jeans. I grin. "Your turn."

They strip, a few meekly, but most with farmboy merriment. Taunts and brags fly every which way.

JOSHUA McCUNE

"You too, Everett," Howard says. "Take off the armor, and show the damsel the bird-man's chest."

"I don't think so," James says.

"The knight's gone chicken," Howard says. The others turn their taunts on James until he relents.

"Thank you," I say as he slips out of his jacket.

"Don't know what you're talking about."

I glance up from the fire, but his face is blocked by the sweater pulled over his head. Fading bruises yellow his stomach and an old scar runs at an angle from his clavicle into the furrow between his pecs. He's got a tattoo of his own. Curled around his left bicep, it resembles one of those tacky barbwire things, but when he turns from me to strip out of his pants, the firelight catches it better.

Letters, jagged and overlapping, circle around to form a phrase. *Drink the* . . . The last part's out of sight.

Then he's off, falling in line with the other half-naked insurgents on a loop around the cave. Others step from their crates to watch. The men stationed at the cave entrance with binoculars and rocket launchers urge them on. The Reds ignore them.

The Silver does not. She's a sheepdog, and the runners are her sheep. She herds them at an enthusiastic gallumph, circling back to exhort the stragglers. Prosthetic Leg Guy, who scoffed at Howard's plea to stay behind, limps along the best he can, but too slow for the Silver. After several nudges met by startled curses, she picks him up and races around the cave until she reaches the fire, where she sets him on his feet, shivering and a bit blue.

"Thanks," he mutters, but the Silver's already rumbling off to help the next laggard. Everybody speeds up after that.

James sprints to the finish ahead of the pack, then doubles over, clutching his knees. I covertly sneak a peek at the rest of his tattoo.

Or maybe not so covertly, because he says, "Drink the wild air."

"The dragon-rider motto?" I ask.

"Something like that." He dresses. "You ready?"

"As I'll ever be," I say, looking toward the far side of the cave. The Reds sit gathered in a circle, heads bowed together. James tells me they're praying for Myra, the faintly flickering dragon that lies in a dark corner.

Religious Reds? I don't touch that one with a ten-foot pole.

"Pretty much the only time a dragon needs your help is when she's having trouble seeing," James instructs as we walk over. "Just talk to them. Describe the situation. Building at two o'clock, three hundred feet below—"

"There's really no need for this. They're injured and—"

"Vestia's not. Anyway, flying heals the soul," he says.

"The easiest way to communicate with a dragon is to address them directly. They'll often ignore you, particularly if they don't like you. We can talk with them one at a time, but they have the ability to carry on multiple conversations at once. It's quite interesting."

"Quite."

He fails to note my sarcasm. "Vestia believes it's a clear indication of their superiority, but . . ."

He keeps talking, but I'm no longer listening. The watching sensation has just bombarded me. Different from Dragon Hill. More aggressive. Evidently the Reds are done praying.

The brightest breaks from the pack, green eyes narrowing on me. The sensation intensifies, the warmth swells, and I break into a furious tremble.

I clench my fists, grit my teeth, but can't control the fear that pulses through me. I tell myself these creatures are not monsters, but my body refuses to believe it. There's too much history to overcome.

Whereas the Silver reminds me of a five-ton puppy, these Reds remind me of my childhood. They were the primary color on the evening news most nights.

"I can't do it," I say, backpedaling. "I thought I could, but I can't. I'm sorry."

James catches me by the wrist. "Vestia won't hurt you."

"Vestia," I mumble, pulling free. Give a monster a name, tell me it prays, does that make it any less a monster?

Give a human a name, listen to it pray and pray and pray, does that make it any less appetizing? The shrill voice sends me stumbling back at a faster clip. I hit a wall. The dragon cranes her neck toward me. Thick swirls of smoke burst from her nose. An image of an enormous hawk scrutinizing a petrified mouse pops into my head.

You think me an animal, do you, human? Vestia says. Her gaze narrows to slits, and she smiles to expose her teeth. *James is right. I won't hurt you.* She chomps. *Wouldn't hurt a—*

A snarl interrupts her. She turns, but too late. The Silver smashes into Vestia, sends her careening to the ground. The Red regains her feet with a quickness that belies her size. She extends her wings, arches her neck, and looses a terrible scream. The Silver adopts a similar position, its glow near blinding. As they circle around, screeching at each other, ripples of intense heat wash over me, followed by blasts of frozen air.

I scramble into a nearby alcove, shallow but too skinny for a dragon to squeeze into. Everybody else—dragons and humans alike—has also gone into full retreat mode.

Except James. I yell for him to take cover, but either he doesn't hear over the roars, or he's too stupid to listen. He falls to one knee in front of the fuming Red, as if he's a beggar beseeching a queen. Vestia lifts her leg and lets it hover a few feet over his head.

James doesn't budge. Instead, he makes an apologetic gesture for the Silver. I assume he's using the same line of reasoning he did with me. "She's a child; she doesn't understand what she's doing."

Vestia listens to him for five seconds at most, then stomps the cave floor beside him. The resulting quake knocks him off balance. The Silver bares its teeth. James jumps to his feet, positions himself between the two dragons, arms raised overhead. Vestia sweeps him aside with her forepaw, gentle enough not to kill him, hard enough to send him flying.

With a mighty bellow, the Silver drives a talon into Vestia's chest. The Red recoils, rises to her full extent, opens her mouth. A fireball forms in the back of her throat.

Vestia, stop it! I implore silently.

The Red prowls forward, her fire rolls to the front of her mouth.

I direct my energy at the Silver, hoping James was right about her liking me. "Stop it!"

She ignores me, too, bares her teeth in full attack mode. Vestia's flames snap out, licking at the Silver's snout. The Silver squeals but doesn't retreat.

"Stop it! Please!"

"Melissa, stay back!" Gretchen calls. She and Howard

are pulling James out of the way. I look around. There is no place to stay back.

I must move or I will die. This is what I tell myself as I launch into a sprint. I can't think of anything dumber than charging into a dragon fight, but that's what I do.

I deliver a sharp front kick to the Silver's mammoth ankle. As a jolt of agony shoots up my leg, she lets out an earsplitting yowl. She couldn't possibly feel anything more than a tiny poke, but her brightness subsides to normal and she draws in her wings. Vestia's glow dwindles, too, and she backs away with a triumphant snort.

The Silver crouches so that we're at eye level, regarding me with an expression of pained confusion.

"You can't do that," I say, feeling a tad ridiculous scolding a dragon. "You're gonna get us hurt."

She slumps down, goes almost dark, and suddenly she's crying. High-pitched, almost inaudible. The screams of a child lost and alone. I press my hands to her icy temples, lean my head against hers.

"I know how hard it is to be without your family," I say. "I know you're scared because I'm scared, too."

Her breathing softens, her whimpering subsides, and her heartbeat stills until I can no longer feel it pulsing. She brightens, slithers backward, and starts to wiggle.

Bath time, Vestia says. *You might want to run, human.*

The Silver bounds forward. I raise my hands, but not fast enough to block her giant pink tongue. She licks me again and again, covering me in cold slobber. I hear a rush of footsteps followed by a chorus of laughter.

James pulls me free of the Silver's affection to applause and more laughter, wraps me in his jacket. As he rubs a semblance of warmth back into me, I locate Vestia. Wings furled, fire swallowed. Smirking?

You are an idiot, the Red says, but not really like an insult. *You know I wouldn't have hurt her? You, on the other hand . . .* she says, almost a joke. Almost. *Be thankful she likes you.*

Despite the craziness of it all, I smile.

12

James cancels our flight plans for that day. Strangely, I'm disappointed. When I mention this, he laughs and blames it on adrenaline and altitude.

"Drink the wild air, right?" I say as we limp toward the cave mouth. Well, he limps.

"Maybe sip it for a while," he says after tossing back a few painkillers. "At least until Vestia forgives me."

I snort. "Forgives you?"

Best you learn your place, too, human, Vestia chimes in. *You should not meddle in dragon affairs.*

"No problem there. Just trying to keep you from burning down the house," I say.

"You don't have to talk aloud," James says as Vestia says, *Picking up some backbone, are you? Good, I prefer you crunchy.*

"I prefer you silent," I say with a wary glance over my shoulder. Vestia and the other Reds surround the dragon in the corner who flickered out a few minutes ago. Their heads move in strange arcs. Their soft mewls echo through the cave.

"You don't have to talk aloud," James repeats. "People will think you're crazy."

"I am crazy. I'm talking to a dragon. A dragon who wants to eat me."

"She wouldn't actually do it. She's a vegetarian."

"Of course she is."

"You'll get used to it. They're not that different from us."

"Minus the flying and breathing fire and ice parts?"

James grins. "Yeah, minus that. It's not normally like this. Today's been a bad day."

"Understatement of the century."

"I'm going to make it up to you," he says, which is why we're hobbling toward the cave entrance.

We exit onto a ledge that faces east. James clears snow from a log for us to sit on. Snow-dusted evergreens and sky-spearing mountains extend in every direction. The wind swirls with a brisk bite, and I can almost forget everything.

"It's incredible." I've never seen so much of the world untouched by war. Not a glimpse of civilization in sight. "Mom would have loved—" I cut off and glance toward James. He's smiling.

Not would have loved. Did love. When James first mentioned an apology and directed me this way, I assumed he was going the farmboy route. Show me a pretty vista in hopes of distracting me.

It's not the first time I've underestimated him.

He indicates a spot between two peaks. "She would often look that way. Usually when she thought everybody was asleep."

His voice softens. "I didn't want to bother her, but this one night she was out longer than normal. I was worried she might catch cold. When I tiptoed out here, she didn't acknowledge me. I assumed she was in conversation with a dragon, but when I draped the blanket over her shoulders, I saw that she was crying.

"There weren't many of us then," James continues. "We had big dreams but little success, and there wasn't much to be happy about. Your mom, though, she could always find the sunshine through the clouds, no matter how thick they were."

"'You got two choices, Mel. Laugh or cry. Always choose laugh,'" I murmur. Laughter doesn't seem possible at the moment.

He shifts position, closer by the sound of it. But I dare not check, dare not move, otherwise I will crumble.

"She started talking about you and Sam," he says, and I

can feel his breath on my ear. It is the only warmth out here. "We all knew she had a family, but she never talked about you before. I thought it was because she wanted to protect you, and that was part of it, but . . . I don't know, Melissa . . . I don't know exactly what I'm saying. I guess I just want you to know how much she missed you."

James leans forward, grimaces when he sees my face. "Tell me those are happy tears."

"I'm not sure."

"Lie to me then. Or I'm gonna feel like a real jerk."

I finally find a laugh, a small one. "Weren't you supposed to help me eliminate emotions?"

"No," he says. "I would never want that. Anyway, it's only the negative ones that open you. Fear, guilt, anger. Nobody knows why, but nothing quite blocks the signal like joy."

"Terrific. Don't suppose faking it works?"

"That would be nice. You've got to find something to hold on to."

"What do you hold on to?" I ask.

"I'm between happys right now," he admits, and for a moment the curtain opens and he's that boy I saw in Mason-Kline, haunted and lost. But it closes even faster, the sadness rolled away off stage, beyond sight and sound.

Thinking of our mothers, I squeeze his hand. "Me too."

✴ ✴ ✴

We go to his crate, where we sit on opposite ends of his cot and get to know each other in a more normal manner. It's nice. Close my eyes to the glow that bleeds through the slats, close my ears to the occasional dragon snorts, and we're just a boy and a girl in an anonymous bedroom somewhere.

I learn he grew up in Calgary before ditching city life for the "friendly confines of stalactites and Porta Potties." He's never read a dragon book and likes Ralph Waldo Emerson.

We swap signs. His Taurus to my Aries. The ram and the bull, always butting heads, he jokes. I tell him he better really watch out, because my moon's in Scorpio. And he says that's okay, because his is, too, but I'm pretty sure he has no clue about astrology beyond the basics.

He's a year older than me, working on a degree in military history via correspondence, though that's on indefinite hiatus. I mention I was finishing up college applications—considering premed—and then get to thinking about how that might never happen now.

Whenever I go glum, he notices and shifts course. This time he starts rambling about his favorite band, some alternative group from England. He plays a sample. I move closer, under the pretense of wanting to get a better look at the background picture, a lonely red maple in an empty field.

The tree is beautiful, the music's awful. I ask if he's got the All-Pinks on there, and it's obvious what he thinks of that. He shuts the music off.

Besides a few books on a caged shelf, there is nothing in the crate to provide me further insight into the boy behind the smile and deep blue eyes. He insists that he maintains a spartan lifestyle because at any moment they might need to relocate, which they do via dragon. Pick up the crate, carry it somewhere else. Pictures and stuff like that would fall, he explains.

So he keeps his life stored in a footlocker. Happens to be the only one with a padlock on it. "Everything's all dusty and disorganized inside," he says when I press him for a peek. "Anyway, I need to have an air of mystery. Otherwise you'll realize I'm entirely boring."

We move on. Any time I touch on anything too personal—his parents, in particular—he changes the subject.

The conversation finally comes around to dragons, starting with the big question. Where do they come from?

"They don't know. They say they can't remember anything before they got here. But they're here now, and we have to learn to live with them."

"You ever wonder what life would be like if they weren't around?"

"Boring."

I snort. "Boring?"

He lies back, closes his eyes, takes a slow breath. "When you're flying a dragon, everything else disappears."

"Yeah, until a squadron of DJs shows up."

He smiles. "Then it's even better. You're on that razor's edge, the world becomes a blur, and you're living a blink at a time."

I laugh. "You're crazy."

"Probably. I don't know. If you don't face death every once in a while, how do you know how to live?"

"Yin-yang, huh?"

"Sure."

"I've had enough death," I say.

He sits up, looks at me. "So, what, you shut down, become a robot, push it all away?"

"Said the pot to the kettle."

He darkens, a pot ready to boil over.

"I don't know, James. I just don't want dragons reading my thoughts."

"You ever consider maybe it's not such a bad thing?"

"Okay, if it's not such a bad thing, tell me what you're thinking. Because it certainly seems like you're trying to keep it all concealed."

He looks away. "I am, but I'm not."

I wait.

He picks at a cuticle, his shoulders sag. "Yin-yang," he mumbles.

I wait.

He shakes his head.

"That's it?" I ask.

"Yeah."

I give him a playful nudge. "Liar."

"It doesn't matter, Melissa."

I inch closer. "Tell me. Please."

He's silent for a long time. Finally he shrugs. "I won't run from death. I won't run from pain or fear. Life hurts sometimes, sometimes so much that you think it's never gonna stop hurting. That's a beautiful thing."

"Beautiful?"

He looks at me, angry almost. "Better to feel something than nothing."

His fierceness makes me smile.

His brow furrows. "What?"

I shake my head, my eyes locked on his. "Nothing."

Definitely something.

Later, as the conversation between us comes easier and the looks linger a little longer, he retrieves a book of poetry. I watch him flip through the pages, surprised at the delicacy in his fingers. Long and lean, like a pianist's. I ask him if he plays, and he says he's tone deaf. I tell him I've been at it since I was six and would kill to have his fingers. He lifts my hand, presses our palms together, and says that his fingers would look funny on me.

He finds the poem he was after. "Merlin's Song." Emerson. He wants me to read it. I try not to skim.

"'Live in the sunshine, swim the sea; Drink the wild air's salubrity,'" I recite as I near the end.

"Brilliant, right?"

"That part, minus the salubrity."

"Different times," he says.

I laugh. "More salubrious, evidently."

"You have a wonderful laugh."

"This coming from Mr. Tone Deaf?"

"My mistake. Your laugh's awful."

I give him a playful eye roll. "You probably tell that to every girl you bring to your crate."

He grins. "Of course. I am the primary recruiter for Loki's Grunts, after all."

"Oh? Is that why you were at Dragon Hill? Might want to work on your routine."

"Hmm. You were off-limits anyway."

"Off-limits, huh?"

"Big time. Keith would kill us if anything happened to you."

I lean back on my arms. "And yet you came up that hill anyway, acting all mysterious."

He cocks his head, amused. "I didn't even know you were there until Cartha told me."

"Did she happen to tell you who set up those decapitated soldiers?"

He hesitates. "She didn't mention it."

"Not Preston?"

"No chance," he says, and tries to change the subject a little too fast.

"But you have suspicions?"

A longer hesitation. "We have a theory."

"I'm all ears."

He's about to speak when the distinctive clatter of a dragon landing on stone reaches our ears. James checks his watch. "Keith."

I'm out of the crate and running in three steps, desperate for good news. But when I catch sight of Keith's somber expression, I know this day's about to get infinitely worse.

13

Paralyzed.

The word crashes over me, a tidal wave on an endless loop.

Paralyzed.

My father, my big, powerful father.

Paralyzed.

The man who never asks for anything, never needs anything.

Paralyzed.

Keith, holding me tight, talks about surgery and treatment plans and how down the road, with God's grace, Dad might recover some movement in his extremities.

Paralyzed.

I hate those surgeons and I hate treatment plans and I

hate God. But more than anything, I hate myself. If I hadn't gotten in that fight with Sam, we wouldn't have been in that tent and maybe Dad wouldn't be . . .

Paralyzed.

"I need to see him. I need to take care of him," I say, pushing away. I must be strong for him. For Sam. I cannot afford more tears. I cannot afford weakness. I must be strong like Dad.

"No, Melissa. I can't let you do that."

"I don't care if they arrest me," I say. "I haven't done anything wrong."

"You helped James escape," he says. "They have video evidence. You were also seen being airlifted from Mason-Kline by a dragon."

"Fine, they send me to jail for a few months. I don't care."

"It's not that easy. They have you listed as a Class One insurgent."

I flinch. Class One insurgent. You can be executed for that.

"We'll figure it out, Mel. It'll be all right," Keith assures me. I wish I were five again and could believe such things. He turns to James. "What's the word on the children?"

"Grackel says a handful can stay aloft for a few minutes. The rest remain grounded. None of them have their ice yet. What's going on?"

"Any more of those distress calls?"

James frowns. "Vestia got one yesterday. She ignored it. Cyrex got one a couple hours ago. He answered."

"I thought we'd agreed on silence."

"You know Cyrex doesn't believe in democracy, particularly not ours."

"He's put us all in danger."

"He's not stupid, Keith. He's setting up an ambush."

Keith's eyes narrow. "We need him and the others on surveillance, not playing chicken with the military."

"What's going on?"

"Just contact him and tell him we need him running eyes on Grackel's perimeter."

"What's going on, Keith?" James repeats, jaw tight.

Keith sighs. "The army discovered the evac tunnels and—"

"I should be out there, running point."

"Your place is here."

"With the wounded? Nobody can fly like Vestia and me."

"We're not talking about this again." Keith notices me listening, scowls. "Drop Melissa off with Howard, then come meet me and Gretchen in the map room. Contact Cyrex and Grackel and let them know."

"Already done," James mutters as Keith strides away. He looks to me. "What do you say we blow this joint?"

I'm confused until Vestia says, *Join us, human. We have a*

flight to make for Myra, and we can roar our grief together.

I can't make sense of her sudden kindness, but I welcome the opportunity to get away.

While I put on goggles, gloves, and a jacket, James retrieves a double saddle from a supply crate, uses a winch to mount it on Vestia, then collects a ladder and places it beside her. Two minutes later, I'm on the back of a red dragon.

"There's no seat belt," I say when James climbs aboard.

"Hold on to me. We won't let you fall."

Vestia flaps her wings. Once, twice, airborne. With a powerful swoosh, we glide from the cave. Seven Reds trail behind us, two of them carrying Myra by neck and tail.

It's an hour after sunset, the moon's a sliver on the horizon, and in the darkness there's not much to see except the shadows of the surrounding mountains and the dim outline of the world below. Far below. I clutch James, dig my feet into the stirrups, and pretend I'm riding a horse. The fastest horse ever, and she's not even pumping her wings anymore.

We alight at the edge of a frozen tarn. My stomach's spinning a nightmare and my head's gone woozy. I wobble down the ladder. Toward the bottom, James grabs me by the waist, guides me to the ground, and gives me a peppermint leaf to chew.

While I struggle to keep from vomiting, the Reds fan out to form an equidistant perimeter around the tarn. Myra's pallbearers, hovering above lake center, lower her to the ice, which splinters beneath her weight but does not break.

Once the two have joined the ring of mourners, Vestia lifts her head and focuses on Myra. *I am Vestia, and I see you.* Her voice resonates in a way I haven't heard before, and I'm guessing she's broadcasting.

The dragon to the left looks up. *I am Syren, and I see you. I am Marrick, and I see you.*

On and on this goes, sometimes with long pauses between proclamations. When I ask James about that, he tells me other Reds are speaking, ones who don't know me and thus do not include me.

Later, my nausea down to a dull ache, I hear the unintelligible but familiar mewl of the Silver, who remained at the cave at Vestia's order. After her cries fade, the Reds who stayed behind with her add their names to the roll call.

Next comes James. "I am James Everett, and I see you," he says aloud, I assume for my benefit. Vestia broadcasts his words for everybody to hear.

Myra would not like this, Vestia says to the group. *She had little respect for tradition, and even less for normalcy. But she is not here to argue, so she gets no choice.*

A guttural rumble echoes through my head. Laughter, I think. Surreal.

A long while back, during a storm of great wrath, Vestia

says, *she got it in her mind to fly the wrong way. As we sane dragons took flight with nature, she worked against it. Quickly she disappeared into the maelstrom. We did not have time to worry. The storm chased us into a valley. We were getting beaten upon with hail when I received her view in my head. The sun, bright and large, shone on a forest of great splendor.* "I won," she told me. "I defeated the wind."

She always fought the wind, Syren says without missing a beat. *I remember when she proposed the idea of mating with the Blues. We called her many names. You cannot talk with your enemy, silly dragon. As for mating, hah! And that's when she introduced us to Cartha and the others. Said she'd known them for years.*

Yes, but she had some standards, another dragon continues. *You remember the time she tricked that dullwit Green . . .*

The moon's near its peak before the story chain arrives at James. "I met Myra four years ago. I was her first talker," he says aloud, his words repeated by Vestia. "Normally, it's a dangerous moment with you guys."

More of that rumbling laughter.

"It didn't help that most of her group had just been killed by the invisible monsters. I had nobody to vouch for me," he says. "Yet she didn't put on a fright fest. Or threaten to eat me."

This time, only Vestia laughs.

"She asked . . . asked me to twirl around." His voice cracks. "Definitely the strangest request I've ever had. But there was something about her . . . so I twirled." He demonstrates. Arms out, chin tilted up. When he finishes his revolution, he's smiling in that way he does when he looks at the Silver.

"I felt like a fool. Then she asked me to close my eyes. 'No peeking.' I was getting dizzy when her glow entered my vision. I figured she was gonna end me, so I peeked. And there she was, dancing." He twirls again and laughs. "Clumsy and awkward and beautiful."

That she was, Vestia says. The Reds around the lake lift their heads skyward at some unspoken signal.

They roar. The sound, a bass-driven orchestra playing a melancholy tune, reverberates through the night. From the distance in every direction, smaller orchestras echo back.

"What did you think?" James whispers in my ear.

"It was nice." I see a flash of disappointment cross his face. I imagine he hoped this memorial service would open my eyes to the humanity of dragons. I can't deny that Myra seemed like a wonderful creature, but even criminals receive kind words at their funerals. How many people did she kill between defeating the wind and dancing with James?

Fifty or sixty that she knows of, and she cried for them all, Vestia says, her voice ripping through my thoughts as her roar goes quiet. I glance over my shoulder, but her glow remains calm, her focus directed toward the stars. *Have you once cried for a dragon, human?*

I snort. *Do you think her victims or their relatives care whether she cried for them? And what of you, dragon? Have you ever shed a tear for a human?*

No, but I do not hate you. Like you, we want to be happy. And we cannot be happy with hatred in our hearts. Live in your dark silence if you want, Melissa Callahan, or let go and roar with us. Roar about us dragons, roar about your god, roar at yourself if you must, roar as loud and long as you can until there is nothing left to roar about. Send all the badness away.

It's a quaint idea, but even if I believed such a thing were possible, there's no way I'd do it with James around.

"It does help some," he says a few seconds later. Vestia must have been in his head, too. I don't know why she cares. Anyway, if it helps so much, why isn't he doing it?

"I'll do it if you do," I say, figuring that'll end the discussion. It does, but not in the way I'd hoped. Without hesitation, James cranes his neck and howls, loud and forlorn.

On the list of things I never thought I'd do . . . At first, I manage nothing beyond a self-conscious squeak. But then I stop thinking about how ridiculous I must sound and start thinking about these past few days. I clench my body, tense up onto my tiptoes, gather everything into my lungs, and open my mouth once more.

The terrible noise that bursts forth is more shriek than roar. James threads his fingers through mine. We hold on tight, squeezing harder and harder as our cries escalate in a painful duet.

It's ridiculous, really, roaring your grief away, but there's something about just letting go completely. There's something even better when there's somebody howling at your side. It comes nowhere close to making me happy, but it helps me feel less alone, keeps me from sinking into the depths, which is about the best I can hope for right now.

We quiet. Our hands slip free; we exchange embarrassed smiles, then look elsewhere.

The dragons lower their heads to Myra. Eight gouts of flame swallow her. They cut off abruptly, and for the briefest moment, the dead Red is bright again, brighter than them all. Then her body dissolves to fiery ash. Steam from the melted ice carries her embers skyward. Winking in and out like fireflies, they swirl higher and higher.

It's the most beautiful thing I've ever seen.

May she fly forever into the next tomorrow, Vestia intones as Myra disappears into the heavens.

When we return to the cave, Keith and Preston are waiting for us, the latter with a bandage wrapped around his head, the former with a sharp scowl, which he directs at James.

"I asked him to take me," I say before Keith can explode, but my lie only makes him angrier.

He glowers at James. "You can't go running off whenever you want. You are too valuable."

"I didn't go running off, Keith. The dragons had a funeral. It's not like I'm doing anything useful here."

Preston pulls at my arm. "Let's go grab some grub and, uh, you can tell me how your crate got blasted in half."

I follow him toward the supply crates but am in no mood for food or storytelling. "James mentioned that you guys have a theory about who set me up at Dragon Hill."

"We're probably wrong," Preston says, but it's obvious he doesn't believe that. I wait. He chews at a fingernail. "I don't want to freak you out."

The Silver bounds over, drops a frozen basketball at my feet. I kick it. "My father's paralyzed. My brother's hurt. My home's destroyed. My best friend's mother is probably dead. And I'm stuck here playing fetch with a dragon. I'd like to know why."

With reluctance, Preston admits he and James were part of a surveillance group that had taken up residence in Mason-Kline. Preston was sent into the school to befriend Konrad Kline in order to hack his father's hard drive for intel.

"About a year ago, the army recollared the Blues—"

"They said it was for comfort or something," I say. Dad applied many of the restrictors himself. "Never believed that."

"Yeah, according to schematics we found, the new collars incorporate telepathy monitoring and control."

It takes me a few seconds to put the puzzle together. "So you think the government was listening in on Old Man Blue?"

"It's just a theory," he says.

And there's more to it, I realize as I recall the BoDA agents who came to arrest me. Those D-men arrived only an hour after the doctored pic appeared in the army system.

"You think the D-men did it," I say.

"Them or the army. If they were monitoring Cartha, they could have coordinated her communication to the time stamp on the photo Trish took. Add in some decapitated toys, remove everybody else, and there you go. You're a 'person of interest' who needs to be brought in."

Last time. My hands are getting cold, I say to the Silver, and toss the ball. I look to Preston with an apprehensive snort. "Then what? They make me disappear?"

Preston, ever-smiling Preston, gives me a frown. "You hear about that 'quarry massacre' in Wyoming a few months ago? That one along the drone zone they blamed on insurgents?"

I nod. Like the reporters, I found it odd a mining operation would be located that far from civilization. The drone
zone is a fifty-mile skirt of land that encircles the evac territories. Nothing illegal about living there, but most consider
it an invitation to disaster via dragon. And that's what the
initial reports indicated. That the facility had been decimated by Red fire.

"It was an off-grid army base, heavily fortified," Preston
says. "We're the ones who destroyed it. We didn't know
there were talkers there until afterward." He blows out a
long breath. "We knew a couple of them. They'd gone off
our radar months ago without a trace. And they're not the
only talkers the army's using. Three weeks back, somebody contacted one of our scout dragons with a distress
call. When he showed up at the rendezvous point, he was
ambushed by the military. A few days ago, Grackel received
one. Yesterday, Vestia—"

"I get it," I snap. If Preston's right, it means the government's rounding up talkers, enslaving them, means I
might never be able to go home, might never see my family again. Two choices. Neither one mine. All-Blacks and
BoDA agents on one side, dragons and insurgents on the
other.

James's words from Dragon Hill leap to mind: "There's
another war coming, Melissa, and you must decide on

which side of the fence you'll stand." I turn on my heel and make a beeline for Keith and the farmboy, who sit alone at a cafeteria table near the front of the cave.

"Where are you going?" Preston asks.

"When I first met James, he told me I'd have to choose sides." I pick up my pace. "He knew what was going to happen, Preston. You all did. You should have warned us."

"It's not like that, Callahan." Preston grabs my arm and I cringe. "Sorry, but you should wait for a better time."

I shake free. "You mean when the war's over?"

"It's not that simple."

The Silver returns with the ball, nudges me into a stumble. "Not now!" She dims and retreats.

"Keith should have told me. Somebody should have told—"

"Don't tell me what to do, Keith. You may be a coward, but I am not!" James's shout rings through the cave. He shoves away from the table, heads for the dragons. Keith follows after him. Breaking into a quick jog, so do I. There's a rapid exchange of words I can't make out. Keith grabs him, pulls him into a hug. James's features soften as tears well in his eyes.

". . . not easy, but it's going to be all right," I hear Keith say as I near. "Let it out."

"You don't understand," James says, his voice breaking.

"You can't understand. You don't know what . . ." He notices me. He flushes and flees to Vestia. She looks at him for a few seconds before scooping him up with a talon. She places him on her bare back, and they fly from the cave.

"You want me to go after him?" Preston asks.

"He needs time." Keith glances up. Dark circles shadow his eyes; he's got a dozen new wrinkles. It must be hard holding on to all those secrets, living a double life.

"You should have told me." I chew my lip. It's all I can do not to yell. "About you and Mom, about Dragon Hole, about everything."

He nods, touches the swords tattooed on his neck. "I'm sure I've told you what these represent."

"Successful missions." I try to bite my tongue, but can't. "More deception?"

His finger somehow finds the last sword in the chain. "Your mother gave me this one. We're not supposed to take them preemptively, but she insisted, and she was a hard woman to refuse." He looks away from me, his eyes pinched. "She wanted me to protect you. I'm sorry things have turned out so badly, Melissa."

He sounds defeated. The little girl in me wants to stay mad at him forever. The not-so-little girl realizes he's like the rest of us. Fallible. Trying to do what he thinks is right, sometimes making mistakes. And I wonder if there is a right path from this darkness. Regardless of the answer, I know I want him by my side for the journey, so I bury my anger and embrace him.

A knock awakens me. 2:14, according to the clock hung between two posters of leggy supermodels. The crate once belonged to a rider named Micah, one of Loki's Grunts' flight medics. It felt creepy taking some dead guy's cot, but Preston assured me Micah would have been thrilled to have a pretty girl in his bed. It was either here or James's crate, and I didn't want to deal with that awkwardness.

A second knock brings me to full alertness. By the third, I realize it's for me. "Melissa, you in there?" Keith whispers as I clamber from the cot.

I open the wall. Keith looks over my shoulder, squinting into the shadows.

For a moment I'm offended. In the next, I'm worried. "James hasn't returned?"

"Neither him nor Vestia. I thought maybe she'd dropped him off and went out for a midnight snack. He turned his radio off, and Vestia's not responding to any of our other talkers."

Vestia, I'm looking for James. . . . Can you hear me?

No response. I repeat my question aloud. Nothing. Am I doing this right? She's pretty much initiated all our previous conversations. When I ask Keith if there's a proper dragon-talking protocol, he suggests I make my request with more deference. "Vestia's a prickly one."

Vestia, we're worried about James. Please respond.

I repeat the call twice more before she answers in a tone well beyond prickly. *The boy does not wish to be disturbed. Neither do I.*

He's all right?

No, he is anything but right. He is human.

Why don't you have him roar his grief away? I return with equal bite.

You are hopeless creatures. I am hungry. I am tired. He knows this, yet he sulks about things he cannot control.

Let me talk to him.

I do not understand.

Can you relay my words to him?

I am no messenger. A moment later, an image pops into my head of a stone watchtower in the woods.

"I think Vestia just sent me a . . . picture." I describe what I saw to Keith.

"Shadow Mountain Lookout," he says. "Ask her to bring him back. Right now."

"What's wrong?"

"It's at the edge of the drone zone," he says. His words invoke memories of news reports that show drone swarms taking down stray dragons who wandered out of the evacuated territories. And of Mom's death.

Vestia, bring him back. Please.

You want me to pick him up and carry him like a little infant? she asks. I can't tell if she's amused or annoyed.

If you have to. Tell him he needs to come back.

You tell him, human. Definitely annoyed. *He does not listen to me.*

She ignores further attempts to communicate.

"We need to get him," I say to Keith.

"Absolutely not. You stay here."

I grab him by the wrist as he turns to leave. "Which one of us do you think he'll listen to?"

"Okay, Melissa. Ask if Marrick will take us to Shadow Mountain Lookout. Tell him I've got five pounds of chocolate for his troubles."

"Chocolate?"

"He loves Hershey bars."

Marrick ignores me until I mention the chocolate. Ten minutes later, we're in the air. While Keith scans the sky for drones, I chew on a peppermint leaf and search for Vestia. We find her hidden in the woods, gnawing on a felled tree. Keith unfurls the rope ladder tethered to the saddle and we dismount.

The red light of the two dragons guides us to the

watchtower, a dark column of stone that looms atop a hill. James appears little more than a shadow on the balcony that rings the tower.

"What do you want?" he calls down.

"I know you're upset, but it's not safe out here," Keith says, glancing skyward. Besides the rustle of trees, it's silent. But unlike jets, drones don't make much noise.

"Hard as it is for you to believe, I can actually take care of myself."

"Please come down, James," I say.

"Melissa? What are you doing here?"

I look at Keith. "I got this." I brace for an argument, but none comes.

"Be quick. I'll be with the dragons."

I head up the tower. James stands at the corner, hands shoved in his pockets, gaze fixed on the stars. I join him at the railing, content to listen to him breathe while I watch the sky for drones.

The far-off hum of insects, the vague scent of the trees, and this tower in particular remind me of my family's trips to the Shenandoah Mountains. A place without television, internet, or phone service, without a connection to the real world.

Upon arrival, Sam and I would race ahead of Mom and Dad to a prayer tower similar to this one, where I would imagine myself a damsel in distress while Sam played Saint

George, stick in hand, protecting me from evil dragons (disguised as cows) that plodded within chasing range. But soon enough we grew tired of the bugs and strange smells. I can't remember one trip where we didn't spend the last several days holed up inside the rental cabin, listening to our iPods and trying not to kill each other.

Here, in the wide, dark middle of nowhere, I finally understand why Mom and Dad kept taking us back to that cabin. It was for them, so they could forget about dragons and war and death.

"You shouldn't be here." James looks at me, his eyes full of hurt, his body shaking. "I'm sorry this happened, Melissa."

"You're freezing."

"I'm fine."

"It's peaceful."

"Mom brought me here when I was younger. She wanted me to learn the stars." He turns away. He wipes at his eyes, then chuckles. "Old-school navigation. I thought it was silly. Just use GPS, right? Eventually I learned some of them. I can show you the major ones, and the oh-so-important North Star." He pauses, collects himself. "Guess she just wanted to spend some time with me."

"Did she have a favorite?"

"Deneb. The brightest star in Cygnus." He looks up.

"She liked swans. They mate for life."

"Which one is it?" I ask, though I already know.

He gets behind me, reaches his arm over my shoulder. I can feel his breath on my neck, in my hair. "There. Next to Draco, my favorite," he whispers.

I turn around. He caresses my cheek, and electric adrenaline courses through me. He leans closer, smiles gently. I shut my eyes and smile back, my entire body trembling. He tilts my head back, his callused fingers moving from my cheek up through my hair, his cool breath tickling my lips. His breathing sharpens—

Dragon screams erupt in my head. Thousands and thousands. James grabs my hand, and we're running, scrambling down the tower.

"Hurry!" Vestia implores. She and Marrick emerge from the forest at full glow, smoke billowing from their nostrils. Keith, sprinting, struggles to keep up.

"What's happening?" he asks as Vestia grabs hold of James and sets him on her back, then launches into the air.

"The children . . . the children," James shouts, his voice cracking. "They found the hideouts. They're killing them. They're killing the children."

We climb aboard Marrick and take flight. Faster and faster we go. Terrifying and brilliant. This must be what it's like to ride a comet.

Keith flips on the radio clipped to his belt. Dragon roars echo from the speaker. "Flash protocol. Converge on alpha location. I'll meet you in the air."

In a matter of minutes, we're back at the cave. The Reds are in fits and the Silver's crying up a storm, but none of that compares to the agonizing wails playing inside my head.

Keith helps me down, then looks to James, who's got a machine gun strapped across his chest. "No, James."

"It's not your call, Keith." He waves at the Reds. "We're going. Don't try to stop us."

Keith tenses, but nods. "Okay, you better get your head straight."

"We're all coming," Preston says. "They need us."

"The injured stay behind," Keith says.

Preston unwraps the bandage from his head. Old blood stains his brow. "I'm not injured."

"I'm not injured," somebody else calls.

"I'm not injured."

Keith holds up a hand before everybody can discard their slings and bandages. "Fine, none of you are injured. And you better damn well stay that way. Follow my orders, know your limits. Preston . . ." He moves aside.

Preston steps forward. "What are all you slackers waiting for? Let's get our Jedi on!"

It's a motley crew, half the riders too wounded to walk

straight. Except for Vestia, Syren, and a few others, the dragons aren't in much better shape. Despite their handicaps, they ready themselves for war with quick precision. Saddles get hoisted onto backs, sometimes by winches, sometimes by other dragons. Harnesses and quivers full of missiles get hung around necks. Saddlebags are loaded with oxygen packs, grenades, and rocket launchers.

Within minutes, they're ready to fly.

Keith kisses my forehead. "We'll be back before you know it."

"You take care of her for us, okay?" James says. I turn to find him staring at me. The Silver cowers behind him.

"You better come back, farmboy. Don't do anything crazy."

"I won't," he says, though his eyes suggest otherwise. He gives me a quick hug. "Let's fly, Grunts! No mercy!"

They mount their Reds and disappear into the night, leaving me alone in a cave with Gretchen, a few of the more seriously injured insurgents, and an anxious baby dragon whose screams soon overshadow the ones inside my head.

14

I mark time by pacing the cave's perimeter, chewing my lip, clenching and unclenching my fists. I pause at the entrance, step onto the ledge, and peer into the darkness, where there's nothing to see but imaginary shadows in a black abyss. When the cold and fear become too much, I return to the fire.

The Silver follows me. If I don't acknowledge her every few minutes with a smile, a touch, or preferably my voice, she starts crying again. I focus on the dragons inside my head, or the lack thereof. This worries me. My attempts to contact Vestia and the other Reds go unanswered, which worries me more.

Every couple of laps, I ask Gretchen if she's heard anything. No. But she's got orders to remain off the airwaves. A couple hours in, she breaks the radio silence. Static. "They must be out of range," she assures me, but keeps the radio on after that.

I bandy names with my dragon tagalong. Tiny head-shakes for Little Blue Eyes and Baby Silver. Shiny Lizard and Annoying Sasquatch result in frosty huffs. Smaug and Saphira draw blank stares. Two laps and fifty names later, I settle on Baby, promising her I'll think of something better before sunrise.

Dawn comes without inspiration or hope. I'm on lap sixty, maybe sixty-one—legs numb, lower lip chewed raw, hands stuck in fists—when the shadows outside turn real and begin to take shape. I move to the ledge, sit on the log, stroke Baby's head as she lies beside me.

Morning fingers of orange-blue light drag the curtain of night back to reveal the pristine landscape. Staggering mountain peaks high above, snow-capped evergreens far below. One way in, one way out. And whoever doesn't have a dragon is screwed.

Baby nudges me, nods toward the horizon. "See something?" I ask.

She shakes her head, flaps her wings.

"You want to fly? Go on. Just don't go too far."

She snorts, rises, and rushes back into the cave. Moments later she returns with a saddle in her mouth.

My flights last night left me queasy, but maybe it won't be

so bad if I'm driving. It would be nice to impress James, or at least show him I won't go green in the face forever. Most important, it will help keep my mind off the fact that they aren't back.

It takes me a couple tries to figure out how to use the winch, a couple more to get Baby's saddle cinched right. I throw on goggles and a jacket, then climb aboard. Her silver scales radiate coolness, but somehow I'm warmer atop her than I was by the fire. She gives a rumbling purr, flutters her wings with increasing vigor. On the fifth beat, we push forward out of the cave.

Stone and snow disappear, and there's nothing but sky around us. Baby banks left and right in slow, gentle arcs. She barely uses her wings, allows the wind currents to carry us in wide loops from one valley to the next.

She's careful, never turning fast or rising sharply. We learn each other's rhythms in a matter of minutes. It scares me how easy this is. Soon I'm ready to kick my dragon-rider training up a level, and there's something in the way she keeps glancing back at me that tells me she is, too.

I tighten my grip on the reins. "Come on, Baby, let's see what you got."

With a gleeful snort, she slingshots forward. Dives fast. Shoots up. Banks hard left. Right. Faster and faster, she follows the track of an imaginary roller coaster. Trees, mountains, sky mix together in a blur of greens, grays, and blues.

We twirl into a steep climb. Over the mountaintops. Higher still, almost vertical, into the clouds. Nausea swells in my stomach, blood rushes to my head. Skin tingling, vision narrowing, sickness coming, I can't stop laughing, drinking this wild air.

She arcs over, rockets down, blisters through sparse clouds, races toward a sprawling landscape of miniature trees and hills. The earth grows larger, my stomach flips inside out. Wind floods my lungs, stings my face. Each time I blink, the fast-approaching world darkens further; fuzzy amorphous stars replace trees; jagged black spots replace hills.

Baby swoops out of the dive. I tilt over, almost fall, and vomit into the valley, which could be a foot away or a thousand. The thrum of her purr subsides. She slows to a flying crawl.

At some point later, when three dimensions become tolerable, my focus returns. And it's cold. Frigid. I press tight to Baby, but whatever warmth she had is gone.

A thunderclap shakes the sky. I glance over my shoulder. Clouds hover above the rim of a nearby mountain, but none of them look like storm bringers.

"We should go back." I look for landmarks, but after our vomit-comet ride, I'm lost. "You gotta lead us home, Baby. And promise not to tell James about this."

She makes a right turn, and her body warms enough to quell my shivers. Pumping her wings every few minutes to maintain altitude, she glides toward a gap between two shorter peaks. The pitter-patter of invisible rain intensifies as we come closer.

I hear a shrill whistle, followed by an explosion. Both came from the mountain bowl. Not from the sky. Not thunder. At the far end, snow and boulders avalanche into the valley. Behind the clamor of tumbling stone, the wind hums, rhythmic and distinct.

I jerk at the reins. Baby jolts, swerves, almost crashes as her wings scrape snow from the mountainside.

"Climb!" I yell. She screeches once, but obeys.

When we're near a peak, my breaths shallow and stabbing, I urge her to an outcropping that affords us an unimpeded view of the bowl. Ten helicopters hover in attack position around a cave. Rubble obscures what's left of several surrounding caves.

A dragon screams, but I can't tell if it's real or in my head. Orange bursts pulse at the cave's entrance. The scream intensifies.

Baby skitters along the ledge. Her scaled skin turns colder. Slivers of liquid ice shoot from her nose.

"We need to leave," I whisper through chattering teeth.

She claws the snowy rock, snorts more ice daggers, but as

the screams die, she settles and some of her heat returns. Not much, but enough for me to feel my toes again.

Several figures appear at the cave's mouth. One of them waves at the nearest helicopter. Three of them look like they're carrying weapons. Not like soldiers carrying guns. More like headsmen wielding axes.

"Come on, Baby, let's go."

But her gaze, like mine, is fixed on the dozen men dragging a large net from the cave. The gunship's side doors open. Hooks are lowered. The chopper lists from the weight, but soon the cargo's loaded, still glowing, and I'm absurdly reminded of chickens, even though I've never seen one get its head cut off.

Two other helicopters retrieve the soldiers. I watch until the last man saunters aboard. No gurneys, no rush, nobody injured. Not a battle. A slaughter. As the two transports move away, my breaths come faster, sharper; my chest constricts.

"Let's go."

I meant for us to retreat, to hide, but Baby launches herself at the nearest helicopter with a sky-shattering howl, followed by a ferocious blast of ice. The gunship makes half a revolution toward us before being swallowed by it.

Its blades grind to a halt. For a half moment it sits there, suspended. I'm close enough to see the soldier manning the side-door machine gun. He's an ice statue, sculpted with mouth and eyes wide open, finger at the trigger.

The frozen chopper plummets; a missile shrieks. Baby reels sideways, sends a funnel of liquid frost at the attacking gunship. Another missile races toward us from the left. Two from the right. I glance back to see the first one spin around.

Baby dives and the missiles follow.

Go cold!

Her skin cools to frigid and her glow brightens to blinding. She dodges three more missiles, heads for the helicopter with the red dragon head. Bullets zip everywhere, a swarm of metal locusts crisscrossing our path.

Baby bucks, bolts, and swerves, always breathing her ice. Ten gunships become five. Missiles churn the mountainside, send fountains of rock and snow hundreds of feet skyward.

In the blizzard of destruction, I lose my orientation. Shadows in the flying detritus could be a thousand feet away or ten, enemies or boulders. I call out every blur, imagined or not, shouting against the thunder until my voice goes hoarse and my lungs burn cold fire.

The explosion hits us from below. Warmth and pain surge through me. Baby tumbles head over tail. My grip loosens, legs slip, head spins.

When my focus returns, Baby's crashing into a mountain and I'm hundreds of feet in the air without a dragon.

15

The Dragon World War—WWD—ended when I was twelve, at least according to Modern History. The end of the fifty-page chapter listed the top ten freedoms we'd sacrificed in our struggle to survive.

Videos accompanied each item. In the middle of the list, a multicolored plane glided through clear skies. An interior shot showed families relaxing to old movies, smiling attendants handing out beverages and blankets.

Until last night, that twenty-second clip was my only memory of flying.

It seemed so peaceful.

"Wake up." The All-Black across the aisle nudges me in the ribs with his rifle.

I open my eyes. "Wasn't sleeping."

"Praying?"

I shake my head.

"That's good. Ain't no prayers gonna save your glowheart."

"Leave me alone."

"Maybe she fancies herself one of them talkers Olshansky was telling us about," he says to the beefy soldier seated next to him. "Huh, dragon sister, you trying to talk to your dragon?"

I don't answer. I do try to contact dragons. Nothing.

The soldier unbuckles his harness, grabs the handcuffs around my wrists, and squeezes until I cry out. He lets go with an approving nod. He leans over, presses moist lips to my ear. "What is it with them dragons? You like Catherine the Great or something?"

I squirm away.

He falls back into his chair. "All I wanted was a thank you. See that, Corporal? No gratitude from the dragon generation."

"We should make her thank us," the corporal says. "Pretty, ain't she?"

"She'd do. Sweet face. Kind of like it with the blood and bruises. Gives her a savage look." He growls at me, claws the air.

The corporal reaches out and strokes my cheek. I flinch

and can no longer hold back the tears. He cups my chin, wobbles my head, worsening my headache. "Look, Sarge, we made her cry." He thumbs the wetness from my cheek.

I spit at him.

In a blink, he's jamming his hand against my cheek, pressing my face to the window. A squad of dragon jets accompanies us and four other gunships over the charred remains of some yesteryear metropolis. Baby is sprawled in a massive cargo net dangling by steel tethers from the other four helicopters. I moan as I spot the spearlike tranquilizers protruding from her glowless back.

The corporal wrenches me back by the hair, shoves me against the seat. "You're disgusting. Good men died today because of you, but you care more about that damn lizard than your own kind. I should have let your glowheart fall."

I had been halfway to the ground, too terrified to scream, when I'd spotted the helicopter diving toward me at a steep angle. An angel of death in his black body armor, the corporal had leaned out from the gunship's berth, his rifle pointed at me.

He shot me. Not with a bullet, but with some net attached to a winch in the helicopter.

"Gotta get Big Bertha sharp," the sergeant says. He retrieves a half-moon ax from an overhead bin, glides a whetstone along the blade's arc. "Cold head. Might take me three chops with such a thick neck. Hope it's not messy."

"You could use one of those electric cutters," the corporal says.

"Clean, but leaves a nasty smell." The sergeant sighs. "Not sure if I should sell it or mount it, Corporal. That's one sizzling piece of coin, but imagine how much tail I'll get with that lizard hung in the entryway."

"What do you think, lizard lover?" The corporal runs his hand along my thigh. I gag and he laughs.

"I tell you, that Silver's gonna make a nice addition to the collection." The sergeant taps one of the two dozen stickers on his helmet—a cartoonish Green's head, a dumb grin on its face, tongue lolling from its mouth. Two axes form the X across its snout. Different kill tokens from those of the Mason-Kline A-Bs, not from actual dragons, but somehow worse.

The corporal touches his own helmet, not as decorated and without any ax kills. "Gotta get some."

The sergeant claps him on the shoulder. "You will. Plenty more slithering around in them caves." He grins at me. "They make the best holiday decorations. You should have seen our last Christmas, dragon sister. My boys put a thousand lights on my largest Red and Green. Lit 'em up bright as the sun. Halle-fuckin-lujah. I played Santa Claus for the neighborhood. Sat right between them. Kids loved it."

"You got pics, right?" the corporal asks.

"Hell yeah. I'll send 'em to you. The Silver would work better for Halloween, though, don't you think?" the sergeant asks me as I begin to cry again. "We'd have to get its glow back. Like a dragon ghost head. That would be some slick-ass—"

"Shut up! Shut up!"

But they don't.

We finally arrive at a massive military base, a sprawling patch of black surrounded by vacant farm fields. The helicopters settle into a hover, dangling Baby above the tarmac. Armored personnel carriers converge. Two tractors pull a rolling sledge from the tallest structure on the base, a ten-story hangar identical to the dragattoir where they executed the Green that killed Mom.

The tractors center themselves between the APCs, and the helicopters lower Baby onto the sledge. Helmetless men in black doctor coats file from the nearest vehicles.

The sergeant scowls. "Mengeles."

"Think we'll at least get our finder's fee?" the corporal asks as the men cut away the netting around Baby.

The sergeant grunts.

We land, wait inside the helicopter while the black-coated men use hoists to withdraw the tranquilizers. One jabs a dragon Taser into Baby's neck. Veins of silver lightning race across her body and vanish at her tail. He waves to an APC. Two A-Bs emerge, each carrying half of a gold dragon collar.

"That a new model?" the corporal asks.

Another grunt. "Probably a cold restrictor."

The men tie Baby to the sledge with straps around her neck, midsection, and hindquarters. The tractors roll at a slug's pace toward the dragattoir.

As we step from the helicopter, the corporal shoves me off to a seven-foot-tall man in a black suit. He's the only person on the tarmac without a gun pointed at me or Baby, but the one who scares me most. He leads me into an Escalade marked BUREAU OF DRAGON AFFAIRS.

"I want to call my father," I say. "Lieutenant Colonel Peter Callahan. I want to call him. I have my rights."

The last part draws the briefest smile, but no response.

We drive to a small building on the opposite end of the base. The silent agent pulls me from the vehicle, leads me past armed guards into a lobby with gray walls, a handprint scanner, and a freight elevator.

"Where are you taking me?" I ask as he places his hand on the scanner.

The elevator door slides open, and he pushes me in. He presses the solitary button on the inner panel. The digital display above the door reads *Going Down* for a long minute, disappearing when we hit bottom.

A black painted corridor with old-school fluorescent lights extends beyond sight, steel doors every few feet on either side. He guides me to the fifth on the right, then forces my hand to the adjacent scanner. When he pulls it back, the top of the display shows my name, national registration number, and birth date.

"Is this correct?" the D-man says.

"Can I call my dad? Please."

He stares at me with hollow eyes. Demon eyes.

I nod, my chest hitching. "It's correct."

He places his hand to the scanner, and a keyboard appears. After he types in a passcode, my picture from last year's yearbook fills the screen. "Is that you?"

Before blood and bruises. I nod. "Please."

He enters another passcode. My chest tightens further when I see what comes next.

Melissa Anne Callahan—Class One Insurgent
Crimes: Murder, Treason.
Associations: Loki's Grunts.
Status: Captured.

"Any other associations?" the D-man asks.

"I'm not . . . I didn't do that. I'm not a traitor. Please."

More typing. The door swings open to reveal a cell

illuminated by glowing red, green, and blue rectangles that dance clockwise around the rim of the ceiling. Padded walls. A cot in the back beneath a giant thinscreen. A rusted shower in one corner, a stained toilet in the other.

"Please," I whisper as he removes the cuffs. "Please don't make me—"

The demon shoves me into hell and closes the door.

16

If not for the thinscreen, I'd lose track of time.

Fifty-three hour-long episodes of TV's most popular program have played nonstop. It's season three now. I never watched the show before because Mom hated it, and when she died, I hated it, but for different reasons. Most everyone else, however, loves *Kissing Dragons*.

From time to time, as I watch the array of lights spin about my black prison, I find myself humming the theme song, a pounding patriotic riff intermixed with techno gunfire and dragon roars. I refrain from roaring, though I want to each time the slot in the bottom of the door opens—every ten episodes—and a paper plate with stale bread and charred meat is passed through.

I try to sleep, but the voices of Frank, Kevin, Mac, and

L.T. (who replaced J.R. after he was killed in season two) wake me. It's never the gunfire or the dragon howls. Always the voices of the four elite All-Black soldiers.

An hour into my captivity, I stopped screaming for help, for answers, for justice. The walls swallow sound. I might as well be on the other side of the universe.

During episodes three and four, I recited the daily tenets of tae kwon do: *ye ui, yom chi, in nae, guk gi, baekjul boolgool.* I stopped at episode five because I got interested in what was happening onscreen. Exotic foreign locales are more interesting than meaningless foreign words.

It's not like courtesy applies in this hole at the bottom of the earth. And look where integrity's gotten me. Perseverance—ha! Self-control, the hardest tenet for me to obey, doesn't matter now.

And indomitable spirit. I soaked that one right up as a gullible eight-year-old. So what if dragons turned our world black? So what if freedom came with a giant asterisk and tons of small print?

But *baekjul boolgool* didn't help Mom or Dad. It's hard to have an indomitable spirit when machines and monsters can destroy everything that's important in a single breath.

Somewhere into episode fifteen, I decided to shower. I know some perv is watching me from a hidden camera, but I've stopped caring. Stripped to my underwear. Washed the shirt and jeans first. Then me. It was cold, more dirt than water, and it switched between jets and sputters, but it was different and I felt cleaner.

The AC turned on after that. No blankets on the lumpy mattress and my clothes were still wet. Three episodes passed before the shivers ceased.

I attempted to break the thinscreen during episode nineteen, but there's some sort of reinforced glass protecting it and I only managed to bruise my hands. Before episode twenty-two, I tried out the toilet, squatting so I didn't have to touch the seat. I tripped over my feet, fell on the floor, and peed myself.

Later I discovered the toilet doesn't flush. I called for maintenance, but nobody's come yet.

My shoulder started to throb somewhere into episode twenty-four. I checked the bandage. It was soggy, the muddied color of dried blood. Didn't reek, though. I remember someone telling me it was bad when a wound smelled. Of course, it's hard to smell anything over the stench of urine.

Five times a plate of food's arrived via the slot. The bread's rock hard and sometimes there are bugs on it, but it's better than the meat, which comes in tiny portions. I can't tell if it's black because of the lighting or because they burned it so bad. It's tough and salty, but I force myself to eat it, even though it makes me gag.

The last time around I hid by the slot to get a peek at my server. But Mr. Food Man was late and showed up when I was getting a drink from the shower. I thanked him anyway. He didn't respond, so I sat on the floor beside the door to eat my dinner and watch my show.

Every twenty-four episodes, the lights and screen go off. I want to sleep but can't. Without the lights flashing, without the screen's loud rhythm, I'm better able to remember my life before Frank, Kevin, Mac, and L.T. (who replaced J.R. after he was killed in season two).

Sam and Dad. Trish. Mason-Kline. Keith. And James. What's happened to them? Do they know what's happened to me? Do they think I'm dead?

Maybe that's better, because what would they think if they saw me now?

Dad would be angry I created so many problems—for myself, for him, for the dragons. Too much like Mom, he'd say. And Trish? She'll hate me forever if her mother was hurt in the attack. James and Keith? Who knows if they're even alive, but if so, they'll never forgive me for losing Baby.

Sam would be the worst. Before he decided to become a dragon jet pilot, he wanted to be a BoDA agent. Would tape a cardboard D to his shirt and roam the house, investigating our actions to make sure we maintained proper compliance to whatever arbitrary rules he'd decreed that day. I couldn't wear red for a week because he found it offensive and would shoot me with his plastic dart gun if he spotted any, yelling for me to surrender when I retaliated against his idiocy. Somehow I ended up being the one who got in trouble because I "should know better."

Now I'm in trouble again. But I don't know better this time. The right and wrong I learned about in school don't make sense anymore. Everything's a confusing shade of gray. Or black.

When the dragons appeared in our world, they wrought death so fast that after the first few weeks, the news started listing towns and cities instead of individual names. Fifteen years later, the world gone black, they're back to names—just a few each week.

And now it's the dragons' turn to suffer. Hunted toward extinction. Slaughtered by All-Blacks or dissected by scientists. Each night at *8/7c*, a government spokesmodel lists the numbers of Blues, Reds, and Greens killed.

They've turned it into a national lottery, most everyone eager to win.

Except for the crazies. Camera crews in tow, one group of nutjobs attempted to commune with a Green hiding in the Appalachians. They were roasted; the Green was executed.

Inspired my new favorite show.

Each episode begins with a warning against amateur

dragon hunts. The next fifteen minutes provide details on the enemy. Number of kills, famous buildings destroyed, last known whereabouts. Show some clips of the monster in action, fifteen minutes of teary interviews with victims' friends and families, then on to the good stuff.

Frank, Kevin, Mac, and L.T. (who replaced J.R. after he was killed in season two) skulk into jungles, rappel down mountains, trudge through swamps. Whispered banter in the early stages gives way to the minor-key soundtrack that accentuates leaves crackling, rocks skittering, water splashing—any noise that might alert the evil dragon and endanger the innocent humans.

Shot in natural light, the armored soldiers are little more than hulking shadows until they come in sight of their glowing quarry, nicknamed Killzilla, the Scarlet Scourge, or something else easily remembered for the tie-in video games played by farmboys across the globe.

The fab four sneak into position. Two quick minutes of gunfire, shouts and curses, and the dragon is hog-tied and collared. The camera zooms in on the monster's snarling face. The soldiers use knives to peel scales from its cheeks. Frank, a ruggedly handsome man, sticks his kill token to his helmet and turns to the camera.

"There are many rules critical for a successful dragon hunt. The first and most important: never wake a sleeping dragon. The sonofabitch's a lot easier to kiss when asleep."

I've heard this rule before. Episodes one, fourteen, twenty-seven, and thirty—the one where J.R. died because he woke the Scarlet Scourge. And somewhere else, too.

An episode later, I remember Konrad Kline and his farmboy advice.

Frank bows his head and leads a brief prayer as Genghis Green writhes in the background. The soldiers gather around the dragon and kiss it while giving thumbs-ups, saluting, flashing peace signs. An unseen photographer snaps pictures. After various poses, the dragon hunters disappear out of frame and a large digital X is stamped across the monster's forehead.

The credits roll to triumphant music. On one side scroll the names of producers, directors, cameramen, and the "brave soldiers of the armed forces"; the other plays a montage of the interviewees hugging their All-Black heroes and laying flowers at graves. At the end, an In Memoriam for the victims.

Who in their right mind could empathize with these monsters after watching an episode of *Kissing Dragons*?

Empathize or not, I beg for their help often. Cover my ears, close my eyes, and concentrate. Send out mental pleas to Old Man Blue, Vestia, Syren . . .

There's never any response. Maybe there's no signal down here. Or maybe the fab four got them.

Midway through episode sixty-seven, the finale to season three—a hunt for twin Reds hiding in the outback—several of the glowing rectangles on the wall flash into letters. *Riley Hanson*. A familiar name, though I don't know why.

Riley scrolls once around the room. Back to the colored rectangles. A second later, another flash. Who is *Johnny Mathers*? Six more unfamiliar names go by, then *Captain Timothy Wright, USAF*. Several more military personnel, followed by dozens of men and women without ranks.

I miss episode sixty-eight watching names. Nobody I know. A glitch in the BoDA entertainment system?

The truth hits me toward the end of episode sixty-nine. Riley Hanson was a Montana ranch hand who spotted the first dragon. Mistook it for a UFO. Became a footnote in history. The first dragon victim.

A dragon kiss later, Mr. Food Man shoves a paper plate into my room.

"You'll have to pick up the pace!" I scream at his boot heel before the slot snaps shut.

I struggle to my feet and wave at *Lance Corporal Edward Hicks, USMC* as he makes his loop around the room. "I'll be dead before you get to Mom!"

Two episodes later, the lights go out, the screen turns off.

"I'm not a traitor," I moan into my mattress over and over.

"Then what are you?"

I look up. Lights still off. Screen, too.

"I'm not a traitor. You believe me, don't you?"

No response.

I stand, shuffle my way around the room with arms extended. Padded walls, toilet, showerhead. Down on my knees, I find the paper plate, chew at the rest of the meat, which tastes better now. Where's the bread? Did I eat it already? Did rats get it?

Sometimes I nap, usually against the wall opposite the screen. It's more comfortable than my bed. And my BoDA landlords are so nice. Once I drifted off with the infrared images of Frank, Mac, Kevin, and L.T. navigating through a field of stalagmites; when I woke, they were still prowling the dark depths of Mammoth Cave.

So maybe I've been here more than a hundred hours, but that's okay. I'm back to season one, and J.R.'s smiling nice and pretty in his unscorched hat. And the names scrolling along the ceiling don't make me sad anymore, except for the Sams, Peters, Olivias, Keiths, Jameses . . .

We're back in season two, episode twenty-eight—J.R.'s been reckless recently. Doesn't bode well for him and his hat—when the lights go white, the screen shuts off, and the door opens.

I'm in the shower, fully clothed, but not at all presentable. Covering my eyes against the brightness, I stare at the shadow outlined in the doorway. "Hello?"

A D-man steps forward. My height. Red hair, a receding hairline. He gives me a towel, which I wrap around my soaked sweatshirt. "Sam?"

I glance at my hands. Pruney. Wrinkled? Maybe I slept longer than I thought.

"Come with me, Ms. Callahan."

Folding my arms across the towel, I give him my stern older-sister look. "This isn't some prank, is it?"

"Jesus," he says beneath his breath, but I hear. "No, Ms. Callahan, this isn't a prank." He gives me a sad look, like he thinks I'm crazy.

"I'm not a dragon talker, Sam. I'm not a traitor. I'm not—"

"Ms. Callahan, I am not your brother."

"He's not dead, is he? I kept thinking his name was gonna appear on the wall, even though I knew it would take years, but I watched for it. You're not lying to me?"

"No. In fact, I'm here to take you to see him." He touches the handcuffs looped through his belt. "I trust you won't try anything rash."

Shaking my head, I squat and grab the plate from where I'd placed it near the drain. I offer it to him.

He blanches. "Thanks, but I've never had the stomach for dragon."

It takes me a couple of seconds to register his words, but when they click into place, I vomit onto his black loafers.

"Baby?" I slide down the wall, clutching at my stomach. No, I mustn't feel sad. "I'm not a traitor, Mr. D-man. I'm not a traitor."

He turns on the shower and washes regurgitated dragon from his shoes. I unwrap my towel and give it to him, nice and proper. "I'm not a traitor, Mr. D-man."

"Of course not." He opens his briefcase, which contains a PDA and a silver circlet that reminds me of a dragon collar, except miniature. He pulls it out, offers it to me like a crown.

I shrink away. "What is it?"

"A CENSIR. It prevents communication."

"I don't have a cell phone. Can't call Dad or Sam or anyone."

He comes closer. "Not that sort of communication."

"Oh. But I'm not a traitor."

"Even so . . ." He places the circlet on my head.

"Does it hurt?"

The D-man gives me a sympathetic smile. "A little at first."

He removes the PDA. I notice words inscribed on the case. CONTROLLER FOR ENcEPHALO SYNAPTIC INHIBITION AND RECORDING. I'm trying to make sense of them when the CENSIR warms and tightens. I groan, scream, beg for it to stop, but it doesn't until Mr. D-man's PDA beeps.

He pockets it, helps me up. "Can you see?"

"Dizzy," I manage to say.

He wraps his arm around my waist. "It'll be a few minutes before you feel right."

Feel right? I laugh, which hurts my head. "Do you even know what you're saying?"

Another sad smile. "We had to be sure," he says, and walks me from the room.

I glance back at the thinscreen. "Will we be back in time before the next episode? It's the one where they go after Abominable Red at Everest. Definitely on my top-five list."

"No. Probably not."

"You're gonna make me miss my show? You're horrible, horrible people."

I say it like a joke, but he frowns and nods, like he doesn't think it's a joke at all.

"Yes, Melissa, unfortunately we are."

17

Beneath sun too bright, but too short-lived, Mr. D-man leads me across a narrow street to another nondescript building. Potted plants, a secretary's desk, and a couple of cheap paintings adorn the lobby.

A receptionist buzzes us through a glass door at the back into a room that resembles a single-person salon, complete with rotating armchair, wash basin, and lighted mirror. An array of beauty products lines the countertop.

Mr. D-man waves at an opaque half globe mounted to the ceiling.

The door at the end of the room bursts open. A short, bespectacled man in a purple silk shirt bustles out, followed by a towering fat woman whose floral-print dress somehow intensifies her double-chinned scowl.

Purple Shirt looks me over, wrinkling his nose. "Strip."

"What's going on?" I ask.

He extends his hand, flicks his fingers in a commanding gesture. The flower lady slaps a rolled-up tape measure into his palm. He uncoils it, steps on one end, reaches up, and presses the other to my head.

"Seventy and one quarter. Come on, girl, strip." The little tailor points toward the door. "You. Out." That was quick. I turn to leave. "Not you, girl. The dragon man."

Mr. D-man releases my elbow. I wobble for a few seconds before finding my balance. "I'm fine." He nods and retreats out the door.

Purple Shirt strokes his goatee, purses his lips. "Strip."

"Why?"

"For your dress. Helga, help her."

I'm out of my sweatshirt before Purple Shirt's fat assistant takes her second step. No way I'm letting that lady touch me. After the jeans come off, the tailor makes fast work of me, barking measurements to Helga. He finishes, hands her the tape measure, then scurries from the room, mumbling about my odor.

Helga bundles my clothes, holding them at arm's length like soiled diapers. She points at the door on the far side of the sink. "You shower now, Stinky."

"What about—"

"Shower." She marches from the room, leaving me alone in my bra and underwear, crusted shoulder bandage, and silver crown. What a monstrous (and evidently smelly) queen I must be.

Bruised, bloodied, subsisting on dragon meat and moldy bread—for how long? Nothing but dirt showers. God help me, I must be worse than monstrous. I make a slow turn toward the mirror to check what's become of me.

The girl gazing back at me shares my startled gasp. She's no older than seventeen, once pretty perhaps, maybe someone I knew.

She looks lost, confused, alone.

"You're not a traitor," I tell her. "You did what you thought was right. *Yom chi.*"

I wipe at my eyes, give her a pained smile. "Not a traitor. Not a victim. *In nae.*"

"That's right, persevere. *Baekjul boolgool*, Melissa, no matter what. Now go get cleaned up. You look like ass."

Hot water, soap, shampoo. Simple things that make me feel almost normal, make me almost forget where I am, what I am. As blood, dirt, and grime disappear down the drain, the fog that surrounds me begins to clear.

I'm considering spending eternity in this shower room when someone with a cigarette voice calls from the other side of the curtain. I peek out. A short woman in a pink pant-suit stands a foot away.

She flings back the curtain.

"They don't pay me to wait." She snatches a towel from a wall hook and thrusts it at me. "Get over yourself, sweet-heart. The longer you gawp, the angrier I get. And me and tweezers don't work well when I'm angry."

I dry off under her intense gaze. "Who are you?"

"Cosmo Kim. You probably haven't heard of me." She gives me a quick once-over. "Definitely don't look like you've heard of me."

"*The* Cosmo Kim?" Über-fashion consultant to the stars. Or maybe it's fashion consultant to the über-stars.

"Not everybody's natural. Some of us require work." She frowns at me. "Some of us, a lot of work. That's enough." She jerks the towel from me, then hands me fresh undergarments.

"What's going on?"

"Do I look like a scale chaser to you? Pink's a dead give-away, I thought. Maybe I'll wear a sign next time. Faster. Can't you dress and listen at the same time?"

She leads me back to the salon, sits me in the chair, and tips my head back into the basin. "Try to relax."

She proceeds to give me a facial, waxes my legs. Next comes makeup, makeup, and more makeup. What the hell is going on? Three times I ask, three times Cosmo Kim suggests I relax.

I drift.

A firm shake awakens me. Helga. She's holding a sleeveless white cocktail dress. Behind her, Purple Shirt's got a silver belt studded with red, green, and blue gems.

"What's going on?"

"Hold still," Helga orders. She unwraps my towel with surprising gentleness and helps me into the white dress. It's tight in the chest, tighter in the hips. She takes the belt from Purple Shirt, cinches it around my waist, then sits me back down and slips a three-inch heel onto each foot.

Purple Shirt claps. "Ah! See, Helga, I told you there was a pretty girl inside."

"One last thing." Helga takes a brooch from her pocket and pins it to my shoulder. "Yes, a beautiful angel," she says, twirling the chair around a hundred-eighty degrees.

I thought I recognized the girl in the mirror before, but this one I've never seen. Her hair's blond and falls in glorious curls around her shoulders. Eyebrows are also dyed, what remains of them. Smoky eye shadow. Enough foundation to fill a grave. Skin a shade between gold and bronze. Midnight-red lipstick to offset the silver circlet nestled in her hair.

And a silver dragon pin above her breast. Anger wells inside me.

I reach for the brooch, but Helga slaps my hand away. "No touch." When I reach again, she jerks me from the chair. I kick at her with my pointed shoes. She spins me around, pulls my arms behind me, and applies a pair of handcuffs.

As Purple Shirt waves good-bye, Helga escorts me into the lobby, where Mr. D-man awaits. He looks at me, smiles. "I preferred you as a brunette."

God, how did I ever think he could be Sam?

He loads me into the back of the Escalade. I squirm away from him, lean against the tinted window, hope he'll stop looking at me.

It's a cloudy twilight now. Parallel rows of ankle-high green solar lamps mark the road. Blue runway lights in the distance brighten as the sun slips below the horizon.

Windowless buildings blur together. Headlights and taillights from other vehicles make irregular patterns. We pass several open hangars, lights on, mechanics and welders busy. Mr. D-man continues to leer.

I attempt to contact dragons, but my silent pleas fall on deaf or dead ears. I check the sky every few seconds anyway. I search the black buildings, looking for the dragattoir, for a hint of silver glow peeking through the darkness.

Nothing.

At another hangar that seems like all the rest, the Escalade makes a left. We park between a black van and a black BMW.

Mr. D-man herds me to the entrance of the adjoining building. One firm hand on my back, the other on my elbow, he leans in, his breath warm and heavy on my neck.

The goose bumps working their way up my arms from the cool night air give way to full-on shivering. I peek over my shoulder. The Escalade's gone.

"Sorry," he whispers. He's close enough for me to feel his heartbeat racing a storm—or maybe it's mine.

"Please, don't do this," I say, unable to keep the panic from my voice.

He squeezes my shoulder.

I raise my foot, ready to slam the stiletto spike through his loafer. Maybe if I hurt him enough, I'll be able to get away. Some All-Black will shoot me, or someone will run me over in the dark, but that's better than this.

Anything's better than this.

18

Abruptly he releases his grip on my shoulder, reaches out, and presses the buzzer.

My relief lasts until the door opens to bright lights mounted on massive video cameras. Mr. D-man nudges me forward. My heel catches on the threshold, and I tumble.

The lights zoom in at me. Mr. D-man helps me to my feet. The cameramen wait for us to pass, then follow close behind. I keep myself steady, hold my head high.

The door at the end of the hallway cracks ajar. Muffled voices come from the other side. The door starts opening again. I chew through a thick layer of lipstick, glance over my shoulder. Mr. D-man and a wall of cameras block any chance of retreat.

When I turn back around, I'm staring at someone I thought I'd never see again.

"Konrad?" I say. Then I notice something that almost makes me laugh. "Are you wearing makeup?"

"Whatever." He checks me out. "Looking good, Mel."

"What are you doing here?"

"They thought you might want to see a familiar face."

Mr. D-man escorts me into some sort of film studio. Cameras, news desk, green screen, several thinscreens. A middle-aged man in a three-piece suit directs Konrad and me to chairs behind the desk.

I glance at Konrad, at my outfit, at the cameras. "This is ridiculous."

"This is reality, Ms. Callahan. I would suggest you cooperate," Three-Piece says. I've never seen him before, but that gravelly, deep-throated voice is familiar. "Stay . . . answer questions to my satisfaction, and be assured that you will see your brother again."

"I want to see him now."

He ignores me, orders the cameramen to adjust their angles. Once they're repositioned to his satisfaction, he turns his attention back to me. "Ms. Callahan, when did you first decide to join the dragon insurgency?" he asks, his voice deepening.

Now I recognize it.

"You're the narrator. Simon something," I mumble.

"Ms. Callahan, when I ask a question, answer it. Otherwise, remain silent." Simon snaps his fingers at me. "Eyes forward."

He repeats his question.

"I didn't join the dragon insurgency. There was an attack on my hometown."

Simon touches his tablet, and video from the Mason-Kline battle plays on the thinscreen behind him. He gestures at the Reds crouched in the cornfield. I don't see the Silver. "When the dragons attacked—"

"It wasn't the dragons. The jets attacked them first."

"Of course they did. Because dragons are peace-loving creatures," he says as the video shows a plane crashing into the housing district, where it explodes in a mushroom fireball.

"That's not—"

He raises a warning finger. "So after this unprovoked attack, you went across town to the medical tent, under the guise of wanting to see your brother."

"It wasn't a guise, you—"

"When actually you were there on a mission to rescue an insurgent from the group that calls itself Loki's Grunts."

"I did not. I didn't—"

The video shifts to shaking footage taken from the bivouac of me freeing James.

"Was that not you, Ms. Callahan?"

"Yes it was, but . . ." But there's nothing for me to say. I glare at Simon. "His mother had just been killed, and they were going to throw him in a hole, just like they threw—"

"Your mother died in a dragon attack, too, didn't she?" Simon asks.

"Leave her out of this," I say. But they don't.

Unlike the video they showed on the news three years ago, shot via cell phone, this one's unedited. The Green glides low, its glow brightening as it emerges from the sparse tree line. It rises up, rears its head, and unleashes a rolling breath of fire that consumes the parking lot of cars stuck on the Wilson Bridge. A few survivors jump from the flaming wreckage into the water far below.

Once again, no sound, but I hear the sirens, the jets, the screams anyway. Fake memories. There were no sirens, no jets. Somehow, without warning, this colossal assassin had penetrated the most protected airspace in North America.

Soon after, All-Blacks and dragon jets scrambled into DC, but the Green didn't head toward the nation's capital. Nope. It went straight for Arlington.

The video shifts to a suburban street, two blocks from where I once lived. Trees in the distance burst into flame. People flee toward homes that aren't theirs, pound on doors, run some more. Never fast enough. The fire vacuums them up.

The newscast that night blurred out faces and bodies, as if that might reduce the horror. Maybe it does for some— Konrad looks as if he's about to throw up. Not me. This unedited version pales in comparison to what's played in my head more times than I can count.

Before that day, I never realized how much noise penetrated a dragon shelter's walls. I couldn't hear the jets or the dragon, just the sirens and the screams. Horrible, horrible screams. Sam, Dad, and I huddled together beneath the dim glow of a lightbulb run by a generator I had once complained was too noisy.

Then I heard the car horn. Not random or chaotic, but rhythmic. Someone trying to draw attention to herself.

Dad promised me it wasn't Mom. Yes, she was coming home from work, but there were plenty of shelters to stop at on the way. And yes, she would hide in one. Because she loved us. She wouldn't jeopardize herself. Sam may have believed Dad's logic, but I didn't. I doubt Dad believed it either.

The footage spins to Mom's VW Beetle—bright fucking yellow—racing straight for the charging Green, horn blaring. Two blocks before they meet, Mom veers to the right and disappears down a street.

The dragon shifts course, belching fire at its new target. The Bug races toward the Potomac, a yellow blur that pops in and out of view. One after another, houses erupt into bonfires, the Green only a half block away from Mom before they disappear off camera.

I close my eyes, shut down the tears, knowing what comes next. A crisp black-and-white military video, taken from a drone, that shows dragon and car exiting the suburbs and crossing barren fields toward the river.

"Whoa!" Konrad says, and my eyes snap open.

The video isn't the one from the drone. It's faster, lower to the ground, swerving back and forth. Tinged at the edges in a green glow. A cloud of fire at the bottom of the screen reaches toward the yellow car.

It takes me a few seconds to find my breath. There was a camera on the dragon. In all that blackness, it should have been disoriented, should have crashed into a building or into the street itself. Yet it never did. The news nicknamed the dragon Leprechaun. But it wasn't luck that kept it aloft.

Someone was guiding it, being its eyes.

The Green performs a midair somersault, turning its attention from Mom's car to the two drones flying toward it. Three missiles blast into its chest. A shaking explosion fills the screen. When it clears, the dragon's on the ground, the camera pointed at the yellow Bug flipped over in a field cluttered with weeds and the remnants of a fourth missile.

The video cuts to static.

"Your mother died saving you, your family, and countless others from that murderous Green," Simon says. "But you don't blame the dragon for her death, do you, Ms. Callahan? You blame the military."

I wipe the tears from my eyes. The makeup job must be ruined, but Simon looks pleased.

"Well, Ms. Callahan?"

"There's plenty of blame to go around."

"But you blame them most," he says.

I don't answer.

He sneers. "Your mother was quite the hero."

They know about Mom. They're going to out her. There's nothing I can do to stop them, but I refuse to give him the satisfaction of seeing me come any more unglued. So I blink away the last tears, and meet him and his cameras with the best go-fuck-yourself face I can muster.

With a tiny smirk, Simon shifts his attention to Konrad. Several minutes of farmboy answers to generic questions. ("She's cute, and I prefer blondes. That's a good look for you, Callahan." "Maybe I should have seen it coming. She tended to be quiet in class. Kept to herself." "I just thought she was stuck up. Good grades, teacher's pet, you know the type.")

Finally, in his concerned talk-show-host voice, Simon asks, "Is there anything you'd like to say to Ms. Callahan?"

"Melissa, I know you're angry. My mother was killed a long time ago by dragons, too. The military's doing the best it can to keep us safe. Sometimes they make mistakes. Sometimes our loved ones die. Sometimes it doesn't make any sense." Konrad adopts a contemplative look that's almost comical. "It's enough to drive someone crazy. You confuse friend—"

"You aren't my friend, Konrad. And I'm not a traitor."

"No talking, Ms. Callahan," Simon says. "Start again, Mr. Kline."

"It's enough to drive someone crazy. You confuse friend and enemy, right and wrong, good and evil. The dragons have taken so much from us, but if we let them take our humanity, if we give up on each other, they win. Mel, I don't blame you for all this. I feel sorry for you."

"You always were an idiot, Konrad."

He shrugs, stands, and removes a transceiver from his ear. "We done here?"

Simon nods.

"Good luck, Callahan. I really do feel sorry for you."

After Cosmo Kim returns me to my dragon-queen best, Simon orders Mr. D-man to handcuff my wrists to the chair arms.

"You don't deserve this," he whispers as he applies the cuffs. He backs away. "She's secure."

"Not yet." Simon pulls a handkerchief from his pocket and stuffs it in my mouth. "Can't have you ruining the surprise."

Sam enters tentatively, shies from the cameras, covers his eyes against their bright lights. I call his name through the gag, but it comes out as a moan.

My brother turns toward me, but Simon and the cameras converge around him and obscure our view of each other.

"Hello, Sam," Simon says. "Do you know who I am?"

"Simon Montpellier. Are Frank, Kevin, Mac, and L.T. here, too?"

"Unfortunately they're out filming other sequences. Ellen explained to you what we're doing?"

"Shooting the pilot for a potential *Kissing Dragons* spin-off. *The Insurgent Epidemic*. That's an okay name, I guess, but I'd go with *The Other Side*. It's simpler, right, and more mysterious."

"It's a working title, but we'll take your suggestion under advisement," Simon says, laughing. "Did Ellen mention why we invited you here?"

Sam gives some answer about discussing the recent attack

by insurgents on Mason-Kline. He doesn't have a clue what they're going to spring on him, *who* they're going to spring on him.

". . . and she told me I'd get to meet one of those bastards. They nearly killed my father, and they kidnapped my sister," Sam continues, his tone shifting from angry to anxious. "Ellen says you guys know what's happened to her. If Mel's dead—"

"She's not dead, Sam," Simon says. He steps back, the cameramen part, and Sam's looking at me.

"Mel?" He turns to Simon. "What . . . what's happened to her?"

"They call it Stockholm Syndrome," Simon says.

"No, not my sister." Sam squints at me, blinks several times in fast succession. "Not Melissa. She hates dragons. They killed our mother."

"Maybe she thought that once." Simon guides him to the chair next to mine. "Who knows why this happens, son? Grief does strange things to people."

Sam sits, looks at me every couple of seconds, hurt and uncertainty in each glance.

Once the cameramen have repositioned themselves, Simon removes the gag. "Don't listen to a thing they say, Sam. I'm not an insurgent. Don't believe them. Don't believe . . ." I follow Sam's gaze to the thinscreen.

It shows the doctored image of me atop Old Man Blue.

"It's a lie, Sam. You know that! Sam, look at me. You know I'm not a traitor. Look at me, dammit!"

But he doesn't. The screen switches to the video of me helping James escape the medical tent. This one's not doctored in any way.

Sam clenches and unclenches his hands, his jaw quivering.

"Sam, they were going to hurt—"

"No!" He leaps up, his face redder than his hair. "You helped him? How could you?"

"James isn't a bad person, Sam, he's not—"

"James? James! What about Dad? What about Dad?" He takes a step toward me, then smashes his fists against the desk.

"I'm not a traitor, Sam," I whisper, but any hope that he might believe me is destroyed when the next clip appears.

Taken at a distance, zooming in, it shows me hanging from the ladder of a red dragon, James holding me. Mason-Kline gets pulverized behind us.

"How could you, Melissa? How could you? After what they did to Mom?"

"Oh, Sam. It's—"

"No, Mel. You don't talk to me." He raises his fist, gives me one last glare, and storms from the room.

"Wait! What about Dad? Sam?"

JOSHUA McCUNE

The slam of the door is the only answer I get.

"I'm done," I say. "Take me back to my hole."

Simon shakes his head. "Patience, Ms. Callahan. Just one more, and you'll be finished."

Finished? All that's left in this puppet show is Dad. He wouldn't believe their lies. He'd trust me, believe me . . . love me.

No matter what?

19

The person they bring in isn't my father.

It's James.

Two agents drag him in, shackles around his hands and feet, one of those metal circlets on his head. He's skinnier than I remember. Sunken cheeks and multiple bruises hide behind a layer of makeup. They've dressed him in a fancy white suit, complete with a silver dragon pin on the lapel.

His brilliant blue eyes burn hatred for everyone in the room, but soften when they meet mine. He doesn't seem surprised I'm here. Just sad. The D-men put him in his chair, then take up positions in the corner of the room.

"What happened?" I ask.

"It was—"

"You two will have plenty of time to chat later, Ms.

Callahan," Simon says. "Until then, speak when spoken to."

"Rot in hell."

Simon reaches into his jacket, pulls out a PDA, taps the screen. My CENSIR delivers an electric jolt that sets my body shaking. Sizzling agony shoots through my head, the world blinks out, and I scream.

"Leave her alone!" James yells.

The pain subsides and my vision returns. Simon's scrutinizing the PDA with an expression of approval. "Are you going to behave, Ms. Callahan?"

I grit my teeth and nod.

"I'm sorry, Mel—"

"Shhh." Simon waggles a finger at James. "I've got you in here, too. Play along now, and we'll be done shortly." He drops into narrator voice. "Mr. Everett, when did you first meet Melissa?"

"At Dragon Hill, several months ago."

I want to correct him—we met little more than a week ago—but the sharp headache behind my eyes convinces me to remain quiet.

Simon indicates the image of me atop Old Man Blue. "Did you take this picture?"

"No, my lieutenant did the initial probing. He made sure she fit our profile before I swooped in."

That's a flat-out lie. It doesn't even sound like James.

Did they stick him in a hellhole too? Are his thoughts still scrambled?

"Profile?" Simon prompts.

"Strong spirit, fragile mind." His expression grows serious. "I thought it would be a run-of-the-mill recruiting trip, but when I met her, she absolutely floored me."

"How so?"

"Look at her," James says. "Not the hair or the makeup or the dress. Look into her eyes. There's something magical in them. I've never met anybody like her."

"What happened after that?"

"I took her back to my cave, taught her how to ride dragons and fire guns. One thing led to another—"

"That's all bullshit—" A sharp jolt from my CENSIR turns the rest of my words into a garbled mess.

"No more interruptions, Ms. Callahan." Simon makes a cutting motion across his neck to the cameras, looks to James.

"Start over. What happened after that?"

"I took her back to my cave, taught her how to ride dragons and fire guns. One thing led to another and, well, you know."

No, he's not scrambled. He's got a transceiver in his ear and someone's feeding him lines. He made a deal with them?

I glare at him, and he has the gall to wink at me. I wonder

if they scripted that, too. He seems to be enjoying himself. "She's quite feisty."

Simon laughs. "Yes she is. And evidently quite talented as well."

"Oh, yeah. She climbed our ranks quickly. She was a natural with the dragons."

Simon plays a clip of me and Baby in our battle with the gunships. Except they've digitized Baby from a Silver to a Red and changed her ice to fire. The shaky video, shot from a cockpit, runs for about a minute showing that I do, in fact, look like a talented dragon rider. Until I get blown off Baby's back.

I can't help laughing.

"You find this funny, Ms. Callahan?" Simon asks.

"Fucking hilarious."

I get a shock for that. I bite hard into my lip to stifle the scream. Out of the corner of my eye, I see James flinch.

"You're going to answer my questions now, Ms. Callahan. You will refrain from using inappropriate language. Do you understand?"

"But aren't I the batshit fragile-minded dragon—"

This shock is sharper. My teeth rattle. James's eyes pinch with worry. He gives a slight shake of his head. I ignore him. "It's gonna be a short interview, asshole, if you keep doing that."

"Good point. We're done with him, however, aren't we?" Simon taps the PDA again, holds his finger there, grins as James spasms. His hands clatter against the tabletop, his feet drum the ground. I stare straight ahead. He begins to groan.

"I'm told that brain malfunction ensues after prolonged exposure," Simon says over the loudening groans. "Or paralysis. The studies are still unclear. You never know what might happen with this new technology."

"You think I care?" I say.

He looks at his PDA. "I know you do. That little crown on your head tells me everything you feel."

I chew the inside of my lip and shrug. "Your software must be glitchy."

"Quite fascinating, really, isn't it?" Simon says, running his finger along the PDA screen. "Maybe his heart will give out first."

James's mouth suddenly falls open in a silent scream. His breaths come in hitching, staccato bursts. His eyes widen. His face vibrates.

I break. "Stop it!"

Simon cocks his head as James's entire body seizes and shudders.

"Stop it! Stop it! I'll do what you want!"

"What did you say?" Simon asks.

"I'll cooperate!" I yell. "Just stop it!"

Simon waits another few seconds before relenting. James goes limp. His head bangs against the table.

"James?" I whisper.

He lets out a soft moan.

"Eyes forward, Ms. Callahan." I comply.

"Go into a close-up on her," Simon instructs the cameramen. He reverts to his narrator voice. "Ms. Callahan, when did you find yourself having feelings for Mr. Everett?"

"What do you want from me?" I ask.

"The truth."

I snort. "The truth is I'm not a traitor. I never meant to hurt anybody. I never wanted to talk to dragons, or—"

"You think you can talk to dragons, Ms. Callahan?"

"She's lost it," James mumbles quickly. "Probably ate too much dragon meat."

"Mr. Everett, remain quiet until further notice or I will turn you into a drooling cripple." Simon steps forward. "Ms. Callahan, answer the question."

"I never wanted to be a part of any of this. I wanted the dragons to go away, the military to go away. . . . Guess I'm screwed."

"So your mother never told you the truth?" Simon asks.

James bursts from the chair, launching himself over the table at Simon. He tackles him, gets his cuffed hands around his neck for all of a second before a pair of BoDA agents are pulling him off. He snarls at Simon. "You promised to keep her out of this!"

Simon picks up the PDA from the floor, examines it with a frown, presses a button. "Let's see if you can play possum with this."

James spasms so hard that the agents lose their grip on him. He collapses to the floor, twitches once, then goes deathly still. The D-men scowl at Simon.

Simon checks James's pulse. "No worries, still ticking. Get him out of here and get him prepped for transport."

They leave.

Simon's eyes narrow on me. "Keep in mind that I can make sure he stops ticking."

I don't know if he's authorized to kill him, but it's a chance I cannot afford to take, so I nod and we return to the farce.

"Did you ever find it odd that your mother was so concerned with dragon welfare?" Simon asks. A picture appears on the screen: Mom at a protest rally. "She saw people killed every day, and while most everyone else thought they were monsters, she never did."

"It's called having a heart."

"A heart of gold . . . or maybe red, green, and blue. Just like her daughter?" he says. "You two were close, weren't you? Similar in so many ways."

"I can only hope so."

He puts another picture up. One I've never seen. The coup de grace.

Mom stands on the balcony of Shadow Mountain Lookout, elbows on the railing, chin cupped in her hands. Tired, but happy. On her left is a black man who looks vaguely familiar, for some reason. James, younger, sits on the railing, legs dangled over the edge. Behind him, a handsome man holds a smiling woman. I don't recognize him, but I saw her a week ago, dead on a gurney.

In the background, through the trees, are six dragons. Five Reds, one Green. A part of me wonders if that's the Green that killed her. Or maybe it's just another fabrication.

"Is that your mother in the picture?" Simon asks.

I don't answer.

He points. "Those are dragons, right?"

I don't answer.

"Correct me if I'm wrong, Ms. Callahan, but it appears that those dragons are wearing harnesses."

Good and evil, right and wrong, all that's gone sideways in my head, but there is one truth I will never surrender. "You can paint her however you want," I say. "But my mother was a hero."

"No, she was a traitor. Just like you, Ms. Callahan. Just like you."

He heads for the door.

"Why are you doing this?" I ask.

He hesitates, turns toward me. "Because lots of us had mothers. Lots of us had sons and wives. You're no different from any of us, except you sided with them. You deserve everything that's going to happen to you, Ms. Callahan. May God save your soul."

PART II
RECONDITIONING

20

A BoDA agent escorts me to an SUV. Minutes later, we arrive at a runway where a cargo plane idles. A dull silver glow comes from inside the cabin.

Baby!

We drive up the ramp that extends from the rear of the plane and park at the top. The agent guides me past several rows of crates strapped to the walls, and there she is. My momentary happiness evaporates. Metal bands around her snout, back, and tail clamp her to the metal slab. The cold-restrictor collar pinches deep into her neck. Tranquilizers protrude from her body.

I call her name several times. Her eyes remain shut, but I'd swear she brightens. I hold on to that as we head to the front of the cargo hold, where James sits shackled in a jump seat. The agent positions me on the opposite side, cuffing me to a railing that runs the length of the plane. The lack of windows gives me the sense that I'm in a giant coffin, and I can't help but wonder where they're going to bury us.

"I'm sorry," James says after the agent backs out of the plane.

"You were trying to protect my family." The ramp closes. Engines roar to life. The plane accelerates. "Where do you think they're taking us?"

He glances at Baby. "A place where dragons go to die."

It's my turn to apologize. "If I'd stayed in the cave, Baby would be safe."

"You didn't do anything wrong, Melissa." He takes a deep breath. "Baby, huh?"

I nod. "It's kind of grown on me."

"Guess that's as good a name as any until she tells us what it really is."

"That how it works?"

"Yeah, usually, but who knows with her?" He frowns. "Doubt they'll keep her around long enough for us to find out."

"What about the others?"

He shakes his head. "I don't know. By the time we got there, it was a mess. Our front squadrons had been decimated. Keith and Grackel ordered us to pull back. Most everybody listened, but Vestia was in a state. So was I," he adds, so softly I barely hear. He gives a strained smile. "Anybody ever tell you that you dress up real nice?"

"This sort of beauty doesn't come natural, you know?" I say with a shrug. "I had a lot of help from Cosmo Kim."

"She was a pistol."

"Did they put you in the hole, too, and feed you dragon meat?" I ask.

"Yep, got my dosage of *Kissing Dragons*, though I avoided the meat. There's something in it that makes you go a bit loopy."

I snort. "I went two loops past a bit."

The cockpit door opens. A man in a flight suit retrieves a couple of plastic bottles from a compartment in the bulkhead.

"Liquid replacement meals," he says. He gives one to James, the other to me, never once looking at us.

"Where are you taking us?" I ask.

"Far." He returns to the cockpit.

James takes a swig. "Tastes like feet."

Worse. "How do you know what feet taste like?"

"A boy's gotta have some secrets." He arches an eyebrow, eyes my feet, laughs.

I grin, raise my bottle. "Here's to feet! May they taste good, be strong, and one day carry us home."

He raises his bottle. "To feet!"

We chat long into the flight, avoiding topics that make us think about our friends or families or the bleak future that likely awaits us. We talk to Baby at regular intervals. Sometimes she brightens, a brief heartbeat of intensity, but that's it. We attempt to contact his dragon acquaintances. Nothing. Either they're dead, or the CENSIRs are blocking us. After a few moments of dreary silence, we go back to rehashing our favorite movies, foods, subjects in school. . . .

I fight sleep, order him to tell me about his childhood. Instead he recites poetry. Somewhere in the middle of Robert Frost's "Fire and Ice," I drift off.

When I wake, I'm shivering. It was nowhere near this cold before. James watches me from across the aisle, his face worn with fatigue. It doesn't look like he's slept.

"I think we've begun our descent," he says.

"Deeper into hell?"

"Something like that."

Within minutes, we touch down. The ramp opens to a cloudless sky and an arctic world. An undulating howl of wind envelops us. It sets my teeth chattering, and in a matter of seconds my fingers and toes are numb.

James tries to smile. "Who knew . . . hell . . . was this . . . cold?"

Four All-Blacks in snow gear rush into the plane, surround Baby, and remove the arm-thick bolts that attach her sledge to the chassis. The scales on their helmets twinkle in the sunlight. Red and green, mostly. A spot of blue here and there. I try not to think that soon silver will be there too.

While a tractor pulls Baby from the cabin, the soldiers bundle us in wool-lined boots, thick gloves, knit caps, and faux-fur jackets. I stop shivering, but the bite of the wind still cuts through everything.

I stare after Baby. "Whatever you're going to do to her, please make it quick."

The nearest soldier glances over his shoulder, frowns, but doesn't respond. They load James and me into the back of a Humvee. The driver, a burly man, pulls the ski mask down to expose his mouth and regards us with eyes as frosty as the weather.

"I'm Major Alderson. You are Talker Twenty-Five," he says through the steel mesh that separates us. He nods at James. "You are Talker Twenty-Six. Both of you have been conscripted by the U.S. Army to help eliminate the dragon infestation. You will cooperate, or you will suffer dire consequences. Welcome to your new home."

"Antarctica," I guess, looking at the hula-girl stick-on clock mounted to the dash. *23:09.* Almost midnight. The sun's out—which must mean we're in the southern hemisphere. Even with the car's heater going full blast, I'm still cold. "Why bring us here?"

"Invisibility," James mutters.

"Correct," the major says. "If you somehow managed to

send one of your fire-breathing friends an image of our location, they wouldn't know where to come rescue you because everything down here in the frozen suck looks the same."

On that wonderful note, the major puts on his sunglasses and backs out of the plane. Dragon jets and artillery flank the runway. We pass a row of hangars, but otherwise there's nothing around us except endless tracts of ice.

The wind moans at us, kicks up snow devils along the runway, pushes the Humvee from side to side. We turn onto a barely visible road that leads toward green and red lights in the distance.

"What are you doing to them?" James says through gritted teeth.

"Research. They have amazing thermal control."

The lights take shape. Dragons. Collared and dying, in giant birdcages. Macabre decorations for the median. A couple of brighter ones scream at us.

The last cage in the line contains a pair of glowless Reds huddled together. "Radio go," the major says. "HQ, we've got snowkill on Dragons Forty-Seven and Forty-Eight. Please be advised."

I grunt and press my head to the window. Our cage may be larger, but what are the odds James and I end up like those two dead Reds?

The patter of gunfire reaches my ears. Along the side of

the road, men fire machine guns at a dimming Green strapped to a freestanding wall. It's muzzled. Blood trickles from its wounds onto a field of snow more crimson than white.

"Isn't it a bit late for torture?" James says.

The major laughs. "No rest for the weary. Gotta get in what we can while the weather's good."

If that steel mesh didn't separate us, I'm pretty sure James would strangle him. I reach for his hand, but he shakes me off. "You're a monster," he says. "You're all monsters!"

"Control yourself, Twenty-Six."

James tugs at the door handle, but we're locked in. He jerks harder, kicks at the steel separator.

The major jams the brakes. The Humvee slides to a stop. James keeps kicking. The major picks up a computer tablet, taps a couple of buttons. James convulses, flails, goes limp. His breaths come in jagged bursts as he continues to glare at the major.

"You're only making this harder on yourself, Twenty-Six." The major shows us the tablet screen. *CENSIR for Talker 26 (Telepathy: Disabled)* is written in block letters above a 3-D image of a brain. James's name, national registration number, and biometric data occupy the top left corner. Flashing red text draws my attention to the right side of the screen. *Current synaptic state: violent, dangerous to others.*

He thumbs the bottom of the tablet. Two columns appear

beside the brain. The first has five buttons: off, record, transmit, inhibit, and incapacitate. The inhibit one is depressed. The other contains a rainbow-colored slider and adjacent button labeled shock. The slider is set to green.

"It can be much worse. Are we clear?" The major adjusts the slider to maximum red, lets his finger hover above the shock button until James nods.

A couple minutes later, we drive through a pair of dragon skeletons held together by wires and rods. Their wings connect in an arch, from which hangs a wooden sign. WELCOME TO GEORGETOWN. Beneath it, in smaller, knife-scratched letters: A NO-FLY ZONE.

Ahead, artillery and missile launchers split the road in two. Buildings press in on either side, rising up from the ice on concrete stilts. Slanted roofs, black, windowless, they are indistinguishable except for their size.

And the trophies. They're everywhere. Smaller bones formed into military insignia on doors and walls. Wings along the longer edifices. A scale pelt here, a mosaic of fangs there.

"That's the cafeteria," the major says. Talons dangle from the eaves. He points across the road at a gargantuan building that spans an entire block and is at least four stories high. Dragon skulls ring the top, hollow eyes looking down on us. "ER . . . Examination and Research. We do some of our most important work in there."

We pull up to a nondescript building. Alderson lets me out, but closes the door in James's face.

"These are the female barracks," he says. "You feel that cold, Twenty-Five?"

I nod.

He walks up the steps, enters a code on the numeric keypad. The door unlocks. He doesn't open it. After a long minute of silence broken only by my teeth chattering, he says, "The closest place that might welcome a stranger is more than three hundred miles from here. That's assuming you head in the right direction and the weather cooperates."

He ducks his head against the wind and ushers me into a room that resembles a small movie theater with a center aisle and beds instead of chairs. The only light comes from a massive thinscreen on the far wall.

I almost scream. *Kissing Dragons*, episode forty-three. Several girls, all wearing CENSIRs and black scrubs, sit on the beds nearest the screen, seemingly enthralled by the hunt for Killzilla, the Terror of Tokyo. Everybody else appears to be asleep.

Major Alderson removes my handcuffs. "Give me your jacket, boots, cap, and gloves."

My heart sinks. It's warm in the room—nobody seems uncomfortable in their short sleeves—but without proper attire, my fairy-tale vision of breaking out, releasing Baby, and flying off into the sunset with James seems even more implausible.

Once I'm down to my white dress, the major leaves. The moment the door shuts, a statuesque blonde claps her hands.

"Wakey, wakey, everyone. Our newest sister is here," she says. I cringe as she checks me out, a smirk spreading across her face.

Lit by the screen behind them, the other girls remind me of ghosts as they rise from their beds. Most of them look my age, though a couple who lurk at the edges are definitely younger.

The blonde positions herself front and center.

"I'm Evelyn, Talker One," she says, emphasizing the title more than her name. She introduces the half-dozen pale girls clustered around her, giving their names, then numbers, which is unnecessary since they're stenciled on their uniforms. They smile at me like I've shown up at summer camp a day late, but don't you worry, we're gonna have lots of fun.

A light-skinned black girl pantomimes turning a dial. "Let's ratchet the freak down a little bit, girls. She's got plenty of scary ahead of her without the Stepford routine."

"Says the drunken whore," Evelyn says, smile never faltering. "We must get you changed." She snaps her fingers. Five scurries off.

"This drunken whore's name is Lorena," the black girl

whispers to me. "I will respond to Drunken Whore, but only on Wednesdays." She runs a hand beneath the number stenciled on her scrubs. "Or Talker Two, if you'd prefer."

I like her. "Melissa."

"Do you believe in Jesus Christ as our lord and savior?" asks a mousy girl with a Bible clutched in her hands. I glance at her scrubs. *Talker 13.*

Jesus Christ.

"Of course she does, Pam," Lorena says as I stumble for an answer. To me: "Dragons are the devil's creation."

Pam scowls. "I wasn't asking you."

"You bet," I say. She doesn't look convinced. Lorena winks at me. I force a smile. "Everybody knows dragons are the devil's creation. Only faith in Jesus can save us from them."

The scowl deepens, but Pam backs off.

Five returns with a pair of black scrubs, which Evelyn presents to me. "You want to—"

A scrabbling noise interrupts her. A child who can't be older than twelve emerges from beneath one of the beds. Her eyes dart everywhere. "She's not a vulture in disguise, is she?"

"No, Allie, she's one of us," Lorena says. "This is Melissa."

"I'm Twenty-One," the girl says. "You don't want to screw with me, no, no."

"Twenty-One, that is not proper language for a young lady," Pam says.

Twenty-One sticks out her tongue, then flips her off. She comes closer, circles around me, sniffing.

"It's best not to agitate her," Lorena whispers.

"You're not a chocolate thief, are you?" Twenty-One asks. She glowers at Sixteen, a girl with a bandage across her nose. Sixteen, who's got at least two years, five inches, and thirty pounds on Twenty-One, shudders and ducks behind Lorena.

"Be nice, Allie," Lorena says.

Twenty-One purses her lips, looks back at me, wrinkles her nose. "You don't smell like one, no, no."

"I'm not."

She shrugs. Her eyes drift to my chest and widen. "Ooh. Can I have that? Can I, can I?"

I follow her intense gaze to the dragon brooch. I'd forgotten about the stupid thing. "Gladly." She runs to a corner, settles into a crouch, and strokes the silver brooch like it's a pet.

"What's with her?" I ask.

"Allie was reconditioned. Sometimes it backfires," Lorena says. She turns to the others. "Back to bed, everyone. Show's over." Evelyn's minions shrink under Lorena's gaze, but don't retreat until the blonde nods her okay.

"You want to sleep on our side, Twenty-Five?" Evelyn gestures at the right half of the room. Based on the silence and stares I'm getting, this is a critical decision. An easy one, though.

"I think I'll stay over here."

Murmurs come from Evelyn's crowd. She raises her hand for quiet. "Nice meeting you, Twenty-Five. Remember, actions have consequences," she says, way too perky, then turns on her heel and marches to bed.

"She been reconditioned, too?" I ask.

Lorena laughs. "Nah, she's just drunk a lot of the Kool-Aid." She nods toward the screen. "We better get moving. This is the last episode of the night. Once the message boards go off, we're in the dark."

I glance at the screen. Frank, Kevin, Mac, and L.T. are skulking up Mount Kumotori. There's a red glow in the distance. Several of Evelyn's girls watch, wide-eyed, hands over mouths or clutched in worry. The fab four open fire, and the girls cheer.

"They're rooting for the soldiers?" I say. "Is that what that crap about choosing sides was about?"

"Pretty much," Lorena says.

"And we're on the other side?"

"No, we're on the stay-out-of-trouble side."

"Sounds like something my dad would say. . . . Where are the adults?"

She shrugs. "Somewhere else. Most of us had parent talkers. One or both. None of them showed up here." She looks away, shakes her head. "Probably a good thing."

She leads me through a door at the back to a restroom with a shower, a pair of stalls, and another thinscreen. A girl sits on the tiles, entranced.

"That's Claire," Lorena says as we walk past. Claire, Talker Fifteen, a thick girl with dark fuzz on her upper lip, waves a bandaged hand at me when I say hi, but otherwise remains hypnotized by the show.

"Reconditioned?" I whisper.

"Yep," Lorena says. I'm about to pile my scrubs on the floor, but she takes them from me. "The first rule of survival here: keep your clothes as clean as possible. Laundry only comes once a week. I'm serious. Lots of things suck here in Georgetown—"

"Suck?"

"Yeah, euphemism, I know. Be happy with what you can, control what you can . . . like your clothes. Unless you're offering an invitation, change here." She guides me to a stained section of tiles adjacent to the shower, motions toward the shadowed ceiling. "Infrared cameras monitor our activities. This is pretty much the only blind spot in this place."

"You haven't tried to escape?" The last word's no more

than a second out of my mouth when my CENSIR delivers a low-level jolt.

"Blind, but not deaf. They got mikes built in." She taps her circlet. "Big Brother's always listening."

She keeps talking while I undress. "It can't read thoughts beyond emotional states. They don't like it when you're upset. When you're in the dragon dicer or battle room, you'll be tuned to a specific dragon frequency. Everything's on an internal line, so you'll be safe."

"Safe?"

"They'll start you in the call center, where you'll be tuned to transmit to the world. You'll be tempted to contact any dragons you know. Don't."

I step into the shower with a questioning look.

She hooks her thumb at Claire. "She was the last one who thought she could beat the system. Her and Twenty-Three."

"That one of the boys?"

She shakes her head. "I've been here three summers. Nobody gets out."

21

The next day begins too early with a fanfare of music, a low-level jolt from my CENSIR, and, worst of all, a chirpy "Wakey, wakey, everyone" from Evelyn. By the time I've opened my eyes, the other girls have gathered near the entrance, a couple nodding in rhythm to the *Kissing Dragons* theme song blaring from the screen.

"Wakey, wakey, Twenty-Five."

I groan into my pillow, then stagger to my feet and join the group.

"Where's Lorena?" I ask Pam. It appears Claire's missing, too. Unless she's still in the bathroom.

Pam shrugs. "Probably in the battle room. Lorena's a top operator."

I start to ask what she means when four soldiers enter the

barracks carrying boxes overflowing with clothes. Evelyn and company fawn over them like they're rock stars handing out autographs, not gun-toting soldiers doling out jackets, boots, gloves, and ski caps. Twenty-One, counting her fingers repeatedly, whispering "Burn, burn, burn" as she does, is starting to look more normal by the second.

Evelyn beams at the thick-necked soldier guarding the door. "Everyone was up on time, Lester, except Twenty-Five."

"She's new here. Why don't we give her a break?" He tosses her a Kit Kat. She thanks him like he just awarded her the Miss America crown. Terrific. Whenever Big Brother's not spying on us, I've got to worry about Ms. Perky and her band of informants ratting me out for chocolate.

The soldiers load us onto a black bus outfitted with monster tires and a snow plow. Inside, a steel grating separates the driver from the rest of us. Evelyn and her crew crowd the front seats, chirping away or flirting with the soldiers, who scan our faces and monitor their tablets.

A half mile down, we debus and single-file it into a mess hall with a small buffet area and several long tables, most of them occupied by All-Blacks. Several leer at us as we enter. A couple hoot or whistle.

One gropes my ass. "Hey there, pretty girl, what's your number?"

I ignore him.

"I'm Lover One," he calls after me. His buddies laugh. Their taunts follow me into the buffet line, where a server loads my tray with runny eggs and overcooked sausages Pam assures me don't come from dragons.

We head for the table farthest from the entrance. Pam indicates a pair of girls seated at the far end. Talker Twenty and Talker Twenty-Two. Each has a Bible laid open beside her tray.

"Would you like to join us?" Pam asks.

I don't, but I don't want to be rude. I bow my head as she recites an opening prayer. "'We rejoice in our sufferings, knowing that suffering produces endurance, and endurance produces character, and character produces hope, and hope does not put us to shame, because God's love has been poured into our hearts through the Holy Spirit who has been given to us.' Amen."

I give the obligatory amen, smile amiably, and dig in.

Breakfast tastes like heaven. While I eat and pretend to listen to Pam lecture on suffering and hope, I scan the table on the other side of the cafeteria where the male talkers sit. I count seven, all high school or college age, none of them familiar.

"Where's James?" I ask Lester, who stands behind us. "Talker Twenty-Six," I clarify when he doesn't respond.

"Best you forget about him," he says.

"What's that mean?"

"Means you should forget about him."

Something tugs at my pant leg. I look down to find Twenty-One beneath the table. "What are you—"

She presses a finger to her lips. "Everyone you care about, everyone you care about, gone. Poof," she whispers. "Make them go. Kill the dragons, or the dragons kill them. Burn, burn, burn. Yes, yes, yes." She nods, spins around, and crawls to her chair.

We're clearing our trays from the table when Lorena, Claire, and two boys enter the mess hall under guard. Though I can't be sure, it appears they're all holding Kit Kats. Claire says something. Lorena slaps her, throws the chocolate at Claire's feet, then storms out of the cafeteria. A couple of A-Bs escort Claire and the two boys to the buffet line as the other two soldiers race after Lorena.

"She's in trouble," Evelyn says. "Actions have consequences."

I imagine stabbing my plastic fork through the smile plastered on Evelyn's face. My CENSIR shocks me.

"Control your emotions, Twenty-Five," Lester says, finger poised over his tablet. "Violent thoughts will not be tolerated . . . even against her."

"I wasn't going to do anything," I say.

Once he's sure I'm calm, we join the others on the bus. As we pull out, I see a soldier shoving Lorena into the back of a Humvee.

"They going to recondition her?" I ask Pam.

"Lorena? She's done worse," she says, then shrugs as if to say "you never know."

Our bus makes a short commute between a pair of missile launchers to the opposite side of the road. We idle close to the entrance of what must be the ER—thankfully out of sight of the parapet of dragon heads. A tractor pushes a flickering Red strapped to a rolling slab up a ramp and into a garage bay.

"Give me fifty on that lightbulb not making it past the flame bath," I overhear the driver say to Lester.

"Only if you're paying triple. That thing probably won't make it past intake," Lester says. "At least it's got a thick head. Should make for a good workout."

They both laugh.

Under the guidance of a couple of soldiers, the slab is maneuvered onto some sort of rail system. Four figures dressed from head to toe in black—faces hidden by goggles and masks, a couple carrying hatchets—walk into view. The slab rotates ninety degrees, pointing the dragon down the length of the ER. A semicylindrical sheath lowers from the ceiling, comes to a stop inches from the dragon. The tractor reverses, the garage bay closes.

The driver opens the bus door. The stench of burned meat wafts in. I hear the faint grind of what sounds like chain saws.

A seat ahead of me, Sixteen tenses.

"One, Five, Twelve, Eighteen," Lester calls.

A chorus of excited thank yous rings out from the front. Sixteen relaxes.

"Kill the dragons, yes, yes," Twenty-One says.

A soldier escorts Evelyn and three tagalongs toward the ER. The girls smile the entire way.

We cross back to the other side of the road to a building decorated with massive dragon-wing skeletons. Must be from a Green.

Or Baby. I swallow. No, they wouldn't have killed her already. They'd want to experiment on her first. Doesn't matter. One day soon, she'll be a trophy on a building. On several buildings, maybe. Will I recognize her?

Lester checks his tablet. "Seven, Ten, Nineteen."

The rest of Evelyn's posse offers up more overzealous thank yous and plastic smiles as they follow a guard off the bus.

"Or the dragons kill them," Twenty-One says with a gleeful laugh.

A block down the road, we stop again.

"Thirteen, Sixteen, Twenty, Twenty-One, Twenty-Two."

"Chocolate time. Burn, burn, burn." Twenty-One bounces up from her seat and skips down the aisle. Pam crosses herself, mumbles something beneath her breath, then follows.

When the bus starts moving again, it's just me, Lester, and the bus driver. "Where are we going?"

"To get you processed," Lester says. "It shouldn't take long. Assuming you cooperate."

We drive to a three-story building that looms at the end of the road between a pair of artillery guns. An American flag flies from the pole atop it, glimmering in the sunlight. We park beside a cluster of cages similar to the dragon ones, except smaller. Exiting the bus, I get a better view of the flag. It's made of dragon scales.

Lester takes me to a top-floor office occupied by a grizzled man, a painting of Saint George spearing a dragon, and a half dozen thinscreens. A couple broadcast the twenty-four-hour news stations; the rest are turned off.

"Colonel Hanks, this is Twenty-Five," says Lester.

"Thank you, Sergeant." The colonel dismisses Lester, then gestures to the chair opposite his desk. I remain standing. His eyes narrow a fraction. "Do you know what we do here, Twenty-Five?"

Horrible things, but I say, "Hunt dragons?"

Another fraction. "We do God's work. And he has granted you a great gift."

"This *great gift* has gotten me into a lot of trouble."

He removes a plaque from the wall, sets it on the desk so I can read it. DO NOT BE DECEIVED: GOD CANNOT BE MOCKED. A MAN REAPS WHAT HE SOWS. GALATIANS 6:7.

I snort. "What does God say about torture?"

"The house of the wicked will be destroyed, Twenty-Five. Whether you are inside or not is up to you." The colonel indicates my CENSIR. "You know why we make you wear that?"

I don't respond. He shows me his tablet. The screen contains my brain image, personal data, and biometrics. I choke off a bitter laugh when I read the words. *Current synaptic state: confused, angry, scared.* No kidding.

"The CENSIR is meant to help you find the righteous path, Twenty-Five. You have been led astray by evil forces."

He switches the CENSIR to record mode. "Be warned, any lie or omission will be detected. Tell me the names of every dragon and insurgent you know."

I hesitate. Colors appear on my brain image, accompanied by text that indicates my reluctance.

"I am disappointed," the colonel says. He uses the tablet to activate a thinscreen. A moment later, Simon Montpellier's awful voice fills the room.

"Sometimes the face of terror is obvious," he says. A

picture of a scowling black guy with a scar along his jawline flashes onto the screen. I squint. The same guy from
the Shadow Mountain Lookout picture? He disappears. A
new image forms, the pixels sharpening slowly into focus.
"Sometimes it's the last person you'd expect."

My junior-high yearbook picture crystallizes.

It's a teaser for that *Kissing Dragons* spinoff.

"Why does a girl destined to be valedictorian, a girl from
a loving, patriotic family, join the other side?"

The screen flashes to the famous clip of Mom leading the
Green away from the Arlington suburbs in the yellow Bug.

Back to my yearbook picture.

"Melissa Callahan, a good girl from a distinguished
family . . . a family with the darkest secret," Simon
says. The image shatters, to be replaced by a video of
me on Baby amid the gunships. They've made her into
a Red. She releases a blast of CGI fire that consumes the
screen. White text appears: *Kissing Dragons: The Other
Side* debuts after *Kissing Dragons*. (Check your loyalty at
www.kissing-dragons.com/check-your-loyalty).

"You know what happens to the families of traitors,
Twenty-Five?" the colonel asks. "Your brother and father
will be eviscerated by the media. . . . What did they do
wrong? How come they didn't see it coming?" He pauses.
"Or maybe they were involved."

My throat constricts. "They didn't know anything."

"I pray that's true. That teaser hasn't gone live. The producers are eager to air the episode, but the army has final say in the matter. Now, Twenty-Five, tell me the names."

Two choices . . .

"Gretchen," I whisper. "I don't know her last name. I don't know if she's alive."

"Please give her description."

I do. Everything I say appears in bold text beneath the image of my brain. Colonel Hanks checks the content, asks a few more questions, then saves everything.

"Who else?"

I go through names and descriptions the best I can remember.

"Anybody else?" he asks.

I shake my head, but my thoughts give me away.

"Twenty-Five, you have taken a step away from the devil's side. Do not fall back."

"Preston," I say. The tablet indicates I'm suppressing something. I clench my fists. "Williams. Preston Williams. He was a transfer student to our high school. Maybe that's not even his real name." God, I hope not.

"Anyone else?"

Yes, one more. The one that hurts most. I scour my mind for a way out, but my mind is the trap.

"Do not make me ask again."

"Keith," I say, feeling like an executioner delivering the death blow. "Major Keith Harden. That's it. That's all of them."

The colonel stands. "Excellent. Be good, Twenty-Five, do what you're told, and God will favor you. You are dismissed."

On the way out, he hands me a Kit Kat.

22

There's somebody in one of the cages. Cap pulled low, jacket zipped to his chin. James. Hugging himself, he bounces from foot to foot.

"What are you doing to him? Stop it!"

"Control yourself, Twenty-Five, unless you wish to join him." Lester drags me into a Humvee.

"Let me talk to him. Please! I can make him cooperate!"

"Sure you can."

"Please. A couple minutes. Give me a chance."

He rolls his eyes, sighs, speaks into his helmet's mouth-piece. "Radio go. . . . HQ, Twenty-Five wants to talk with Twenty-Six, who is currently in a Smurf pen. She believes she can persuade him to behave." A brief response from the other end. Lester nods to me. "You have five minutes."

I realize why they call it the Smurf pen as I get up close. James's cheeks and nose are tinged blue. He squints in my direction but looks confused. I call his name three times before his eyes find focus on mine. I reach between the bars and press my gloved palm to his face.

He flinches, loses his balance for a moment. "It burns . . . burns. How . . . can burn . . . and be . . . so cold?"

I unwrap the Kit Kat, press it into his hand.

"This is what they give you when you're good," I say as he struggles to chew and I struggle to keep it together. "Doesn't seem quite fair, does it?"

He tries to smile, but it must hurt too much.

I bite my lip hard. "Just do what they want, James. Please."

"They . . . will . . . have . . . kill . . . me first," he stutters through chattering teeth.

"They won't do that. They'll recondition you."

"Maybe . . . that's . . . better."

Despite my best efforts, I start crying.

"Don't." He takes my hand between his. "What . . . was . . . phrase . . . you . . . told me . . . about . . . the spirit one?"

"*Baekjul boolgool*," I whisper. "Please, James."

"It's time to go, Twenty-Five," Lester says from behind me.

"I'm . . . sorry." James releases my hand and turns away.

"James, don't."

He ignores me.

Lester grabs me by the arm.

"Please. Just a few more minutes."

"Don't make this difficult, Twenty-Five." He pushes me into the Humvee. "You should forget about him."

"Stop telling me that."

"Just trying to help."

"I don't need your help."

"You need all the help you can get out here, Twenty-Five. Actions, consequences, it all boils down to this, the most helpful piece of advice anybody will give you: don't make the mistake of thinking you're brave." He points a thumb over his shoulder toward the Smurf pens, grimaces. "It won't end well."

We drive to the building where the bus dropped off Twenty-One and Pam. At the door, I hear a boy's muffled cries from inside. "I'm scared, I'm scared. Please, I need your help. The invisible men are after me."

"Join us or die!" somebody else shouts.

"Burn, burn, burn!!!"

"What's going on?" I ask as Lester types in the passcode to the door.

"Greasing the scales," Lester says.

As he ushers me inside, other voices rise and fall, some with anguished pleas, others with growled commands.

After hanging our coats on a communal rack and stuffing gloves and hats into marked cubbies (25 for me, L. ROGERS for him), I follow him down a short hallway that ends in a fluorescent-lit office crowded with a dozen cubicles, most occupied by an All-Black and a dragon talker. The soldiers monitor tablets while the talkers beg and growl at computer screens.

Major Alderson watches intently from the front of the room. *Actions have consequences* and *Weak links break chains* are written on the whiteboard behind him. Beneath that is a list: *3, 4, 6, 9, 11, 13, 14, 16, 20, 21, 22*. Red and green tally marks adjoin each number. Eleven has the most, with seven reds and two greens. Twenty-One's right behind, with six reds and two greens.

"Cube twelve," the major says, writing *25* at the bottom of the board.

Lester guides me to the cubicle adjacent to Twenty-One's, then sits me on a folding chair in front of a computer.

Target: Pravik (Red)
Call frequency: Unknown
Last known whereabouts: Central Canada
Known dragon associations: Calixis, Korm*, Oryson, Ulg[†]
Known insurgent associations: None

Your name: Sandra Bynum

Your location: Sioux Falls, South Dakota
Your insurgency group: The Nebraska Reds

"A star by the name means that association is deceased," Lester says. "A cross indicates that the dragon is imprisoned. Never mention a captured dragon to the target. Here's your script."

He hands me a couple sheets of paper. I'm supposed to start by introducing myself as an insurgent in need of a temporary hideout. If the dragon agrees to help, I ask for a location image. If the dragon hesitates, go to the rebuttal section, which has a dozen options depending on the dragon's response.

Several places in the script require me to fill in the blanks with my or the target's information. Beside each section, handwritten notes instruct me to *Pretend you're scared!* or *Get angry*. It seems ridiculous the dragons would buy any of this, but by the time Lester comes back with a cup of coffee, Major Alderson's already added another green tick to Twenty-One's tally.

Lester taps the transmit button on his tablet. Three choices appear. *1-to-1, Partial, Full*—grayed out. He selects *Partial*. The CENSIR loosens slightly.

"Go time, Talker Twenty-Five," he says. "Speak everything aloud. Any attempts at silent communication will be punished. Stick to your lines until you become familiar with protocol."

"Pravik, Pravik, are you there?" I read from the script. No response. I continue, *Add urgency!* "My name is Sandra Bynum, a talker with the Nebraska Reds. Korm told me that you are a friend to the cause. I tried reaching him, but he's not responding. Please, I need your help. The invisible men are after me."

The Red never answers. Lester inhibits me, offers pointers on inflection and emphasis. The information on my monitor switches to Kworl, a Red last seen in Idaho.

Kworl snubs me, too. I plead harder, louder. Another three dragons ignore me.

I'm about to ask Lester what I'm doing wrong when I notice the timer on the computer. Previously, he ended our calls and moved to the next target after a minute of silence, but we've been waiting on Demodek for over five minutes.

I look over my shoulder. Lester's sipping his coffee, chatting it up with the A-B a cube over, not paying me any attention. The tablet that controls my CENSIR is tucked beneath his arm. More importantly, I think he's forgotten to inhibit me.

Maybe a better opportunity will present itself down the road, maybe James will come around and decide to cooperate, maybe Baby will figure out a way to escape on her own. And maybe Santa Claus is real.

I focus on Syren, the only dragon I can think of who knows me and might still be alive. *Syren, this is Melissa*—

"Hum—" I hear her begin, then my CENSIR constricts. Blinding pain shoots through me. I crash to the floor. Screams echo everywhere. Mine?

When I come to, it feels like somebody's taken a hammer to my skull. My head throbs, my vision's murky. As the world slides back into focus, I see Major Alderson hunched over me with an amused smirk. A boy stands beside him, stiff and expressionless.

"Welcome back, Twenty-Five," the major says. "That first one's always a doozy. Trust me, the second one's worse. Eleven, how many times did you try to warn the dragons?"

Confusion fills the boy's face. "Warn them? Why would I do that?"

"You'll have to forgive him. His memory's a little spotty." Major Alderson holds up three bony fingers. He jabs my CENSIR. "This precious piece of metal around your thick skull has several wonderful features about it." He jabs harder. My headache accelerates, the fading spots in my vision swell and swarm to the center. "One of my favorites is that when you're in transmit mode, it autosenses any attempt at silent communication. Doesn't mean anything necessarily. You could be trying to talk to God, for all it knows. Thing is, God doesn't listen. Worse for you, if you get a return signal of any sort"——he claps his hands together an inch from my eyes——"talker goes down."

He jerks me to my feet. "Now, Twenty-Five, what did you say?"

I tell him.

"No harm, no foul," he says. "Here's the thing, Twenty-Five. You're a needle in a frozen haystack out here. So even if you got a message out, even if the dragons decided to put their lives on the line for a human, the chance of them finding you is . . ." He holds out his thumb and forefinger, then presses them together. "But even those odds I can't afford. Don't make me recondition you. You won't like it."

That much we can agree on. But that's not my main concern.

"I'll behave," I whisper, thinking of Dad and Sam.

He pats me on the head like a dog. "I know you will."

Over the next hour and a half, twenty more dragon names cross my computer screen. All ignore me.

"Why aren't they answering?" I ask Lester.

"Because they don't know you. Or because they know about our little operation," he says. "It's the ones that do want to help that we have to worry about."

Fifteen more dragons go by before I make contact with Najla. *It has been two white moons and you are the fifth human to aggrieve me with your whines. I grow weary of all this begging. What is wrong with you humans?*

Everything she says appears on my screen in a rolling scroll of text a moment after I hear it in my head. The call frequency field updates from *Unknown* to *97.386 iGHz*.

I scan the script for what I'm supposed to do but can't find anything that applies. I look to Lester with a shrug. He indicates the section near page bottom—*For arrogant or annoyed dragons.* "Please help me. I am weak. Without your help, the invisible men will—"

You sound fearful, but your mind is closed, human. I do not trust you.

Further attempts at communication go unanswered.

Ten silent dragons later, I get my first Green. Bryzmon has just one known dragon association, registered dead. Lester hands me a different call script. A single page with two paragraphs of text. One for introduction, one for rebuttal. Only one fill-in-the-blank (my alias) and one handwritten note (*Growl as you speak*).

"Bryzmon, my name is Christina Grace, I am a member of the Diocletians," I say, adding a throaty rumble to my words. "Join us or die."

The Green responds immediately in a guttural voice that spikes a shiver through me. *I will enjoy sucking the skin from your roasted body, human.* His call frequency updates to 98.667 iGHz.

The rebuttal section—*When the dragon threatens to devour you*—is simple. "Join us and you can eat well every day without fear of—"

I am not afraid, but you should be, human. You sound delicious.

That's the end of that conversation.

"Be more assertive with the Greens," Lester says, and we move on.

Over the next couple of hours, a dozen more dragons answer my calls (thanks in large part to hungry Greens) and I learn a thing or two about my telepathy curse. If a dragon's on the line, you hear a subtle ringing noise, imperceptible unless you concentrate. Though I can initiate the conversation, only a dragon or Lester seems to be able to end it.

Despite my improved contact rate, I have yet to get a mark on the board. The responding Reds don't trust me, and the Greens want to eat me. Lester, who seems unconcerned with my lack of results, assures me that success will come, then promptly tells me to try harder.

But I can't. I'm already putting everything I have into it. I growl assertively at Greens, pretend I'm scared for Reds. Except it's not pretend anymore. Not even close. I'm so worried failure will result in punishment that my urgent pleas have turned real.

I'm near tears, desperate not to disappoint, when I make

contact with Eck, a Red from Colorado whose known associations are all dead. Immediately I know he's different by the sadness in his voice. Without much prompting, he tells me about his friends, how they were killed by the invisible monsters, how he's alone and scared.

I scan the script, choke up when I find the appropriate response. "I'm afraid, too, Eck. But together we can be less afraid."

An image of a snowy mountain range pops into my head. *May the wind be at your back,* Eck says in farewell.

The CENSIR tightens. Lester shows me the tablet, which displays a picture identical to the one Eck sent me. "Twenty-Five, you just bagged your first dragon," he announces. A couple of soldiers clap as Major Alderson puts a red mark next to my number.

"What's going to happen to him?" I ask.

"We'll sync the image to the military database. They'll bring him in or dispose of him."

My gaze returns to the mountain in which Eck hides, and memories of gunships and that headless dragon flood my mind. Maybe there's a girl near Eck's cave—wrong place, wrong time—who they'll capture and stick in a hole before sending her to this frozen hell. And it'll be my fault.

"He's not dangerous," I say. "He won't hurt anybody. You don't need to kill him."

Lester scowls. "Maybe he is some decrepit recluse content to live out his days in the evac territories. But he's just as likely a clan leader or elder trying to play us. Look, Twenty-Five, you don't have to like what you do, but it's your job now, so you better do it well. Remember, actions have consequences."

As the afternoon wears on, I get better at suppressing the guilt, better at deceiving dragons. Whenever I locate one, Lester congratulates me with kind words or a warm smile. I tell myself the momentary satisfaction I experience comes from the knowledge I'm protecting my brother and father.

By the time Major Alderson calls an end to the day, I've located three more Reds, all of them seemingly old. I'm in last place, but I gained a spot on Fourteen since sitting down at my cubicle.

Alderson dismisses the boys first. They line up in ascending order against the wall adjacent to my cube.

"The next time you see James—" I start whispering to Three.

"Who?" he says as the line starts to move.

"Twenty-Six."

"Shh," Four says.

"I don't think he's coming back," Three says.

My CENSIR jolts me. "No fraternization, Twenty-Five," Lester says. "Move along, boys."

The major stops the line at Eleven, offers him a Kit Kat. "For a job well done."

The boy shakes his head. "It was a privilege, sir."

Fourteen, chewing at a fingernail, glances at the candy bar, then to his feet. The major pockets the Kit Kat, claps him on the shoulder. Fourteen stiffens. "You barely reached the minimum standard today, Fourteen. Your performance continues to lag. Remember, weak links break chains."

Eleven glares at him.

Fourteen nods rapidly. "I'll do better tomorrow, sir."

"You've had plenty of chances. You will resume your duties in the ER."

Fourteen blanches. "Please, sir. I'm not—"

"Enough. Fourteen, you are dismissed."

Then it's the girls' turn. I get behind Twenty-One, who bobs her head from side to side. "Kill the dragons, yes, yes. Chocolate for me. Burn, burn, burn."

"Hush now, child," the major says, extending a Kit Kat. She snatches it from him and sticks it into her waistband. Alderson frowns. "What do you say?"

"More, more!"

His frown deepens. "Not today."

"Burn, burn, burn," she says, and skips after the other girls. I try to follow her, but Alderson blocks my path.

I expect another lecture for my behavior, but instead he

says, "I heard about what you did for Twenty-Six. Trying to persuade him to our cause. I appreciate that. Unfortunately, some are too stubborn to break by conventional methods. . . . I'm glad you have seen the error in your ways."

I want to slap that smug smile off his—

My CENSIR jolts me.

Chuckling, the major steps aside. "We'll work it out of you, don't you worry. Have a good dinner, Twenty-Five."

As I climb the steps onto the bus, I glance toward the Smurf pens. Empty.

I join Twenty-One in the front seat behind the driver. She clings to the steel grating with one hand; the other's clutched around the dragon brooch I gave her. "I'm sorry, I'm sorry," she mumbles to it. She notices me, follows my gaze to the Smurf pens. "Crawl, crawl, crawl. Burn, burn, burn."

Her knuckles go white around the brooch. She sniffles and looks back to me. "They're always talking, always talking. We can't get rid of them." Her eyes widen with expectation. "You'll help us get rid of them, won't you?"

I stare out the window, at the empty cages shrinking from view. What choice do I have?

23

When we return from dinner, the barracks are frigid. I check the screen, worried I'll see my interview on display, but it's just episode fifty-two, "Kissing Viridescia." Lorena, who wasn't at dinner, sits on her bed, shivering in her blanket.

"Weak links break chains," Evelyn says. Her girls repeat the phrase in hushed whispers while the soldiers collect our jackets, gloves, and hats. Once they're gone, the whispering ceases and everyone makes for the warmth of their beds.

I wrap a blanket around myself and join Lorena. "You okay?"

"Just a bad day. Sorry."

"For what?"

"It's my fault it's cold in here."

"Weak links break chains," I mutter.

"Yep. Another reason to do what you're told. Check that. Do what you're told and be happy about it."

"If it makes you feel better, it might be my fault." I tell her about my attempt to contact Syren.

"Nah, it's not your fault." Her upper lip curls into a sneer. "Almost everybody tries to call out at some point. They expect it. I think they like it. They want to break you. We're nothing but animals. . . ." She stops talking, takes a deep breath.

"You should roar," I say, thinking of Myra's funeral. "Let it out. I'll roar with you. Bet Twenty-One would, too." The girl, counting fingers on the floor beside us, raises her head and howls at the ceiling.

"No!" Reconditioned Claire screams. She leaps from the bed closest to the screen and lumbers toward Twenty-One, murder in her eyes.

"Stop them!" Lorena says to the camera in the ceiling corner. She steps in front of Claire. "It's all right, Claire. She's not a real dragon, she's a hu—"

Claire plows through her. Lorena falls hard. I lunge for Twenty-One, intending to pull her out of Claire's path, but she springs up too fast. She darts away from Claire's bull rush, sucks in a lungful of air, and releases a louder roar. Claire wheels around.

Twenty-One flaps her arms, circles the larger girl. "I'm a

dragon, I'm a dragon. Burn, burn, burn!"

Claire's face goes crimson. Her nostrils flare. Her bandaged hands lock into fists. She swings out, misses. Again. Twenty-One circles her, roaring and taunting.

"Kill the dragon, Claire! Kill it!" Evelyn shouts from her bed. Her minions take up the chant. Some of them laugh.

Lorena, back on her feet, scowls at Evelyn, then directs her anger back at the camera. "Dammit, Jim. Stop them!"

Twenty-One glances at Lorena. "No, no, I'll be good, yes, yes!" She pantomimes locking her lips, makes a choked roaring sound.

Claire pounces from behind. She whips Twenty-One around, clobbers her with a blow to the forehead that sends her crashing to the floor. The dragon brooch tumbles from her hand.

"Stop her!" Lorena begs the camera. She grabs for Claire, gets elbowed in the jaw, staggers backward. I side kick Claire in the flank. It should debilitate her, or at least slow her, but she barely flinches. She snarls, whips around, drills me in the sternum. I fall to my knees.

As I gasp for air, she straddles Twenty-One, hits her once, twice, then rears back with a banshee wail that turns into a terrible sob. Her shoulders slump, her eyes widen. She looks around frantically before her gaze lands on Twenty-One. Squinting, she grabs her by the shoulders, shakes her.

"Wake up! Wake up, Twenty-One! Wake up!"

Lorena, massaging her cheek, puts a hand on Claire's shoulder. "Let her sleep, Claire. She's tired."

"Nobody wake her then!" Claire says with a glare at the other girls. They all nod with deference, though Evelyn can't keep from smiling. Claire returns to her bed, where she crosses her legs beneath her, rests her chin on her hands, and resumes watching *Kissing Dragons*.

I grimace. "She safe?"

"For now," Lorena says, checking Twenty-One's pulse. "It's a damn game to them."

"I'm sorry, I didn't realize. . . ."

"A party every night around here." She scoops Twenty-One into her arms and carries her to bed.

I'm retrieving the brooch from the floor when a soldier enters the barracks. He's portly with shaggy hair. Definitely not your typical All-Black.

Lorena emerges from the bathroom with a wet rag and a bottle of painkillers. She sees the soldier, freezes. "Asshole."

He taps his tablet and she spasms. "Watch it, Lorena. I have my orders."

"They're not guinea pigs, Jim. You knew very well what would happen. You should have incapacitated them."

"Too dangerous. We almost killed Eleven the other night. Major A thinks the reconditioned are more susceptible."

"Or maybe you just like watching too much. You sick—"
She spasms.

"Don't push it. I did try to shock Claire several times. She didn't feel it." He waves a hand. "Whatever, Twenty-One's fine. I am, of course, going to have to report this."

She frowns. "What's the situation on Big Bro?"

"I'm the only one monitoring you ladies tonight."

"Shocking." She rolls her eyes. "What's it gonna cost?"

Jim nods at Twenty-One. "She's already on the shortlist. Major Alderson will likely want to give her another dose of reconditioning if he discovers she instigated another fight."

Her eyes narrow. "What's it gonna cost?"

"Whiskey's running low. Three freebs."

"Two, and I want some minis. I know you've got them."

"Three and I'll bring you six."

"Turn up the heat and you have a deal."

"See you after lights out, princess." He tips his cap and leaves.

"I'm sorry," I say.

Lorena shrugs, sits beside Allie, presses the rag to her reddened face. "Forget about it. I needed to resupply anyway."

The heater ramps up.

Evelyn's voice rises from the opposite end of the room. "Strike another deal, Two? Seems like Twenty-Five should be the one paying the toll."

I clench my fists, step toward her. Five and Seven close ranks. I sneer. "Good dogs."

A loud beep echoes through the room. A bed over, Sixteen ducks beneath her blankets, the playing cards from her game of solitaire scattering across the floor. Everybody else turns toward the screen, which switches from the hunt for No-Tail Nelly to news. An anchorman and a congresswoman from New York discuss a newly passed bill that authorizes the extermination of all dragons, regardless of color, age, or location. The congresswoman, who formerly opposed the idea, cites "the recent tragedies in the Midwest" as the reason for her change of heart.

The program shifts to silent aerial footage of Mason-Kline, post-stampede. I recognize the high school in the distance, but the rest of the town's been churned into an undulating landscape of fractured ground, crumpled houses, and trampled corn.

I fully realize why Lorena calls the screen the message board when names and pictures of victims start scrolling down the side. Each familiar face drives the knife of grief a little deeper, but none so hard as *Major Amy Potter (Army)*, Trish's mom.

The message is loud and clear: dragons destroyed this town, snuffed these lives.

As the list continues, Pam gathers her Bible trio, has

them join hands and close their eyes. She quotes Scripture from memory, something about being at home with the lord. A couple of Evelyn's girls cry. A sniffle here, a tear there. Along with several colorful curses.

Claire begins to moan.

"Watch Allie." Lorena hands me the rag. "She can be a bit disoriented when she wakes from something like this. Just try to keep her calm." She grins. "No more roaring.

"Hey, Victoria, the military killed those dragons. They're all dead. They're not going to hurt you . . . ," Lorena says as she approaches Sixteen's bed.

I press the rag to the bruise on Twenty-One's head where Claire hit her. Her left cheek's puffy, her eyelid's swelling. I peek beneath her shirt and find several bruises, half bluing and new, the rest yellowed with age. Yet her chest rises and falls with ease, her face is at peace.

She's so young.

"I'm sorry," I whisper as I place the dragon brooch beneath her pillow, beside a stash of chocolates.

"Go away!" Claire yells. I tense, but she's not coming for Allie. She launches herself at the screen, smashes her fists against it over and over. Blood seeps through her bandages.

Lorena, in the midst of a card game with Sixteen, races over. "Frank and the others will be back soon, Claire. The dragons will die." She restrains her with a hug from behind, gets bucked about for a bit, but finally coaxes her into the bathroom.

The list of pictures and names end a few minutes later. *Kissing Dragons* returns. The intro music blares. Images of the fab four in action flash across the screen. Most everybody cheers.

"'The house of the wicked will be destroyed, but the tent of the upright will flourish,'" Pam announces. After a group amen, her prayer circle returns to their beds to watch.

Evelyn cuts her a glare, then bounds to her feet with a syrupy smile. "We've got a new episode tonight. Remember, ladies, we must not dwell on the past, but focus on the future."

She nods to Twelve, who uses several napkins to wipe Claire's blood from the screen. The music crescendos. The show starts with a decade-old clip of a Green destroying Disney World. Boos cascade through the room.

Simon interviews a man whose wife and two children were killed on vacation by One-Eyed Willy. Then on to the hunt.

Midway through the fab four's trek into the crocodile-infested swamps of the Everglades, Twenty-One stirs.

"Mom, it's coming. It's coming to burn us. It told me. They always want to burn us," she mumbles. Her eyes dart beneath closed eyelids, she shudders. "We need to get away."

She frees her arms from the blanket, paws the air above her in quick, rhythmic strokes. Her knees join in. Her breaths come fast and shallow. "We need to get away. They're going to burn us. We need to get away! They're going to burn us!"

I shake her, but she doesn't wake. Her air-crawling accelerates. Like a bug turned upside down. I look for Lorena, but she's still in the bathroom.

"You have to soothe her," Twenty says. She and Twenty-Two sit huddled together two beds down. Twenty appears to be massaging circles on Twenty-Two's forearm.

I mimic the motion. "It's not working."

"Try something else." With a shrug, Twenty continues to massage Twenty-Two.

Thinking of Mom, I glide my finger from Twenty-One's chin to her forehead. Calms her some. Onscreen, the fab four open fire. Gunshots echo around the room. Several girls clap. Twenty-One's eyes spring open. She clutches my shirt. "Run!"

I pull her to me. Her knees push against the bed; jagged fingernails drive into my skin. One-Eyed Willy tumbles from the sky; the gunfire quiets. Twenty-One's grip loosens, and she ducks her head under my armpit to watch.

"No bad guys, only victims?" I wonder aloud.

"Yes, yes," Twenty-One says, then cheers with the others as the fab four hog-tie One-Eyed Willy.

While Kevin, Mac, and L.T. plant smooches, Frank drives a ceremonial sword through the Green's skull. The Saint George routine must be a new addition to this year's show.

"There are many rules critical for a successful dragon hunt," Frank says, "but always remember this: no matter what a dragon looks like, no matter if it has one eye or none at all, that sonofabitch's fire will scorch you dead in under a second. Never let your guard down."

As the credits roll, Evelyn steps back in front of the screen. "Let's put our hands together for Eighteen, who helped make the world a safer place by locating this abomination. This is her third televised one," she says with an impressed nod. "She needs a few more to catch me, but let's wish her the best."

Eighteen takes a bow to applause and congratulations, which only end when the music shifts to the dirge that accompanies the In Memoriam. Pam leads a prayer for the dead.

The next episode starts. Seventy-two, "Kissing Red Rover." A rerun. Not a very good one, either. Most of us watch anyway.

24

They come when it's dark.

The door closes softly, flashlights turn on. A tablet activates, its eerie glow illuminating the faces of Whiskey Jim, Lester, and an A-B I don't recognize. They strip off jackets and hats and gloves.

I close my eyes, steady my breathing, and drool onto my pillow.

Footsteps approach.

"You bring my minis?" Lorena asks.

Glass clinks.

"What about the new one?" I don't know the voice. But it's close. Too close. Stinks of alcohol. Light shines through my eyelids. "Cute."

I tense.

"I don't think she likes to play," Lorena says. "Leave her alone."

"Doesn't hurt to ask." A hand pushes aside my hair, blistered lips press to my ear. "Twenty-Five, you home in there?"

"She's awake," Lester says. "No point faking it, Twenty-Five. If it makes it easier, you can pretend he's James."

"Get away from me," I say.

"Feisty ragger." The unknown soldier runs his tongue along my earlobe. "You might like it. Never hurts to have a friend in these parts—"

I thrust my elbow toward his voice. It connects with bone.

"Bitch!" His hand clamps around the back of my neck, and he jams my face into the pillow. I struggle, but he's got a death grip on me.

Whiskey Jim laughs. "Guess she doesn't like to play. Back off, Corporal. There are plenty of other willing participants."

"The bet was for—"

"I don't care what it was for. We can't afford another Twenty-Three."

The corporal releases me, and I start breathing again. "Bitch could use a good reconditioning."

He slaps my ass, laughs, strides away.

I bite my lip hard until the threat of tears passes. I duck beneath my blanket, pressing it tight to my ears. It's not enough to block out the noise that soon comes from the bathroom. Pam starts reciting verse. Others hum the *Kissing Dragons* theme song.

For the life of me, I can't remember another tune, so I join in.

We're on our third refrain when somebody lifts the blanket off my feet. I stifle a scream as a small hand pats my ankle. "It's just me, silly."

I unclench my fists, squint into the blackness. "Twenty-One?"

"Yes, yes." She crawls up onto me, drapes an arm over my stomach, settles her head on my chest. "Don't worry, Twenty-Five, the fuck vultures don't stay long. You want to come to my island with me?"

"Your island?"

"It's pretty exclusive. No vultures or dragons can come. We allow monkeys, though. They're part of this killer bongo band. . . . They tend to get a bit sulky, though," she adds in a hushed voice, as if she's afraid the monkeys might overhear.

"Is it warm?"

"The warmest. Coconut trees everywhere. The dolphins swim right up to the beach and carry you into the ocean. You want in or not, Twenty-Five? This is a one-time offer, yes, yes."

I laugh. "Yeah, I want in."

As she tells me about her island, I close my eyes, picture it in my head. The sounds of sex and humming fade. Her voice carries me to sleep.

"Wakey, wakey, everyone."

It's Monday. I think.

Technically, I've been here a week.

Feels like forever.

James isn't at breakfast. Every time the door opens, I look up from my food, but it's always somebody else.

When I arrive at the call center, I check the bottom of the board. *25*, but no *26*. At the end of the day, I ask a couple of the boys about him. They pretend not to hear.

Lester laughs. "This is getting old, Twenty-Five. You'll see him soon enough, but I promise you, he won't see you."

He's not in the cafeteria for dinner.

"You need to let go," Lorena says, not for the first time.

I nod, push at my spaghetti, wait for the door to open.

It's never him.

That evening, Lorena takes me into the bathroom and shares a bottle of whiskey with me. Jameson. Figures. I turn the label away and drink.

"Thought you were running low."

She winks. "Yeah, but I'm Jim's favorite customer."

I grin. "Whore."

"On my good days."

"How long's it take?"

"Don't think about it, Melissa. He won't be the person you remember."

"How long?"

She drinks. "Two weeks. Three max."

"Maybe he's stronger than the others." I drink. "Maybe it'll be forever."

"Maybe."

The thinscreen runs a clip of Reds destroying Denver.

"My mom was there," I say. "After the attack. I miss her—"

Twenty-One bursts through the door, her fist clenched around the dragon brooch. "How many died, how many died today?"

"Nobody," Lorena says. "It's old footage, Allie."

"Doesn't look old, no, no."

"Yesterday, today, does it make a difference?" I say.

Lorena snatches the bottle from me. "Quitting time."

I give a bitter laugh. "Running low on Jameson."

Twenty-One stares at me like I'm the crazy one.

"Go away!" Claire bellows from the main room. The wall shakes with her pounding.

Lorena rises. "Duty calls." She takes the bottle with her.

When she returns with Claire a few minutes later, a rivulet of blood's running down the side of her face, and she's singing the bigger girl a lullaby. She dresses Claire's bloodied hands with excessive slowness until the screen switches from the news back to *Kissing Dragons*. A season one rerun, episode twelve, I think. Lorena ties off the bandage and whispers something in Claire's ear.

Claire claps her hands, spins around, plops to the ground. She points at the screen. "J.R."

"J.R.'s her favorite," Lorena explains as she applies a Band-Aid to the gash over her right eye. "Thankfully they don't play episode thirty anymore. . . . I'm not sure she realizes he's dead."

We sit on either side of Claire, who stares wide-eyed at the screen, smiling from ear to ear whenever J.R. and his cowboy hat appear. Twenty-One, using my lap as a pillow, counts her fingers with the tip of the dragon brooch, happily whispering, "Burn, burn, burn."

Tuesday, a new episode, number one hundred seven, of *Kissing Dragons* premieres. After Evelyn takes credit for the slain Green, we get our nightly message board reminder— Reds bombarding Moscow. Claire goes into psychopath mode. Lorena gets her into the bathroom.

"How many died today, how many died?" Twenty-One asks me.

The Moscow video's several years old, but there's no convincing her of that. "Too many."

"Burn, burn, burn." She points at the smoky remnants of the Kremlin. "Is that a circus?"

"No. It's the—"

"I read about circuses, yes, yes. Mom said we could never go because it was too far away. Can I put it on the island?"

We spend the rest of the night deciding what attractions our Kremlin circus will include.

Wednesday, Twenty-One ties a call center record, earning herself a bag of Kit Kats and our barracks a day off from our duties. That night, the fuck vultures return. She and I huddle together and decorate the Kremlin's beach-front. She opts for rainbow-colored huts. I almost go with vulture guillotines, but decide on pink beach umbrellas instead.

Thursday, we get to sleep in. After breakfast in a nearly empty cafeteria, they bus us to the rec center. The attendant at the front desk glares at us, gestures dismissively at a nearby bin full of T-shirts and athletic shorts emblazoned with U.S. Army logos.

"Always a pleasure to see you," he grumbles to Lester as we collect clothes. He waves at the screen behind him, which reruns episode ninety-eight, where the fab four head to Mexico in search of La Chupacabra. "The Yanks had the bases loaded, too."

"Yanks?" I whisper to Lorena.

"They've got a strict policy on what we can see," she whispers back. "Whenever we're here it's *Kissing Dragons*. Can't have us watching baseball games because it might somehow tell us what's happening in the real world."

"Two outs?" Lester asks the attendant.

"Don't you know it?"

"I'll save you the suspense. They choked."

"You serious?"

Lester shrugs, laughs.

"Asshole."

"Yep."

A stocky man with a skin graft across his left cheek and a droopy eye jogs over from the basketball court. He feigns a punch at Lester, who flinches, then grins and hits him twice on the shoulder before looking at us. "Who can we blame for our topside freeze this time?"

"Me, me, me!" Twenty-One says.

"Overachiever."

"Yes, yes. You have chocolate?"

The man smiles. "Maybe. You better bring your A game. Don't make me wait too long."

"No, no," she says, and hurries past our guards toward the locker room.

"Already causing problems," Lester says with a half grin. "One and Two. You have five minutes." Evelyn and Lorena follow after Twenty-One. A pair of soldiers takes up position outside the door.

Twenty-One emerges no more than a minute later, tugging at Lorena's hand. Only Twenty-One's wearing shorts. The bruises on her knees stand out in sharp contrast to her pale skin. "Hurry it up, Talker One, yes, yes!" she bellows into the locker room at least ten times before Evelyn comes striding out. Like Lorena, she's kept her scrub bottoms on.

The next three numbers are called. Twenty-One exhorts them to hurry, to the chagrin or amusement of everybody within earshot.

Twenty-Two and I are the last to dress. I don't know much about her. She's one of Pam's crowd. Never talks, except for polite yes, sirs and no, sirs to the soldiers. After hanging her coat in locker twenty-two, she strips out of her scrub top. I notice a tattoo on her ribs. Three names, each listed with date ranges. None older than twenty-five. The death dates are identical, little more than a year old.

"Why don't you take a picture?" she says with more sharpness than I expected.

"Must have hurt." I strip out of my scrub bottoms and show her my tattoo.

She shrugs, slips her T-shirt on.

"I'm sorry," I say.

She turns to me, eyes narrowed. "What's my name?"

"What?"

"Do you know my name?"

Based on her tat, I'm pretty certain her surname is Hernandez, but I can't recall her first. Did she even introduce herself the day I arrived? I can't remember.

She purses her lips. "That's what I thought. I don't know you and you don't know me. It's easier for everybody if we keep it that way. Got it, chica?"

She sweeps past me before I can respond.

"Hurry it up, Twenty-Five, yes, yes!"

As I exit the locker room, I hear a couple of snickers from the other girls, a few whispered jabs about Bigfoot. Besides the reconditioned, I'm the only one who decided to don shorts. Claire, whose hairy legs could very well belong to a sasquatch, thrusts a fist at me. I recoil. Then I see that she's extended her pinky and thumb. It takes me a couple of seconds to realize why that looks so familiar. It's J.R.'s signature celebratory move.

I give her the expected fist bump. Twenty-One joins in for a three-way.

I catch Evelyn smirking at us. I smirk back. "Got your eye on somebody out there, Talker One?"

Evelyn nods at my exposed legs, arches an eyebrow. "Some of us have standards, Twenty-Five."

Lorena nudges me. "Let it go."

I ignore her. "Last I heard, your standards led to a trip to the infirmary and a prescription for some antibiotics."

A couple of girls laugh.

Evelyn reddens. "Story time, is it, Two? Should we inform your little sidekick of your daddy issues?"

"Leave it alone," Lorena says.

"Oh, yes, can't drink or blow your way out of that, can you?"

"That's enough," Lester says. "Go on, gals, go enjoy your day."

"Yes, yes, I gotta kick Julio's ass," Twenty-One says, and sticks out her tongue at our escort, who responds with a smile.

"Language, Twenty-One."

"I've got to kick Julio's ass. Better, yes, yes." She laughs, flips off Pam, then rushes past some cardio equipment before disappearing around a corner.

Lester grabs my arm. "Stay here."

"Weak links break chains," Evelyn says on her way by, with a little wave. Her minions echo the gesture.

I expect him to shock me for all the violent thoughts running through my head, but he doesn't.

"I didn't do anything wrong," I say once we're alone.

"Maybe. I know these first couple of weeks haven't been easy on you. They never are. But if I was you, I'd be very careful with Evelyn." He looks away, blows out a breath

JOSHUA McCUNE

through his nose, looks back at me with pursed lips. "She's not anybody's friend but her own."

I squint at him.

He darkens. "It's not like that. Never mind. Get out of here, Twenty-Five." Again I expect him to shock me, but he merely shoos me. "It's your day off. Go have fun."

Fun?

A few of the girls are working out on cardio equipment, but most have congregated in a game room at the back of the rec center. I find Twenty-One hunkered over a chessboard. She controls the white army. The guy with the droopy eye plays the black side.

"I'm killing the dragons, yes, yes," Twenty-One hisses to me, then swipes a black pawn (a smallish dragon with folded wings and red ruby eyes) with her white pawn (a soldier with a machine gun strapped across his shoulder). Licking her lips, her gaze darts to the three large Snickers lying on the table in front of her opponent.

"Not yet, little one," he says. He kills her pawn with a larger dragon (this one with green eyes).

"Burn, burn, burn," Twenty-One says, and makes her next move.

Back and forth they go. Soon pawns are dying left and right, and the board's rather empty. I rise from the couch, look for something else to do.

Five, Ten, and Eighteen are playing hearts at a poker table with a couple of our guards. Claire lounges in a recliner, watching *Kissing Dragons*. I wander to the other side of the room, where Lorena and Pam fling taunts across an air-hockey table.

Lorena scores. "What's God have to say about that, Bible Girl?"

Pam grins, knocks in the puck a second later. "Through God we shall do valiantly."

They drop the puck again. Lorena glances my way right as Pam strikes. The table dings. Game over. Pam bobs her head from side to side. "And it is He who will tread down our adversaries."

Lorena fake pouts. "Adversary? Don't take that shit out on me. God obviously loves me."

Pam waggles a finger at her. "Come on, Lorena. No swearing for a week. We agreed."

"Fine, fine. How 'bout double or nothing?"

"Okay, but if I win, no consultations for a month."

"My consultations got you your Bibles."

"Your soul is worth more to me than any book, even God's."

Lorena sighs, hands the puck pusher to Twenty-Two. "Maybe next time."

"I'm going to hold you to that. No cursing."

"What did she have to give up on the off chance you didn't lose?" I ask Lorena as she cedes the table to Twenty-Two.

Lorena shrugs. "Telling people not to swear."

"Which is like her favorite thing to do," I say.

She smiles sadly. "Yep."

"You okay?"

"Terrific." She points across the way to the basketball court. "You any good?"

"Horrible."

"Me too."

Evelyn emerges from the throng of players, spotting up for a three. A soldier passes her the ball. Nothing but net. High-fives all around.

"I would not have pegged her for a basketball player."

"More the cheerleader type, right?" Lorena grins. She takes my hand, tugs me toward the court. I resist. "Come on, Melissa, it'll be fun."

I pull free. "I'd rather watch Twenty-One kill dragons."

"Huh?"

"Never mind."

"You know what a foul is?"

I nod. "I play soccer. . . . Played."

"You ever play against anybody who wasn't very good?"

"Yeah. Made me thankful for shin guards." I laugh. "You're wicked."

"Hey, I don't know about you, but I just want to learn. Good thing about basketball, they don't hand out red cards."

"I think I like being your sidekick."

Lorena indicates a skinny guy dribbling a ball on the side of the court. "That's Billy, another Big Brother." She winks. "He knows how we like to play."

We recruit Sixteen and Twenty to fill out the other two spots for our team.

Except for Billy, none of us has any clue what we're doing. We get clobbered.

But the next morning, there is no "wakey, wakey." In fact, Evelyn's the last one out of bed.

In the cafeteria, I manage to eat breakfast without peeking once toward the boys' table. At some point, the door opens. I ignore the impulse to look up. In the call center, I don't check the board for his number. I keep my head down and duck into my cubicle. I tally five dragons that day, a mediocre showing, but my personal record. Lester gives me a Baby Ruth. I give it to Twenty-One. She stuffs it beneath her pillow.

We're discussing graffiti decorations for the cliff we erected behind the Kremlin when a beep sounds.

"How many died, how many died today?" Twenty-One asks.

"Too many." I glance toward the screen, expecting video of Blues stampeding through Rio or a Green assaulting Mecca, but today's message looks current. A journalist clad in body armor describes how a group of Greens opened fire on a Tiny Tots child-care center.

"Please be warned, the footage you are about to see is intensely disturbing," she says.

Watching dragons incinerate people is terrible, but we've all seen it before, sometimes with a much larger victim pool. No, what makes this homemade video particularly chilling are the white-cloaked dragon riders. With shocking ruthlessness, they machine gun any adult or child who escapes the wrath of their mounts.

Most of us weep. Twenty-One laughs until she sees me, then she starts to cry, too. Claire shouts curses as she beats on the screen. I expect Lorena to pull her back, but she's nowhere to be seen. She must be in the bathroom.

The video ends in a blaze of crackling fire.

"A group of insurgents who call themselves the Diocletians claim responsibility for the attack. Casualties number over one hundred, most of them children. Dozens remain unaccounted for," the reporter says. "The leader of the group, a former All-Black by the name of Oren White, released a statement."

A video pops up. It's that guy with the scar on his face,

TALKER 25

the guy from the Shadow Mountain Lookout picture. "The government recently destroyed the Blues sanctuaries, knowingly murdering hundreds of dragon children. Until they admit to this genocide and cease all hostilities, your children will continue to die."

After a brief discussion between two wise-looking veterinarians, who determine dragon breeding is impossible, the screen returns to episode thirty-two, "Kissing Big Blue."

Normally, the girls would go quiet, but tonight they're abuzz with horror over the idea of dragons breeding. I'm trying to get Twenty-One to stop crying when I hear Evelyn mention something about a Silver she saw in the ER.

"They told me it was an albino, but I don't buy that. For one thing, it wouldn't talk to me. I don't think it could," she says as I approach. She notices me, fake smiles. "Can I help you, Twenty-Five?"

"You saw the Silver?"

"Why do you want to know?"

"Is she alive?"

She waves at the screen, all her phony perkiness gone. "How can you be a glowheart after you saw what they did?"

"That Silver is a child, just like those children."

Evelyn stares at me like I've grown another head, then turns away. I grab her wrist. "What's going to happen to her? Please, Evelyn."

Her smile returns. "They're going to chop its head off. Usually with a chain saw. But I bet the soldiers will want to test their ax out."

I flinch. "When?"

She wrenches free. "Tomorrow, after they're done with their experiments. Don't touch me again."

After checking on Twenty-One, who's curled up in the corner with the dragon brooch, I head for the shower, the one place where I can drown out the sound of the television and the other girls, and, if I'm lucky, memories. Each night, except when we're under punishment, we get one hour of hot water to share. According to the schedule on the bathroom door, it's not my turn until tomorrow, but some of the girls skip their days.

When I enter the bathroom, Lorena's lounging against the wall beneath the screen, knees tucked to her chest. A cigarette dangles from her lips, a close-to-empty bottle of whiskey sits beside her. She's been crying. If it were another girl, this wouldn't be unusual, but the worst I've seen from Lorena is a disapproving frown or a sad shake of her head.

I sit beside her, grab the bottle, and take a long drink. "You all right?"

She inhales, looking toward the ceiling. "You know, when I first discovered I could communicate with dragons, I thought I was losing it. I didn't tell anybody because you're not supposed to have imaginary friends when you're thirteen.

"I later learned that dragons don't just talk to you out of the blue." She blows out a stream of smoke. "It was my dad who told them about me. He was a frontline A-B, you know? I thought he hated dragons."

She snorts. "I didn't find out the truth until Mom died. The letter the army sent us called her a hero. For dying? How fucking stupid is that? Dad burned that letter, burned the flag they gave him after they buried her. Then he burned down our house."

I wrap my arm around her shoulder. "I'm sorry."

Lorena shakes her head. "I've seen what he's done, but I always had some stupid hope that he might be able to come back to . . . I don't know. Normal, I guess." She glances up, and more tears come. "How could he do that? How could he murder all those children, Melissa?"

I gape. "Him?"

She squeezes her eyes shut. "How could he do that?"

Now it makes sense. Horrible sense. Oren White, the leader of the Diocletians, is Lorena's father.

I fetch another bottle of whiskey from beneath her mattress. We drink until memories fade and blur and disappear. Then we drink some more.

25

"Five, Seven, Fifteen, Twenty-Five," Lester says from the front of the bus. "Twenty-Five!"

I think my CENSIR jolts me, but it's hard to tell because my head's been aching something fierce since I staggered from bed this morning.

I look out the window. The battle room? "Why am I being transferred?"

"Because," Lester says. Typical.

I'm not sure what to expect as I follow the others off the bus. Only Lorena, Claire, and a few from Evelyn's crew have worked the battle room before. Lorena never talks about it. Evelyn's girls don't interact with me anyway, but they always seem pleased with their efforts.

Lester leads us into a dark room of thinscreens and

electronic equipment. We pass a digital map with seven blinking green dots, each located in one of three lakes. Adjacent to a satellite image of an unfamiliar city, Major Alderson and several soldiers operate a massive touchboard. One side's dominated by indicators, radars, and maps; the other's split into eight sections, each showing the CENSIR controls of the talkers in here.

Four boy talkers sit in a row of lounge chairs. They wear wraparound sunglasses. I do a quick search of faces. No James.

Lester hands me over to Major Alderson, then leads the other girls to a row of chairs on the opposite side of the room, where they're given sunglasses.

Soon after, a soldier announces, "We are green for mission go."

"Activate talker VR-HUDs," Major Alderson says.

The thinscreen that comprises the wall in front of us turns on. Seven columns of radar images and data appear— coordinates, altitude, speed. It reminds me of something I've seen in one of Sam's video games, where he plays a jet pilot in search of dragons to destroy.

"Enable communication," the major says.

At the touchboard, soldiers operate the CENSIR controls of the seven seated talkers. An eighth section, sandwiched in the middle, displays my CENSIR panel. I focus on the adjacent screen as Claire's overseer touches the transmit button and selects the 1-to-1 option. A list of names appears with Rs or Gs beside them. He selects Korenth (G).

Beneath Claire's readout, the dragon's info appears.

Dragon: Korenth (Green)

Call frequency: 93.461 iGH₂

Location: Latitude 50.847°; Longitude 100.371°; Altitude 5,397'

Fire status: Inactive

I look back to the map and radar, confused. The green dots are positioned in a jagged semicircle about fifty miles outside of the city.

Seven of them.

One for each talker.

I'm barely able to stifle my gasp.

"Talkers, please initiate communication," Major Alderson says.

They growl out their commands, which are relayed to their CENSIR readouts as text.

Seven: *Ugarth, we fly today. Behave, and the glory of flame will be yours. Do not, and you will die.*

Seventeen: *Fly straight and fast, Morth. Obey, and you will eat well tonight. Remember what happened to Valryn.*

The others also balance their threats with promises of rewards for good behavior. Except for Claire: *You better listen, Korenth, or your head will find its way off your neck.*

The dragon responses appear in dialogue boxes beneath their names on the touchboard.

If I ever break these bonds, the glory of my flame will find you, human.

I tire of your words and this smell. Perhaps Valryn had the right of it.

Korenth's the only Green who doesn't respond.

"Activate eyes," the major says.

Seven videos pop up on the front screen. Each shows the inside of some sort of metal compartment occupied by a dragon. I can see wings pressing up against walls, animal carcasses littering floors.

At the major's command, the compartments split open. Seven Greens launch skyward. Soldiers call out instructions— shifts in direction, altitude, speed—to the talkers, who relay them to their dragons. Korenth glances over his shoulder. It takes me a few seconds to spot the camouflaged compartment floating in the lake from which he emerged.

"Discard the packages," the major says.

The compartment explodes down the middle and sinks into the lake.

Following Claire's barked orders, Korenth ascends above the clouds, where he's joined by the other six Greens. They line up side by side, no more than a few hundred feet separating them. As they fly, I catch glimpses of cameras on the other dragons, affixed to abnormally bulky collars that Alderson informs me are modified to control their fire and reinforce compliance.

He indicates my CENSIR. "Like this, but with a lot more kick."

And they need lots of kicks. The Greens lurch and bolt at each other constantly. Talkers order them back into formation, but if they don't fall in line (they usually don't), they get an electric shock. The stunned dragon, lightning rippling through its body, plummets from the sky for a couple of seconds before the paralysis wears off. With curses and threats, the dragon gets back in line and behaves. At least for a minute or so.

I'm praying one too many shocks will permanently immobilize them when, in near unison, their gazes shift groundward. Through thinning clouds I see scattered homes and a couple of lonely roads.

I smell them. It is time to eat appears on Seventeen's screen.

Seventeen's response: *Not now, Morth. Stay on target, and you will eat better soon. Smell what lies ahead.*

The other talkers give similar orders.

With the promise of the feast to come, and perhaps the scent of it in their nostrils, the dragons raise their heads and focus forward. According to the map, they'll reach the city in five minutes.

Seven ravenous Greens. It'll be a massacre.

"Enemy fighters incoming, Major," a soldier announces.

"Activate fire for Three, Six, and Seven," Major Alderson says. "Draw them away from the rest of the group."

Seven: *Ugarth, the invisible monsters come. Let us show them the glory of your flame.* Ugarth and the other two selected Greens swoop from the pack to intercept.

Black jets race into view on the displays of Three, Six, and Seven, who shout frantic orders at their dragons. Fire geysers, missile blurs, and bullet tracers flash across their screens. Planes plummet left and right, streaks of smoke and flame that fade into the background until they explode against the earth.

The remaining jets regroup and direct their attacks at Six's dragon. He dodges the first several missiles, but then one catches him in the chest and the video signal blacks out. I can't contain my smile.

Alderson scowls at me. "What's happening, Six?"

"I've lost communication."

"Redirect the Templar to confirm," the major says. The satellite image shifts from the city to the countryside and zooms in on a dead Green among crushed trees. He nods to the soldier monitoring Six. "Initiate cleansing."

The collar explodes, severing the dragon's neck. Major Alderson looks at me. "The first rule of the battle room: cover your tracks. No more—"

"We've entered the blind zone, Major."

While Three and Seven continue their battle with the remaining planes, the other four Greens advance on a thickening checkerboard of black homes and buildings. In rapid succession, orange bursts of fire explode from artillery and rocket launchers hidden in the dark city.

The talkers give fast instructions. *Swerve left, barrel roll left, dive, climb! Fire, fire, fire!* Flames, smoke, sky, and buildings whirl together.

"Switch the Templar to thermal," Major Alderson says.

The satellite image, clouded with gun smoke, shifts to a color map. Among the buildings, bright red dots appear. Hundreds of them, maybe thousands, packed in tight bunches. On the display, it doesn't seem like they're moving fast, but they're all moving in the same direction. Away from the dragons.

People.

"I'm losing him!" Seventeen bellows. I check his screen. Blinding bright, Morth plunges through the clouds, swerving and bobbing in wild gyrations, ever downward despite repeated shocks and Seventeen's orders to regain altitude.

The major draws my attention to Morth's dialogue box. *I smell them. I smell them. I will eat human. I will eat well now.* "The second rule: if a dragon gets out of line, make an example of it for the others. Cut off transmission."

The soldier monitoring Seventeen's CENSIR inhibits him.

"Activate Morth's fire," the major says.

My throat tightens. "What are you doing?"

"He's beyond control and would undoubtedly be at full flame by now."

Morth unleashes his inferno toward the meal he can smell but cannot see, for all the black buildings that blind his view. Through the fire and smoke clouding his screen, a sky-scraper rushes into view. He crashes through the top story in a rush of flames, glass, and office equipment.

He tumbles out, regains speed, and immediately plows into another high-rise. I bite hard into my lip. Five long counts later, the building about to crumble atop him, the Green emerges from the other side, staggering on the edge, glow gone dim, fire down to weak plumes, one wing shred-ded. Major Alderson orders another collar decapitation. The video signal dies with Morth.

"Why didn't you do that earlier? There could be people in there!"

"Plausible deniability—"

"That's bullshit. Greens don't fly in packs. They don't fly in formation."

"They do if they're Diocletians."

So they're the scapegoats in this. I wonder what else they'll take the blame—

Suddenly it all seems so familiar.

My stomach lurches.

My chest hitches.

I forget how to breathe.

"Arlington?" I croak.

"What?" Major Alderson says, his gaze locked on the satellite image to our left.

"Arlington?"

"We are in attack range of the target, Major."

"Mom?" I find a breath. Not much of one, but enough. "Did you kill my mother?"

"Arlington was a mistake," Alderson says. "That Green went wild. We've taken measures to ensure that will not happen again."

"How big of you." I fight back tears, focus on the rage. "Now your killing's intentional."

"Control yourself, Twenty-Five, or we'll do it for you."

The dragons drop through the smoke and glide several stories above the streets. I can see the people now. Sprinting, looking over their shoulders, stumbling . . . often over each other. It's a stampede. And the dragons haven't even done anything—

"Activate Five, Nine, and Fifteen. Open fire," Major Alderson says.

Flames appear on each screen, growing funnels that blast into the crowds. The video cameras don't have audio, probably because it would make everyone's job harder, but you can see the people screaming, almost feel it through the silence broken only by All-Black commands and talker voices.

"They're innocent people. Please stop," I say. "You can't do this."

"Control yourself, Twenty-Five," Major Alderson says. "This is what it costs to keep your family and mine safe."

I think of actions.

I think of consequences.

I think of Mom. And I make my choice.

On my CENSIR screen, the *Current synaptic state* blinks bright red, and the text beside it shifts from *angry, sad* to *violent, dangerous to others*.

As the major reaches for the handcuffs on his belt, I slam my heel into his shin. He doubles over, grabs for me, but not fast enough. I tap the incapacitate buttons for Nine and Fifteen before someone cracks the butt of a machine gun against my skull.

26

I killed Claire.

Nine remains unconscious in the infirmary. Evidently, going from transmit to incapacitate causes serious injury, or worse in some cases.

After a nurse bandages my head, Major Alderson takes me to view the body. Claire looks monstrous in death, her eyes wide, mouth open in a silent scream, upper lip snarled.

"You know, all you've done is delay our timetable," the major says. "More will die now because we'll have to come in over the main district. Good job, Twenty-Five."

It takes me a while to speak. "Go to hell."

He gestures at Claire. "Looks like that's where you sent her."

"Do whatever you're going to do to me and get it over with."

He sighs. "Not my call." He grasps me by the shoulders, regards me with a paternal expression that sickens me. "You've got spirit . . . and talent. But you need to channel it in the right direction. We don't want you to end up like this one. We really don't."

When we return to the barracks, most of the girls are gathered in excited conversation around Five and Seven. Major Alderson clears his throat. They notice us; the chatter dominoes to silence. Five and Seven glare at me. Evelyn wears a tight smile. "Welcome back, Twenty-Five. We weren't expecting you so soon."

"Today was not one of our finest, ladies," Alderson says. "Unfortunately, until Nine recovers, shifts will be lengthened by two hours. Good night."

The moment he's out the door, the hateful whispers begin.

"Thanks a lot, Twenty-Five."

"Should have reconditioned your ass."

"Who you gonna murder next?"

I want to shrink into the corner and disappear, but before I've gone two steps, Evelyn raises her hands. "Now, now, everyone, let's calm down. In fact, I think we owe Twenty-Five a round of applause."

"What?" Five says.

"Yeah, that stupid bitch could have killed us," Seven adds.

Evelyn raises her hand, but Seven waves her off. "No, she needs to get a goddamn—"

"Do not profane the—" Pam starts.

"Shut it, Thirteen," Seven says. "Twenty-Five, maybe you don't like us, but you better start caring about us, because we're the only ones who have your back. We're your family now. Even Fifteen. You should have seen her flopping on the floor. They say she choked on her own tongue."

I bite into my cheeks, clench my stomach, desperate to keep from crying.

"Submit yourself to God, Melissa," Pam says. "And the devil will flee from you."

"Leave her alone," Lorena says, grabbing my hand. I squeeze it like a lifeline.

Evelyn nods. "I'm sure Twenty-Five has learned her lesson. Let's not dwell on the loss of our sister or the punishment she's inflicted on us with this unfortunate occurrence. Let's find the silver lining, girls."

"Silver lining?" Seven hisses.

"Yes, think about it. We won't have to worry about Fifteen bothering us with her incessant pounding, getting the screen bloody, or sitting all retarded in the restroom."

"And I'll get more chocolate now!" Twenty-One says from the corner.

It's too much. I race into the bathroom and collapse against the wall.

Lorena enters soon after, an Almond Joy in hand.

"I can't . . . I'm sorry. I didn't mean to kill . . ." It hurts too much to say her name. "I'm sorry."

"You did her a favor."

I shake my head, unable to speak.

"You know how many times I considered interfering?" Lorena says. "I couldn't, though. I was scared. Terrified. We all are. I know it feels like they're against you now—"

"The entire world."

She laughs. "Yeah, them, too. They'll hate you for a while, but deep in that buried part of them, from the time when they were names, not numbers, they know what you did was right. That goodness you showed today will give them something to hold on to."

"Bullshit."

"Know the difference between fairy-tale heroes and real heroes?"

I think of Mom. "In fairy tales they don't die. Why did she have to die? Why did she leave me alone?"

She hugs me. I sob into her shoulder.

I compose myself, push away. "For the record, you suck at pep talks."

She laughs. "I can only be so perfect. Now eat up. . . . Take it, Melissa. Allie will be annoyed with both of us if she finds out you rejected her donation to the Make Melissa Feel Better Fund."

I bite into the candy bar. Close my eyes, pretend I'm on Twenty-One's tropical island . . . no All-Blacks, no dragons, no battle rooms or CENSIRs—

A beep sounds. I stop chewing. It's not a news clip this time, but the premiere of *Kissing Dragons: The Other Side.*

I watch in numb silence as they transform me from an all-American girl to a delusional insurgent suffering from what a famous psychiatrist calls "dragon exposure." Watch farmboys lie and smile and lie some more. Watch Sam go from confused to enraged to repulsed all over again.

"This is what becomes of traitors," Simon says. "They don't just ruin their own lives, they ruin the lives of those closest to them. But is Melissa truly the one to blame? Maybe her transformation didn't begin after her mother's death. Maybe it began much earlier. . . ."

Unveil Mom's treachery.

Starts with a montage of her on various salvage missions.

Fast forward to protest rallies.

End with the photo taken at Shadow Mountain Lookout,

where she's standing beside Oren White, the Diocletian leader responsible for the recent terrorist attacks on day-care centers.

Simon interviews a stern-faced general who looks familiar, though I don't know why until they show a picture of him handing Dad a folded-up American flag at Mom's funeral.

"What do you know about the relationship between Olivia Callahan and Oren White, General?" Simon asks.

"Major Callahan and Sergeant White worked together at several points in their careers," the general says. "After the sergeant's wife died, he snapped and joined the other side. We believe he recruited Major Callahan. It's unclear when exactly this occurred, but we do know it was well before the attack on Arlington."

"Why does that matter?" Simon prompts.

"We believe she and Sergeant White used their specialized background in military intelligence to hijack the national defense system."

"So you're saying that Olivia Callahan, a decorated war hero, instigated the attack on Arlington, an attack that killed more than twelve hundred people?" Simon says.

Play cell-phone video of the Green roasting victims on the Wilson Bridge.

"We believe their actual intent was an attack on Congress or the president."

"With a dragon? There was nobody flying it. It couldn't know where it was going."

"It knew exactly where it was going. When we examined the creature's corpse, we found a high-resolution camera attached to a high-tech collar."

Switch to a "live" shot of Simon, brow pinched. "General Sparks allowed me to see some of the footage recovered from the camera. Though much of it remains classified, he has given us permission to share a sample. Please be warned . . . what you are about to see is not for the faint of heart."

Show Wilson Bridge massacre from the dragon's perspective.

Back to the general. "Originally we thought they wanted to record their efforts for propaganda, but when we investigated the collar, we discovered a remote sonic communicator—an advanced dog whistle for dragons. With video and acoustics, they could tell the dragon where to go."

"It went the wrong way," Simon notes.

"Either it got confused, or, as we believe, it decided not to listen."

"But if they initiated this murderous strike, why would Major Callahan have sacrificed herself to divert the creature she was supposedly in league with?"

Run clips of Mom steering the Green away from the

suburbs toward the river, first from a drone's perspective, then from the dragon's.

"Her family lived two blocks from the dragon's fire path," the general says. Show snapshot of burning suburbs, highlight our house in neon green. "You do the math."

"What do you think of the general's claims, Ms. Callahan?" Simon asks.

"My mother was a hero." He never asked me that question, but those are my words, spoken with absolute certainty.

"In some ways, she was," Simon says. Back to the Shadow Mountain Lookout photo. Flames appear at the edges and slowly consume it. "A hero for the dragons. Now she's dead and her daughter's in a mental institution. This is what happens when you join the other side."

The credits roll.

"I didn't realize your mother knew my father," Lorena says, the first words either of us have spoken since the episode started.

"Honestly, I don't know what's real anymore."

She squeezes my hand. "Your mom was a good person, Melissa. Nobody will believe that stuff about her attacking Arlington. That's crazy."

I want to believe her, but I know it's not true. We're no different from dragons to them.

Villains.

No.

Monsters.

I pull Lorena into the blind corner of the bathroom, employ a tactic I've seen a couple other girls use. Since we're not allowed any writing utensils—Eleven was reconditioned because he stabbed one of the ER Mengeles in the eye with a pen—they converse by finger drawing words on their blankets or body parts. Slow going, but safer.

I trace out the word on my arm. *Escape.*

She shakes her head.

I have a plan.

It takes a few tries before she deciphers my words. She taps her CENSIR. "Doesn't matter."

"I have to try."

"Others have tried."

"I have to."

"What if . . ." She writes the number *15* on my forearm.

I can't wait to die here.

27

Two nights later, Big Brother Billy has a midnight date with Lorena. Lantern in hand, he beelines it toward the back. Lorena intercepts him. She runs one hand along his pants, grabs the lantern with the other, and sets it on the floor. Several girls start humming. Kissing him, Lorena strips him from his winter clothes. He kicks off his boots. She grabs his hand and pulls him toward the bathroom.

"Hold up," he says. He grabs the lantern. In its light, his grin is wicked. "I want to see you."

As she enters the bathroom, Lorena looks back at me and gives a little wave. Then the door shuts and darkness returns.

Hands extended in front of me, I look for Twenty-One. She's not in her bed, nor in the corner where she sometimes sleeps. "Twenty-One? Allie?" I whisper several times. No response.

Billy's quieter than the others, and I can't hear him or Lorena over the humming. He's only visited once before. Lorena said she'd delay him, but for how long?

Something rustles beneath my bed. "Twenty-One? Allie?"

She doesn't respond. Asleep?

I lower myself to the ground, reach for her. Our hands meet. Hers is cold and soft. So small. She opens my fingers, places the dragon brooch in my palm.

"Keep it safe for me." I give her the brooch back, curl her fingers around it. I hear her sniffle, then retreat. "We'll get to that island."

I scramble to my feet before my resolve fails me.

I find Billy's pile of clothes. As I change into his jacket, the humming intensifies. Are the other girls actually covering for me, or am I just imagining it? Billy's boots swallow my feet. His gloves come past my wrist. I search for keys in his pocket, have a moment of panic before remembering that most military vehicles don't use keys.

I feel my way to the door, enter the key code, the one I've seen Lester use every time we return from dinner. Locked.

"Reverse it," Evelyn says from the nearby bed.

It works.

I glance over my shoulder. In the haze of sunlight,

Evelyn's expression is distant, unreadable. Has she tried this before?

I squeeze out the door, squinting against the brilliance of blue sky. Other than the whip of sharp wind, the world is silent. I slip into the Humvee, teeth chattering, and almost crush a pair of sunglasses on the seat in my rush to get out of the cold.

Dad once let me drive one of these behemoths down Reservation Road. I don't remember much about the controls, but I remember enough to get it started. I max out the heater, put on the sunglasses, and accelerate toward the glow of caged dragons in the distance.

I need a long-range radio or a sat phone, something that will allow me to contact the outside world. Antennae sprout through dragons skulls from several of the buildings near the cafeteria. One of them must be a communication station, but it's undoubtedly manned 24/7. My best bet is the hangar.

The speedometer needle hits fifty-five, doesn't want to go much higher. The engine whines and whirs, the Humvee trembles. As I race through the dragon skeletons that mark the entrance to Georgetown, a gust of wind crashes into me, sends the Humvee sideways several feet before I regain control. Thankfully, the road's deserted except for the caged dragons.

Their choked roars follow me, a rumble of angry noise that cannot keep up with my heartbeat.

Tick-thump, tick-thump, tick-thump.

Any moment now, Billy will find his clothes missing, the Humvee gone.

I swerve onto the runway. The hangars are too far away. The Humvee's too slow. If I actually do contact somebody, what do I tell them? I'm in Antarctica. Where? An entire continent of tundra and ice. No visible landmarks.

Tick-thump-tick-thump-tick-thump.

Major Alderson was right. I'm a needle in a frozen haystack. This was a mistake. I should turn around. Maybe I can make it back in time.

But I don't slow, I don't change course, and I reach the first hangar.

The code doesn't open the door. Nor the reverse code.

Tickthump-tickthump-tickthump.

I push another four numbers. Then another four . . . my fingertips go numb. Breathing hurts. My vision blurs. I steady myself against the wall, manage another four numbers. No, I already did those. A tear freezes on my cheek, makes me laugh, which stings my lungs. I laugh some more, slam my palm into the keypad. Pain sizzles up my arm.

The door opens. A man in a flight suit and bomber jacket stands there. He holds a wrench in his left hand.

He gapes at me. In his eyes, I see confusion and what I pray is sympathy.

"Help," I mumble.

He reaches for me, and I strike with a side kick to his stomach. He doubles over; the wrench skitters across the floor. I follow with a knee to the chin that knocks him senseless. On a nearby workbench, adjacent to a soldering iron and some rubbing alcohol, is a box of tie wraps. I use thick black ones to bind his hands and feet.

There are two gunships in the hangar. The engine's open on one, a ladder beside it. I spot an array of electronic equipment on the bench against the far wall, including a phone attached to a metal controller of some sort. Terms like x5 DATE/REM and MODE: P1-P6 cluster around numerous dials and pronged interfaces.

I flip the various controls, but don't hear anything. I check the adjacent computer, but it's password protected.

Tickthumptickthump-tickthumptickthump.

I sprint back across the hangar, where I retrieve the wrench. Overhead vents blast heat everywhere, but I'm shivering more now than I was outside. I clutch the wrench tighter, consider using it to ring his doorbell, then remember the bottle of alcohol.

I pour half of it onto his face. He startles awake, curses, blinks back tears.

I tap his forehead with the wrench. "Tell me how to use the radio."

"Huh?" He continues to blink rapidly, his face squeezing up as he tries to look at me. "Who are you?"

I jam the wrench handle hard into his thigh. He cries out. "Tell me how to use the radio."

"Who are you trying to contact?"

I raise the wrench over his kneecap.

"Look, girl, you can bludgeon me to death, but without a little information, I can't help you."

"I need to contact somebody in Michigan."

"We've got a thousand-mile throw on our signal. You aren't reaching topside. You'd be lucky to reach McMurdo."

"What's that?"

"A civilian research outpost. Come on, girl, put the wrench down. Let's figure this out. I can help you."

"You have no idea who I am, do you?" I jab the wrench at the gunship. "Can you fly me there?"

"To McMurdo? What's going on? Why are you so scared?"

"You won't fly me?"

"I'd need clearance. Without it, they'd shoot us down."

Tickthumpthumpthumptickthumpthumpthump.

I use a pair of sharpened pliers to cut the tie wraps around his feet. "Fine, you're gonna contact McMurdo for me. Hurry."

He squirms to the wall, edges himself up. "What's going on? Who are you?"

I wave the wrench toward the radio. "Hurry."

"What do you want me to tell them?" he asks as I follow him past the gunships.

I consider. "Tell them that they've imprisoned dozens of boys and girls to help them kill dragons. That they torture us if we don't help."

He grimaces. "You're serious, aren't you?"

I pull back the jacket to show him the TALKER 25 label on my scrubs. I lower my hood to reveal the CENSIR.

"What is that thing?"

"The torture device." We reach the radio equipment. He extends his bound hands. I want to trust him. Need to. This is already taking too long. I cut him free.

His gives me a rueful smile before sitting down at the radio. He picks up the phone, plugs in a cable, adjusts a couple of dials. "Come in, Mac Ops, this is Golf Tango One. Urgent. Over."

I lean closer to hear. A reply comes in through the receiver seconds later. "Reading your five, Golf Tango. What's the emergency? Over."

"Prisoners treated outside the boundaries of the Geneva Convention. Over."

"Say again."

I snatch the phone from him. "The military's enslaved a bunch of kids and is torturing them. Over."

"Copy. You are OTG. Not sure how we can help. Over."

"Off the grid," the pilot explains at my questioning look.

I hand the phone back. "Give them our coordinates."

He swallows, looks toward the ceiling, whispers something I can't hear beneath his breath that sounds like a prayer. Finally he puts the phone to his ear. "Come in, Mac Ops. Relay as you see fit. Coordinates to follow. Wait."

He accesses the computer beside the radio, navigates to a map. He types in a command and hundreds of multisized squares appear, most located in the United States. Greens, reds, blues. A handful of black ones are scattered in remote locations across the globe. Georgetown, the largest black and the only installation in Antarctica, sits in the southern middle of the continent.

He clicks on the Georgetown square. A password entry box appears. BLACK LEVEL. From his pants, he pulls a metal rectangle. A digital bar across the middle displays a super-long array of numbers and letters. A few seconds later, the readout shifts to something new. He hands the rectangle to me. "We have a minute before the passcode updates again."

I read aloud. "A—7—5—T—R—H—1—2—K—"

My CENSIR shocks me.

"Captain, you've been decommissioned." The words echo through the end of the phone. The voice belongs to Major Alderson.

The front of the pilot's head erupts in a spray of blood. The computer screen shatters. I hear the whistle of a bullet an instant later.

I whirl around. Alderson, a sniper, and some guy with a metal backpack stand near the hangar entrance. Alderson hands the phone to Backpack Guy. The sniper redirects his rifle at me.

"She's far too valuable for that," the major says to the sniper as he strides toward me.

He lifts the pilot's head by the scruff and turns him so I can see the carnage. "Well done, Twenty-Five. You have helped us deal with a dangerous security threat."

Bile rises in my throat. I swallow it back, breathe through my nose, force a smile. "Glad to be of service."

He wraps an arm around my shoulder. "I think you deserve a reward."

I expect him to take me to some reconditioning dungeon, but we return to the barracks. He activates overhead lights with his tablet. Several of the girls wake up too quickly to have been asleep. Twenty-One rushes over and grabs my hand. "You're back. Can we go to the island now?"

"Not yet," I whisper.

"Keep getting those dragons, and you'll be on that island in no time, child," Alderson says. "Sorry to disturb you so late, ladies, but I've got some good news. Thanks to

Twenty-Five's diligence, we discovered a weak link in our chain. She has earned you a day off from your duties. Good night, ladies. Sleep in."

A cheer goes up. He leaves. In the second before the lights go off, I see Evelyn grinning at me.

I want to cry and roar, but most of all, I want to hit something. Somebody. My CENSIR shocks me. I repress the urge, focus on the mental image of the captain's head exploding. I wait a few minutes before slinking from my bed. I can't see anything, but I know this room inside and out. I know where Evelyn sleeps. I tiptoe forward so her guard dogs won't notice me.

On a good day, I might give the queen bitch a chance to defend herself.

I don't remember the last time I had a good day.

I'm almost there when my CENSIR shocks me again. But it's not just me. Other girls are stirring. A beep sounds, the screen turns on. I freeze.

The video on the screen, shot via drone and labeled 25, is focused on the sidewalk adjacent to Confections of a Chocaholic. I last visited my aunt and uncle in Ann Arbor five years ago, but I remember that candy store vividly. I loved the chocolate-covered raspberries; Sam preferred the double-stuffed turtles.

Apparently, he still does.

The drone tracks him from the store to a house a couple blocks away. It zooms in on a window, shows Sam sitting on his bed. He's waving.

"He knows it's watching him?" Lorena says. Her arm's around my waist. I don't remember her putting it there.

I shake my head as I try to calm my breathing. I force myself to swallow. "Mom used to do that as a joke. 'Say hi to the camera, everyone!' He and Mom made a game of it. Punch buggy with drones."

The screen switches to different drone footage, dated six months ago, labeled *21*. Lots of open farmland. A glowing green dot appears on the horizon. Moving fast toward a dilapidated house. An old man steps onto the porch, a rifle in hand.

The viewpoint shifts to the dragon.

The man gets off three useless shots before the Green sets everything aflame, including him.

"Is that real?" I say. "Did they really do that to her family?"

It's not Lorena who answers, but Twenty-One. "Yes, yes, yes. Burn, burn, burn!" She's clutching the dragon brooch so hard that the tail's pierced her skin. "Kill the dragons, yes, yes. Kill the dragons, or the dragons kill them."

28

My CENSIR shocks me awake.

"Wakey, wakey, everyone."

Almost a month.

I'm out of my bed faster than everybody except Evelyn, but I still get a second shock.

Almost a week of that.

"Faster, Twenty-Five," Lester says.

On my way through the cafeteria serving line, I peek toward the boys' table. I tell myself I'm looking to see if Nine has recovered yet—he hasn't—but my gaze lingers on the empty seat next to Eleven.

"Scoping out your next target!" Four shouts.

I cast my eyes floorward, see a pair of boots coming my direction. I glance up. The A-B pretends not to notice me.

I dodge, but he adjusts, just enough to clip my shoulder. I catch myself from tripping, but my tray tips and breakfast tumbles to the floor.

"Watch it, talker girl."

My CENSIR shocks me.

"Stop antagonizing the soldiers, Twenty-Five," Lester says.

"I'm sorry, sir," I say. "It won't happen again."

But of course it will. Sidelong glares, muttered curses, lewd catcalls, sometimes physical retribution. I ignore it the best I can, and when I can't, I apologize because I know it rankles them even more. They want me to lash out, to prove that I'm some heartless monster, maybe. I will do everything they ask of me, but I refuse to let them break me.

The grind of metal biting into scales echoes from the far end of the ER, a dragattoir bigger than the Air and Space Museum I visited on a field trip a lifetime ago. Instead of old planes, space modules, and tour guides, we've got torture slabs, computer-controlled "test" apparatus, and Mengeles.

And chain saws.

Lots and lots of chain saws.

The dragon being sliced and diced on the slaughter slab by a half dozen All-Blacks glowed out at the Electrics station five minutes ago.

On the slab to my left, a car wash of flamethrowers drenches a Red in fire that looks green through the tint of my safety goggles. The filtration mask I wear beneath my jacket hood cannot block the stench of charring flesh.

To my right, mechanized syringes insert a human-length needle into a Green's neck. Veins of viridescent light race through its broken body before vanishing at its tail stump. The Green flickers off and on, arrhythmic. I see Fourteen flinch. A soldier laughs, another pantomimes a spasm. The Mengele controlling the syringe system gives a thumbs-up.

"Clear!" shouts Patch, my Mengele supervisor.

I turn my attention back to my victim, a Red named Ryla. I clamp the hood of my jacket tight to my ears. Nothing in this place is as loud as Mjöllnir. Well, almost nothing.

The giant hammer swings down from the wall onto her left shoulder. Bindings rattle, bones shatter. Her eyes burst open.

Despite my improvised earmuffs, despite her muzzle, I hear her anguished squeal anyway, though it is a whisper compared to the scream that blasts through my head.

I breathe through my mouth, slow and deep like Lorena told me as I exited the bus this morning. Doesn't matter. Breakfast rises in my throat. I swallow it back for the third time today.

Patch shows me an incomprehensible graph on his tablet. *Subject 247-R (Ryla): Impact Force.* "It's got brittle bones, this one." He pulls up another graph. *Subject 247-R (Ryla): Telepathic Volume.* "It maxed out at one hundred and twenty-two decibels. We're getting to it." Using the computer console adjacent to the slab, he repositions the hammer over the Red's right shoulder. "Ask it again, Twenty-Five."

"Ryla, what are the names of your friends?"

"Kill me."

In my head, her voice remains defiant. From the speaker in Patch's tablet, the words are robotic, monotonous.

"Tell it this is not a killing blow," he says. "Tell it if it continues to resist, we will prolong its suffering."

I tell her.

"Kill me."

Patch taps his goggles. Lester and Tim, the other A-Bs from our research team, bound onto the slab. From a tool chest, Lester retrieves a device that resembles a trowel. He uses it to peel back the dragon's eyelid. Tim draws his combat knife. Modern-day executioners. With the filtration masks, tinted goggles, and floor-length jackets—everything black—we look quite the part.

I shut my eyes.

My CENSIR shocks me.

"We talked about this, Twenty-Five," Patch says.

"But she can't even see me."

"She can sense it," he says.

"Stop being the weak link, Twenty-Five," Lester snaps.

I force myself to think of Sam waving at the drone. I will be strong for him. I have to be. I open my eyes.

One quick thrust. One gigantic scream. I fall to my knees, clutching my head. Breakfast fills my mask. Ryla dims.

Patch jerks me to my feet, hands me a splatter rag. "Get it together. Ask it again."

After cleaning my mask, I repeat the question.

"Kill me," she mumbles between soft mewls.

I think of Sam. "Answer the question."

"Please, human."

"We've almost broken her." Patch points at her other eye. A vicious thrust later, Ryla's blind and screaming again. I tremble, but keep my balance. Thankfully my stomach's empty. Empty enough.

"What are the names of your friends?"

"Kill me."

"Tell her that if she continues to resist, we will prolong the suffering of every dragon in here."

I do.

Patch gets in my face. "Do it with conviction, Twenty-Five. Don't be a glowheart."

I pretend I'm talking to him, put violence into my words.

Ryla brightens momentarily; her nostrils flare. "Kill me."

We crush her tail, then a wing, cut off two of her feet with a hatchet, pausing after each blow for me to ask my question. Her glow fades, but she's done screaming. Her responses turn to groans. Two-syllable groans.

A buzzer goes off. The flamethrower car wash shuts down. That dragon still glows a semihealthy red.

The overhead loudspeaker activates.

"Teams, please proceed to your next station. Team One, return to Intake. Team Four, take over at Chemics."

My CENSIR warms and tightens. Patch snatches the radio from his belt. "Why are we being swapped?" Something from the other end.

Patch frowns. "The colonel?" He glances at me. "You're sure?" Another glance as he shoves the radio back in his belt. "Let's go."

The intake bay opens. A Red is towed in, pulsing brightly, lips drawn back in a snarl as far as the muzzle will allow.

"A rager," Patch says. "Your lucky day, Twenty-Five. Even you can't screw that up."

Evelyn saunters from the opposite direction with Team Four. Blood stains her jacket.

I hug myself against the cold. With the flamethrowers off and Ryla's warmth dwindling with her glow, the cold draft that blows through the ER has become noticeable.

"Still don't have your Antarctic skin, Twenty-Five?" Evelyn says.

"What's the scenario?" Team Four's Mengele asks Patch.

"It's stubborn. Probably in shock. Give it some adrenaline and some hallucinogens."

"You think it's crackable?"

"In the right hands." He shakes his head at me. "My talker's a little too much of a glowheart, though."

Four's Mengele laughs. "Taste of a rager will work that right out of her."

"One can hope."

Evelyn pulls a half-eaten Baby Ruth from her pocket, unhooks her filtration mask, and takes a bite. She offers the rest to me. "You look hungry, Twenty-Five."

My stomach knots up. "I'm fine."

She shoves the rest into her mouth. I force myself to watch until she's finished. She gives this phony embarrassed smile, straps her mask back into place. "Don't worry, Twenty-Five, I'll pick up your slack."

Our team returns to the beginning of the torture line, where our newest victim awaits, shiny and whole. Patch lowers the cylindrical sheath over the dragon's body. It hovers there, emitting a low hum for a couple of seconds before rising back to the ceiling.

His tablet beeps. Two 3-D scans of the dragon appear. *Subject 249-R (Name Unknown): Luminal Map/Thermal*

Map. He beams. "Haven't seen a Red this bright in a while. Approach, Twenty-Five."

As I enter the dragon's line of sight, its glow dims. I mount the slab and take my mark on the X, a dozen feet from its snout. Though it shouldn't be able to see me, its green eyes track me the entire way. Its snarl fades. Warm puffs of breath wash over me in gentle waves.

"Ah," Patch says. He runs the scan again. He looks from me to the dragon, then back to me. He taps his tablet. My CENSIR loosens slightly. "Initiate communication, Twenty-Five."

"What's the dragon's name?" I ask him.

"It's a battlefield recovery. We don't know . . ." If he says more, I don't hear it.

"Hello, Melissa Callahan."

I gasp. I recognize the voice.

My CENSIR tightens. Patch looks smug. "Tell me its name, Twenty-Five."

"Vestia."

"One of your friends."

Not a question, but I answer anyway. "Yes."

"Proceed." He puts me back in transmit mode.

Painted on the wall behind her are three columns of questions. I recite the words printed above the red column. "Vestia, answer our questions truthfully and we will limit your suffering. Do not, and you will beg us to die."

"It hurts?"

Her question catches me off guard. "Yes. They will hurt you very much if you do not cooperate."

"No, that is not what I mean, human. It is strange. I cannot sense your thoughts, but I can . . . smell them. Do not hurt for me, Melissa Callahan. I am tired of this world. The next tomorrow awaits. I go to it with joy."

I try to think of something happy, something to somehow alter my scent, but every memory that pops up—Mom teaching me the piano, Dad pulling me out of school early to go see a movie, Sam hiding with me in the attic during a thunderstorm—is fleeting and bittersweet.

"Hurry it up, Twenty-Five," Patch says.

I look down the wall, focus on the questions. "Vestia, how old are you?"

"I do not know." The same answer Ryla gave. And Blaklik before her.

"Where do you come from?"

Sadness creeps into her voice. "I do not know."

"How long have you been here?"

"Two hundred three cycles of your moon." Two moons longer than Ryla and Blaklik.

"How did you get to our world?"

"I do not know."

"Where did you arrive?"

"I woke here." She sends me an image of a forest. Ryla and Blaklik came from the mountains.

"What was your role in your clan?"

"Warrior." The sadness deepens. "Paladin."

"What is the status of your clan?"

"I do not know."

"How many dragon holes are there?"

"There were five. They are gone."

We continue like this. I ask, she answers. Not once does she ask me anything. Nothing about James, nothing about Baby. At first I figure she's trying to spare her own emotions, but at some point I realize she's probably trying to spare mine. This gives me no joy, but it does give me courage, which I desperately need as I ask the final question on the list.

"What are the names of your friends?" Out of the corner of my eye, I see Lester grab a hatchet from the wall. The opening salvo. Didn't work on Ryla or Blaklik, but that's not the point.

Vestia does not hesitate in her answer. "I have none."

I brace for her pain, but Patch waggles a finger at the soldier. "Tell your dragon friend that if it wishes to fly into the next tomorrow with the glory of flame, we need to go no further."

"I do not understand," she says after I tell her.

"Fight for us, and you will get to die in battle," Patch says.

As I relay his message, Lester runs the edge of his hatchet along Vestia's snout.

Her lips peel back in what I believe to be a smile. "Tell the invisible men that they are not worthy of death in battle. They are not even worthy of a funeral by worms. How many of their brethren have passed through my belly?"

An instant after the robotic voice speaks the words from Patch's tablet, the hatchet is embedded halfway into her snout. I flinch, but she does not. Tim rushes her with his knife.

"Halt, you fools," Patch orders. "It's baiting you." He looks to me. "It's sure?"

"She's sure," I say.

My CENSIR shocks me. "I didn't ask for your interpretation, Twenty-Five."

I repeat the offer.

"Tell the invisible men that they reek of cowardice. In the next tomorrow, I will pray that their god grants them courage."

"Ground it," Patch says to the A-Bs.

"Gladly."

They use the serrated portion of their knives and start

sawing into her wings. I try to shut my eyes, but Patch shocks me. When I take a step back from my mark on the slab, he shocks me harder.

He doesn't have me interrogate her any further. We just watch.

It's slow going. The membrane slices apart with relative ease, but the bone's tough. Vestia flares here and there, sometimes I hear the slightest grunt, but her smile remains as they treat her like poultry.

They switch out their knives halfway through for fresh ones. Vestia's wings flicker on and off. By the time they've winked out, the various experiments have shut down. The chain saws have gone quiet.

The other teams meander over.

"I got a Benjamin on Tim!" somebody shouts.

"Double on Lester!"

The pace picks up, a race with eager spectators cheering them on. Tim wins. The other A-Bs swarm the slab. They grab hold of Vestia's attached wing. Twisting, tugging, wrenching, they tear it free, along with a good length of bone.

Lester wipes the blood from his gloves, pulls a camera from his pocket, pushes it at me.

"Rot in hell."

Evelyn bounds up beside me. "I'll do it."

After removing their goggles and masks, the soldiers gather beneath Vestia's wings, some with hands beneath chins and mile-wide grins, others making peace signs and goofy faces. In the middle, blood pumping down her scales onto the slab, glow fading fast, Vestia continues to smile.

And if she can smile through all this . . .

I pull back my filtration mask, suck in a lungful of frigid air, and loose the loudest roar I've got.

A sharp jolt from my CENSIR drops me to my knees, a brilliant explosion of light blinds me, a wave of heat washes over me. At first I think it's the CENSIR's doing—maybe a malfunction—but then somebody cries, "I can't see!" One of the soldiers posing beneath Vestia's wing, I think.

The light fades. The cold returns.

"A death nova," Fourteen says, excited.

Soldiers curse at me. Patch delivers a few more shocks.

As I blink back the black spots in my vision, I hear Vestia's voice in my head. She sounds a universe away. "Just because the wind fights you, it does not mean you are flying the wrong direction. Thank you, Melissa Callahan."

Her voice plays from the tablet speakers, monotonous, before turning to static. I smile. Vestia has moved on to the next tomorrow.

29

After Patch announces that both the girls' and boys' barracks will be on heat reduction through the night, he sends me to the "principal's" office.

"You've had an interesting few weeks here, Twenty-Five," the colonel says from behind his desk. "You have proven inadequate in the call center and troublesome in the battle room. Your willfulness has cost me the life of one of my pilots and the skills of one of my finest talkers. And now I understand that you've caused a disruption in the ER on your very first day."

"What do you want from me, Colonel?"

"Tell me, if you were in my position, what would you do?"

I don't answer.

Colonel Hanks cups his chin, rubs his lower lip with his

finger. "Major Alderson is convinced that our family would be better off if we rectified your behavior. Maybe he's right. Families need to get along, otherwise families get hurt."

"I'm doing the best I can. If that's not good enough, recondition me. But leave my family out of this."

"We're not the ones who put them in this situation. Who knows where their allegiances lie these days? We must be vigilant, Twenty-Five. Surely you understand that?"

"What do you want?"

His eyes narrow. "You're asking the wrong question, Twenty-Five."

I stare at him.

"You should be asking, 'How do I make myself a valuable member of this community?'"

I roll my eyes.

"I have been lenient with you, but do not make the mistake of thinking yourself irreplaceable."

He turns on a thinscreen, taps at his tablet. I expect another terror video, maybe a doctor holding a syringe at my father's throat or something. What pops up isn't much better.

A flashy, silver-themed website. Dedicated to me, or the TV version of me. The site already has over a hundred thousand followers.

And based on the comment wall, almost everyone sympathizes with my plight. Most because they think I'm crazy, though a few admire me for flying a dragon or sticking it to the government or for just being "hot."

I almost laugh.

The colonel turns on another screen, which displays an overtanned man with a face stiff from too much Botox. His smile makes me think of Evelyn.

"Hello, Melissa. I'm Hector, the director of *Kissing Dragons*. First off, well done. You absolutely smashed the ratings. . . . We'd like you to reprise your role in a crossover show with the fab four. A redemption episode."

I almost cry. "Seriously?"

"It'll afford you some time off from your other responsibilities," the colonel says, as if he's doing me a favor. "Who knows? If things go well, maybe we can figure out a way to better accommodate your talents."

I do laugh. "Quite a coincidence, don't you think?"

"What's that?"

"Vestia."

"Oh?"

"Oh." I smile at him.

He smiles at me. "I am sorry you had to witness that."

Super sorry. Asshole. I shrug. "What about my family?"

I intended the question for the colonel, but Hector's the one who responds. "We hope to incorporate your father into the episode."

I look to the colonel for the answer I want, but he only says, "Consider this your opportunity to make things right."

"Right?"

"A lot of these people blame you, Melissa, for what happened," Hector says.

I gasp. "You're doing the episode on Mason-Kline?"

Hector nods. "It's where your journey to evil began. It's where your journey to redemption will end." He lays out the details. I stop listening.

If the situation weren't so ridiculously horrible, I'd laugh. Agree to this charade and suffer the wrath of Mason-Kline, never mind helping to fund the military. Or decline, and hope that my decision doesn't result in my family's demise.

"I need some time to think about it." I need forever.

"This isn't open for discussion," the colonel says.

"Then you better go ahead and recondition me."

"We'll let you know, Hector." Scowling, Colonel Hanks shuts off the screen. He checks his tablet, then picks up his phone. "Major, who do you have on the Duckworth assignment? . . . Hold off on that. I want Twenty-Five to handle it. . . . Yes, Major, I'm sure."

The colonel hangs up. "I've got another battle-room mission for you. It's simple but important. I know you won't disappoint us."

Elvin Duckworth, the ranking senator from Alaska—the only state untouched by dragon flames for the past decade—is the sole member on the Armed Services Committee who voted against the bill to exterminate dragons. In and of itself, not a big deal, but since he's the chair of some military research subcommittee, Major Alderson and his superiors fear the senator's decision will lead to a cut in funding.

I'm not sure why the major tells me this. I guess to justify what he wants me to do, or maybe just to pass the time while we wait for mission clearance. Duckworth's nephew, a thirtysomething councilman from Anchorage, is on vacation in Jamaica.

Which means he's ripe for the torching.

An easy assignment, at least according to Major Alderson. All I need to do is fly my dragon into Montego Bay, a coastal resort town, and instruct it to open fire when Alderson gives the order. Get in, get out. A few deaths, for sure, but that's the cost of victory.

"We are green for mission go." Lester's voice echoes through the battle room. It's practically empty in here. Just me, Lester, and the major.

Alderson hands me a pair of those wraparound sunglasses. "Enable communication and activate VR-HUD."

On the lenses, a herky-jerky video appears—from the camera attached to my dragon assassin, a Green named

Almac. He's inside one of those compartments. Animal remains, dragon crap, and something I'm guessing is vomit cover half the floor.

"Initiate communication."

My CENSIR loosens. "Hello, Almac."

The dragon scans the compartment, looking for something. Me, I suppose. *What do you want, human? Where is Lorena?*

"I'm in charge today," I say. "You ready?"

To kill humans? Always.

Grimacing, I give a thumbs-up.

"Release the hound," the major says.

The compartment hatch opens from the top, revealing an expanse of gray sky. Almac launches himself toward the clouds, then glances back. The compartment bobs up and down with the roll of the ocean.

"Discard the package," the major orders. Seconds later, the evidence is gone. "Twenty-Five, have your dragon bank left to a due south heading."

"Almac, bank left . . . level out."

Where are the humans, human? I want to kill humans. He scans the darkening skyline, searches the seemingly endless ocean. *Where are they? Where is my fire?*

"He's getting angry," I say to the major.

"It's thirty minutes before landfall. Tell him to keep

his temper in check until then."

Almac continues to grumble, but stays on course with an occasional shock and reassurances of the slaughter to come. I tell myself that this is nothing more than a video game, that the bloodthirsty dragon and the wicked major are characters in some twisted plot; I must carry out this mission with them to keep my brother and father safe. No do-overs. No extra lives.

Besides, if I don't take out the senator's nephew, some-one else will. That's the piece of this puzzle that doesn't fit. "Why aren't you attacking the senator himself?"

"*We* are not attacking Senator Duckworth because he's a powerful man with powerful connections," the major says. "It would be in our interest to gain his allegiance."

I grunt. "So you're going to show him how dangerous the dragons are."

"He already knows how dangerous they are. He just doesn't consider them much of a threat anymore. It's out of sight, out of mind for him. We want to open his eyes."

"You ever wonder if what you're doing is wrong?"

I expect him to reprimand me, but instead he says, "Every day, Twenty-Five. That's what makes us different. You believe you've got the world figured out, you—"

"I don't have anything figured out," I say with a bitter laugh. "Less makes sense today than it did yesterday. But I know what you're doing is wrong. What *we're* doing, I guess, but *we* only help you because *we* have little choice. You do."

"The world's a dark place. Sacrifices must be made for the greater good. I don't always agree with them, and I don't often like them, but every atrocity you think we commit here, I see as a means to an end that gets us closer to the light at the end of this dragon-riddled tunnel."

"A brave new world, huh?"

"No, Twenty-Five, a peaceful one. Let's focus now. *We* have work to do."

In short order we reach land, veer south toward rows of brightly colored villas and homes . . . none of them black. Guess these people never worried about dragons. Not until today.

"Activate Almac's fire," the major says, and my heart jumps into my throat. "Tell him to open fire, Twenty-Five. . . . Open fire, Twenty-five . . . think about your family."

Almac, your fire's active, I whisper.

It's about time, human, he says, then goes silent because I guess he can't talk and incinerate at the same time.

At the major's orders, I direct Almac lower, until we're skimming the rooftops. We create an ocean of flame that consumes everything. People spill into the streets. My attempt to convince myself that this is just a video game collapses when some of the victims look over their shoulders. I see the stark terror in their faces; they know they're going to die. And then they do. I force myself to watch the first few melt into the dragon's fire, to implant the memory of my horrible crime.

I close my eyes for the rest of it, ordering Almac to shift course at the major's discretion. The dragon doesn't talk while he works, but I hear a funny noise in my head, something between a growl and a purr.

"Target neutralized," a soldier says.

"Contact the *Gerald Ford* and launch DJ countermeasures," Major Alderson says.

"Dragon jets have been launched, Major. Anticipate intercept in two minutes."

"Set Twenty-Five to inhibit," Major Alderson says.

I open my eyes. Half of Montego Bay still burns. The rest is charred ash. Soon the resort town will be nothing but black death. Almac spins around. From the distance, five dragon jets zoom toward him. *I can hear the invisible monsters! Where are they, human? Where are—*

My CENSIR warms and tightens; the line goes dead. The dragon sweeps his head back and forth to create an arc of fire in front of him. Useless. The jets disappear off the video, but I can see them on the radar, yellow icons closing in on the green target.

Almac dies fast, in a blur of gunfire and missiles. Tumbling head over tail, he crashes into the jungle. His collar explodes; the video blacks out.

Major Alderson jerks the video glasses from my face. "Good job, Twenty-Five," he says in the same sardonic way he congratulated me for killing Claire. I don't know why he's not happy. We destroyed the town. We destroyed everything.

"I didn't do anything. . . . I did nothing," I mumble. Nothing at all.

"You don't know much about dragon talking, do you?"

"More than I'd like. What's your point?"

"Greens feed on talker emotion. It fuels them, literally. We figured Almac would destroy half the town before he ran out of juice, but he obliterated everything and caused far more collateral damage than was necessary because you couldn't get it together."

"Don't you blame this on me! I did everything you told me. You could have launched those jets at any time. Turned on his fire restrictor—"

"That would not have been within the scope of reality." He waves Lester over. "Sergeant, remove Twenty-Five from my battle room. Take her back to the barracks and let her think about what she's done."

That evening, as I get drunk with Lorena, we watch a news report about an unprecedented attack on the heretofore dragon-free nation of Jamaica. The Green that perpetrated the massacre was shot down by dragon jets launched from

a nearby aircraft carrier. With the help of the U.S. government, the Caribbean islands are now scrambling to institute
a mass blackout policy.

"You didn't do anything wrong, Melissa," Lorena says,
not for the first time.

I thump my head against the wall. "How many people
did I kill because I want to keep Sam and Dad safe?"

"Forget about it if you can. Otherwise, drink up."

I cough against the burn in my throat. "Maybe it's easier
to just be another bobblehead number. Blondie Number One
certainly seems to have it figured out."

"Gimme a break." She shoves my shoulder. "This is what
they want. You're gonna really piss me off if you give them
what they want."

I shove her back, a little harder. "Says the drunken
whore."

"I am who I am. Who are you?"

"A mass murderer. A pretty pawn. Pick your poison."

"Huh?"

I fill her in on my fan website and the show they want
me to do. I take a swig, snort. "The redemption of Melissa
Callahan." Another swig. "You know, my mom used to
always say that there are no bad guys, only victims."

"Deep."

"It's bullshit."

Lorena squeezes my arm. "Don't give them what they want, Melissa."

"Easy for you to say. They're not dangling your family out there on surveillance footage."

"Lucky me," she says. I start to apologize, but she interrupts. "Sorries don't matter in the frozen suck. You just gotta survive to the next day."

"You're drunk." I shake my head. "Forget it, I'll figure it out."

She taps her temple. "It's not about in here." She taps my chest. "It's in here. Look, Twenty-One's family were known insurgents. That drone video was just a scare tactic to string you along." She sticks out her tongue at one of the cameras watching us. "They'll fuck you up, but they won't do anything to your family."

I'm not sure I believe that, but it's a chance I have to take.

I cannot be a victim, I cannot be a bad guy. I cannot be Talker Twenty-Five.

I have to be Melissa Callahan.

30

When I inform Colonel Hanks that I won't do the show, he pulls a weathered brochure from his desk. A vacation advertisement for a place I've never heard of called Fiji. "Doesn't have a Kremlin circus, but the weather is a bit more hospitable."

He hands me the brochure. Based on the swimsuit styles of the models lounging in seaside hammocks, it's over a decade old. Fiji must be one of the forgotten islands that went off the grid after the dragons showed up. With no commercial airplanes or cruise ships, nobody could get there anymore. Except the military.

"A week in the warmth, all expenses paid," he says.

I set the brochure on his desk. "Sorry, too many vultures."

His brow furrows. "Fiji doesn't have vultures."

I restrain a smile. Big Brother listens but doesn't always hear.

"I'm sure it does," I say, thrilling in his confusion.

"You have until tomorrow morning to change your mind," the colonel says in dismissal.

While Lester and I wait for the elevator, the colonel picks up the phone. He glances my way and gives me a look that warns me he has an ace up that starch-pressed sleeve of his.

Unless they produce James out of thin air—an unre-conditioned James—there's no bait big enough to hook my cooperation. But I know that won't happen. Someday soon he will show up at the cafeteria, call center, or ER, no longer the farmboy I remember. Will he even remember who I am?

Thankfully, he's not in the ER today.

Lester and I suit up in our protective gear, then meet Patch and Tim at Station One. A couple minutes later, the hangar doors open, and a dimly lit Red tied to a slab is towed in via tractor.

Even before I attempt communication with the subject, I know by the look in his eyes that he's what Lorena calls a grandpa, an old dragon who's ready to die because he's sad, lonely, and tired of living in a world with invisible monsters.

"Hello, Curik," I say after Patch puts me into transmit mode. "My name is Melissa."

"Hello, Melissa," he says right away. "This isn't going to be painful, is it?"

"It will hurt less if you cooperate. I'm sorry."

I get a CENSIR jolt for apologizing, but I don't care.

According to the adjacent computer screen, Curik's responsible for hundreds of deaths in Minnesota and Michigan. I don't know how the military determined this, but I don't doubt that he's killed at least a few people in his time.

I go through the standard list of questions. Most of his answers are variations of "I don't know."

"Curik, please give me the names of your dragon friends."

"Where do I begin?" Curik says, his words echoing from Patch's tablet speaker. "There was Kald. He was great. Once, when we were flying over the ocean, he saw this group of dolphins. I was hungry and wanted to eat them, but he thought they were graceful, so he made me go swim with them."

"He's dead?"

"Two years ago, your invisible monsters found him in the woods. He was trying to talk to a bear. He always had this way with animals, but till the end, none of them ever spoke to him. Foolish dragon."

"Hurry it up, Twenty-Five, we don't have all day," Patch says.

"Who else?" I ask.

Curik starts in on stories of his many friends, but I cut him off because the Mengeles don't care about anything but their names and their death status.

"What about your human friends?" I ask when he can't think of any other dragons.

"One spoke with me a few weeks ago. Scarlett Graves. She was so scared. The invisible monsters were after her. I wanted to help her. She seemed nice."

Scarlett Graves—that's one of Twenty-One's call center aliases. "Yeah, she is nice. Anybody else?"

"No, other than you. You seem nice, too."

"That's all for now, Twenty-Five," Patch says.

"They're going to silence us, Curik. I'll be back when we change stations."

"Could you continue to talk with me?" he asks. "I like hearing—"

My CENSIR tightens.

"Can I keep talking to him?" I ask Patch.

He growls a sigh. "You have to stop sympathizing with these monsters, Twenty-Five."

"I'm not sympathizing. It will make him more cooperative," I say.

"He's not giving us anything useful. Besides, you're both inhibited. It won't hear anything you say."

"That doesn't matter."

He waves an impatient hand. "Fine."

Tim and Lester whisper roars at me, make sawing motions with their knives.

Ignoring them, I mount the slab and sit beside Curik. He smells of rusted iron and radiates a pleasant heat . . . though in a few hours, he'll reek of smoke and chemicals, his warmth will be to embers, and he very well might not have any wings.

Ever since my "outburst" with Vestia, Patch has insisted on studying "the acoustic-emotional resonance of a dragon in a weakened state." To the amusement of everybody within hearing distance, I've roared at more than a dozen wingless subjects. A couple brightened a smidge, according to Patch's tablet, but none has come close to a death nova.

If you can somehow hear me, Curik, let go. Fly into the next tomorrow as fast as you can. . . . I'm sorry about your friends. I miss mine, too. I think of Trish. *I'm not sure what's happened to her. Our town was destroyed by a stampede of Blues. Her mother died. She probably blames me—*

A buzzer goes off.

"Twenty-Five, time to move," Patch calls.

The door at the opposite end of the hangar opens; the disposal trucks enter. After All-Blacks load crates full of a Green's body parts onto the trucks and the bloodied slab on which it was dismembered is hauled away, the remaining dragons are slid down the line to make room for the next victim. Our team follows Curik to Thermals, where he's scheduled for a low-degree flame bath, which is one of the more pleasant experiments, at least to a dragon.

A buzzer later, on our way to Impactions, the overhead speaker orders my team to switch places with Evelyn's, which is rotating from Electrics to Station One for the next intake interview. A talker swap's not abnormal—sometimes a dragon's personality jibes better with one talker than another—but Curik and I get along well, and the Green Evelyn was working on is already dead and halfway toward decapitation via an All-Black with a large ax.

"Be gentle with him," I tell Evelyn. "He's doing his best to cooperate. Sometimes he gets a little addled, but—"

"I know how to deal with these monsters, Twenty-Five." She smiles at the surrounding A-Bs. "Once a glowheart, always a glowheart. She probably still thinks her CENSIR's a dragon-queen crown."

"Control yourself," Lester says, grabbing my arm before I can retaliate. "It would serve you well to ignore her."

"It would have served me well if she'd been in the battle room instead of Claire," I snap.

"Families need to get along—"

"Yeah, I know, otherwise they get hurt. Why don't you

go lecture her for a—" I break off as the hangar door opens and a silver glow suffuses the area.

Baby. I thought she was dead. . . . I should have known better.

Scars and gouges cover her from tail to head. Her wings are frayed and bent at awkward angles beneath the metal straps. Her glow's a ghost of what it should be, but when her eyes find mine, she brightens. My lungs seize up, but I force myself to smile at her.

This is the colonel's ace in the hole.

Two choices. Reprise my dragon-queen role and keep Baby on life support until my fifteen minutes of infamy are up, or let her die on my watch right now.

It's no choice at all.

"I need to speak with Colonel Hanks."

31

After a seemingly interminable plane flight, a sleepless night in a normal prison cell, and a breakfast I couldn't bring myself to eat, I find myself back in the Fort Riley salon. Purple Shirt the tailor—in green today—and his hefty apprentice, Helga, check my measurements to ensure that the costume they've designed for my redemption episode will fit.

Purple Shirt scowls. "You're skinnier."

"They don't serve burgers at the rehabilitation institute, and I don't get much chocolate." Purple Shirt and Helga share a phony laugh, then hurry from the room. Next up, Cosmo Kim.

"Well, you just like to make us feel like we're earning our money, don't you?" She drops her bag of supplies on the floor beside my armchair, puts a warm towel over my face. "Try to relax."

Not a chance that's gonna happen, because this time I know what awaits me on the other side of the makeover. Last night, Hector the director provided me with my plotline for today's taping.

I'm on leave from a maximum security mental hospital at the request of my psychiatrist, who believes confronting the survivors of Mason-Kline will help my rehabilitation process. Overcome with remorse by this experience, I join the A-B dragon hunters during the climactic scene, in which Frank plunges his sword through the target's head.

Old Man Blue. That's the target. I figured she was killed during the Mason-Kline battle, but Hector informed me otherwise. She was wounded, near death. He intervened before she could be shipped to a dragattoir for disposal; now she's sedated in a hangar-turned-production-studio, awaiting "a fitting execution."

Kim finishes her work with an hour to spare. I'm the blond, bronzed girl again. Crazier this time. Hair puffed and wild, eyes overshadowed with red, blue, and green glitter, lashes longer than spider legs.

Purple Shirt and Helga return with a silver jumpsuit and matching slippers that remind me of something the female inmates would wear in one of those B-movie prison flicks

Sam might watch when Dad's not around. Even with me skinnier, it takes lots of squirming and sucking in to wriggle my way into it.

I glance at myself in the mirror and snort. They're not dressing me for redemption. They're dressing me for slaughter.

Helga fits my feet with matching slippers. "What's funny?"

"Aluminum foil isn't this shiny."

She purses her lips, giving her the appearance of a blowfish. "You look wonderful."

I don't argue, because I know it won't do any good; I'm stuck in this thing, literally and figuratively. This outfit will surely go over well with my so-called fan base, but they're not the ones I'm worried about. Facing the families of Mason-Kline's gonna be hard enough, but now I've got to do it dressed like some sort of futuristic streetwalker.

And Dad. Hector wouldn't tell me if he's going to show up. "When the door to the room opens, we don't want you to know who's coming in," he said last night, when I begged him for the participant list. "My script paints the picture, but it's emotional truth that brings it to life."

Pain, rage, hatred. That's what they want. The families will provide their emotional truth in spades, but their wrath's a candle flame to the inferno that would be Dad. Maybe he won't come, though. Maybe he's too injured.

Or maybe he refused. As Mr. D-man loads me into the Humvee for the trip across base, that's the hope I cling to. I can make it through everyone else. Grimace and bear it. *In nae.* Persevere. But, God, just don't let Dad be there.

When we arrive, the interview room's empty except for Simon and the cameramen. Three rows of seats form a semicircle around a solitary chair, to which Mr. D-man shackles my hands.

Simon shoves a tiny transceiver into my ear.

"When I speak, I am God and you are my disciple who must do as you're told," Hector says through the earpiece. "We're clear on that, right?"

I chew at my lip. Last night, Hector mentioned a loose script that needed to be followed. The transceiver's his safeguard to ensure story continuity and prevent any misunderstandings. Should I behave inappropriately or go off my spoon-fed lines, he will incapacitate me, sending me into spasming fits that will be attributed to my psychological instability.

"Are we clear, Melissa?"

"Yes," I whisper.

"Excellent. The party's going to begin soon. . . . You look terrified. That's good, but try to back it off a little bit. You're sad afraid, not scared afraid. You don't want to meet these people because you know the damage you've done, but as the show goes on, you find relief in admitting your guilt."

While Simon fine-tunes the camera positions, Hector continues his ridiculous coaching. I keep glancing at the door, expecting it to open any second. By the third time Hector tells me to calm down, my heart's ready to explode. Is this what it's like to be in the electric chair?

The door opens. My breath catches in my throat, but it's just Kim, here to touch up my makeup. Ignoring the stylist's orders not to wrinkle my face, I shut my eyes tight and pray that when I open them I'll be in my bed in Mason-Kline and the world will be halfway right again.

"Bring them in," Simon says. "One at a time."

"Open your eyes, Melissa," Hector says. "Don't hide from these people. You owe them your shame."

I obey and find a camera a few feet from me, focused dead on my face. "My shame is agreeing to this lie."

"Keep those opinions to yourself."

Karlton Smith is first. The class valedictorian the year ahead of mine. A physics genius. I had a serious crush on him. Once upon a time, I thought he might have even liked me.

He stops in the doorway and stares at me for what feels like hours, his left eye twitching every few seconds.

"Karlton Smith's twelve-year-old sister, Julia, died of smoke inhalation during the first wave. Her family called her Chipmunk," Hector tells me. "They said she smiled all the time. Her cheeks would puff out, big and happy."

I don't doubt it. Karlton didn't smile much, but when he did, you couldn't help but notice, especially if it was directed your way. As Simon's assistant points him toward a chair in the back row, I wonder how long it will take before Karlton remembers how to smile.

Lieutenant Mickelson's next. The balding history teacher doesn't crack an expression. He was always a bit bland, but now he seems completely lifeless.

"Geoff Mickelson's wife, Laurie, was killed outside the Walmart when the dragons stampeded," Hector says. "It was three days before their anniversary. During Christmas break, they had planned to celebrate with a vacation to Mexico. It was going to be their honeymoon because they couldn't afford one when they got married."

Lieutenant Mickelson shakes his head at me, then takes the chair beside Karlton. I'm counting them, wondering if all will be filled, when a middle-aged woman enters, her mascara already in ruins from crying.

"How could you?" she blubbers.

I recognize her, though I don't know why until Hector provides her name. "Cordelia Simpson's daughter, Cynthia, was attempting to free their horses from the barn when she was caught in the flames of a red dragon. For her senior service project, Cynthia organized a cow-pie bingo fund-raiser for cancer patient Wyatt Nelson. . . ."

I flinch at the memory. The entire community gathered at the soccer field, which had been sectioned into a massive bingo grid. Dad bought a number for both Sam and me. Pictures of a healthy Wyatt scrolled across the scoreboard. One included him playing Knights and Dragons with Sam. From his wheelchair on the sideline, Wyatt released the cow. To cheers, laughter, and a few directional prods, it plodded around the field until making its deposit.

". . . Wyatt died two days after the attack from burn wounds."

The roll call continues. Most I know by face, if not by name. For each, Hector provides a tragic story about a life cut short, families unmade.

Everyone's in funeral black. A few mutter curses and some admonish me with finger waggles—I'm not sure if it's for my assumed actions or my getup. Probably both. But for the most part they just seem in a state of shock or grief.

I manage to keep my own tears at bay, even though Hector urges me to let loose. I can't, though, because once I start, I'm not sure I'll be able to stop. I know I didn't destroy these people's families, but they think I did. I can feel their hatred.

Almost all the chairs are occupied when Trish enters. My

heart falls through the floor. Any sign of our friendship is gone, replaced with stark contempt.

"Trish, I'm so—"

With a primal scream, she hurls herself forward, black hat flying backward at the cameramen swarming behind her. She smashes into me. As we tumble to the ground, she rams her fist into my bicep. Something sharp pricks my skin. A needle.

She shoves it farther into my arm, I squirm but can't break free.

She drives her knee into my stomach. "Stop struggling, you dragon whore!"

Mr. D-man jerks Trish off me. A rivulet of blood trickles down my arm, but the needle's disappeared into her fisted hand. Thrashing wildly, she gets in a couple of good kicks and curses before he drags her from the room.

Simon comes over and rights the chair. "Can't say that wasn't interesting. A bit overdramatic, but it should play well. I thought she was your friend."

The dam collapses, the tears flood out.

"She was," I manage to say. My best friend.

He wipes the blood from my arm with a handkerchief. "That's a nasty scratch she gave you." He calls for Kim.

As she applies foundation to my "scratch," I wonder what Trish injected into me. Poison, disease? I consider telling someone, decide against it. Nobody would care. If anything, they'd approve.

Kim finishes, leaving my face a tear-streaked mess at Simon's command, and the few remaining family members trudge in. All the chairs are taken, except for one—Trish's—when a nurse rolls my father in via wheelchair, one of those specialized models for the severely disabled.

I have played this moment a thousand times over in the past hours, but it hasn't prepared me in the least. I start to hyperventilate as the nurse turns him to face me. He's even more broken than I imagined. Only his eyes seem to work, but the muscles around them are frozen, so I can't even tell what he's thinking.

Hector's saying something in my ear, the nearby camera's coming closer, but nothing seems real other than the person in the wheelchair who's supposedly my father. He looks like him, but Dad can walk and talk. He can yell at me, tell me how mad he is, tell me that no matter how much I fucked things up, that he still loves me.

I struggle against the handcuffs. "Let me see him. Please!"

Simon nods to Mr. D-man. The lock clicks and I bolt for Dad, the cameras converging around us.

I have to squeeze my hands between his back and the chair to hug him. He's limp and heavy. I press my face into his shoulder, my tears soaking into his hospital gown. "I'm sorry, Dad. I'm so sorry."

He lets out a low gasp. I back away, afraid I'm hurting him.

"He wants to talk," the nurse says. She extracts a small tablet from the back of the wheelchair and inserts it into a tubular column a few inches from my father's face. A digital keyboard appears on the bottom half of the screen. Using rapid eye movements, Dad types a message onto the top half. It plays from the tablet speakers in a robotic voice identical to the one I hear in the ER when I'm interrogating dragons.

"You do not need to be sorry. How are you doing?"

I bite my lip until I taste blood. "Okay."

"You look like you have lost weight. Have they been treating you well?"

I nod. I can't let him know the truth. I've already caused him too much pain. "I'm sorry, Dad."

"You are a good girl."

"So you don't hate me for what I did?" Hector says in my ear, causing me to flinch. I forgot he was there. "Ask him that."

I hesitate. The cameras come in close. The heat from their lights warms my face.

"Melissa, I won't ask twice."

Deep breath. "You don't hate me for what I've done to you and Sam?"

"That's not what I told you to say," Hector says. "Don't ad-lib."

"I would not have come if I had known it would hurt you so much," the robotic voice says.

"What about Mom? You're not upset about Arlington?" Hector says.

I clench my fists. "You're not upset about Mom?"

"Your mom was an angel in a world of demons. She only ever did what she thought was right. You are a lot like her."

My smile vanishes when my CENSIR jolts me.

"That was your last warning, Melissa," Hector says. "Ask him this. It doesn't bother you that Mom killed all those people? Ask him. No changes."

"I love you, Dad. If you talk to Sam, tell him I never meant to hurt anybody."

Rising, I remove the earpiece. I'm about to throw it to the ground when searing pain blasts through my head. The world goes dark.

32

"Has the bleeding stopped?"

Hector's voice pulls me from the void. Floaters flash behind my eyelids. I struggle to open them but can't. My arms and legs are equally useless. A drumbeat of pain ignites in my skull and accelerates into a pounding throb. Somebody's pressing a wet towel to my temple.

"You're hurting me," I try to say, but manage only a groan.

The pressure abates, the pain intensifies. A warm gush of blood spurts from somewhere above my CENSIR. I choke on bile.

"It'll be a while before it clots. We need to take it off to stitch her up," a woman says. The towel holder, I think. Seated beside the bed. A doctor? She reapplies pressure.

"Absolutely not." Colonel Hanks's voice sounds staticky.

"We can't do the show with her bleeding all over the place," Hector says.

"Then you won't do the show," the colonel says.

"We have a contract."

"It's not coming off. She might communicate—"

"She's in no condition for that," the doctor interrupts. "Even if she were, we'll hit her up with meds. She'll be completely knocked out."

"She won't be able to communicate?" the colonel asks. "You guarantee that? Your job's on the line, Captain."

"She'll have the functionality of a corpse." Pause. "She might be able to receive messages."

"But she won't remember anything, anyway, would she?" Hector says.

"We'll use an amnestic, but that's for standard cognition. I'm not familiar with this condition."

"What's the worst that could happen?" Hector says. "A few dragons sing her lullabies?"

After a long silence, Colonel Hanks says, "Make it quick."

. . . The armies gather. We will come . . .

The words fade as I regain consciousness. Somebody's pressing on my head again, but I barely feel it.

"Give her another dose," Hector says, from what sounds a mile away.

A cool sensation streams up my arm. My eyes blink open and, after a couple of seconds, focus on Cosmo Kim. She sits at the edge of the hospital bed, dabbing at my temples with a makeup sponge. "You're a piece of work."

"How are you feeling?" the doctor asks from the other side.

"Confused," I mumble. The armies gather. We will come. A dream?

While Kim fixes my face and hair, the doctor removes my IV, has me follow a penlight, stethoscopes me, tests my reflexes. Once Hector's sure I won't be a drooling Frankenstein, he orders everybody out.

"We're going to try this again. Colonel Hanks informs us that you two have a deal. If you're not on your best behavior for the rest of your visit with us, Melissa, that deal is forfeit."

The deal. Keep Baby alive until I return to Georgetown, let me say good-bye to her, execute her when I'm not around. Not the greatest bargain, but it was the best I could get.

Hector tosses me my streetwalker outfit, then leaves to let me change. There's a small window in the room. It takes me a good minute to get out of bed, another to cross the ten feet to the window.

The armies gather. We will come. A message?

Outside, it's night. Real night. With darkness and moon and stars. I scan the sky, but the only visible specks of light remain white and miniscule. I lift my gaze from the horizon to the heavens.

Long time, no see, Mom. There's this baby dragon I know. She's the reason for this horrendous outfit, so keep that in mind if you've got TV up there. I don't know if she'll be around here much longer. I hope you two get to meet. I think you'll hit it off.

"How much longer, Melissa?" Hector calls.

Gotta go. Love you.

As I turn from the window, I catch my reflection in the glass. Barely visible stitches, covered in bronzer like me, peek out from beneath the CENSIR and run from the middle of my forehead halfway to my left ear. Otherwise, I appear undamaged. If only memories could be fixed so readily. A few sutures here, some makeup there, and all the ugly goes away.

I've just slithered into my whorefit when Hector and Simon barge in, followed closely by their production crew. They place a green screen against the wall and set up the interview chair in front of it. Hector positions me at an angle that favors my stitch-free side, and we're ready to continue the charade.

Simon goes into narrator question mode. Hector feeds

me the answers. Without Dad here and the family members staring at me, it's easier to repeat the lies, to accept blame for actions I never committed, to condemn the insurgency and the dragons, to beg for forgiveness.

Some of my responses are directed at the families ("I'm sorry about your wife, Lieutenant. If I'd known how dangerous the insurgents were, I never would have helped them."), others to the viewing audience ("I don't blame my mother for how I turned out. She was always troubled, and I guess that made her into a monster. But to me, she was always just Mom."). Some questions I answer over and over because I don't get the tone right or I start crying too early or too late.

A long time later—voice hoarse, eyes aflame, head throbbing—it's over.

Next stop, the Fort Riley draggatoir, where I get to watch the fab four kill Old Man Blue. She's fastened to a slab surrounded by production lights, cameras, green screens, and All-Blacks. Frank, Kevin, Mac, and L.T. lounge in makeup chairs.

After introducing me to the four dragon hunters, Hector seats me beside Frank so a beautician can fix my face.

Frank notices my tear-streaked makeup, frowns at Hector. "You should feel ashamed, maricón." He sounds different from TV. Nicer. Which is strange, because I always imagined him to be a jerk.

"You worry about your job, pretty boy, I'll worry about mine." The director turns to me. "There's been a slight change. When I give you the signal, I want you to run up to Frank, who'll have the sword positioned over the dragon's head, and take over."

"You want me to kill her?"

"I want you to redeem yourself." He waves at the dragon. "This beast murdered dozens of people in your community. What better way to prove your remorse?"

"She was just trying to protect the children."

"I don't care, it's what you're going to do. Now get it together. I don't want you crying up there."

I stand off to the side while the fab four gather around the dragon and congratulate each other on a hunt well done. Hector orders an adrenaline injection for Old Man Blue to liven her up. Her eyes open, her glow brightens. Take away the scars, gouges, and spatters of fake blood that cover her body, and she looks almost like she did that night atop Dragon Hill.

The fab four repeat their congratulatory act. Ceremonial sword in hand, Frank positions himself beside the dragon. "We've got a special guest for you, old man," he says in his gruff TV voice.

"Melissa, move toward Frank," Hector orders. "Back it up. Be more confident. Shoulders back, hold your head high."

I obey.

"Pick up the pace. Close your mouth. Snarl a bit. Tell him that you want to kill the dragon, then take the sword."

"I want to do it," I say.

"No, no, no!" Hector bellows. "Add more oomph. Like you actually mean it. Start over."

A dozen or so start-overs later, I manage an overwrought rendition he finds acceptable.

"Now kill the damn thing," he says.

I grab the sword from Frank, its tip balanced on the middle of Old Man Blue's head. Sweat slickens my shaking hands.

No.

Not like this.

I roar—

My CENSIR shocks me.

"What the hell was that?" Hector says.

"I was improvising . . . um . . . releasing my wild side."

"Interesting." He purses his lips. "Okay. Try it again. More natural. Less screechy."

Asshole.

I give it everything I've got. If anything, Old Man Blue dims.

"Let's kill it for real this time, people," Hector says after another adrenaline injection.

I take a deep breath. And another.

"Push in a little bit. It'll help with the nerves," Frank whispers.

Bye, old man.

"Good-bye, Melissa," I hear her say. A memory. Back when I thought there was nothing worse than dragons.

Now there is only silence.

Then Hector: "Hurry it up!"

I close my eyes, tighten my grip, press down, feel the blade slide in through her scales. Far more easily than I expected. I stop.

"Do it, Melissa. Straight down!"

"The dragon's almost dead," Frank whispers. "It won't hurt him."

"Her," I mumble. "It won't hurt her." My arms lose their strength. The sword wobbles, my vision blurs. "I can't."

"Frank, help her out," Hector says.

Frank draws his pistol and shoots Old Man Blue in the side of the head. Her glow disappears, the hangar darkens.

Hector climbs onto the slab, his Botoxed face gone red. "What were you thinking? I meant for you to help her push the sword through, not shoot the damn thing." He wheels on me. "And you—"

Frank steps between us. "Leave her alone. You can add the glow back in post-production."

"Fine. Makeup! Get it under control, Melissa."

"No makeup," Frank says. "You let her cry. CGI it out if you want, but you let her cry."

With Frank's help, I drive the sword deep into Old Man Blue's head. While Frank gives his sign-off, I sit beside the dead dragon, thinking about her last words to me.

In the end, she died to protect those children. If she were human, she'd be given a ceremony and medals. But she's just a slain monster who will be remembered for the lives she took, not the lives she sacrificed herself to save.

And all for nothing. As far as I know, Baby's the only one left, and she's on borrowed time.

The armies gather. We will come.

But they're not coming. Not now. Jets would be scrambling, sirens would be blaring.

In an hour, I'll be on a stealth transport back to Antarctica. A few hours after that, Baby will be dead. An ax to the head, maybe a chain saw. Wings ripped off? I wonder if they'll have a talker roar to her before—

No! The dragons will come to Georgetown, they will find us. So what if those words were nothing but figments of desire or anesthesia? So what if we're a needle in Major Alderson's frozen haystack? So what if the only dragons Lorena's seen there in almost three years of endless days and endless nights are those brought in strapped and collared?

Doesn't matter. Rescue will come. Maybe not today, maybe not tomorrow, but it will. It must. I look to Old Man Blue. She did her best. She and Vestia and Keith and James . . .

And Mom.

Now it's my turn.

Colonel Hanks will only keep Baby alive as long as I have bargaining power. And my sole currency is popularity. I recall the messages on that fan website he showed me. Melissa's supporters love her because she's crazy.

I can't disappoint them.

I wrench the sword from the dragon's head, slick with blood, and clamber atop her.

"Get out of my shot," Hector shouts, reaching for the tablet that controls my CENSIR.

As soldiers run toward me, I raise the sword. "There are many rules critical for a successful dragon hunt, but always remember this: dragons bleed just like we do," I shout, then tilt my head up and open my mouth to catch the acrid blood dripping from the hilt. "Dragons feel pain, just like we do, and dragons die, just like we do!"

I plunge the sword into Old Man Blue again and again until Frank pulls me off.

A beaming Hector scuttles over. "That was absolutely brilliant."

"I want to be your official dragon slayer," I say, wiping blood from my face.

"We'll have to see how the ratings track and get permission from the colonel. Why the change of heart?"

"For the children, of course."

It's midday when the plane lands in Georgetown. After A-Bs unload several supply crates, Lester uncuffs me and herds me into the Humvee. On our way toward the base, I spot Baby in one of the dragon cages. Unlike the other captives, she thrives in the frigid climate. Seeing her alive and semi-healthy puts a smile on my face.

"Enjoy your vacation, Twenty-Five?" the sergeant says.

"Oh yeah, I had a blast. How things been down here? Still killing everything you can?"

"Hoo-rah."

We visit Colonel Hanks. I give him a rundown of my performance. "Hector's thinking about making me a regular on the show."

The colonel frowns. "We'll see. I don't want this interfering with your duties."

"I mentioned that to him. Said you'd probably want a larger cut, too. He didn't like the idea, but I think he's open to it. Depending on the ratings, of course."

The colonel stares at me for a while, then laughs. "I

don't know what they did to you topside, but I approve of it."

"I saw the Silver in the cage on my way in," I say. "Can we keep her there?"

"For the time being."

"Thank you, Colonel," I say.

"Thank me by doing your job well," he says, beckoning Lester. "She's at the call center for the rest of the day."

The hint of a smirk plays on the sergeant's lips.

I don't understand his amusement until we enter the call center. The voices echo around me, but one stands out above all else. He's the talker leading the weekly tally board with twenty dragons located.

26.

James.

33

I go through the motions of locating dragons, but can't focus because I'm trying to convince myself it's not James I hear. Lester chastises me often. Harsh words, a CENSIR jolt here and there. Makes little difference. It takes me three hours to contact my first dragon (who hangs up on me within seconds), another hour to get an old Red to reveal his location.

Numerous reprimands later, Major Alderson announces an end to the workday. It's Tuesday, which means it's the girls' turn to leave the building first, but as we're getting up, Major Alderson raises his hand.

"Twenty-Five, you will remain here until you hit the minimum daily standard. Your barracks will be on heat reduction until you are successful. The rest of the girls are dismissed.

"On a good note," the major says as the girls file out, "Twenty-Six set a call center record with eighteen targets located in a single day. Weak links break chains . . . strong links hold them together. Twenty-Six, please stand."

He's in a cube at the front. I can't see his face.

The major tosses him a bag of candy. "To further show our appreciation, I have decided to give all the boys tomorrow off, with provisional access to the rec center. You are dismissed."

The boys rise. Cheerful murmurs percolate through the group as they form their exit line. I expect James to be crazed like Claire or scattered like Twenty-One, but when he comes into view, he appears no different from the farmboy I remember.

He doesn't so much as glance my way as he passes.

Perhaps he didn't recognize me. I'm skinnier than the last time we saw each other, and my hair is blond. I see him whisper something to a soldier. Then he turns around and stalks toward me.

He opens the bag of candy and tosses one at my feet.

"You fed me in the cage," he says. "I don't want to be in the debt of a glowheart. We square?"

I bite my lip, give him a curt nod.

"Good. And try to do better, Twenty-Five. Weak links break chains."

*   *   *

That evening, when I finally return to the barracks, nobody's watching *Kissing Dragons*. Nobody seems to mind the chill, either. They're all too busy talking about him.

Lorena wraps me in a blanket hug. "Welcome back."

Twenty-One tugs at me. "He's your friend, right?"

I swallow. "No."

"But I heard he gave you chocolate."

"Go count your stash, Allie," Lorena says.

Twenty-One sticks her tongue out. "Already done. I like him, yes, yes. He gave me some of his chocolate, too. Told me to keep up the good work. Can he come to our island?"

"You bet," I whisper.

She points a finger gun at Evelyn. "We'll have to kill her first, though."

"That's enough, Allie," Lorena says.

Twenty-One sulks. "He gave her more than he gave me."

I can't help myself. "He did?"

"At dinner. He came over to our table. Said he wanted to share," Lorena explains. She rolls her eyes. "'With those who deserve it.'"

"So much for no fraternizing, huh? That's good," I say. "They deserve each other."

Lorena shrugs. "Try not to think about it."

"You figure out what you want to put next to the carousel?" Twenty-One asks.

Jesus. I force a smile. "Not yet. I will. Promise."

"Yes, yes. Maybe something for Twenty-Six. Like a basketball court. He can play with the monkeys."

He prefers soccer. Doesn't matter anymore, I suppose.

"Wakey, wakey, everyone."

I don't know what day it is.

I hear the excited whispers as we dress. Sometimes his name slithers over, snakes its way into my ears.

I retreat to the bathroom and almost run into Evelyn, who's soaping up her armpits, a stupid smile on her face. Not her fake, bullshit smile either. Well, not until she sees me.

On the bus, the whispers are louder, the smiles wider.

"Maybe we should do it," Evelyn says.

Seven laughs. "You're crazy."

"James is fine." She grins. "Mighty fine. Bet they've worked out the kinks."

I'm tempted to encourage her lunacy. Twenty-One may be addled beyond repair, but she's not an emotional zombie who feeds on dragons. Sure, he may be perfect for Georgetown needs, but once they no longer need him, Twenty-Six will shrivel away and there won't be anything left.

I suddenly find it difficult to breathe.

Twenty-One squeezes my hand. "You okay, Twenty-Five?"

"I'm fine." I don't know why it hurts. I barely know him. Knew him.

Eyes down, I enter the cafeteria, get my food, quickstep it to the girls' table. I sit in the far corner with Lorena and Twenty-One, try to ignore the laughter that comes from the other end.

I'm squashing peas into mash when I hear footsteps, then his voice. "Good morning, Sergeant."

The table goes quiet. Boys aren't allowed over here.

"Good morning, Twenty-Six," Lester says. "Can I help you?"

"If you don't mind, I'd like to borrow Talker One to ask her about examination techniques."

"Of course," the sergeant says without hesitation.

I peek askance and see the whore rise. She looks like a dog ready to fetch a bone. He looks eager to throw it. I clench my fork. It snaps. Twenty-Six notices. "You want to join us, Glowheart? You could use some pointers."

Evelyn's scowl almost makes me take him up on it, but I shake my head and return to stabbing peas with my shard of fork.

My CENSIR shocks me. "Violent thoughts will not be tolerated, Twenty-Five," Lester says.

"Bet he's got a pecker the size of a thimble," Lorena says. I almost choke on my milk laughing. She scoops up some of my mash and stuffs it into her mouth. "Think about it, all that chocolate he's giving Evelyn is gonna make her fat and ugly."

"One can hope."

Twenty-One pouts. "How come he doesn't want to make me fat? I'm a better talker than she is, yes, yes. The best."

I ruffle her tangled hair. "Yes you are."

"They're always talking, always talking." She leans over conspiratorially. "We need to get rid of them. Talker One, too, yes, yes."

Lorena grins. "Maybe she'll have a reconditioning accident."

I glance toward Evelyn's minions, who cluster together in excited conversation. "If she ended up like Claire, you think they'd take care of her?"

Lorena's grin fades. "Claire used to be her best friend."

"Really? How come you were the one taking care of her, then?"

"Somebody had to."

"You'd take care of Evelyn, too," I say, more statement than question.

She arches her eyebrows. "I don't know. That's a lot to ask."

"She's got toothpick arms," I point out. "Wouldn't hit you as hard as Claire."

"Yeah, but she's got that whiny-ass voice. And if she started screaming at the message board . . . have you ever heard her scream? Sounds like a dying whale." She mock shudders.

The chatter from the other end of the table stops. I glance over to dare them to say anything, but it's not our conversation that drew their attention. Twenty-Six and Evelyn are on their way back. Behind them, the boy talkers are clearing their table. I pretend to watch them, pretend that I don't care, but my eyes keep returning to Twenty-Six and Evelyn. They look so damn happy.

I focus on my tray.

"Dying whale," Lorena whispers, then makes a little squeaky sound. I want to laugh, but I can't seem to remember how.

"Thank you, Sergeant, it was very helpful," Twenty-Six says. Then, a smile entering his voice: "I'll see you soon."

I look up. He's gone. But Evelyn won't stop talking about him. His name follows me out of the cafeteria onto the bus. James this. James that.

James doesn't exist anymore, I want to yell. James is gone!

Why can't he just be gone?

"One, Seven, Thirteen, Twenty-Five," Lester announces as we pull up beside the ER.

"Kill the dragons, yes, yes."

"I think I'd be more useful in the call center, Sergeant," I say.

My CENSIR shocks me. "I'm tired of your attitude, Twenty-Five. We go where Major Alderson assigns us."

After putting on our filtration masks and goggles, my team heads for the Chemics station to finish off a tabun regimen on a now-wingless Green.

A soldier retrieves a hatchet from the wall, points it across my face. "Looks like your boyfriend found somebody more to his liking."

"Good for him." I avoid looking at the Electrics slab until the A-B's attention is elsewhere. Twenty-Six is crouched in front of a flickering Red's scorched snout. Evelyn lingers close, no doubt giving instructions he doesn't need.

"Pricklers are green for go," Patch says from the Chemics control console. The mechanized syringe system extends from the wall and injects a needle of adrenaline into the Green's back. Seconds later, its eyes pop open.

"Proceed, Twenty-Five," Patch says.

My CENSIR loosens. I repeat the same question I asked a hundred times yesterday. "Velmar, where are the Diocletians?"

"I do not know Diocletians," he says. The subsequent growl that rumbles through my head comes out as harsh static from Patch's speaker.

A talon gets hatcheted off. Velmar's growl deepens.

"Velmar, where are the Diocletians?"

"I do not know Diocletians."

A lie, at least according to the drone video Patch showed me. Velmar was shot down in a recent ambush by the Diocletians on a supply convoy traveling through the evacuated territories. The jagged scar of glowless flesh along Velmar's back is unmistakable.

After another talon amputation, Patch injects the Green with a high dosage of tabun. Velmar dims, the growl becomes a whine.

"Velmar, where are the Diocletians?"

"Open yourself to me, human, and I will show you the truth."

Not the first time I've heard that from him, either. Other Greens have said similar things. Creeps me out. I asked Lorena about it once. She acted like she didn't know, but I think it had something to do with her father.

"Do you know what he means?" I ask Patch as he ups the dosage.

"It's just trying to scare you. Don't worry, Twenty-Five, it can't hurt you."

I don't know if he's trying to be comforting or ironic. I assume the latter.

The loudspeaker turns on. "Team Three, please proceed to Chemics. Team One, stand down and observe. You will remain after hours to account for the backlog."

"Dammit, Twenty-Five," Patch says. "Stop making my life miserable."

"Feel free to transfer me at anytime," I say, knowing very well that he can't. He can, however, shock me.

I stifle a groan, which has less to do with the pain from my CENSIR and more to do with Twenty-Six sauntering toward me. At least he's alone.

"Hey, weak link," he says. "Can't squeeze the juice out of this lime?"

"I didn't need any help with Vestia," I say. "She was beautiful, you know?"

I hope for a flinch, some sign of the farmboy I once knew, but his coldness remains steadfast. "Vestia was weak, with too much sentiment and not enough sense. Reminds me of a certain underperforming glowheart I know."

"Bite me, asshole."

"Control your emotions, Twenty-Five. They tend to get you in trouble."

The soldiers laugh.

With another glare for me, Patch cedes control of the

Chemics console to Team Three's Mengele.

"Watch and learn, Glowheart." Twenty-Six turns to the dragon. "Velmar, where are the Diocletians?"

Velmar's words play from the console speaker. "Did I scare the girl away?"

"Perhaps."

"Too bad. She smelled delicious. You smell delicious, too."

"I'm sure I am. But have you ever tasted a human child?" Twenty-Six asks.

Velmar groans through his bindings. A purr almost. "Often."

"Recently?" Twenty-Six asks.

Velmar doesn't answer.

"The smell of their skin, the softness . . . ," Twenty-Six says, as if describing a delicious delicacy.

"Twenty-Six, what are you—" Patch starts, stops as Velmar brightens.

"There is nothing so glorious as fresh flesh," Velmar says.

Whispered conversations end abruptly. Somebody gasps. Several A-Bs draw knives. A couple pull their sidearms.

Twenty-Six waves them off. "Surely you took some of these fresh kills back to your lair."

"I surely did, but I will not tell you where."

"Are you a good little dog, protecting your pack?" Twenty-Six says.

"I am no dog. I have no pack."

"Yes, but they know where you live, don't they? That fresh flesh will be theirs. Your bounty."

Velmar pulses. "Mine."

"Show me where it is."

"Open yourself to me and I will."

"It is too late for that. You know how this ends, Velmar. Show me. The invisible monsters will bury your treasure in an avalanche, never to be shared."

"You can promise this?"

"Yes, but you must hurry."

An image appears on the console computer screen. Some mountain range. Then another. Inside a cave. I look away too slowly to avoid the corpses. Little corpses.

"That's as close as we're going to get," Twenty-Six says to his Mengele. "Now, if it's all the same to you, I'd like to chop this bastard to pieces. I'm tired of looking at him."

A soldier hands him a hatchet. The other A-Bs join the impromptu dissection. For once, I don't mind.

After another long day in the call center, in which I came in last again and had to spend two extra hours to reach the new minimum daily standard—raised from two to four because of Twenty-Six's successes—I return to the barracks to find my *Kissing Dragons* episode playing.

The screen fades to the credits as I go apeshit with the sword on Old Man's Blue head. Evelyn bounds to her feet. "Let's put our hands together for Twenty-Five, who has turned the corner and helped make the world a better place. If only we were all lucky enough to be given the chance. How did it feel slaying that demon, Twenty-Five? Was it spectacular?"

"You want to know how it felt?" I say, closing the distance between us in three quick strides. She senses my fury an instant too late to raise her hands. After the first punch, I expect my CENSIR to shock me silly, but nothing happens. Must be Whiskey Jim running Big Brother patrol tonight.

I get in a couple more straight punches before Seven and Ten pull me off and shove me away. I glower at Evelyn. "That was spectacular."

She wipes blood from her nose. "You're in trouble."

Lorena shakes her head. "Anybody asks, you fell." She leans in, her voice little more than a whisper. "Otherwise, I'm going to let Allie know who took her Kit Kat the other night."

"That wasn't me," Evelyn says.

Lorena glances at Twenty-One, who's huddled in the corner, grinning at us. "Who you think she's going to believe?"

"Thanks," I say on the way back to our beds.

"You need to get it together," Lorena says, taking me by the arm. I cringe. Her fingers probe the bump on my tricep where Trish injected me. "You should see one of the doctors."

"I'm fine."

"It's not getting better. What if she poisoned you?"

I pull free. "Then you won't have to worry about me anymore, will you?"

"Sulk on your own time, Twenty-Five."

"Fuck you, Two. I'm doing the best I can."

"No, you're not. You've got to stop being a weak link. They already hate you enough without this."

"This?"

Lorena waves at the screen. "I didn't tell anybody why you went off base. They thought you were in trouble. That made them happy. But now they see you were hanging with All-Blacks and killing dragons."

"You think I enjoyed it?"

"You don't get it. You could have gotten us days off, better food, anything. But all you cared about was that stupid baby dragon of yours."

"Be careful unless you want to get hurt, too."

She steps back, disgusted. "You need to do better."

"Or what?"

"Or I'll tell Allie who really took her chocolate. She won't attack you like she would Evelyn, but she'll hate you forever."

Twenty-One had been sleeping in her corner. I didn't want to steal from her stash, but I'd missed dinner again. "I'm going to replace it."

"How you plan on doing that when you're dragging your feet all the time?" She shakes her head. "You don't have many friends, Melissa. Don't throw us away over a boy who's no longer here."

As much as I hate her right now, I know she's right. Tonight, as with every night since Twenty-Six showed up, I go to bed hoping that when I wake in the morning, James will be left behind in my dreams. I'm not sure he exists anywhere else, and I need to stop looking for him.

34

"Teams, please remain at your current stations. Team Three, please head to Electrics for dragon disposal."

Terrific. Team Three is Twenty-Six's death squad. And I'm at Electrics. "Shouldn't we head for Station One?" I ask Patch.

"We're supposed to wait here until this lightbulb's taken care of," he says as the ER door at the end of the facility retracts.

I glance at the flickering Red on the slab, praying he glows out before Team One arrives.

No such luck.

"We've got a live one, boys!" Twenty-Six says. The A-Bs split into two groups, dismemberment and collection, arming themselves with chain saws or large plastic bags.

Twenty-Six struts toward the dragon, a hatchet in one hand, an ax in the other.

He climbs atop the slab, then raises the hatchet. "Should we go with the piranha?" He lifts the ax. "Or the shark?"

Most everybody shouts for the hatchet.

"Just kill the damn thing."

James sets down the ax, covers his brow with his hand, like I'm not in plain view. "Is that you, Glowheart?" He points the hatchet at me. "You want to come do this? We don't have a sword, but you seem capable." He grins. "Or maybe you want to roar at it some more."

As several soldiers tease me with howls that are more wolf than dragon, I look toward the slaughter station. Men are unloading crates from a cargo van onto the slab where a dragon normally goes. The disposal trucks are nowhere in sight, which means Twenty-Six can take his time torturing the flickering victim.

I step forward. "Yeah, I'll do it."

"Keep one hand on her CENSIR," an A-B says.

"Can you wear that outfit of yours?" another one calls.

"I bet she can't even lift the shark."

"Sounds like a wager to me," Twenty-Six says. "What will it be?" He feigns deep thought, then raises his finger. "I've got it. If she can get through the lightbulb here in ten strikes"—he pats the dragon on the head with the butt of the hatchet—"she gets a reward."

"What sort of reward?" someone asks.

"Does it matter?" another soldier says. "There's no way she's getting through that neck in twenty strikes, much less ten."

"A day off for the barracks," I say, glaring at Twenty-Six.

He nods to Lester. "What do you say, Sarge?"

Lester taps a message into his tablet. "I believe Major Alderson will find that acceptable."

"Outstanding," Twenty-Six says. "Now for the good part. What should her penalty be if she fails? Standard punishment would be the easy choice, but poor Twenty-Five's been failing a lot recently, and that would be like adding a grain of sand to a mountain."

The crowd laughs.

"No, we need a special prize," Twenty-Six says with a smirk. He listens to several suggestions ranging from me wearing a necklace of dragon talons to doing something called a polar run. "Those would be outstanding, but how about something beneficial to us all?"

He waits for everybody to quiet. "If Twenty-Five is unsuccessful, she must become the official ER slayer."

The crowd approves with rowdy enthusiasm.

Patch does not. "That will interfere with her examination duties."

Twenty-Six snorts. "So what? The only monsters who ever talk to her with any consistency are the decrepit, and they're information wastelands. She'll be doing something useful for once, giving the rest of us more time to do the real work around here."

He's so damn sure I'll lose. "I've changed my mind."

"Surprise, surprise. Are—"

"I want a week off for the girls' barracks when I win."

Lester taps at his tablet, gets a notification a few seconds later. "The major will allow you five days, but no more than two in a row. If you fail to sever the head in ten strikes, you will become the headsman of the ER until the slaughter slab area is made available again. Are we in agreement, Twenty-Five?"

I nod, then climb onto the slab and pick up the ax to whistles and catcalls. It's heavier than I expected, but once I get it propped on my shoulder, I find my balance and shamble to Twenty-Six's side.

Twenty-Six grins at me. "You probably think you're helping this monster by doing this. An ax ain't a sword. You know how many blows it will take someone of your stature to hit something vital?"

The words hurt, not so much because they might be true, but for the delighted malice with which he delivers them.

"You're the monster," I whisper as I raise the ax. I push

away my sorrow, gather my rage at Twenty-Six and the jeering soldiers, and throw it all into the swing.

The blade clanks off the dragon's scales; shock waves reverberate up my arms and laughter plays loud in my head.

"She may have scratched it," Twenty-Six says. "Perhaps we should have made the bet for a hundred. Come on, Glowheart, you can do better. Pretend it's my neck on the block."

I do. Every time. On the fifth blow, I break through the scales. On the eighth, the dragon stops glowing. On the tenth, I'm halfway through. My hands ache with the promise of future blisters, my arms burn, my scrubs are soaked through with sweat. Dragon gore covers my ankle-length coat from hem to neck.

"What are you waiting for, Glowheart? Back to work," Twenty-six says.

I drop the ax. "Give me a chain saw."

Lester shakes his head. "Actions have consequences, Twenty-Five."

Twenty-Six hands me the ax. "Chop chop, Glowheart."

Over the next ten attempts, the soldiers go from heckling me to encouraging me to offering help.

Twenty-Six puts a hand on my shoulder. I flinch. "What do you say, Twenty-Five? Do you need someone to finish this monster for you?"

"Back off." I squirm free of his touch and drag up the ax.

Six cuts later, my hands and shoulders aflame, my rage exhausted, I break through the other side. After an A-B uses a hoist to remove the head from the slab, the dismemberment crew swarms the carcass. As I totter from the carnage, Twenty-Six strides toward the wall of chain saws, eager to join in. A man in a hooded fur coat—not military issue—approaches him and strikes up a conversation.

Lester withdraws his pistol and hurries toward them. "Who gave you permission to be here?"

Twenty-Six and the stranger turn, enough for me to make out a middle-aged man with near-wrinkleless features.

Hector.

He speaks briefly with Lester, then waves me over, a curious smirk on his face. "Saw you working up there with that ax. Interesting technique, but I'd stick to the sword if—"

"Why are you here?"

"The colonel didn't want you off base again." Hector gestures at the crates on the slaughter slab. "We brought the mountain to you."

I look at my bloodstained jacket and croak out a sardonic laugh. Thanks to my efforts to protect Baby, the cameras and lights have come to Georgetown. And because I lost Twenty-Six's bet, I'll not only have to execute dragons for TV, but also for the daily amusement of my captors.

"You don't have to look so happy about it," Hector says. He glances at his watch. "Sergeant, could you get Melissa a clean coat and meet us at the colonel's office?"

"Us" turns out to include Twenty-Six.

I chew at my lip. "Why's he coming?"

"The producers have wanted to reach out to the female demographic since season two. James here is pure double-X heroin, and because the audience is already familiar with him, he's gonna be easy to inject." Hector grins. "Plus, you're cheap labor."

"And what exactly is my role?" Twenty-Six asks before I can.

"You're Melissa's love interest." Hector looks from Twenty-Six to me, his smile fading. "You guys still like each other, right?"

35

As Hector and Colonel Hanks discuss the logistics of our participation, I stare at the painting of Saint George on the wall behind them. The dragon slayer appears happy in his shiny armor and flowing cape, but maybe that's Painting George and not Real George. Maybe the artist told Real George to suck it up and smile, otherwise Real George's baby dragon friend would be next in line for the spear.

It's all stupid ridiculous, but nobody cares what I think. Read my lines. Follow Hector's direction. Execute dragons. Pretend to like Twenty-Six. A lot.

I peek over at him. He's examining the script binder on his lap. Why does he have to look so much like James? He catches me watching, grins.

It's a half hour later according to the clock on the wall,

though it feels much longer, when the meeting ends. On our way out of the building, I squint against the brightness of the sun and scan the sky for the slightest hint of red or green glow.

Empty. The armies gather. We will come. Nothing but imaginary words by an imaginary dragon. Anyway, this is the frozen suck, far off any dragon map. I'm not sure even imaginary dragons could find—

"Waiting for a miracle, Glowheart?" Twenty-Six says.

"I don't know what you're talking about."

"*In nae,*" he says. I glance back. He's got that evil smile on his face. "Any chance you could hurry it up, Glowheart? I'm getting cold."

"You're far past cold," I mutter.

We head to the rec center for wardrobe and makeup. The clanging of weights and pounding of basketballs fade to near silence when we enter. Soldiers in drab workout clothes track us as we make our way to the parlor on the far side of the gym, which has been transformed into a temporary salon.

At the first station, a thick-necked barber sets up shop in front of a mirror and a faceless dummy mounted with a blond wig.

"Run out of hair dye?" I ask with a smile that comes out more a grimace.

Hector follows my gaze to the wig, explains that the

writers decided James and I should lose our dragon crowns. Because I'm not a good little slave (my term, not his) like my better half (his term, not mine), I must still wear my crown. Just out of sight.

While Twenty-Six changes in the locker room, the barber goes to town on my head. I ignore the hum of clippers and the falling clumps of hair the best I can. He spins me around to face the mirror.

Nothing remains but a few sprouts poking out around the CENSIR. Gaunt and almost hairless, execution gore splattered on my neck and one cheek, I resemble a cross between a cancer patient and a mad scientist.

I'm searching for something I recognize in my reflection when a sour-faced production assistant hands me a garment bag at arm's length and directs me to the showers.

I spend the first part probing my head, which is bumpier than I'd expected. I lather my hands up with shampoo, realize I've got far too much, squeeze back tears. Once I've come to terms with my new look, my thoughts turn to the show.

Three episodes over three days, culminating in the midseason finale. If the ratings track well, Hector assures us our contract will be renewed. If not, Baby's back on the chopping block.

Just have to make the world believe Melissa loves James.

Crazy I can do, but love? The concept seems as invisible and distant as the stars. How do I fake something so far from sight?

I take a deep breath, turn off the water. Three days. That's it. I can make it through three days . . . one kiss at a time.

I towel off and change into my outfit, a monstrosity of red, blue, and green dragon scales that makes me sparkle like a disco ball.

When I return to the salon, Twenty-Six is reading his script, getting powder applied to his cheekbones. He's dressed in a black jumpsuit, and they've styled his hair to make him seem rebellious and intense.

He looks up from the binder, and his piercing blue eyes ensnare me for a second. Then he winks. "Get a look at this, Lester. I barely recognized you, Glow—"

"For this show to work, James, you need to be nicer," I say. His name seems foreign on my tongue.

He waves his binder at me. "Hello? That's kind of the point of the script . . . Melissa."

"All the time. Fake it if you have to."

"Some things you can't fake."

I chew at my lip. "Pretend I'm somebody else if you have to."

He considers. "That might work. What's my CENSIR say, Sergeant?"

Lester examines his tablet. "Still annoyed . . . nope, now you're okay."

Twenty-Six nods, looks at me like I'm not a bug in need of crushing, then gives me a kind smile that calms my nerves. "How are you doing, Evely—Melissa?"

"Terrific."

"Do what I have to," he says. "Want to read lines with me, Melissa?"

I sit in the adjacent chair. "Everything but the execution scene."

"Too bad. That's the best part."

I ignore his grin, open my script binder, and start reading.

Makeup done, hair in place, and lines half learned, we're escorted by Lester to a building with biometric scanners protecting both the outer and inner doors. Given the extra layer of security, I expect to find something interesting inside.

But besides some scanner-protected wall cabinets that ring the square room, everything I see appears to be part of Hector's traveling studio. Lights, chairs, green screen, a tripod-mounted camera. While a couple of production assistants adjust the lights, a stone-faced A-B guarding the door at the back pretends to ignore us.

"We'll do James first," Hector says, stepping behind the camera. "Take a seat. Lester, please remove his CENSIR . . . careful with the hair!" He places a chair next to the tripod.

"Melissa, sit. Look at her, James. . . . Melissa, on my cue, read the narrator lines from James Scene One. Don't worry about cadence or anything. We'll blend in Simon's voice later."

He taps his tablet, and the lights in the room dim. "Okay, James, you're in a bittersweet state with an undercurrent of anticipation. You were locked up in solitary, then you saw Melissa on the show and had a there-is-a-god epiphany that dragons are evil. You've volunteered to help the A-Bs hunt them down in hope of redemption. But of course, the best part about this opportunity is that you might get to see Melissa again."

"Of course. Without the memory of her to keep me strong, I would never have made it through the darkness," he says, repeating the final line from this scene.

"Brilliant," Hector says. "Let's roll."

I read the first narrator line: "When you think about everything that's happened, what do you regret most?"

"There are lots of things. When you're up there on a dragon, you can't see the faces of the people you kill or know the grief of their family members," James says with perfect solemnity. "You get all worked up for the cause and you're going so fast . . . so damn fast. . . . You don't really consider the consequences until it's too late."

His expression darkens, his voice softens. "But if I had to

choose what I regret most, it would be Melissa."

He pauses, smiles as if recalling a fond memory. "She came into my life like a tornado of energy . . . unexpected . . . powerful . . . with this raw fire inside her. It overwhelmed me. I should never have let her join the cause, but once she was in my life, she was the air to my lungs. . . ."

On we go, moving from our fabricated insurgency story to his confinement to his rebirth, everything centered around our romance. Hector wanted female heroin; James gives it to him pure. Every sappy line he delivers seems to come from the soul. And with his intense eyes locked on mine, I can almost forget Twenty-Six and convince myself the words are for me.

I come to the last question in the scene: "If Melissa were here right now, what would you tell her?"

"So many things. The first would be . . . thank you," he says, followed by a dramatic pause. "Without the memory of her to keep me strong, I never would have made it through the darkness."

He's supposed to end there, but doesn't. "She once told me this phrase, which I never forgot. *Baekjul boolgool*. It means indomitable spirit." He looks at me. I see passion, warmth, truth. I tell myself it's an act. "It means the world to me who she's become."

"Brilliant," Hector says.

Lester puts James's CENSIR back on. "Had me believing."

Twenty-Six grins. "Once we get rid of these monsters, maybe I'll go to Hollywood."

Hector has us swap places.

I can't recall a single line. After I stumble over several attempts, Hector jams a transceiver into my ear and hisses my lines at me. My scene's half the length of James's, but with all the retakes and coaching from Hector, it takes three times as long.

Last, and by far the worst, the final scene for the day. In our script, it's labeled Grand Canyon Red Execution, but in my mind, it's The Kiss. Two lovers reunite, make out, then kill a dragon. On the list of terrible ideas, this has to be near the top.

An audience awaits us in the ER. Soldiers, scientists, talkers. Most everyone's here for my embarrassment, even Colonel Hanks. I scan the talkers for Evelyn but can't find her. Too bad. Her presence might make this experience a smidge tolerable.

We're almost to the front of the murmuring crowd when somebody yanks my arm. I glance back. Twenty-One's looking up at me.

"They're always talking, always talking," she says. She flies the dragon brooch in front of her face, then smacks it into her palm. "Kill the dragons, yes, yes, or the dragons kill them."

"Yes, yes," Twenty-Six says, pushing past. "We're going to kill them all soon enough."

She sulks. "He doesn't mean it, does he? Not everyone should die."

"Of course not," I say, for lack of a better lie.

Lights, cameras, green screens, and soldiers surround the bright Red pinned to the slaughter slab. Hector positions Lester and three other volunteers around the dragon's snout as stand-ins for Frank, Kevin, Mac, and L.T.

After removing Twenty-Six's CENSIR, Hector hands him a sword and orders him to a marker near the edge of the slab. He turns to me. "You're beside the dragon, expecting Frank to bring you the sword. On my cue, you notice James. This is where you go all giddy. Woman giddy. Not teen giddy."

I don't know what he means by that, but he'll be lucky if I can muster any giddy.

Once we're all positioned to Hector's satisfaction, he orders our jackets off and demands quiet from the crowd. He calls my name through the earpiece, and the butterflies in my stomach become wasps. "You see James now. You're startled, overjoyed. Fly into his arms. Then kiss."

Nothing to it. Pretend it's the real James. Take a step

toward him. And another. Away from the dragon, I start to shiver, even though it's not that cold yet.

"Don't think, just do it," Hector urges.

I clench my fists, rush forward. James drops the sword, strides toward me, eyes lit with joy. How can he be so good at this? He enfolds me in his arms. My shivers cease, my stomach settles, my heartbeat intensifies.

"I never thought I'd see you again," he says.

He draws back, cups my face, and looks at me with the same fierce passion I remember from Shadow Mountain Lookout, when I so wanted him to kiss me. How can he look at me like I'm the center of his universe, this same person who treated me so awfully this morning?

Who are you?

I shut my eyes. His thumb traces my lips. He lifts my chin, glides his other hand up my face . . . and through the hair of my wig. The touch of his fingers on my naked scalp breaks my trance.

I remember our audience, my outfit, our purpose on this slaughter slab.

I turn away, and his lips meet my cheek.

"Cut!" Hector bellows. "What the hell was that?" he asks through my transceiver.

"I can't do it," I say.

"It's okay, Melissa, I won't hurt you," James says softly.

Hector growls something unintelligible, then stands up and orders everyone but his production assistants to clear out. Once the hangar's empty of spectators, we start again.

"It doesn't have to be a magical kiss. It's just a simple peck. If more happens, great. If not, fine. Don't think about it. Close your eyes and let him kiss you. Don't make it so damn difficult."

A simple peck. Run forward. A simple peck. Embrace. A simple peck. Close my eyes. A simple peck. Coming closer. A simple—

I push myself away. "I can't do it."

Hector scowls at me. "Melissa's got stage fright, so we'll come back to the kiss later. For this take, do the scene without it. Hug, look at each other lovey-dovey, kill the dragon. Can you handle that?"

"I'll try."

"Try correctly."

Without kissing, the hugging and gazing go fine. After retrieving the dropped sword, we stroll hand in hand to the dragon. James gets on one side, I get on the other.

"Together, we can destroy this monster and begin to cleanse our hearts of the evil we've done," Hector says in my ear.

I repeat the line, say a silent apology, and press the sword tip to the dragon's skull. James wraps his hands around mine.

Hector makes a cutting motion across his throat. "Make it pretty."

James looks from me to the dragon. An expression of absolute hatred contorts his face as his hands crush mine. Not an act. He loathes dragons with every ounce of his soul. Unexpected relief floods me, quickly followed by a storm of fury over the way he's played my emotions these past hours.

How could I have been so gullible? He's a monster.

I tighten my grip on the sword. The blisters on my palms burn hot against the hilt. I tell myself the wetness in my eyes comes from the pain in my hands, and I squeeze harder to drive back the pain in my heart.

Twenty-Six wipes a tear from my cheek and I recoil. "Let go, Melissa. I can do this without you," he whispers with Jamesish precision, as if he actually gives a damn.

"So can I," I hiss, clenching hard until the fiery agony pulsing through me becomes too much. I let out a scream and thrust the sword deep.

When my vision clears enough for me to see, the dragon is impaled to the hilt.

"That was brilliant," Hector says. I grab the earpiece, knocking the wig askew in the process, and hurl it at him. My CENSIR jolts me to my knees. I push myself up, my wig falling over my eyes. I rip it off, ready to fling it, too, when inspiration strikes.

I march over to Hector. "I'm not kissing him."

"It's a simple—"

"Fine, have someone else do it."

He frowns. "No."

"Why not?"

"Because a kiss is a close shot. How 'bout you let me direct and you just try to figure out how not to screw up my scene?"

"It'll look like I'm kissing my grandmother," I say. "Don't you want a good one?"

"You're a thorn in my ass, you know that? I could do an over-the-shoulder, maybe pull out to medium," he mutters, more to himself than me. He shakes his head. "It won't work. We'd need a stand-in, and there's no time."

"I know someone perfect," I say, jiggling the blond wig at him.

36

Everyone gawks when I enter the barracks. I left my scrubs in the rec center bathroom—Lester wouldn't let me retrieve them—so I'm stuck in my dragon-scale out-fit until tomorrow. After everyone gets their disapproving looks in, they return to watching a new episode of *Kissing Dragons: The Other Side*. I don't see Evelyn, which means either she's decided to undergo reconditioning, or she's in the bathroom.

I hurry through the door at the back. Red-eyed and puffy, she sits against the wall beneath the screen, blubber-ing something unintelligible to Five and Seven. She notices me, wipes quickly at her eyes.

"What do you want?" she snaps.

"I kind of like the waterworks." I remove some gauze

and ointment from the medicine cabinet. "Almost makes you seem human."

Five and Seven rise to her defense. I raise a hand in peace. "I have an offer for your queen."

"What could you possibly have that I want?"

I nod at Five and Seven. "Evil stepsisters, clear out."

"They stay," Evelyn says.

I make to leave. "Okay. I'll give your regards to James."

"Hold up," Evelyn calls, her voice breaking.

I spin around, bite back my smile. "Yes?"

"Wait outside," Evelyn says to her girls.

While I wrap my blistered hands, I explain the kissing situation to Evelyn. By the time I'm finished, her mood's at full perky.

"Of course," I say, "I need something from you. Do you or your sorority sisters have any chocolate?"

Comprehension dawns on her face with a devious smile. "So you're the one who stole Twenty-One's Kit Kat."

"Answer the question."

"No," she says. "But here's what I'll do for you. I won't tell her or anybody about your mistake. It'll be our little secret."

"I'm not your enemy, Evelyn."

"Actions have consequences, Twenty-Five. You'll learn."

"One day, when you're alone and nobody can hear

your screams, I'm going to enjoy hurting you," I say on my way out the door.

Twenty-One's waiting for me on my bed. "You look nice, Melissa."

"Don't remind me." I sit beside her. Deep breath. "Twenty-One, I need to talk to you about—"

"The monkeys are depressed."

The monkeys are always fucking depressed. "Let's plant a pumpkin patch or build a dolphin-shaped swimming pool."

"Who likes pumpkins? And why would we need a pool when we live by the ocean?"

"I'll come up with something better tomorrow. That's not what I needed to talk about."

"Is this about the Kit Kat you took?" She doesn't seem upset in the least.

"You knew?"

"Yes, yes. I smelled it on you the next morning."

Evidently reconditioning made her a bloodhound. "How come you didn't say anything?"

She looks at me like the answer's obvious. "You were hungry."

"But I stole from you."

The first hint of anger flashes in her eyes. "Only bad people steal. You're not a bad person, are you?"

A couple of months ago I knew the answer. Now . . . "I'm not sure."

"I am." She smiles up at me with such affection that I almost lose it. She doesn't care that I'm a weak link or a glowheart or a thief. She accepts me unconditionally.

She whips the dragon brooch from behind her back. "Soon the dragons will come, yes, yes, and they can take us to our island and we can be happy. We need to find something for them to eat."

"But I thought dragons aren't allowed on our island," I say, my attention drifting to the screen. Simon's interviewing the insurgent of the week, some middle-aged guy made to resemble a cross between a biker and a vampire.

"We should let Arabelle visit. You like her."

"Arabelle?" For a second, I think it's Keith. But it's not, thank God.

"The Silver," she says with a dramatic huff.

"I'm sorry, did you tell me that already?"

"No. She only learned how to talk this afternoon, yes, yes. She said you'd want to know."

"Yeah. Thanks."

"She told me you came up with some pretty silly names for her."

"She did, huh?"

"Little Blue Eyes, Smaug. She did not like those."

My focus snaps to Twenty-One. "How do you know that?"

"Arabelle told me. She says you can keep calling her Baby, if you—"

I press my palm to her mouth. Given her penchant for rambling nonsense, I doubt Big Brother monitors her too often, but it's not her mike that concerns me.

"Vultures in the sky. Gotta stay sharp," I say.

She doesn't catch my meaning, but at least it distracts her. Her eyes dart around in suspicious little bursts. She settles her glare on Evelyn and friends. She shapes her right hand into a gun. "Their stench offends me, yes, yes. They're upsetting the monkeys."

"We'll hum to them. That always makes them feel better." I start in with a lullaby; she chooses the *Kissing Dragons* theme song. We're both off-key.

I tug a blanket around us, keep it clasped tight with one hand to conceal my movements from the cameras. With the other, I press my finger to Twenty-One's left forearm and scrawl *How can u talk to dragons?*

She squints, shakes her head, hums louder. We repeat this several times before she nods acknowledgment and responds on my arm.

Three tries later, me mouthing out guesses and her answering "yes, yes" or "no, no," I correctly decipher: *Can hear. Can't talk.*

Is her CENSIR malfunctioning? But . . .

How can you hear Baby? She's collared.

"It doesn't work the same on us. We're different."

They'll kill Baby if they discover this. And they might very well do the same to Twenty-One. *Island secret.*

I don't think she notices my words, though, her attention back on Evelyn. "We could have the dragons throw them in the ocean, yes, yes. They'll freeze." She clenches the blanket in her fists, trembles violently. "Or burn them! Burn, burn, burn!"

I embrace her until she calms. "Shhh. The monkeys are still upset." Ignoring the agitated looks of those near us, I resume my awful hum. *When do dragons come?*

"A few—"

I tap her arm.

A few days. I think.

Is Keith with them?

She shrugs. *I don't know much. I think they're worried I'll blab.* "But I haven't blabbed about you, no, no."

I press a finger to her lips. *Me?*

"Follow the Silverback's trail, yes, yes." I shush her again. *That's what they call you.* "Because of Arabelle."

How could they follow my trail? Maybe they tracked the airplane or . . . It doesn't matter. Rescue's coming. It's actually coming.

I kiss her forehead. *Island secret.*

She pantomimes locking her mouth and throwing away

the key. We practice shooting vultures until she drifts to sleep.

After a breakfast that doesn't taste quite so bad as normal, Evelyn and I meet up with the makeup artists at the rec center. While she changes into a spare outfit, a production assistant preps me for today's shoot. I'm getting eyeliner applied, reading over the script, when Twenty-Six shows up.

He glowers at me, grabs his binder from a table, and slumps into a nearby chair. "What problems you going to cause today, Glowheart?"

I tap the script. "This is good stuff. While I'm off foraging for berries like your good little cavewoman, you get to show Frank the best way to skin a dragon. Doesn't that make your blackheart extra happy?"

He frowns. "You're in a good mood."

Even Evelyn emerging from the locker room, bouncy and bubbly—far more suited for the tight jumpsuit than me—can't ruin it. I suffer a momentary prick of envy, but it disappears fast when the barber informs her she needs a haircut.

"Did I not mention that?" I say. "Whoops."

"But I'm blond already," she whines.

The production assistant steps in. "It needs to look the same. We have an extra wig for you."

Evelyn's eyes go buggy as the barber gives her the sheep treatment. She catches me grinning at her reflection in the mirror. "I'm telling Twenty-One about the Kit Kat."

"Does this mean we're not friends?"

After Evelyn's wigged and prepped to resemble me, and James is properly sultrified, Lester chauffeurs us to the slaughter slab. Hector's got everything set up, including a live dragon to replace the one I slayed last night. Twenty-Six and I hug, gaze longingly at each other, then Evelyn steps in, and they kiss.

And kiss. Hector gives them a "Brilliant," repositions his cameras, and has them go at it again. I grit my teeth. Only two more days. Maybe less. I glance up at the ceiling. Maybe the dragons are already on their way. While Twenty-Six and the strumpet continue their lovefest, I contemplate what I'm going to do once I'm free of this hellhole.

I won't be able to return to the old world. No more high school. No college. At least not until my name and face are forgotten. I'll probably have to be a crate-in-a-cave nomad for several years.

It'll be a far different life than I ever imagined growing up, but it will be mine. No CENSIRs. No A-Bs, no Major Alderson. No call centers, ERs, or battle rooms.

"Brilliant, brilliant, brilliant."

No TV shows.

For episode two, we help the four A-Bs track a reclusive Green responsible for the destruction of a million acres of

African flora. And, oh yeah, he's also killed a bunch of people, but the show's more focused on his ecological impact because, according to Hector, the environmentalists are another demographic they're attempting to snare.

After filming the preexecution bullshit, we return to the ER to slay the Serengeti Savager. Twenty-Six hands me the sword, and we kill the dragon. Evelyn steps in, does her thing, and we're done before dinner.

"Excellent job," Hector says, though I know his praise is meant more for Twenty-Six. "I'd like to invite you all to dinner, if that's all right, Sergeant?"

"The major shouldn't have a problem with that," Lester says.

I grab my script binder from a chair. "If it's all the same to you, I'd rather not."

Hector shrugs. "Don't worry about those lines. We're changing the script."

"Why?" Twenty-Six asks.

"Major Alderson had a plot idea I found quite appealing. That man is brilliant."

If brilliant equals evil, I'd agree. But I don't care anymore. I can do anything that sick bastard can dream up, because rescue's coming. And in a few days, if things go according to my imagination, Major Alderson will be dead. That would be brilliant.

I join Twenty-One at the cafeteria table. Hunched over

my tray, I use my plastic knife to score out letters on the paper napkin. *News?*

She looks both ways and in a quick hush says, "No, no."

"What are you two up to?" Lorena asks, sliding over.

"Nothing to see here, no, no." Twenty-One ducks beneath the table.

"I thought you weren't talking to me," I say.

Lorena squints at the napkin. The letters have faded too much for her to decipher. She frowns at me. "Melissa, don't do this to yourself."

"I don't know what you're talking about."

Lorena rolls her eyes, sticks her knife into my tray. *Rescue.* "Ring a bell?"

Despite her exasperated expression, I can't contain my smile. "They're coming."

She shakes her head. "No, they're not."

"But Twenty-One said—"

"She comes up with this type of thing all the time. Sometimes it's the dragons who are going to save the day, sometimes it's her parents, who happen to be dead. You can quit it with all this cloak-and-dagger—"

She cuts off when she sees my new message: *21 talked to Baby.* "She knew something I never told anybody."

Lorena gives me a sympathetic look. "It doesn't matter, Melissa. Ever since Allie was reconditioned, she's been like that. They're just jumbled voices in her head. She can't make sense of what's real and what's not. Maybe it's a good thing for her, these stories she fabricates, I don't know, but you can't trust what she says." She grips me hard around the wrist. "It's only asking for trouble. For her, for you, for all of us. You have to let go."

I can't. Rescue will come. Someday, somehow. I have to believe that. *In nae.* I bite at my lip, manage a weak smile. "Well, at least I'm finally over James. That's something to be happy about, right?"

She releases my wrist. "We will have to celebrate properly when we get back to the barracks."

"You sure you want to be seen with me? What was it Pam called me?"

She grins. "The rainbow whore. Kind of has a ring to it."

I laugh. "Wait until you see Evelyn."

On our way to the bus, Twenty-One tugs at my jacket. "Thursday."

"Thursday?"

She nods with excitement. "Arabelle says Thursday, but she's scared, yes, yes."

"Why is she scared?" Lorena asks, as if she's talking to a kindergartener. She shoots me a warning look.

Twenty-One waits until we're past the guard at the front of the bus. "Because they're moving her."

"Tell her not to worry," Lorena says. "Melissa's doing everything she can to protect her." Another pointed look. "And we trust Melissa, don't we?"

"She's one of the good ones, yes, yes," she says, plopping into her seat. She pulls out her dragon brooch, waves it through the air, hums the *Kissing Dragons* theme song with a jovial "burn, burn, burn" thrown in here and there.

Watching her, I realize Lorena's right. It's one thing for me to hope and scheme, another to involve Twenty-One. I only risk endangering her.

When we enter the barracks, I pull Twenty-One aside. "So I was thinking we could discuss more decorations for our island tonight."

"For the dragons?"

I shake my head. "If they come, fine, but right now it's just you and me."

She nods, shrugs out of her winter clothes, then races to the far corner.

I toss my jacket into a box and slump onto the bed beside Lorena. "Sorry."

"Don't be. You didn't know."

"That's not what I'm sorry for."

"I know." She smiles. "We all have our moments."

"Hurry it up, ladies," Lester says from the doorway.

I'm pulling off my boots, extra slow because of the blisters on my hands, when Twenty-One starts bawling.

"Control your emotions, Twenty-One." Lester shocks her, which only gets her crying harder.

"Leave her alone," I say, hurrying over. "Twenty-One, what's—"

She slaps me hard across the face with the brooch.

"You're not a good one, no, no!" I stumble back, half in pain, half in shock. She hurls herself at me with a mournful wail, fists flying. I hug her tight, get punched in the nose, kneed in the thigh. Lester jolts her again and again.

"Leave her alone!" I say.

"You're supposed to protect her!" Twenty-One cries, then goes limp in my arms.

"Give her here, Twenty-Five," Lester says as I check her breathing. Alive.

Lorena steps between us. "Sergeant, we can take care of her. She gets like this sometimes. When she wakes up, she won't even remember it."

"Don't make this harder than it has to be."

Lorena settles her hand on his wrist. "There's nothing we can do, Sergeant?"

I try to mimic her seductive smile. "Anything?"

Lester pushes Lorena's arm away. His face hardens. "Twenty-Five, the girl."

"Do what the sergeant wants, Melissa," Lorena says.

I kiss Twenty-One's forehead, whisper "Remember the island," and give her up.

When they leave the barracks, I collapse onto my bed. A rerun of *Kissing Dragons* plays, followed by propaganda that shows a trio of Reds bombarding London. Evelyn finally returns and her girls go gaga over her new look.

"Don't any of you people care?" I shout, rising to my feet. "She was one of us, and we just let them take her because she had a bad moment. We've all had our issues."

"Yeah, like killing Claire?" someone says.

"Slut."

"Hate me all you want, but she's a child who needed our help," I say. And I didn't do anything either. Just handed her over like a sack of grain.

Lorena hugs me. I weep into her shoulder. "She's not coming back, is she?"

"You won't recognize her. . . . I still can't figure out what set her off."

I feel at the bruise on my face where she hit me with the dragon brooch. The silver dragon brooch. "You're supposed to protect her," I mumble, then let out a bitter laugh.

"What is it?" Lorena asks.

"It's Baby."

37

The next morning, I request a meeting with Colonel Hanks. Lester happily obliges.

"We had a deal," I say when I enter the colonel's office. But it's not Colonel Hanks sitting behind the desk.

Major Alderson looks up from his tablet. "Can I help you, Twenty-Five?"

"Where's Colonel Hanks?"

"On leave. While he is away, I am in charge."

My heart sinks. "You can't execute the Silver."

"Found out about that, huh?" He shrugs. "The thing just wouldn't die out there in that cage. Then this show of yours comes along and throws a big wrench into my ER. And when I met with Hector the other night, I learned that if things go right, he and his crew will be back for the long term, causing logjams and distracting my men. I needed a solution that would satisfy everybody."

"I had a deal with Colonel Hanks."

"I'm not Colonel Hanks. You don't have a deal with me."

"I won't kill her," I say. "And you can't do the show without me."

He nods with feigned concern. "That could be a panty twister." He raises a finger, makes a phone call, puts it on speaker mode. "Hector, I've got Twenty-Five here with me, and she says she doesn't want to do your show anymore. Is that a problem?"

Hector doesn't miss a beat. "I'd prefer for Melissa to do it, of course, but if I do long shots and some CGI touchup, Evelyn will work fine."

Evelyn. The grave of my hope. And I have nobody to blame for digging it but myself. "She can't do the preexecution stuff," I say, knowing I'm grasping at invisible straws.

"We can do those scenes when you're in a better frame of mind," Hector says.

"I'll never be in a better frame of mind, asshole!"

My CENSIR jolts me. "Control yourself, Twenty-Five," Major Alderson says. "Melissa will no longer participate in the show. Can Evelyn replace her for the other scenes, too?"

"I'll need some time," Hector says. "Is the Silver in place for this afternoon's shoot?"

The major checks his tablet. "That's an affirmative."

"Let's run that now. It'll give me some wiggle room, particularly since my writers are still tweaking the front end."

"Works for my schedule." The major hangs up. "Well, looks like we're all settled up here. Sergeant, please conduct Twenty-Five to the ER for the Silver's execution. Need to remind her who's in charge around here. Can't have the inmates running the asylum, can we?"

Soldiers and scientists assemble around the slaughter slab. Excited murmurs follow Lester and me as we push our way toward the silver glow. I wish I had a gun with an endless supply of bullets. Bet their smiles wouldn't be so broad if they had blood leaking from holes—

My CENSIR shocks me. "Control your emotions, Twenty-Five."

When we get to the front and I see Baby surrounded by the lights and cameras, thoughts of retribution vanish. For a moment, maybe ten, my mind, my lungs, my heart seem to stop working. There's so much fear in her eyes.

"Baby!" She brightens. "It's gonna be okay. It's gonna—" My CENSIR shocks me. "Be okay—" Another shock.

"Control your emotions, Twenty-Five."

"I'm not doing anything wrong."

My CENSIR shocks me.

Evelyn saunters to Baby's side. She waves to the cheering crowd before turning her eager gaze on Twenty-Six, who seems fixated on the sword in his hands.

Baby deserves a better end than this.

"Hector!" I shout.

The director gets out from behind the camera. "If you cannot control her, Sergeant—"

"Let me do the execution," I say.

"Evelyn will do fine."

"Yeah, she's a good kisser." I snort. "But I don't think that's what you want right now."

He glances toward Evelyn, then his eyes narrow on me. "Why? I was told this creature was your friend."

"She is," I say. "If you knew your friend was going to be executed, would you want somebody who hates her to do it? Or would you rather suck it up and do it yourself because you know you'd make it as painless as you could?"

"That would be scene appropriate." Hector beckons a production assistant and a makeup artist. "Get her outfit. You, cover that welt on her cheek. Otherwise, keep it minimal."

While I'm getting my face done, he waves for Evelyn. "Take five. Melissa's gonna do the scene."

"What?" Twenty-Six looks up from the sword, as if he just noticed I was here. "She'll screw it up."

Evelyn storms over. "She's only doing this because she

wants to say good-bye to her precious little Silver."

"I don't want to do it with her," Twenty-Six says as Evelyn and I glare at each other. "She's unreliable."

"Just bring me the sword, Blackheart. I'll do the rest."

Goose bumps prickling every inch of my body, I change behind the wardrobe screen set up behind the slab.

Hector gives me an earpiece. "One miscue, and you're off my set."

When I get close to Baby, I can hear her mewling through the bindings around her snout. I run my hand along her icy head, which calms her a bit.

"It'll be over soon," I say.

"Let's roll!"

Twenty-Six begins a slow death march. With every step he takes, my heart seems to beat faster, louder.

"You're more sad than happy," Hector whispers through the earpiece. "This is the dragon you grew up with. A friend—look at her—but she's too dangerous to let live. You know that now. With her death, you will be free of attachment to dragons and you will be redeemed. Feel free to cry. That would be appropriate at this time."

It requires all my willpower not to chuck the earpiece. I chew hard at my lip. I will not cry. I need my strength to make this as painless for Baby as I can, and I will not give Twenty-Six or Evelyn or any of these bastards the pleasure of seeing how much this hurts.

Baby's staring at me, her eyes full of question. I mustn't cry.

I smile at her, hoping that when her life flashes before her eyes, it ends with the memory of us soaring over the mountaintops without a care in the world. A slice of dragon heaven before everything went to—

"Don't smile," Hector says. "You're sad."

I clench my fists. Why is Twenty-Six taking so long? I look up. He's only halfway to me, all solemn faced. He doesn't notice the camera cable and trips over it. The sword goes clattering and the crowd snickers.

"Cut! What's going on, James? You're a zombie out there."

"Hurry it up," I say. "I'm getting cold." As if that matters.

Twenty-Six glances at me, shakes his head, and returns to his mark.

This time, there are no mistakes, though he still takes an eternity getting here. But now that he's actually on the other side of Baby's head, offering me the sword hilt, I wish he'd taken longer.

"You meant so much to me, but the world will be safer without you," Hector says to me. "Then lean down and kiss her."

I repeat the line to perfection. Safer, but not better. I touch my lips to her head, squeeze back the tears. "I'm sorry, Baby. I'm so sorry." I don't know if I'm supposed to take the sword now, but if I have to wait any longer, I won't be able to do it.

As I grab the hilt from Twenty-Six, he stumbles toward me. I'm not sure whether momentum carries him into the sword, or if I push the sword into him because I'm trembling so much. Either way, the blade slides into his stomach.

He doesn't retreat and I don't pull back. I feel drunk, like my body's acting a second faster than my brain and everything's happening sideways.

All I can think about as I watch the blade disappear into him is that human skin's a lot softer than dragon scale. And then my hand reaches his stomach, and there's no more blade left, except for what's sticking out his back.

He grunts something, then goes quiet.

For a moment, I wonder if I killed him. I imagine I should be happy, but for the most part, I'm confused. I don't think I started out stabbing him, but I definitely didn't try to stop.

In the next moment, I spot soldiers running toward us, hear shouting and screaming. At gunpoint, Lester orders me to release the sword. I didn't realize I was still holding it. When I let go, he taps his tablet, and pain detonates behind my eyes.

I blink once and see Twenty-Six lying beside me with a sword sticking out of him. When I blink again, I'm in complete blackness, surrounded on all sides by the wails of dying people and the roars of furious dragons.

A nightmare. But I'm not asleep. My reconditioning has begun.

38

A dragon screeches somewhere to my left. I can't see it. But I hear it—I hear everything, every damn thing. Behind and above me, the crackle of impending dragonfire blisters my ears, the reek of char clogs my nostrils, so I crawl through trampled brush and moist leaves, toward the whimpers of a woman. To my right, a man orders people to a dragon shelter.

In waves, they shriek their deaths. The reek intensifies. Suddenly, blinding images flash all around. A snarling Green to my left, fire bursting from its throat; a scorched man to my right; three women aflame in front of me.

I tell myself they're not real, yell it sometimes, but each image takes longer to go away than the last. They stick in my vision, specters of death that follow me as I turn and flee.

The ghosts finally vanish. The blackness returns. But

the roars and screams continue, the scent of death lingers. I crawl into a swale. The brush dwindles; the ground hardens to asphalt.

Whenever I shut my eyes too long, my CENSIR jolts me. Whenever I cover my ears, my CENSIR jolts me. Whenever I attempt to stand, whenever I stop crawling to rest my knees and hands—

My CENSIR jolts me.

Asphalt becomes gravel. Pebbles dig into my palms. Every few seconds, I extend a hand in front of me or to my side to protect myself from the obstacles they've put in my path. I skirt mounds of rubble, the metal frame of a car, something that I think is a roadblock.

I never find a boundary to my prison, though. They make sure of that. This time, I'm maneuvering across uneven concrete when my CENSIR shocks me in fast succession, jerking me to a halt.

I must change course. Left, right, backward, it doesn't matter. The dragons chase me wherever I go.

Sometimes it rains. Not water. Too salty. Like Gatorade, except thicker. Early on, I thought it was liquefied dragon meat mixed with water, but I'm beginning to think it might be blood. From dragons . . . from victims?

Best not to think about it. I get so very thirsty.

Whenever it stops, a strong gust of hot air envelops me.

In those minutes, as my scrubs dry and stiffen, as the liquid clinging to my skin evaporates, the clamor of murderous dragons and dying humans subsides.

And that's when I hear the girl. Weeping, moaning, or screaming. Unlike the other noises, she seems far away. Or maybe it's my own torment echoing back at me. Before I can ever decide, the dryer's hum shuts off and the reconditioning cycle starts over.

My knees and hands ache, my head throbs, my eyes burn. I crawl on. The rain comes and goes. The dragons roar longer. The people die louder. Bodies pile up around me.

Always screaming.

They're everywhere.

A dozen Reds burst forth. I turn away, attempt to stand, crash back to my knees. Skyscrapers burn all around. I scurry around a burned-out minivan. A businessman leaps from a window. He gets swallowed halfway down.

"Not real!" I shout, can hardly hear myself over the din.

My knees scrape against asphalt as frenzied footsteps surround me. A townhome collapses. I crash into a pile of rubble, jam my finger.

A flash to my left. An All-Black exhorts me to hurry, waves me toward a public dragon shelter. I adjust course, accelerate. The heat intensifies. Sweat drenches me. Flames roil in. People melt. I beg them to get down, but they never listen. A Red decapitates the soldier. His headless body bleeds out beside me, wetness seeps through my clothes, splatters my face.

The corpses dissolve, the screams fade, but the stench and wetness remain.

It's raining.

I can hear it. The pitter-patter. I stop crawling. No shock. I fall to my back, drink as I pick away gravel embedded in my palms. Are they done? No . . . I don't hate dragons yet. A glitch?

I need to sleep. I curl up—

Wait. A girl's sobbing. I dab at my eyes. Not me. A hallucination? Or maybe this is phase two. This girl could be the daughter of someone from Montego Bay, of someone Baby iced. Listen to the child, Melissa. Alone, helpless. That's the dragons' fault. That's your fault.

I cover my ears. Silence.

I pull my hands away. The girl's gone. A trick of my captors, my mind?

I sleep. It seems that I've barely closed my eyes when my CENSIR jolts me awake.

A round later, I hear the girl again. She needs to shut up so I can rest. I try to tell her so in various ways, but whenever I open my mouth to speak, my CENSIR shocks me.

I start toward her cries. My CENSIR jolts me. I grit my

teeth and try again. Another jolt, sharper. My arms give out, and I collapse onto asphalt. On my third attempt, I almost pass out from the shock wave that ripples through my head.

And I scream, in a voice I barely recognize as my own. Whoever's controlling my CENSIR does nothing to stop me. Lying there on my back, legs and arms twitching, I listen, but the girl's no longer crying. Maybe she's on the other side of this place. Maybe she's trying to talk, but they've got her CENSIRed—

Twenty-One.

I flip onto my stomach, put one arm down, then the next. My entire body trembles as I push myself up. I slide a knee forward. I wait, but nothing happens, so I keep crawling. On a couple of occasions, when I'm reaching out, hoping that my hand finds hers, my CENSIR fires in quick staccato bursts until I change course.

They will never let me find her. Nonetheless, I crawl on.

Eventually I fade into a dreamless sleep cut short by a pandemonium of roars.

Behind the dragons, there's a low rumble. A gravel road appears. APCs with red crosses painted on their sides maneuver through a mountain pass. My CENSIR shocks me. I start right, it shocks me again. I go left, up a small rise through the wild grass that skirts the road. It tickles my nose.

Five Greens erupt from behind a mountain. Saddled,

harnessed. Their riders wear white cloaks and wield machine guns and rocket launchers. A cascading rumble of dragonfire thunders in front of me. I flinch, spin around. An explosion ignites.

The thunder crescendos. Gunshots echo. Car horns blare. Soldiers scramble from the wreckage of APCs.

I crawl beneath one as the Greens converge.

I squeeze my eyes shut, cover my ears. Doesn't matter. I still see everything, hear everything.

Something shocks me. I retch.

Men in white cloaks sift through the carnage. I hear laughter.

"Not real." I collapse. Another shock. I crawl on.

Blues charge through the streets of a small town. The road cracks beneath me. Soldiers fire weapons. Reds and their riders battle dragon jets overhead.

A Red swoops in behind a squadron of soldiers using a scorched minivan as cover from the Blue stampede. The rider fires his rocket launcher into their huddle.

I get a closer look. Bandanna over an oxygen mask. Beady eyes barely visible behind goggles. Familiar?

The word Jedi leaps to mind, though I have no idea what it means.

The world spins. I'm in an explosion crater. Beside me, I find a severed hand holding a picture of a family.

"Not real," I mumble.

The earthquake subsides. The sky shades bright green. Growled roars blast from above. The temperature swells. Tornados of fire erupt. Gunshots ring out. Explosions detonate.

I wipe sweat from my eyes. Through wisps of smoke, I see hills of rubble. A Tiny Tots child-care center sign dangles from the blown-up remnants of a roof. A firefighter emerges nearby, a crisped body in his hands.

A number pops into my head. "Twenty-One?"

A man dismounts from his Green. He looks familiar, though I don't know why. He aims his machine gun, shoots. The firefighter falls, full of holes. The dead child tumbles from his hands.

"Please don't be real."

I hear singing in the distance. Coming closer? Nursery rhymes?

A school bus appears at the end of the street.

"Faster! Drive faster!" I implore, but instead the driver stops, his jaw slack, his focus on the sky. I look over my shoulder, see only the sun. There. Two spots of red breaking the corona. They take shape. Wings tight to bodies, they dive in fast.

"Turn around! Run! Go away!" I scream at the driver.

Nobody ever listens.

I try to crawl toward the bus, but something holds me

back. A sharp throb ignites in my head. I turn left, scurry down a side street, jump to my feet, get knocked down.

"Over here!" I yell, flourishing one arm overhead.

The dragons swoop in low. Their riders rise from their saddles, aim their weapons. I wave more frantically, yell louder, but they don't notice me. I whirl to my right, just in time to see a torrent of bullets rip through the bus.

"No, no, no. Not real!"

My world blurs. I blink. Shattered glass everywhere. The Reds pick through the wreckage of the overturned bus, gorging themselves. Their riders watch from the steps of the adjacent school building, goggles on their heads, oxygen masks unstrapped. A man and a woman. A cigarette dangles from her mouth. He's smiling, pointing at his neck. Closer, I see the tattoos. Little swords.

I crawl forward for a better look at the woman. Olive skin, dark hair pulled back in a tight bun, a faint tan line around the ring finger on her left hand.

"Mom?"

No, Mom didn't smoke. . . .

At least I don't think so.

"Not real!"

I scream it at her, flee as fast as my aching knees and hands can take me.

Asphalt gives way to gravel and gravel mixes with grass,

then back to gravel and asphalt. I feint left, take a sharp angle right, whirl around, then do it again, push up a rise, circumnavigate a scorched APC, scurry through wild grass into gravel. . . .

She meets me at every turn, follows me across the broken world through rain and darkness, sometimes on foot, sometimes atop her dragon, sometimes beside the man with tattoos.

My knees go numb, my palms turn bloody. I push on. Crawl and crawl and—

I tumble into a trough, face-plant in wet grass. I struggle to my knees. My wrists buckle. I lie there. At some point I realize my eyes are closed. Yet I still see her. Delivering death in a thousand different ways. I cover my ears, but it doesn't matter. They're part of me now.

Not real, not real, not real.

But what if it is?

Dragons murder people. Insurgents murder people. Maybe in the deep dark of my soul I knew the truth. Maybe I've gotten mixed up backward because I couldn't handle the fact that Mom was evil—

"No! No!"

It takes me a while to visualize her face, her real face, but seeing her there, smiling at me, floods me with good memories. I hold on to them as I drift to sleep, because I know it won't be long before I hate her forever.

An explosion rattles me awake. I'm lost in darkness.

A second explosion sends me skittering sideways. The sirens cut out. Something clanks beside me. My head starts to throb as the *boom boom boom* of anti-dragon artillery fire goes off.

New sounds, new sensations. Same terror. Unable to find my balance with the ground trembling beneath me, I fall onto my stomach. I lie there, but receive no CENSIR shock. No need to crawl, I guess, when they can throw me around at their whim.

Or perhaps I'm not supposed to be fleeing dragons this round. Maybe I'm stuck in a gen-one dragon shelter, buried beneath tons of concrete. It's getting colder in here. Breathing hurts.

A deafening blast pitches me sideways into a wall.

A wall? Real? The throbbing in my shoulder definitely is. I reach out to check, expecting to be CENSIRed, but receive no jolt, and my fingers find a glassy surface. I quickly run my hands along my scalp until they meet atop my head. No CENSIR. I do it again, just to make sure.

I'm wobbling to my feet, steadying myself against the wall because my legs are weak and the ground's still shaking, when a door opens. The haze of distant daylight illuminates a swath of asphalt spattered with gravel, the shadowy edge of a roadblock. A silhouetted figure appears in the doorway. The blinding beam of a flashlight swings my way.

Two things occur to me in fast order: whoever opened

the door did so without hesitation, like he knew what waited on the other side; I should move.

I dart sideways as a gunshot echoes through the room. A sting of hot pain slices across my upper arm. Fear and adrenaline suffuse me. I duck low and race toward a nearby mound of rocks.

"Take your medicine like a good girl, Melissa."

Major Alderson.

He fires again. The bullet whistles past.

Someone screams. The major shifts the flashlight to a grassy knoll on the opposite side of the room. With my eyes adjusting to the light, it takes me a moment to spot the girl peeking out between thick shoots of brush. Twenty-One. I'd forgotten about her.

"Kill the dragons, yes, yes!" she hisses at the major.

Alderson aims the gun at her.

I rush around the roadblock. "Over here, asshole!"

He spins toward me, but not fast enough. I kick him square in the chest. He smashes into the doorframe, dropping pistol and flashlight. I scramble for the gun, but he catches me by the ankle and twists.

I flip over. He punches me hard in the face. Starbursts explode in my vision. Straddling me, he puts his massive hands around my neck.

I kick and flail, but it's useless.

Like ink spreading fast through water, my vision clouds dark until I see nothing but Major Alderson's eyes. My legs and arms spasm; the world spins. Faster and faster. Blackness engulfs me, but it's silent—no dragons, no insurgents, no victims.

Peacefully, wonderfully silent.

"Kill the dragons, yes, yes." A whisper at the edge of consciousness.

Abruptly, the major's hands loosen. I gasp for air. Liquid sprays my face, clogs my throat, makes me cough more. Alderson lets go altogether and lurches back. Sensation crawls into my body, and I knee him in the groin as hard as I can. It's not much, but it's enough to weaken his leghold around my waist. I squirm out from under him.

As I scrabble backward, groping for the gun, my vision returns. The major's close to dead. Twenty-One sits on his back, stabbing him with the tail of the dragon pin I gave her in another lifetime. One side of the major's neck resembles a field of tiny crimson flowers. Blooming, then wilting. I watch the last trickles of life pulse from his wounds.

"Kill the dragons, yes, yes." Twenty-One grins and continues to gouge the dead major. "Or the dragons kill them."

39

I no longer hear the buzz of jets amid all the dragon howls overhead. The artillery's gone silent, but otherwise the battle carries on. Bullets, missiles, dragonfire. Roars, yells, screams.

Real?

I peer past Alderson and Twenty-One into a smaller room cloaked in shadows. Beyond its open door, a hallway leads outside. I can see columns of smoke and the front of a Humvee. Several soldiers rush past, followed by a crackling cone of flame.

"Allie . . . Twenty-One?" I say. She looks up, cocks her head.

I edge closer. "Do you know who I am?"

"Yes, yes."

I crouch down, close enough to hear her mumbling to herself.

"The dragons kill them, yes, yes. Yes they do."

"I'm sorry about Baby . . . Arabelle," I say.

She glances at me. "Why?"

"I couldn't save her," I whisper.

"No, no." She drives the pin deep into Alderson's neck, then laughs. She jerks it out, wipes it clean with her shirt, and offers it to me.

I'm not sure what just happened, but it doesn't matter. We're friends again. "You keep it safe." I retrieve the flashlight and gun. "Right now, we've gotta go check on the others."

She helps me strip him of his clothes. I put the helmet on—God, it smells like him—and slip into his jacket. It reaches the floor and could fit a girl twice my size, which is perfect. I wrap the excess around Twenty-One. She peeks out, mumbling to herself.

We shuffle around Alderson. A dragon roar sounds somewhere behind me. I hesitate in the doorway, waiting for the screams, but none come. Real? Or is everybody dead?

I look behind me with a sweep of the flashlight. Massive screens form an octagon around a grid of cracked streets and crumbling sidewalks. Gravel pits and undulating stretches of brush fill the adjacent lots. Scattered rubble piles dot the terrain. I focus the beam on the charred minivan crashed into the roadblock, then onto the mangled APC a dozen feet away in a field of wild grass.

I release the breath I didn't know I was holding. Set pieces. Not real. No corpses in sight. Other than Alderson.

I level the gun at his head. I want to shoot him, shoot his face into a bloody pulp, shoot him until nobody, not even his family will recognize him.

I force myself to look away. Might need the bullets. I kick him hard in the ribs, stub my toe, curse him.

Following the brightening swath of sunlight, we creep down the hallway. I clamp my jaw to keep my teeth from chattering. A couple of soldiers flash past the open door-way, but they're too busy fleeing or shooting at the sky to notice us.

Nearing the exit, I look up through the fog of smoke and almost remember what happiness is. Tracer bursts and strings of fire make chaotic patterns as dozens of insurgent-mounted Reds and Greens zip across the sky. Gunships weave among them, blasting away.

Machine-gun fire snaps my focus back to earth. It seems to be coming from the opposite side of the road, but a billow-ing wall of smoke obscures my view of everything but the dragon skulls atop the ER.

A Humvee's parked a few feet away, undamaged. I peek

out the door to get a better view. Overturned vehicles, dead dragons, and scorched corpses litter the road. No live A-Bs I can see.

I pocket the flashlight, duck low with Twenty-One, and scurry to the Humvee, sloshing through half-melted ice. We get in fast, shut the door faster. The heater's at full blast. The hula-girl clock on the dash reads *2:31*. The talkers should be in the barracks.

It takes me a couple tries to maneuver past a nearby crater. I spot a few A-Bs hiding in doorways, several running in the opposite direction, but they don't seem to notice us. I check the rearview mirror, but don't see any signs of those soldiers.

I don't see the crater either, but it's hard to tell with all the smoke. I take a long blink and focus forward.

The closer we get to the barracks, the quieter it becomes.

At two thirty-four, we arrive. The door's open halfway, enough to see three scrub-dressed bodies inside. I can't make out the faces.

"Stay here," I tell Twenty-One as I scan the area. Another Humvee idles two blocks down in front of the infirmary. The battle rages on behind us. Otherwise we're alone . . . I think.

"Hide now."

Twenty-One hunkers down, eyes darting about. "Vultures?"

"Everywhere." I point to the floorboard. "They won't see you there."

She scoots off the seat and scrunches up into a ball.

I get out of the Humvee, take several breaths of cold air to numb my senses, and enter the barracks.

Five, Seven, and Ten lie nearest the door in an expanding pond of blood. Noses and cheeks bluing, eyes glazed, torsos riddled. Twelve, Eighteen, and Nineteen are sprawled behind them, facedown, shot in the back.

These were Evelyn's girls, the ones who'd convinced themselves the soldiers were their friends. Twelve, Eighteen, and Nineteen probably realized what was happening and fled. All of three steps before they were cut down.

Gunfire erupts nearby. My legs wobble, the room spins. Men in white cloaks burst from the darkness in front of me, firing away. I drop to my knees, crawl through blood. "Not real!" I squeeze my eyes shut. The noise fades to the distance. I open my eyes. The men have disappeared, but the girls remain.

I rise, force myself to look at them. Evelyn's not here. Maybe she escaped. Maybe others did, too. I check in, around, and beneath each bed. No more victims in the main room.

Five in the bathroom.

Lorena's there, her face ripped apart. Sixteen, Twenty,

and Twenty-Two appear asleep on the floor. Pam's propped against the back wall, Bible clutched in her hands.

I shut off the flashlight, lean against the wall. It hurts too much to cry. They weren't supposed to be dead. That's not how rescue works.

Footsteps. I raise the gun, touch my finger to the trigger, and peek out. Twenty-One. Shivering and giggling, she raises her arms. "Don't shoot."

I enfold her in the jacket. "I told you to stay put," I say, almost yelling.

"I needed my chocolate. For the island." Knowing I can't convince her otherwise, I help retrieve her stash.

We're almost back to the Humvee when two All-Blacks emerge from the infirmary. The taller one's limping. They head toward the thinning wall of smoke that splits Georgetown in half.

A missile blisters overhead. I grab Twenty-One tight, tuck in, and brace against the Humvee. The infirmary explodes. Another missile. Another earthshaking detonation. A wave of heat warms my face. Staying low, I open the Humvee, load Twenty-One in, crawl in behind her.

I've just shut the door behind me when the barracks gets pulverized. Rubble pelts the windshield and chassis of the Humvee, as rapid as a machine gun.

I floor the accelerator. Buildings blow up left and right.

The world becomes a jumbled nightmare of fire and smoke. The hailstorm of debris intensifies. Louder. Louder. Louder. We slide from side to side. I glance in the rearview mirror. Through the haze, I see four gunships closing in, unloading their arsenal. A half-dozen Reds pursue at full flame, their riders launching their own rockets.

"Watch out!" Allie screams.

I snap my gaze forward. A dead dragon blocks our path. I jam the brakes, swerve hard right. Fishtail. I throw the wheel left. Too much! The Humvee tips.

We roll.

Glass shatters. Pain ignites. Screams everywhere. The world unravels.

Blackness.

Wake up, human.

I know that voice.

Wake up, Melissa Callahan.

The armies gather. We will come.

Blink.

Red glow.

A screech of metal.

Blink.

The Humvee roof peels away.

A dragon's looking at me. I shudder.

"Hold still." Two pairs of hands grab me by the armpits,

haul me from the wreckage. "You look like hell, Callahan." He injects me with something. "Don't worry, we'll have you patched up in no time."

As they load me onto some sort of stretcher, I see the infirmary. With effort, I turn my head, squint. The barracks are there, too. "They blew them up. I saw it. They blew them up!"

"Calm down." He holds my head still, puts a bulky collar around my neck, straps me down so I can't see anything but the smoky sky. They bind my legs and hands.

They lift the stretcher, start walking. A dragon lumbers beside us.

"Al—"

"Everything's gonna be fine. You're safe now. Just calm down."

"Allie?" I groan. "Allie? Where's Allie?"

"The girl? A few scrapes, but she's Jedi. You took the lion's share. . . ." He continues to talk, I drift.

"Can I see her?" Her voice awakens me. A small hand touches my cheek. "You want some chocolate, Twenty-Five?"

I squeeze back tears, open my eyes. Her face bounces in my vision as she walks alongside me. She's got scratches on her cheeks, a black eye, a lopsided grin. "You okay?"

She nods. "You're not a very good driver, no, no."

"I'll work on it." My laugh turns into a grimace.

"Really, you have to take it easy, Callahan."

The person at the other end of the stretcher chuckles. I don't recognize him. "You'll have to excuse Preston. He's very concerned about his balls right now," he says.

"Trish didn't threaten to castrate *you*," Preston says.

"With a butter knife, I believe she said. What was it? 'If you don't get Melissa out in one piece, I'm gonna—'"

"Trish?" I interrupt.

"Diva Trish," Preston says. "Acts like she did all the hard work. Biotracer was my idea, thank you very much. Don't let anybody else tell you otherwise."

My head swims. "She's one of you?"

"An honorary Grunt now."

"Need to get her to do a Loki run," the other guy says.

"For sure. First thing when we get back."

"We really need to recruit more chicks. . . ."

They continue their chatter. At some point I notice that Allie's no longer at my side. The smoke that clouds the sky has thickened, but it's now somehow brighter, too.

We pass through a jagged opening into a building. I hear footsteps and conversations. Becoming louder. Somebody kisses my forehead, murmurs my name, says he'll be back. I glimpse the sword tattoos on his neck, and then he's hurrying away, shouting orders.

"Where are—" I start.

The room brightens, illuminating winches and cranes overhead. The power's out, but it's getting brighter. Doesn't make sense. We're headed toward the slaughter slab.

It keeps getting brighter. So bright.

"She's got her light saber up for you," Preston says. I can hear the smile in his voice.

Hope sneaks in. "Baby?"

Melissa?

She has the voice of an angel.

"Let me see her."

"You need to stay immobilized until we can fully evaluate you," Preston says.

"If you don't let me out of this thing, I'll castrate you the first chance I get, and I promise you, you'll be *wishing* I'd used a butter knife."

The moment I'm loose, I stumble from the stretcher. She's strapped to the slab, cameras and green screens still around her, her wings so broken. But she's licking Allie into hysterical giggles, looking at me with those beautiful blue eyes. And glowing. Glowing so bright.

I laugh and I cry and my body almost gives out. Preston tries to help me, but I shrug him off and run. And it hurts. Everything hurts. So fucking much. But she's alive and she's glowing and she's fucking alive.

So fucking alive.

At least two dozen insurgents surround her, some taking pictures, others tending her wounds and removing her bindings. I'm pushing through the crowd, am almost to her when I see two All-Blacks huddled together at the other end of the slab, backs to me, heads bowed together. The shorter one looks my way.

For a second, I don't recognize her. She seems too haunted. Too human.

Evelyn.

We stare at each other—different strangers than before. Then she turns back around.

"He'll get better, Melissa," Allie says from beside me. It's the first time she's ever used my name. Sounds odd.

"Who—"

A chain saw revs up. I flinch. So does that soldier next to Evelyn. He turns his head halfway to glare at something I can't see.

I stop breathing.

I thought I'd killed him.

For the briefest moment, he focuses on me, and I'd swear his scowl softens and his eyes brighten. In that glance I recognize the boy from Shadow Mountain Lookout. Then he looks away.

"Arabelle has some silly ideas for the island," Allie says. She sounds excited.

An ice cave is not silly, Baby says. Based on Allie's snort, I assume Baby's in broadcast mode. *And don't forget the snow-field where we can play ball.*

"Snow will melt."

Not if it's cold.

"It's cold here. I don't like the cold, no, no."

Somewhere else, where it's a nice cold.

"Tell her she's silly, Melissa."

The chain saw goes quiet. Nobody else seems to notice.

Real? Not real?

What about him?

I just don't know anymore.

I'm not sure I ever did.

I turn back to Allie and Baby. "Wonderfully silly."

I grab Allie's hand, press my forehead to Baby, and find something happy to hold on to, something I know is real.

So very real.